Praise for the Retrievers novels of
laura anne gilman

Staying Dead
"An entertaining, fast-paced thriller set in a world where cell phones and computers exist uneasily with magic and a couple of engaging and highly talented rogues solve crimes while trying not to commit too many of their own."
—*Locus*

"An exciting, fast-paced, unpredictable story that never lets up until the very end...I highly recommend this book to fans of urban fantasy, especially [the works of] Jim Butcher, Charlaine Harris, Kim Harrison or Laurell K. Hamilton."
—*SF Site*

Curse the Dark
"Gilman has managed the nearly impossible here: a cleverly written and well-balanced fantasy with a strong romantic element that doesn't overpower the main plot."
—*Romantic Times BOOKreviews* [4½ stars]

"With an atmosphere reminiscent of Dan Brown's *The Da Vinci Code* and Umberto Eco's *The Name of the Rose* by way of Sam Spade, Gilman's second Wren Valere adventure...features fast-paced action, wisecracking dialog, and a pair of strong, appealing heroes."
—*Library Journal*

Bring It On
"Fans of Charlaine Harris, Kelley Armstrong and Kim Harrison will find *Bring It On* a very special treat. The author is an expert worldbuilder and creates characters that are easy to care about."
—*Affaire de Coeur* [5 stars]

"Gilman has outdone herself…The revelations are moving, the action is fantastic and the ending is something that makes you wonder what will happen next."
—*In the Library Reviews*

Burning Bridges
"Wren's can-do magic is highly appealing."
—*Publishers Weekly*

"This fourth book in Gilman's engaging series delivers… Wren and Sergei's relationship, as usual, is wonderfully written. As their relationship moves in an unexpected direction, it makes perfect sense—and leaves the reader on the edge of her seat for the next book."
—*Romantic Times BOOKreviews* [4 stars]

"I've been saying it all along, and I'll say it again, this is an excellent series, well worth picking up, and I haven't been let down yet."
—*Green Man Review*

"Valere is a tough, resourceful heroine, a would-be loner who cares too much to truly walk alone. A strong addition to urban fantasy collections."
—*Library Journal*

Free Fall
"An intelligent and utterly gripping fantasy thriller, by far the best of the Retrievers series to date."
—*Publishers Weekly,* starred review

"Compulsively readable, fast-paced and deadly serious… Wren continues to be an engaging and likable protagonist, one the reader can root for with all her heart."
—*Romantic Times BOOKreviews*

bring it on

laura anne gilman

LUNA™
www.LUNA-Books.com

LUNA™

Recycling programs for this product may not exist in your area.

BRING IT ON

ISBN-13: 978-0-373-80296-8
ISBN-10:   0-373-80296-X

Copyright © 2006 by Laura Anne Gilman

First mass market printing: March 2009

First trade printing: July 2006

Author photo copyright: © by Peter R. Liverakos

www.LUNA-Books.com

Printed in U.S.A.

Dear Reader,

Some people say that New York City is a magical place. They're right. Some people also say that magic died in the modern age. They're wrong....

And, with that, a Public Service Announcement: People have asked me if it's possible to use the places and names in the Retrievers series as a map for visitors to Manhattan. You *can,* but I wouldn't advise it, as the contents tend to shift during reading. More to the point, the West Village, where Wren lives, is merely odd in fiction: in reality it's a neighborhood of strange turns and three-cornered buildings, where West 10th Street intersects with West 4th...and you never know who—or what—you may meet on any given corner!

So venture forward and have fun...but turn the page—and corners—carefully!

And don't miss Wren's other adventures in *Staying Dead, Curse the Dark, Burning Bridges* and *Free Fall,* available now, and *Blood from Stone,* coming in May 2009.

Laura Anne Gilman

For my Muse.

Without whom I might sleep better at night,
but not have such interesting dreams.

Acknowledgments

Again, a shout out to my editor, Matrice, and my agent,
Jenn, who are lovely, patient, kind, considerate, patient…
Did I say patient?

Deb Grabien, who is a goddess—quite mad, of course,
but all the best goddesses are.

And to my "baby bro" Keith, who was there, every time.

bring
it on

No one gets to miss the storm of
What will be
Just holding on for the ride…
—Indigo Girls, "The Wood Song"

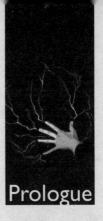

Prologue

Darkness. Not merely night, which mankind had banished ages ago with the first, stuttering campfire, but an absolute, terrifying dark. No moon sailed, no stars glittered. No light reached into the cold heart and set the blood to pumping again.

"Do so swear to it." One voice. Confident. Neither demanding nor coercing, not inviting or seducing. It did not echo in the darkness but rather settled into the corners, softening the edges, herding those within hearing distance into a tighter group, although few of them did more than shuffle in place.

"I do so swear." More than one voice, less than a dozen. Muted, one or two uncertain, but all with an underlying note of—determination? Fear?—carrying them forward. Like most initiations, it was less about wanting to belong, and more about the fear of being left behind—or left out.

"Then I hereby declare the overwrought and pretentious portion of this meeting to be concluded."

Faint, relieved laughter, and the lights flickered and came up, revealing an open courtyard surrounded on three sides by thick stone walls, the center one with a simple doorway set into it. Directly opposite it, similar stones framed an open window running the length of the wall, showcasing what, in daylight, would have been an impressive view. Tonight, the river below glimmered darkly, black against black.

"Please, come inside and join us." The woman who had spoken last came forward. A tiny, elegant silver-haired woman, immaculately dressed in a gray wool suit and sensible heels, she made a welcoming gesture that included everyone. Turning with the assumption that they would all follow her, she walked through the door in the far wall. The stones underfoot were smoothed with generations of use, and as the others followed, expensive suits and elegant dresses mingling in a casual dance of friendly power, one might think it was the opening moves of an ordinary cocktail party, lacking only the waiters passing trays of canapés and champagne.

As they left the courtyard, something sparked in the distance, over the river flowing below them. Thunder, or an electrical fire on the other side, or something else. One of the participants turned to look, barely a twitch in the middle of conversation, and frowned, as though suddenly reminded of a minor chore left undone.

"Has any of this been discussed with the Others?" he

asked, the capitalization plain in his tone.

"Those avenues were explored." The response was smooth, cool, conciliatory.

"Indeed?" He sounded surprised. "I had heard nothing—odd, as my contacts on that side of the river are usually quite vocal about everything."

That got him some appreciative, and sympathetic, laughter. He went on, warming to the topic. "I would hope that each of those *avenues* was indeed thoroughly explored, as you say. I would not want to go home and discover that anyone had—"

The knife appeared between heartbeats, turned under the third rib, and shoved in deep.

"We cannot afford to be distracted," his killer said calmly, as the knife withdrew and disappeared back from wherever it had appeared. "All avenues are closed to us now, save this one."

The three remaining conversationalists in that group stifled whatever reaction they might have had, and merely nodded, stepping over the body to continue their move into the mansion.

Without seeming to look, other attendees managed to somehow stream around their former fellow initiate, moving past him without hesitation; his body might have been one of the stone columns framing the room for all the attention they gave it. The message, if messy, had been perfectly clear. Accept your status as one of the elite—or lose it, and more.

The body lay on the stones as the courtyard emptied. A moment passed, then another, and the blood pooled, congealing even as more flowed from the wound. Another woman came out, this one dressed in a simple scarlet dress that set off her brunette curls to perfection.

"Idiot," she said to the dying man, not without regret. "You should have known better. They'll only replace you with someone less prone to asking questions."

Shaking her head at the stupidity of it all, she placed her hands, palms down, in the air over the body.

"Allow no secrets uncovered, no confidences broken, no vows released, but hold this body to the darkness until time has time to erase the traces."

The body shimmered with a faint silver glow, then disappeared. In the distance, there was the sound of a faint splash, the kind a fish might make as it leaped into the air and crashed down again. Or a body, slipping deep into the waters, might make as it sank and was carried out into the ocean.

"It's too late to change course. Too much has already been done."

The woman went back into the mansion, leaving the courtyard completely empty, even the pool of blood gone as though it had evaporated entirely in the cool autumn air. After a few moments, the lights slowly began to fade out, until only one illuminated the doorway. Soon enough, it too went out.

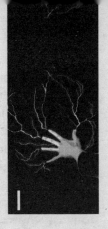

The demon in her kitchen was making a peanut butter and jelly sandwich.

"How the hell did things get so bad, so fast?" Wren asked him, staring down at the sheets of paper on the table in front of her. Nothing to make her break into a cold sweat, on first or even second glance. It was just paper. Nice paper, but nothing expensive. Three double-spaced sheets, neatly typewritten, with decent margins. It had arrived in a manila envelope with her name written on the front in dark blue ink, carried in a courier bag slung over the shoulder of the demon, who had handed it to her wordlessly and then gone to investigate the in-nards of her refrigerator.

"Do you really want me to answer that?" the demon asked now, curious. The butter knife looked odd in his clawed paw, as though he should not be able to handle it, but he wielded the dull blade with surprising dexterity.

"Only if you're going to reassure me that everything's peaches, and the city's about to break out into spontaneous song and dance," she said. "And I don't mean *West Side Story* kind of dancing, either."

She forced her eyes away from the letter, and looked at her companion. There was a smear of jelly on the counter, and another one in his coarse white fur. And he had used the last of the peanut butter. So much for a midday snack. She sighed, and looked away again. Other than that, it was the kind of late autumn day that Wren Valere loved the most: cool and crisp, the sky a bright blue, what little of it she could see out her kitchen window and past the neighboring buildings. Almost like Mother Nature was apologizing for the hell she had put everyone through over the summer.

And, as always, thoughts of that summer made Wren close her eyes and take a moment to center and ground, emotionally.

The entire summer had sucked. The deal with the devil that her business partner Sergei had made with his former employers to keep her safe when the Council of Mages had threatened her and her livelihood had come back to haunt them—literally. The Silence—a group of mysterious do-gooders with a sizable checkbook—had offered what had seemed like a lifesaver of a job, but—

Her grounding faltered, then came back.

Lee's death during that job hadn't been her fault, no. But it was her responsibility. And the simple fact of it made her core—the inner storehouse of magic that every Talent carried within them, like a power pack—seethe under the weight of the guilt she carried. It felt like snakes in her gut, tendrils in her brain. It felt like—

"Ow!"

A furry, leather-palmed paw struck the side of her face, not as hard as it might have, but harder than a love tap.

"What the hell was that for?" she asked, her hand going to her face as though expecting to feel blood, or at least heat rising from the skin. Thankfully, he'd kept his long, curved black claws away from delicate human flesh.

"Self-pity." The demon climbed back onto his chair, bringing his sandwich with him and watching her with those dark red eyes that were the mark of his breed. "Doesn't look good on you."

"Great. The entire lonejack community is freaking out over what might or might not be Council-directed attacks on them, the fatae are claiming that humans are targeting *them,* my love life is going seriously weird, and I'm getting slapped for self-pity by a four foot tall polar bear with attitude. Who has jelly in his fur."

P.B. took a bite out of his lunch, and swallowed, ignoring her last crack. "You're wallowing, Valere. Lee's dead. He's gone. Move on, or you're going to be distracted at the wrong time, and get yourself dead, too." He relented, only a little bit. "Damn it, I liked him, too. I trusted him."

"You didn't get him killed."

"Didn't I?"

That made her look up and meet his gaze.

She had known the demon presently sitting in her

kitchen for years. Almost ten, in fact. In all that time, he had been effective in his job as courier of privy information and items, witty in his comments, and aggressive in his refusal to get involved in anything other than his own life. In short, the perfect lonejack, even if he was a fatae, one of the non-humans who were part of the *Cosa Nostradamus,* the magical community.

All that had changed over the past six months, when P.B. had somehow, for some reason, gotten tangled up in the vigilante attacks against other fatae; human vigilantes, preaching hate with guns and bats.

Wren had friends among the fatae, more than just this one demon. She was ashamed now to admit that she had shrugged the first attacks off as random violence; not acceptable, but normal enough. Prejudice happened. Violence happened. That was life, unfortunately. She had been angry—but not proactive. The question of who these humans were affiliated with, how they knew about the fatae: those things hadn't been dealt with the moment the severity of and prep behind the attacks became clear. The fact that she had been ears-deep in a job was no excuse.

She *had* been worried enough to ask her friend Lee to keep an eye on the demon when she and Sergei had left for Italy to Retrieve the Nescanni parchment, the "little job" the Silence had hired them for. But that had been just to keep her friends out of trouble. P.B. had then inveigled Lee into helping him with his investigation into the human vigilantes who seemed to be targeting the non-human population. That investigation had led to the two of them meeting with various fatae leaders, trying to prevent the anger against humans—specifically, Talents—from growing out of control. What had been a relatively simple case of hate crimes then blossomed into a potential *Cosa*-wide chasm.

And then a fatae had tried to kill Wren, for some reason seeing her as the human behind those meetings, and Lee paid the price for being in the wrong place at the wrong time.

"Grow up," P.B. advised, not unkindly. "You did everything you could do, more than anyone else bothered to. If you want to beat yourself up because you're not some perfect goddess of unfailing generosity and loving kindness, do it when I'm not around. That sort of thing makes me sick." He took a bite of his sandwich and said again, "Really. Grow up."

"Growing up sucks." It really did. "And you still have jelly in your fur. Left shoulder. Messy eater." He was right. Miserable bastard. She wasn't any kind of goddess. She was a selfish, self-interested, puny excuse for a sentient being. She also couldn't change what had happened.

Nobody had enough current to do-over the past.

She picked up the paper and stared at it again. *Deal with what's happening now, Valere.*

The paper still said the same thing it had the first three times she read it. *Another Talent has gone missing. Tally up to seven. WTF is going on? And why? Are you doing this? Godless bastards, why?*

Not on those words, of course. Not to the Council.

The language was formal. The wording was polite. The passion behind it unmistakable. And the paranoia practically leaking out of the ink. A manifesto, if ever she'd seen one. Which, actually, she hadn't.

The Talents who had drafted this document weren't calling it that, of course—they fell back, as Talents tended to do, on historical precedent, and called it a—she checked to make sure she had the wording correct—"a petition to address the grievances of," etc., etc.

This wasn't exactly unexpected, even if it was annoying. Fatae were blaming all humans for the attacks on their kind. Lonejacks were blaming the Council for Talents who had gone missing, or were otherwise assaulted. There was just enough truth in all their suspicions to make violence in return seem like a logical response.

Wren didn't know who the Mage Council was blaming for what, but she was pretty sure it was someone, for something.

"Am I the last sane person left in this city? Don't answer that," she warned the demon. "A petition to the Council—Jesus wept. All right, all right. I don't know what they think this is going to do, but…" She made a few final additions in the margin with a red ballpoint pen, and then signed her initials next to them in a small, neat hand. She wasn't ready to sign onto this version, not yet. But if they made those changes, moderated the paranoia, asked for specific things rather than a blanket admission of guilt that hadn't been proven yet…

"Take this back. Tell them to…don't tell them anything, just give it back to them." She caught a glimpse of the small, battery-operated clock on the far wall. Almost 4:00 p.m. "And scoot. I have a client coming."

"Here?"

"Yes, here." She picked up the courier's bag from where he had dropped it, and handed it back to the demon, giving him clear indication that this conversation was over. He looked as though he might argue, but simply sighed and took the bag from her. Dropping the paperwork into the internal pocket, he slung it back over his shoulder.

"Go. Get paid. Go home. And next time you have to deliver anything here," she said as he crawled back out the small kitchen window onto the fire escape, "bring your own damn lunch. Or at least clean up after yourself!"

The mess actually wasn't too bad; P.B. was a mooch, but not a slob. Wren had managed to give the entire kitchen a wipe-down, throw the dark green coverlet over her bed—covering night-rumpled sheets—and straighten the books and papers in her office before the client was actually due to arrive. Not that the client should be seeing either bedroom or office, but her mother's training seemed to kick in at the most inconvenient times. God forbid someone should be in the house when a bed was unmade.

The buzzer rang before she could start to contemplate the state of the kitchen floor, all five square feet of it.

"Is this…do I have the right address?"

The voice on the other side of the intercom was female. Attractively nuanced. Young. Educated, but not hoity-toity, to use one of her mother's most annoying phrases. You could tell the difference, if you listened. People gave so much away in their voices, you could close your eyes and see their emotions in the tenor of their throat. And that had nothing whatsoever to do with current.

Wren waited.

"Is this The Wren?" The voice was coming as though from farther away than street level. "It's Anna Rosen. We spoke yesterday?"

Upstairs, Wren leaned against the wall, pressing her forehead against the cool plaster as though to ward away the headache that had kicked in the moment the buzzer sounded. Bad sign. Very, very bad sign.

Finally her hand came up and—despite the headache, despite the forebodings—hit the door buzzer, letting the client in.

The intercom was new. Or rather, not new, but newly working. Sergei had hired an electrician to come in and fix it after years of waiting for the landlord to do something, paying triple-time to get it done over Labor Day weekend, and making her promise to use it. No matter who she knew was coming, no matter how silly it made her feel.

The fact that the first time anyone used it was a potential client, a potential client that she was meeting behind his back and without his knowledge, wasn't something she was willing to think about, yet. Maybe not ever.

She hadn't had a secret—a real secret—from Sergei since she was twenty-four.

Rosen took the stairs at a decent pace, and wasn't

breathing heavily when she stood in front of the apartment door. Wren gave her points for that, then promptly took those points away when she saw the ridiculously expensive and useless shoes the client was wearing. Still, if she could afford those, she could afford Wren's fees. And then some. Well-heeled, you betcha.

Young, maybe midtwenties. Long, naturally blond hair pulled back into a thick braid, classic Princess WASP features enhanced by just the right amount of cosmetics, darkening the blond eyebrows and enhancing the pale peach mouth to be noticeable but not stand out. Everything about the girl said Money—but her dark green eyes were sharp, and showed a wry understanding of where she was and what she was doing.

Hiring a Retriever.

"You're…The Wren?"

"None other." And she didn't offer any more information than that. Within certain ever-expanding circles, her identity was well-known, but for various reasons she preferred to go by the nickname she worked under.

And you screw all secrecy-for-a-reason by inviting her to meet here? In your home?

Shut up, she told the voice, and focused her attention outward, honing herself into a version of Sergei's "All Business, All The Time" persona, as best she could. Beside. Wasn't as though the Council didn't know where she lived. The Silence, too. And pretty much every fatae in the city, since this summer and Lee's wake, which she still sometimes had nightmares about. Might as well just put a sign over her door: Wren Valere, Available Here.

Focus, Valere.

Miss Rosen's peach mouth quirked into a smile that showed perfect, perfectly white teeth and meant absolutely nothing. Wren returned the same, aware that her own beige features—brown hair, brown eyes, and pale beige skin—never made that much of an impression. Curse and a blessing: if asked by anyone Official, this Anna Rosen wouldn't be able to remember anything about Wren that could be used to identify her. She hoped.

"Come in," Wren said, opening the door all the way.

The apartment was large by Manhattan standards—three tiny shoebox bedrooms off a narrow hallway, a kitchenette to the right, and one large main room to the left of the front door—but it was almost painfully bare of furniture. Despite living there for dog years, Wren had never really had the time to think about buying chairs. Or a sofa. Or putting anything on the landlord-white walls.

Clients never, but never saw her home. She had lived here a year, in fact, before anyone other than her mother and Sergei walked through the door. There had been more people in this space in the past four months than in all the time previous, and Wren *hated* it. But it also made her look around and notice that her nest was missing a few items most folk would consider essentials. Like, oh, furniture.

Given the choice of using the two narrow and more than a little beat-up chairs in the kitchen for this meeting, or sitting on the floor, Wren had finally broken down and, after confirming the appointment, bought a small wooden table and two reasonably comfortable wooden chairs to go with it from a secondhand junk/antique dealer a few blocks away. Those, and the overstuffed upholstered chair that had seen better decades, were still the only pieces of furniture in the main room, other than the stereo system set against the far wall, and two extremely expensive speakers in either corner.

Maybe the client would think that she rented the place. That would work, yeah.

"Nice system. Acoustics must rock."

Rosen looked to be in her midtwenties, but she spoke younger. Twenty-three, according to the dossier Wren had put together after the initial contact. Not as complete as what Sergei could have done, but she'd done all right, if she did say so herself.

"Anna Rosen. Born in Glendale, raised in Madison, went to school in Boston, came home to work at the law firm of which Daddy was a partner two years ago, just before his death of a heart attack." There. Taking control of the meeting. Establishing herself as the person with the knowledge.

"Alleged heart attack." Rosen took the left-hand chair and sat down without being asked, placing her oxblood briefcase by her expensive shoes and resting her well-manicured hands on the table surface. "He was murdered."

Wren stood in the doorway and looked at the client. "I don't do murders."

Not intentionally, anyway. Not by name, as such. Only the dead never seemed to stay properly, quietly dead, around her.

"Not asking you to." Rosen looked at Wren directly, then; the humor in her eyes was muted by pain that hadn't had the chance to scab yet. The death hadn't been that recent; she was carrying around some significant emotional issues, then. "I'm Null, not stupid."

Wren opened her mouth, then snapped it shut. There wasn't anything she could say at this point that wouldn't come out all wrong, anyway, even if the girl had been looking for soothing platitudes.

Null meant a human without any Talent, without the ability to channel current, or magic. Almost half of her jobs came from the Null world. They hired her as a thief, not a Retriever, but that was a distinction without a difference to most people. In fact, it probably only meant something significant to another Retriever, and there were only a dozen or so in the world, as far as Wren knew.

The fact that this Miss Rosen used the word Null with such casualness meant that she was aware of Talents, by reputation if not personally. Interesting. Possibly totally irrelevant, but interesting. Wren filed that fact away for later contemplation.

The fact that the client had contacted her directly in the first place might be a little more telling—people who heard about her via the Talent gossip networks usually knew to approach Sergei, first.

She was starting to get too well-known. She'd been too high profile, lately. A good Retriever wasn't in the spotlight. A good Retriever—a successful Retriever—needed to be invisible, known only for her actions, not herself. Wren wasn't much for game-playing; she left that to Sergei. Except here she was, playing games, inviting clients into her home, buying furniture that didn't suit her...

"Let me get directly to the point," Miss Rosen said, crossing her legs in a ladylike fashion, the sheen of her shoes expensively muted.

Thank God, Wren thought, forcing herself to gather her scattered thoughts and pay attention to what was going on in the here and now. *Focus! Don't screw the pooch so early in the game, Valere!* Damn it, she wasn't a negotiator. She didn't even like to debate. Her thoughts scattered again like butterflies in the wind. Why had she agreed to meet with this chick anyway, instead of handing it over to Sergei the moment the nibble came in? This was his job, his part of the partnership, to deal with the prejob details.

But the call had come directly to her, and she had taken it on directly. So there wasn't any Sergei here to fall back on. Her choice, so hers to deal with. *Grow up,* she heard P.B. say again.

"My father was killed last year. His will entered probate." Rosen spoke without emotion in that lovely voice, as though all that had happened to someone else. "Now his widow is claiming that a particular piece of jewelry is hers, not mine. It belonged to my mother, and *she* has no claim to it."

There was more emotion in the last sentence than the girl had shown, total, up until then. Whatever the piece was, it meant a lot to her. And she really, really didn't like her stepmother. Did she suspect the woman in her father's murder? *Not your problem, Valere.*

Not Wren's business, who felt what about who, except as it impacted what she was hired to do. Her business was the job, and only the job. "She has it in her possession?"

Rosen nodded. Apparently, the widow did.

A straight-ahead break-and-grab. Nice, Wren thought to herself. Just what the doctor might have ordered, to keep her mind busy while she waited for the Talent-storm forming overhead to either break or disperse.

"I want to keep this low-key," the girl went on. "She's going to know it's me—there's no way she can't know. But without proof, without a way to trace it back to me, she won't be able to do anything about it. That's why I came to you."

"Because I'm a Retriever?"

"Because you're the best."

All right, that was a fact Wren wasn't going to argue; although she could name half a dozen non-*Cosa* thieves who were at least as good at lifting things, they weren't always as careful about giving the merchandise back over to the client. It was a highest-bidder market out there, for items without clear ownership and no binding contract.

That was the difference between a Retriever and a thief. Not just current, but good work ethics. A Retriever, once bought, stayed bought.

"I need the best. I also need someone with a connection to magic. Can you, I don't know, do something so that she knows magic is used? To throw her off my trail?"

Covering her ass. Wren could approve. But she hated having anyone tell her how to do a job. Not even Sergei ever did that. If it called for current, she used it. If it called for the more pragmatic, practical skills she had picked up over the years—lock picking and door-jimmying—then she used those. That was what made her the best, not just an accident of Talent.

Wren didn't say any of that, however. She avoided sitting in the other chair, feeling more comfortable on her feet. At just over five feet tall and otherwise unmemorable, one of the best ways to keep someone focused on you was to present a moving target. Make them just nervous enough to pay attention.

"I am the best, yeah. I'm also not inexpensive." Okay, so that wasn't patented Sergei Didier smooth. She wasn't Sergei, and she did things her way, damn it. "I'm not going to insult you by suggesting that you can't afford me, but are you sure that this is going to be worth it?"

"You're suggesting that I shouldn't hire you?" Rosen seemed less surprised than amused, like her pet dog had done something cutely annoying.

Wren shrugged. She found it hard to care, one way or another, what this girl did. *Fake that sincerity, Wrenlet,* she could hear Sergei say in the back of her mind. *Clients love to believe you're giving two hundred percent.*

"I hate buyer regrets. Especially when I'm the one getting regretted."

Whatever Rosen was going to say in response was drowned in the blast that reached the building just as she opened her mouth.

What the hell?

Wren grabbed the girl by the shoulders and had them

both flat on the hardwood floor by the time the shock wave hit them completely.

"What the hell?" Rosen echoed Wren's first thought.

"Shut up." Every sinew in Wren's body was trembling, far in excess of what the noise should have caused. She willed herself to stop shaking, but couldn't do anything about the cold sweat on the back of her neck. Current sizzled inside her, and she wanted, very badly, to throw up from the pain expanding inside her head.

"Something…" The girl was clearly puzzled by the strength of Wren's reaction, proving that she was, in fact, completely Null. "Something hit us. The building. Was that an earthquake?"

"Not an earthquake," Wren said, not sure how she knew but knowing, without hesitation. "Not even close."

That was current. A lot of it. And all of it sent with nasty intent.

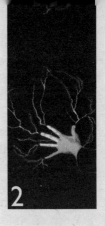

2

Nothing in the apartment seemed to be broken, although a stool in the kitchen had fallen over, and Wren didn't want to think about what her research library, a bedroom in the back of the apartment, toward the front of the building, might look like. Some of those books were old, and expensive, and damned rare, and a lot of them were only on loan from people who would kill her if anything happened to them.

"Stay here."

"But…" The client looked around, clearly remembering the shock of the explosion, and decided that obedience was the smarter move right now, no matter how unfamiliar the sensation might be. Walking cautiously down the hallway, as though an additional attack might come at any second, Wren did a once-over of the rest of the apartment.

Amazingly not only were all the books still on the

shelves in the first bedroom, but nothing had even slid off the desk in the second room, which served as her office—and when she booted up her computer, holding her breath and mentally reciting prayers to whatever saints she could recall, it came up without a hitch.

"Oh thank you, God." If that blast hadn't been current-shaped, she'd hand in her lonejack ID. Somehow, though, it hadn't done what current typically did, which was fry every bit of electronics in the vicinity.

Wren didn't know why she had been spared; she was just thankful.

There was no dial tone on the phone when she first picked it up, but as she held it, thinking that maybe she had given thanks too soon, the tone came back.

"Well, that's a switch," she said in mild surprise. Typically things broke when she held them, not the other way around and getting fixed. Putting the receiver down before it changed its mechanical mind, Wren reached over to shut down the computer. Other people might have the luxury of leaving their system up and running all the time, but not Talents. Not even in this seemingly super-insulated building, bless its pre-War, plaster-coated walls.

Giving the room another quick once-over to make sure that nothing had moved since she came in, Wren went into the third and smallest room, the one she used as a bedroom. Her wind-up alarm clock had stopped ten minutes ago, and the water glass on her nightstand had cracked, but thankfully she had downed the last of the water in it that morning.

This room seemed to be less protected. And yet, there was nothing different about it from the first two rooms in terms of construction. In fact, there was nothing at all that should have attracted current—no electronics, no magical implements, no tools of the trade. Not where she slept, where unconsciousness might allow current to slip in or out unguarded.

"Um, excuse me? Hello?"

The client, her voice wavering down the hallway. Damn it. Wren needed to get the girl out of there. She needed to think, to find out what had happened, and there was no way she could do that with Miss Old Money pacing the main room. A Null who knew she was a Null was still a Null. Sergei was the only non-Talent she trusted with lonejack business, and even then it was with regret, because he just wouldn't stay out of it.

"Hello?"

"Yeah, it's okay. You can get up now."

If it hadn't been okay, they'd both be dead by now, anyway.

When she went back into the main room, Rosen had picked herself up and was dusting nonexistent debris off her slightly mussed outfit with an expression of distaste on her face. Guess the client didn't like being tossed to the ground, no matter what the cause. Some people were just so picky.

"Is your building often bombed?"

"Yeah. All the time." She was channeling pure P.B. now, and Wren made a conscious effort to choke that back. One was not snarky to the client, no matter how much their tone pissed you off. *About* them, yes. But not to their faces.

Thankfully Rosen's livery driver had been waiting around the block reading a newspaper when the shock wave hit her building. Wren waited while the client paged him, then helped her down the stairs, carefully not answering the girl's questions beyond a vague "This sort of thing, Manhattan, you know. It happens."

No New Yorker worth her Metrocard—even ones with hired cars—could deny it. Things happened in Manhattan.

Wren waited while the livery car—a clichéd black Town car with smoked windows, so ordinary and commonplace it always raised curious eyebrows—slid down the narrow street and stopped in front of them. Packing the girl into the back seat, Wren started to close the door, but Rosen pushed a hand against the frame to stop her.

"You're taking the job, then?"

Wren stared at the girl's pretty green eyes, and thought about it for a second or three. "Yeah. Yeah, I'll take it." She wasn't so far out of the financial hole the bastards on the Council had dug for her this summer to turn down work, especially something as basic as this sounded.

"I can write you a check—" Rosen started to say, but Wren waved her off. She didn't want to be bothered by actually dealing with the nitpicky business details now. Not when she was this jumpy, and the client had already verbally agreed to whatever price Wren set. Bad business, but right now she had other things on her mind. Like getting this Null child the hell out of range of…whatever it was that had just happened.

"Make a deposit to this account, in this amount." And she jotted down the numbers for the blind account she and Sergei used to accept funds, plus her usual retainer fee to get things started. "I'll be in touch with the rest of the details as soon as I have a better feel for the job."

Not satisfied, but realizing that she wasn't going to get any more out of her new hire right now, Rosen tucked herself all the way into the car and allowed Wren to close the door.

Wren stared down the street, watching but not really seeing the brake lights of the Town car, itching to find out what the hell had happened upstairs. She was beginning to run through places to start asking questions, when someone came up behind her on the street. She heard the footsteps, aware that there was no threat-aura to them, and dismissed them from her awareness with a skill that was more classic New Yorker than Talent. The tap on her shoulder, therefore, startled her so violently that she almost let loose with a spray of current: full fight or flight reflexes kicking in.

"Christ. Jumpy much, Valere?"

Her almost-assailant backed up and leaned against the building behind him, arms crossed against his oh-so-pretty-if-you-liked-beefcake chest. If she didn't have a pounding reaction-headache, she'd have appreciated the visual more.

"Danny." Cowboy boots and dress shirts worked better in Houston than they did in Manhattan, but Danny still managed to make them look good. And the boots had the advantage of hiding his hooves.

"Danny," she said again, this time in a different voice. Shaking off the quiver of nerves, she looked around for the first time at the mild disaster the blast had left: car windows blown out, tires flattened, trees wilted. Whatever *hadn't* hit her apartment had done some significant work just outside it. Interesting. "What the hell happened?"

"I was going to ask you that."

Glass crunched under his heels as they walked together, both of them checking out the damage. Wren was thankful she'd thought to pull on work boots before coming downstairs. Her usual soft-soled loafers wouldn't have offered as much protection from the sharp-edged shards.

"No sign of explosives," Danny went on as they walked down the street, past her building and down to the end, then started back again. Of course he'd already done a preliminary sortie. She didn't ask how he'd gotten there so quickly. That was what Danny did. "No car bombs, no blown manhole covers, no dead guy bits with wires and whatnot strapped to him. Nobody heard a thing.

"And yet, every single Talent in the area felt the blast, and hey, look at that, half a dozen car windows got blown out. Right in front…" He paused for dramatic effect as they reached her stoop. "Of your building. That sort of narrows it down, don'tcha think?"

Danny had been a damn good beat cop, before tabloid-driven pressures made it tough for fatae to advance in the ranks. He made an even better insurance investigator. His network of Talents in the NYPD was the match of any small-town gossip chain. In fact, in a lot of ways it *was* a small-town gossip chain. When something weird happened, they let him know. And he got to be piggie-on-the-spot, asking all the nasty questions.

"So who in the *Cosa* you piss off this time?"

Like that one. The *Cosa Nostradamus*: the magical community, the human Talents and the supernatural fatae, with or without usable magics. The "family" part was closer to Manson than Brady, unfortunately.

"You been tuned into some other universe the past couple of months?" The only people in the *Cosa* she hadn't pissed off lately were the ones from out of town. And maybe she'd annoyed a few there, too.

"If I knew how to get out of this one, I'd buy you a ticket," he said, proving that he had too been paying attention lately. "One-way. You're becoming a target for way too much shit."

Ow. "Not my fault this city's going to hell," she said defensively. It wasn't. In fact, she was part of the reason it hadn't gotten a hell of a lot worse. The vigilantes? Guilt aside, she had been one of the first to figure out the connection between the "exterminators" advertising with their cryptic flyers, and the attacks on the nonhuman members of the *Cosa*. The surge in general crankiness that couldn't be blamed on the heat wave? She was the one who had gotten rid of the semisentient manuscript that incited and fed off increased levels of negative emotions. The Mage Council going after the lonejacks to prove who was top dog in the city? No way that she was taking the shit for whatever was chewing at *their* brains.

"And yet…" He looked around and gestured tellingly at the dark blue mailbox directly in front of her door, crushed like it was made of tinfoil instead of riveted steel. "Someone was sending you a message of some sort. Sounds like 'back off' to me."

She didn't even try to deny the fact that she had been the target. "Damn it, Danny. I didn't ask for any special attention from anyone. It just…happened."

He snorted like the centaurs of his paternal line. "Nothing just happens, Valere. Nothing ever just happens."

"City filled with Yoda wannabes, and I gotta look like a swamp. Go catch a criminal, Danny. Leave me alone."

"Valere." He touched her arm. Danny didn't touch anyone, much. "You got a headache?"

"Yeah."

"So does every Talent within five blocks, I bet. And this was a bitty baby psych-bomb. A warning shot.

"Twelve months ago, the biggest talk in the *Cosa* was who was sleeping with what. Six months ago, we were talking about those damn vigilantes, targeting us."

By us, he meant the fatae, the nonhumans of the *Cosa.* No Talents had been attacked by that particular group of bigots, as far as Wren knew.

That fact had been the beginning of the split in the *Cosa,* along racial lines: us versus them. Well, that and the fact that most Talents were selfish and lazy, and couldn't be bothered to deal with something that didn't affect them directly. Wren wasn't particularly special, in that regard.

"Four months ago, it was the flameouts." The wizzarts, or crazed Talents, who had been killed by someone or someones still unknown. Wren had tried to find the killers, but had only been able to force them out of town. But Danny didn't know that part of the story. She thought.

"Today?" he went on. "Today we're talking about Talents gone missing. Fatae gone dead. You—and a bunch of others—getting blacklisted by the Council. The fact that there's been a Talent Moot, and you knocked heads together."

Wren winced at that. The Moot, or gathering, had been a bad idea, and her telling them all it was a bad idea had been an even worse idea, for all that it made sense at the time. All it did was bring her notoriety she didn't want and couldn't use. And, if Danny was right, which she suspected he was, had led to this.

"What it all comes together as, girl, is you in the middle of shit, like it or not, want it or not. You is standing there with a great big red target painted on your nice peachy-skinned forehead."

"So what do you think I should do, oh wise one?" She was trying for sarcasm, but it came out too sincere a question for comfort.

Danny didn't hesitate. "Run, babe. Run like hell."

By the time she got back to her apartment and tossed her boots back into her bedroom closet, the news trucks had already shown up. They were cruising up and down, narrowly missing the cars parked on either side, looking for some hapless passing pedestrian to interview for the news. The timing sucked for witnesses, though; the lunchers were back in their cubicles, and the afternoon dog walkers hadn't started hitting the streets yet. They were probably going to be stuck interviewing the same firefighter or cop on every channel.

Run, babe.

She had never run in her entire life. Not when she discovered what she was, not when her mentor disappeared on her, rather than risk exposing her to his madness, not when the Council had first targeted her, not even when the relatively low-risk life of a Retriever started getting downright dangerous.

If it was just herself, she'd be rabbiting like a, well, like a rabbit. But it wasn't just her, was it?

She made a bet with herself—a water main break, something serious but impossible to blame anyone for—and sat down on the bed and waited for the phone to ring.

It took seven minutes after the first camera set up and started broadcasting live. She picked up the phone and held it a cautious distance from her ear.

"Damn it, woman, what have you been doing?"

That was her partner, always willing to give her the benefit of the doubt.

"Water main break, or electrical fires?"

There was a pause, then the muted sound of the television in the background. "Manhole cover explosion, no suspicious activity suspected."

Wren wondered sometimes what might happen if a Talent decided to go terrorist. So far—and by that she meant the entire history of Council *and* lonejacks—it hadn't happened. Not even the IRA or PLO had ever claimed a Talented member. Something about channeling current, it seemed to burn out any kind of political or nationalistic fervor. Thank God.

"So what's going on?" Sergei asked again, this time with an edge to his voice. Bless the man, he *did* worry.

"Buy me dinner, and I'll tell you all about it." What little she knew, anyway. Hopefully, by then, she'd know more. Or at least, what to tell him.

His immediate reaction was a long, drama-queen sigh. "Why is it that I always seem to end up buying you dinner?"

She had actually opened her mouth to respond when he added, "Don't answer that. Make it early. I was too busy talking at my lunch meeting today to actually eat anything."

Wren hung up the phone without saying goodbye, and stared at the wall in front of her. She really needed to hang some artwork. She really needed to buy some artwork. The place really did look like she rented it. Her partner ran a damned art gallery, and her walls were bare. What was she waiting for? Some windfall of millions? To move to some larger, better-lit space? To suddenly develop artistic taste? None of that was going to happen, not in this lifetime.

"And this suddenly bothers you now, why?" she asked herself out loud. "Because some chickie comes in and sneers at your apartment?"

Or maybe, a little internal voice suggested, because this was the third time in less than a year someone had maybe-probably tried to seriously harm her. She had always acted like life was long and amenable to planning. Maybe it was. Maybe it wasn't. She'd gotten Sergei into bed on a whim, and that had worked out well, hadn't it?

Hadn't it?

The little voice had nothing to say on that matter.

Enough of that. She had four hours before she had to meet Sergei for dinner. Work to be done. First up, send out some feelers on the client, see if anything ugly came back before she actually cashed the retainer check. Paranoia was a lovely thing, and so useful, too. Then, maybe a wander down to the usual cafés, have some coffee, see if anyone else had gotten a package via demon-courier…

"Nope. Not a thing. Guess they don't think I'm important enough."

"Oh, give me a break." Wren downed the last of her coffee and made a grimace. That was her fourth cup of the afternoon, it having taken this long to get her companion around to the topic of interest. She should probably switch to decaf at some point. It wouldn't taste any better, but she'd feel a little less spring-wound.

"Seriously, Wren." Bill leaned across the Formica table, his black eyes intent on her face. "Last I heard of any of this, you had shot all the battle-mongers down at the Moot. Things quieted down after that. I thought that was the end of it."

She'd thought that was the end of it, too. The Moot had been a meeting between the local lonejacks that had taken place over the summer, to discuss what to do about the apparent aggression the Council was showing against lonejacks, in general and in particular. She'd pointed out then, rather dramatically, how piss-poor of an idea trying to fight the Council was. No lonejack knew a damn thing about organizing, or, more importantly, was any good at it. Lonejacks were all about individual action, individual concerns. The Council was where all the joiners landed. The followers, the order-takers. No less selfish…just differently oriented with it.

For lonejacks to form some kind of Talented militia, that was just asking to get stomped on by the big kid on the block, especially when the big kid's already got stomping boots on. She'd believed—she still believed—that their best chance to survive the Council's newfound aggression was to stay true to who they were, and not make big honking red-shirted targets of themselves. The Council would burn off whatever insanity was infecting them, and everything would go back to normal.

But when the joiners start looking cross-eyed at the individuals, even the most anti-organizational types can get nervous. Especially when violence—even unproven—gets added to the picture. And nervous made for snap decisions. But sometimes, she was starting to think, that was what the job needed.

There was no proof that the Council was behind anything that had and was happening. If you wait around for proof, sometimes you get it—and sometimes you got dead.

"Would you have signed it?" she asked him now, after the fact.

Bill relaxed back into the hard-stuffed bench of their booth, and shrugged. "Dunno. Maybe. Probably. What's been going down, it's some scary shit. Making a scary noise back might not do anything, but sitting around waiting for them to come for me? Lost most of my family, that way."

Bill looked Generic WASP, down to the Top-Siders on his feet and the natural blond of his hair, but his genetics included a long line of steppe-riding wildmen and witches, only some of whom had made it to America on the last *Cosa* express out of Germany in 1939. He was also the best damn Translocator in the city, which had earned him the much-hated nickname of "Scotty." One of the few who could—or would—create spell-sticks for Talents like Wren, for whom Translocating was, at best, a chancy operation.

If she were part of a group looking to garner support among the lonejacks, Bill would have been at the top of her list. The fact that he hadn't been approached meant—what? That they had no interest in this letter being circulated among lonejacks. That they had no intention of building a consensus, or circulating it further. That the people putting it together—otherwise intelligent, if hotheaded Talents—had an agenda that probably did not include getting the Council to back down, but rather force their hand.

She hoped to hell the Council didn't take the bait, but suspected they rather would. And that that had been the plan all along.

And you fell for it. You went along and blithely jotted your initials on the damned thing without thinking it through, giving them your fingerprints over the damn thing, which could be just what's needed to make the Council move overtly—and therefore make a lonejack coalition needful. Brilliant, Valere. Fucking brilliant. You got played.

She downed the last of her coffee, and waved the waitress over for a refill, already mentally composing the "stop the press" response she was going to scorch into their hides, via demon express. She'd do it herself, if she thought they'd left themselves open to any kind of directed attack. But they were smart, these bastards. Almost smart enough to pull it off, worse luck.

The bells from the church up the street were tolling six when Wren came up out of the subway. She was late. As usual. Knowing her partner, he had arrived exactly on time.

At some point, they had stopped even specifying where and when they were going to meet for dinner. Before they were sleeping together, but after she'd moved into the apartment on Hanover Street. And wasn't it sad, that she marked her life not by years, but events? She couldn't even remember, without looking at her lease papers, what month she had moved in. Autumn, she knew that, because her mother had been worried about an early snow or some other insane thing interrupting the move. All four pieces of furniture she had, at the time, and two suitcases of clothing…

Things like that, now, made her laugh. God, what she wouldn't give for a life where a little snow was a major catastrophe.

She caught a glimpse of herself in the window front, and paused to check her teeth for lipstick. She still hadn't gotten used to wearing it. She still wasn't sure why she even bothered. Even if he noticed, he never said anything.

Of course he notices, she told herself with mild irritation. *Sergei notices everything. Even me.*

"You're late," Callie said when the Retriever walked through the front door. It was early enough that the restaurant was mostly empty, the very last of the very late lunchers cleared away but the local dinner crowd still caught in their nine-to-whenever office jobs.

"I'm always late," she said, and then, just to get it over with, "No, don't bother to get up, I'll find my own way."

The hostess/waitress just waved an indulgent hand in acquiescence as Wren moved between the tables of the small restaurant, moving unerringly to the table for two at the back corner where Sergei was already waiting. Her partner was reading a paperback while he waited, which was unusual. Typically he had his face buried in one of the endless trade rags the art world produced, or the apricot-colored pages of the *Financial Times*. The years had been gentle on him; the guy she had met more than a decade ago had worn his hair shorter, carried a dozen fewer pounds around the torso, and had more of a military precision in his posture. But the lines of the jaw were still as square and clean, and his wide-set brown eyes still had that same pale glow to them.

Or maybe it was just the way he looked at her. *Saw* her, the way the rest of the world seemed incapable of managing. It was, damn it, sexy as hell.

"Hi."

"Hi."

"I ordered you a diet ginger ale. I thought you might need it, to ease the headache."

They had been partners for almost eleven years now. Lovers for less than a year. She really did love him for his mind.

And, okay, the bod that housed that mind, too. But mostly his mind. And the way he did shit like that.

"Headache, huh? Someone's been doing some research while they were waiting." Good. If he knew what was going on, that would make life easier for her, in the "what the hell is going on" category. And maybe he could explain the "why" of it to her, too.

"Actually Doblosky called me, after we talked." Ben Doblosky was a beat cop in the Midtown South precinct whom they had met three—no, four jobs prior, when the vigilantes were still a new threat on the block. He was also a Talent, and so part of Danny's network. "All he said was that you were going to have a nasty current-backlash headache, and would probably need a place to crash, somewhere out of attack-range of your apartment."

His tone was still mild, but there were undercurrents there only someone who had known him a long time would hear; striations of, "Were you going to tell me you were the target?" blended with, "Are you sure you're okay?"

She sat down and picked up the menu, just to have something to do with her hands. "I really wish that people would stay out of my personal life. I already have a mother, and she's more than enough." Wren didn't appreciate people deciding that she needed taking care of. Not even Sergei. Especially not when she was fine, damn it.

Her mom went through fourteen hours of labor to push Wren into the world. She got dispensation to fuss, much as she wanted. Nobody else.

She looked around. "Where's the chalkboard?" The specials were always written on a chalkboard.

"Broken. There's a sheet in the menu."

She signed, opening the menu and staring at it. She didn't know why she bothered. She had been on a veal kick lately, and that's what she had gotten the last six times they were in. Or maybe seven.

"The incident outside your apartment, the one on the news. It was—"

"*Cosa* business." Wren suddenly wasn't in the mood to discuss it. She hadn't been able to figure out why the blast was bothering her so much. Or, not the blast, but the *why* of it. "Just someone being cranky."

"At you." Sergei stared at her over the top of his reading glasses.

"Probably." Definitely. Danny was right, there wasn't

anyone else the message could have been for. She was the only lonejack on her street, unless someone had moved in over the summer. Council members waging a little intramural rivalry she'd gotten caught up in? Unlikely. Council membership had its perks, and one of them involved protection from things like this—both from other members, and from outsiders. That was the appeal of the Council, the carrot they were offering lonejacks.

Ignoring the fact that the main problem they seemed to be offering protection from was—according to lonejack paranoia—the Council itself.

"Some sort of mini-blast. Danny stopped by. He's looking into it."

"You're staying with me tonight." Sergei caught himself before she could even give him a Look, proving that he knew exactly how she was going to take that particular pronouncement. A deep breath, his hands flat on the table, fingers not clenching by sheer force of will that she could appreciate. "If you want to stay with me tonight, I'd be glad of the company. I'm a little unnerved by anyone setting off explosives in your general vicinity."

Slightly mollified, Wren lifted her water glass and studied the way the fluid inside it moved around the ice cubes. "You think they're not going to set them off if you're around?"

"My building is a little more secure. Not to mention my apartment's farther from the street."

A psi-bomb could be set off right next to his window. Right next to his bathroom sink, if he'd left the window open even a crack. No need to tell him that, if Doblosky—that blabbermouth—hadn't.

"You gonna cook me breakfast?" He might be the master negotiator, but she could haggle a bit, too.

"I think I've got a few eggs I could scramble, somewhere in the fridge, yes. You'd know that, if—"

"Don't go there, lover."

There was no way she would ever give up her apartment, bare walls and unnerving memories aside. But even at her most stubborn she had to admit that there were real plusses to Sergei's place, not the least of which was a state-of-the-art kitchen, and an owner who knew how to use it.

"Let me guess." Callie appeared tableside, despite the fact that Wren still had the menu open. "You're going to have hanger steak, rare, and she's going for the veal scaloppine. You want a glass of wine, too?" That last was to Wren.

"No, I'm good, thanks." Callie was a professional waitress, not an actor-waiting-break. More, she was a New York professional waitress. But as used to them as Callie might be, they were accustomed to her as well, which took half the fun out of it. She just nodded like some sort of benign dictator, picked up the menus, and walked away.

"Now that that's settled. What *kind* of *Cosa* business, that involves things exploding and Ben worrying about your safety?"

Figured. Trust Didier not to be distracted, not when it involved her. She had to give him something, or he'd be impossible. Make that *more* impossible. "The kind everyone tells me they want me to stay out of while they keep dragging me *in*. P.B. came by earlier."

"Oh?" He took a sip of his wine, swallowed appreciatively, and raised one narrow, probably professionally plucked eyebrow, inviting her to continue.

In for a dollar, in for a euro, or whatever the saying was. She took a deep breath, let it out. "Some of the more usual suspects have put together a letter to the Council, wanting to know if they're behind the recent…problems. Walks a real pretty line between threat and whimper, I have to admit. And despite my advice to the contrary, I suspect that they're going to send it." Hopefully a revised version. Hopefully using her suggestions. If not…

Sergei digested that; she could almost see the wheels and gears turning in his brain. "And it will do…what?"

Wren drained half her water, and put the glass down with a thunk on the table. "Not a damn thing, if we're lucky. If we're not, which we never seem to be, it's going to piss off the Council, whether they had anything to do with the disappearances in the first place or not. And then the real fun begins. Not. Fuck. Look, you've reassured yourself that I'm okay, can we just drop it?"

Sergei frowned, wrinkles forming between his eyes as he stared at her. She met his gaze with as much inner calm as she could manage with her head still aching, willing him to accept the fact that she was okay, all right, present and accounted for.

She knew what he was afraid of. Had been afraid of, deep down inside that stoic business-guy exterior, ever since all this began, six months ago.

Afraid that the lonejack paranoia was true. That the Council *was* behind the disappearances of the Talents. That the Council *had* been behind the attacks on the fatae, had been funding the so-called vigilantes. That they—the Council—*were* plotting something. And that Wren, by taking a public stand against them and winning, during the Frants case, had put herself on their to-do list.

And that their *do*-ing was of the fatal kind.

She didn't know how to reassure him. She wasn't immortal. She didn't even heal particularly well. And Lee's death over the summer had just driven that home all the harder. No matter that the other Talent had died because of fatae politics raising its ugly head at exactly the wrong moment, or that the violence had been driven by the malign influences of the job she had been working on, an influence now, hopefully, locked away in a lead-lined, current-sealed box and sunk a mile deep into the floor of some cold ocean somewhere.

Death sobered you. It made you think about things like the people you loved, term life insurance, next of kin, and how badly your friends were going to screw up your wake if you didn't leave them explicit instructions.

"Y'know what I really want to do?" she said suddenly.

"Get dinner in a doggie bag, go back to the apartment, and screw like maddened weasels?"

Wren widened her eyes in mock shock, even as she felt the heat rise in her face. "I was thinking about getting a hot fudge sundae for dessert, actually, but that sounds good, too."

Sergei smiled, that half grin that made her insides do a nice-feeling woogly, and gestured for Callie to make their order to-go.

She really did love him for his mind. Really.

"Did she give you a message?"

P.B. didn't like this guy. At all. The feeling seemed to be mutual, from the glare the human was giving him. Maybe he was a bigot. Maybe he just didn't like demon. Maybe he glared that way at his mother, too.

"No, she didn't give me a message. She gave me the paper, which I gave to you. That's what I do." The rhyming pattern, unintentional, made P.B. think of the spells Wren used to direct her current. She didn't rhyme, but the words always had this singsong pattern to them. If he had access to magic, he'd use it to turn himself invisible and get the hell out of here. "Here" being a small, smoke-filled room like he didn't think they made anymore, with way too many hard-eyed humans who smelled like stale fear.

Demon didn't sweat. When nervous, P.B. blinked a lot. He hoped that these humans didn't know that, and ascribed his constant twitch to the layers of smoke.

"What did she say?" That gravelly voice belonged to a seated human; grossly overweight, like Santa gone bad. He might have been jolly once, but not now. The stub of a cigar rested between thick pink fingers.

"She didn't say anything," P.B. started to explain again, when he realized the man was speaking to the guy holding the papers.

"That we were idiots, but if we were determined to slit our own throats, she wouldn't stop us." He looked past the scrawled note on the top sheet and skimmed the rest of the papers. "She marked up the actual letter with red pen, made some suggestions about wording."

"And…?" A third human, this one covered in dark hair like a badly evolved orangutan and a surprisingly squeaky voice. It should have been funny, but P.B. didn't ever want to meet that guy in a dark alley.

"And nothing. That's it."

"She won't sign on with us?" Human #4, with skin as black as P.B. could ever remember seeing, and deep green eyes that were absolutely not natural—and not colored contacts, either. The Force was strong in that one, and it was Sith, all the way. "Even after they tried to kill her?"

"She didn't say she would." Back to the first speaker, who held the papers.

"Damnation! We need her!"

"She didn't say she would," the fifth and last man said. A small, weedy, whiskery-looking man, wearing Bermuda shorts that showed off impressively knobby knees, he held a cigar that was still unlit, and looked like it had been chewed at by a nervous rat. "But does she say that she *won't?*"

The four other men and one demon stared at him. He shrugged, twirling the cigar idly. "If she says she will, she will. If she says she won't, she won't. If she hasn't committed…she's thinking. She hasn't ruled either answer out. She's being a smart lonejack, and keeping her options open and her opinions to herself." He sounded like he envied her. From what P.B. knew of lonejacks, he probably did. The first order of business was something like "don't take jobs you hate," or something like that.

"We don't have that option anymore."

"Neither does she," the fat man said. "Demon, thank you. Payment will be made in full, by the end of the workday. Now, go."

P.B. would have hung around, despite the smoke and the glare from Human #1, just to hear what was being said. Even if it hadn't involved Wren, knowledge was currency. Especially these days. But the choice wasn't his.

The door of the town house shut firmly behind him, and the demon took a breath of the relatively cleaner air outside. But the stink of smoke clung to his lungs, and made him feel dirty.

"They're going to get themselves killed. All of them."

Not that it should matter. Humans, even Talents, even lonejacks, were none of his concern. He was demon, the stepchild of the fatae. None of them were his concern, just like he had never been theirs. Wasn't just lonejacks who played by those rules.

For most of his life, all he had wanted to do was survive. When the vigilantes started targeting the fatae last year, he had thought about leaving town. But he had stayed, to help the only fatae breed more helpless, more friendless than he was: the piskies.

And then, when Wren had been targeted by her own kind, he had come to her aid. He had brought her information and watched her back, hers and her partner's. He hadn't even seriously considered abandoning her, not while she needed him. Not only because she had played fair with him all the years they'd known each other. But because he *liked* her.

That had been new. Nice, but new.

And when the other fatae had started coming to him—to *him!*—with their worries, their concerns, he had listened. And done something, become part of bringing the lonejacks and fatae together, using Wren to create the possibility of…something. A bridge. A chance.

The ties he had avoided for so long were tight around him now. And he still didn't know how it had happened, or why.

Or maybe, he thought, looking down the street and watching the usual flow of bodies and cars doing their usual oblivious-to-each-other dance of the crosswalks, he did.

Whistling a disturbingly cheerful dirge, P.B. put his slouch hat slantwise on his head, and set off down the street, confident in the fact that this was New York, and nobody would even take a second look at a four foot tall white-furred demon walking past them. In their minds, if they processed it at all, they'd shrug and think "well, why *shouldn't* there be something that looked like that walking down the street?"

This was *his* city, damn it. His home. If it was going to go down in flames, he would go down with it.

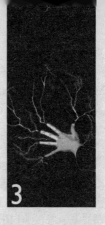

3

She is in her apartment, filled with twisted bodies, sweat-sheened faces, like something out of a mid-Level of Hell: cocktails and damnation. She turns, looks for the door, and suddenly there's something holding her, pulling her arms off like a little boy tugging fly wings. It hurts. She twists, trying to get free, back arching until her leg muscles strain in sympathy, tendons snapping, sweat pouring off her, and the current would. Not. Come.

"Help me!" A silent scream, and she aches worse than her body inside to answer that plea. But she can't do more than twist in death throes, unable to do more than relive the agony of realization, the moment of Lee's death, even knowing that this wasn't how he had died, this wasn't the way it went at all—

Her arms finally free, her body falling forward, landing hard on the floor, and she inches forward like a worm to the tall, bleeding form and looks on his face to say goodbye, and...

The face that looks back at her, eyes wide and staring with madness, isn't Lee's but John Ebeneezer's. Her mentor. Her father, in all the ways that mattered.

And he stares at her, and says:

You killed me.

Sergei's bed took up most of the sleeping loft of his apartment. It was huge, comfortable, and damned difficult to get out of in the morning, like a feather-bed hug. He was a solid lump of heat, and the urge to snuggle in next to him, rest her head on his chest and go back to sleep, was so overwhelming Wren almost gave in.

Almost. Not quite. Not after that particular nightmare.

Easing out of bed with more care than was needed—he could sleep through an earthquake, when he was in his own bed—Wren located the nearest shirt from the pile of hastily dropped clothing on the floor and slipped it on over her head, then went down the spiral staircase that led from the sleeping loft to the rest of the apartment. Large, open and modern, it was the total opposite of her own place. Hi-tech, carefully furnished, and very, very expensive.

She liked it, but always felt like she was going to break something by accident. Like, oh, the coffeemaker. He'd upgraded from the piece of shit percolator he'd bought when he realized she wasn't much more than a lump of mobile meat without real caffeine, and every time she looked at the gleaming testament to fine Italian caffeine know-how, she wasn't sure if she was supposed to press a button or genuflect.

She settled for measuring out the coffee, adding water, then pressing the right buttons and walking away to let it do its magic. Let the blessings of the kahve rain upon her, and all would be well. Or at least washed clear for the day, so she could do what she needed to do.

Sergei's laptop was set up on a sleek Danish Modern desk in a far corner of the loft, surrounded on all sides by ledgers and paperwork. Sergei might make a sizable chunk of money moonlighting as her business manager, but the Sergei Didier Gallery—Fine Art and Collectibles—was what the taxes were taken out of.

She walked cautiously over to the desk. What was once a simple wireless setup had been complicated in recent months by a tangle of surge protectors and duct tape. The surge protectors weren't actually hooked into the wall outlet—they weren't meant to protect the computer from wild energy coming in through power lines, but from *her.* She had a much more intricate system set up on her own computer, as well as the phones, her stereo system, and the toaster. She didn't even dare have a television—one moment of irritation with network programming, and there went the entire set, shorted out under peevy current.

Sitting down and logging in, she checked her e-mail. Nothing. Not even her usual mailing lists were stirring, much less any response to the feelers she had sent out yesterday on the client.

There was, however, an e-mailed sighting of that damned stuffed horse she'd been chasing for too many years. Another pin in the map that had too many pins already. Someday she was going to catch that bansidhe in equine-and-sawdust form, and stuff it back into the glass museum case it came from, be damned if she didn't.

Next step was her bank account. Yes, there it was: a lovely, lovely overnight deposit. Bless Miss Rosen and her bank of good repute, neither of whom had wasted any time despite Wren's short-tempered, high-handed manner. That went a long way toward improving her mood, dissipating the last remnants of her nightmare.

What that meant, however, was that Wren was now officially on the clock.

"All right. First things first."

She called up her preferred search engine, and typed in "Melanie Worth-Rosen." The hits that came back seemed to indicate that the grieving widow was a woman of some social distinction and obligation. Vice president of the Gotham Historical Center, Secretary for the Uptown Foundation of Arts, quite hoity-toity, but also Secretary of the Manhattan Mission for Animals… and chair for the local Literacy Campaign. "All that we're missing for you to be All American is a stint as the May Queen. So, was this paragon of virtues on the so-cialite's parade float, or did she get down in the trenches, protesting the imperialist waste?"

A few more searches gave her the answer.

"Protesting. Good for you!" An arrest back in college, for trespassing with intent to distribute pamphlets. An actual arrest, even if there was no conviction on-file, so somebody made a bargain. Wren was impressed. Back then, companies hadn't been so lawsuit-shy; they'd actually sent lawyers after penny-ante offenders like that, giving them their day in court—and in the newspapers. Protestors got media-savvy, and the corporations got weaselier, exchanging prosecution for no video footage on the evening news…but to stand there, back then, and give The Man the finger—that took guts.

So. Wren pushed back a little from the desk in order to think. A widow, younger than her husband and older than her stepdaughter, within socially acceptable parameters but a bit of a conscience as well. Attractive woman: not a blonde, which showed a refreshing change. Auburn, maybe; it was difficult to tell in the photographs. Decent bone structure, and wonder of wonders, a smile that didn't look like it was about to crack her face. Wren suspected that this was a woman who knew how to laugh.

In several of the photos, Anna Rosen and Melanie were together. In one, they had their arms around each other, with body language that seemed neither forced nor uncomfortable.

All right, that was significant. Anna had not given off warm and fuzzy vibes towards stepmomma when she hired Wren, but there they were, chummy-buddies and smiling, not just for the cameras. So why was Melanie holding on to the one thing that darling stepdaughter wanted? Where had it gone wrong? With Daddy's death? Or after, when the will was read out?

Knowing the answer might not make any difference. Not knowing the answer might make all the difference in the world. That was the thing about Retrievals. You never knew what was important until you realized you didn't know or have it. Better to be safely obsessive, and end up with useless trivia. Might come in handy some-when else, you never knew.

Hitting the print key for several different screens, Wren got up to go check on the coffee's progress.

"Bless you," she said to the machine, grabbing one of the black, surprisingly delicate-looking china cups from the cabinet and pouring herself a long dose. It needed sugar, but for now, this was manna from the gods just as it was.

The computer was still printing—the photos were taking forever—so she headed for the sofas, curling her feet under her and making sure to set her cup down on a coaster rather than directly on the surface of the cof-fee table. Sergei protected the high-gloss surface of the furniture with the ferocity of a momma bear protecting cubs. She didn't understand it—growing up, a coffee table was what you put your feet up on—but she was willing to humor him, within reason.

A flash of recent memory—she grabbed the headboard, arching back, thankful the bed was wood, and sturdy, as they rocked back and forth. His teeth were bared in a fierce, taunting, smug grin that made her want to wipe it off through sheer exhaustion.

"You like that?" he asked. Totally unnecessarily, in her opinion. She wasn't sure what she had been vocalizing just now, but she was pretty damn sure it hadn't been "stop."

"Not bad," she managed to say, then rocked forward again, rewarded by his hiss of purely physical satisfaction. Current stirred within her, woken by the intense emotions

running her brain. Normally she could only "see" them when she was in a fugue state, but the sense of them was always there, in this particular instance dark blue and purple strands eeling around her inner core, sparking and sizzling in her arousal.

"Lyubimaya. Yessssss." Sergei was practically crooning his approval as she moved on him, and the current reacted to that, streaking up and out, exiting her pores like highly charged mist. Where her skin met his, flesh sizzled, and his croon became a loud, exuberant yell of climax as he thrust upward and came, almost violently, within her.

The memory ended abruptly, Wren shaking herself out of the reverie she had fallen into. *Coffee. Drink coffee, Valere. Then back to work.* Only she knew from experience that she wouldn't get much work done, not with a still-naked, warm, sleepy and morning-eager Sergei still in bed. Sex was just such a great way to procrastinate.

Drinking her coffee, she went back into the gleamingly clean kitchen to find a piece of paper and a pen to leave a note. By the time she had figured out what to say, gone back up the staircase, found her clothing and—quietly—gotten dressed, the printer had finished kicking out her materials. She gathered them up, shoved them into a folder, and let herself out of the apartment. After a moment of indecision—library? Starbucks? Home?— she headed back downtown to her own place, where she could spread out without fear of interruption or over-priced coffee-lures.

* * *

"Zhenchenka?" A hand reached out from underneath the sheets, stretching blindly into the space where Wren had been sleeping. It patted the mattress, as though thinking the body might still be there, then gave up.

Rolling over, Sergei Didier opened his eyes, blinking against the faint sunlight reaching up into his sleeping loft, and calculated the time. The semifamiliar smell of coffee rose from the main level. So much for an early morning roll call.

Getting out of bed, he noted that Wren's clothing was gone from the pile. Tossing his castoffs into the laundry basket, he pulled fresh socks and underwear from the dresser drawer, and went down to shower. The burns on his chest and thighs were tender, but already healing.

He knew it worried Wren, the way her current would occasionally overflow while they were making love, but he didn't mind. Yes, he knew what current could do. He had seen the remains of the wizzarts killed by the over-rush of current, during that case last year. On her insistence, he had even read a book about electricity and the ways it had been used to kill, over the years. Interesting book. That probably hadn't been the reaction she had intended to provoke in him.

He trusted her, even when she wasn't sure she trusted herself, not to hurt him.

Much, anyway. And a little pain mixed in with the pleasure…well, sometimes, with the right person, it just added to the pleasure. That was a new realization for him, and he was still poking around the edges of it. Carefully, the way he did everything, but not shying away from the facts, either.

He turned on the water, and stepped under the spray.

Besides, she'd been grounding in him for years. He doubted that had left him totally untouched—his most recent medical exam had shown some interesting striations on his kidneys that hadn't been there before that fiasco in Maine, and the incident in Italy over the summer couldn't have helped any.

No job was without risks. So why not take the benefits, too?

Not that he was going to tell her any of that. The last thing she needed to do was start pulling back in the middle of a job because she was worried about his internal organs.

Resting his head against the wall and letting the hot water pound against his skin, Sergei tried to force himself to relax. Wren was going to be okay. She was tough; toughest woman he'd ever met, in some ways. Lee's death was a blow, but she'd recover. All he had to do was keep her busy, somehow. Find her a job. Keep her body going—jobs as he can, sex when he can't. It was all he could think of, and it wasn't enough to stave off the feeling of disquiet he had, holding her while she slept, watching while tears flowed from under her closed eyelids.

A shudder swept over him, like a horse trying to shake off flies. In all his life, Sergei Didier had only failed once. The thought of it happening again—losing someone because he wasn't strong enough to save them—wasn't one he could accept.

By the time he came out of the shower, tying his robe around his midsection, the smell of coffee had faded, and the apartment was completely quiet, the way only a very expensive, modern building could manage in the middle of a bustling city. So he knew, even before he saw the note on the kitchen counter, that she was gone.

A scrawl on the back of a used envelope. *Stuff's cooking. Nothing to worry, just details. Thanks for dinner—and dessert! Will stop by later.*

And that was all. Vague even for Wren, who thought you should never preface anything with more than, "Hey, watch this!"

Rinsing out the coffeepot and setting it out to dry, Sergei put on the kettle for his own tea, toasted a bagel, and spread it with a schmear of cream cheese, and went to check his e-mail. She had left the machine on—unlike her. Very unlike her, normally as cautious around expensive electronics as a soldier in a minefield.

It had taken him longer than he liked to admit to Talent-proof his apartment for Wren, and the sight of the surge protectors and add-ons still made him do a faint double-take of "how'd that get there?" The kitchen had likewise been proofed, although it was less visible there. Expensive and unsightly, but the ability to use his electronics was one less excuse Wren could use to rush home, rather than staying the night. He'd found that he liked having her stay until morning. Purely selfish, and he made no excuses for it.

Plus, he liked his apartment much more than hers. A better shower, for one, and a much larger, more comfortable bed. At five-foot and inches, she could get away with a twin mattress. He was considerably taller, and liked to sprawl.

"Incoming!" the computer sang out, and he looked to see what had landed in his in-box. Most of it sorted into "gallery" files, some to "clientele," which meant potential jobs or leads for Wren, and the rest went directly into the main folder to be sorted by hand.

One of those e-mails was red-tagged as urgent. The return-reply name was simply "bossman." That was enough.

Sergei opened it.

We need a meet. Sigma GG.

That was all it said, and all Sergei needed to read. "Bossman" was Andre Felhim, his former superior officer and current contract liaison with the Silence, the organization that had saved their bacon last year and then tossed it right back into the fire with the Nescanni Parchment job. The job that had—indirectly—gotten one of Wren's best friends, Lee, killed, and landed Sergei in the hospital with severely bruised kidneys the doctors were at a total loss to explain. Wren had treated him like he was made out of spun glass for a month after that.

Turnabout on the traditional role-play, he supposed, and no more than he deserved, but it had made him even more determined to keep his partner as far away from the Silence as he could. Just the mention of his former employer made her eyes go cold and hard in a way that wasn't natural to her.

No, even without the GG coding—Greta Garbo, for "tell no one, come alone"—he wouldn't have mentioned it to his partner. Keeping her busy was only part of the plan. Keeping her unstressed, so she had time to work through her thoughts, that was key. She wasn't the type to talk it out, or act it out, or any other "out." All you could do was stand by and wait for the storm to pass.

Deleting the message, and then wiping it from his system seven ways from Sunday, so that only the most determined snoop would be able to reconstruct it, Sergei started to reconfigure his workday. He needed to be able to get away long enough to meet with Andre without either Wren or his gallery assistant noticing that he was missing. Sending the revised schedule to Lowell for him to sync with the gallery's computer, Sergei browsed the morning's headlines, did one last check of his e-mail, then shut down the computer and went back upstairs to get dressed.

The last thing he did, before leaving the apartment, clad in his usual expensively subdued suit and tie, was to retrieve the delicate-looking but vicious handgun from his lockbox, count out a handful of bullets, and place the pistol in the holster snugged into the small of his back. You didn't call for a meet—something outside of the office—without there being trouble. And trouble, when it came from Andre, meant going armed.

I hate that thing. Wren's voice, floating around inside his brain. She had a more than decent touch of psycho-symmetry that made her actively ill around guns, especially this one, which had his touch all over it. She didn't like to be reminded of the fact that he was capable of taking life. Even when it was to save her own.

Don't go. Her voice again. *Or, call me. Let me be your backup, not that thing.*

"Sorry, Wrenlet. But there are some parts of the Silence you still don't know about. And that's how I'm going to keep it."

He owed her that much. It was his fault the Silence had found her at all. It was his fault that Lee was dead.

So much blood staining his hands, no matter how much he tried to step away from it all.

But he was a loyal dog. Always had been. And Andre had been his master, once upon a time.

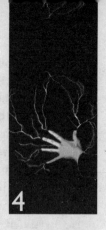

4

The man sitting behind the mahogany desk might have been carved out of the same wood, so still was his expression and body. Only his eyes moved, black pupils bright and alert.

The messages had all been sent. Some would come right away. Others would play out the anticipation, measuring the years and the miles between against the urgency of his request. But they would come. They would all come.

Andre knew his people well. Had chosen them, trained them. In some cases, let them go. All, always, waiting against a day like this.

The location of his office had once been a matter of significance to him; a corner space with a custom-made desk, and an in-box that was constantly filled with urgent projects and situation files. And when he had demanded extra filing cabinets moved into the office, so that he didn't have to wait for someone else to look something up, they had arrived paneled in matching wood.

Now, those filing cabinets mocked him, filled with information from past situations, solved situations. How much of that had been complete? he wondered. How many of his situations could have been closed sooner, if he'd gotten more, faster, more accurately? How many of the situations still open could have been closed, if he'd gotten one piece of information withheld? Who was behind this? What was their goal?

How soon would he go insane, wondering what-ifs without any basis, replaying scenarios without ever knowing for certain?

Andre Felhim was not a man who lingered overmuch on "what-ifs." He dealt with facts and responsibilities. Actions and counteractions. Situations and solutions.

He saw the road, and took it.

"Sir?"

The voice that broke into his thoughts came from Darcy Cross, standing in the doorway. Brilliant, dedicated Darcy, who never failed him, not once. His office manager, Bren, lurked behind her, the Amazonian blonde towering over tiny, sparrow-boned Darcy. Andre had trained more than a dozen field agents in his career, knowing that most would come and go, but these two were his constant. He would have been hard-pressed to replace either one of them.

"Come in, both of you. Sit, please. Would you like some tea?"

Darcy and Bren looked at each other, then nodded.

"Yes, please," the researcher said. "Would you like me to pour?"

"Please."

The teapot was an elegant silver Art Deco set, the tea poured into tall glasses with silver chasers. Sugar lumps, not packets, from a silver bowl. Bren poured out, and sat back with the glass balanced easily on one knee, waiting for it to cool. Bren, bless her, was dog-loyal. He had no doubts of her.

"Sir?" Darcy asked again. She moved the glass from one hand to another, her delicate hands making the glass seem oversized. He hated to see that look of fearful anticipation in her hazel-blue eyes. Still, she was valued within the Silence not for her courage, but her almost frightening ability to uncover things other people tried to hide. If Darcy did not know something, there was nothing to know. Her knowing; that made it real. She knew that there was a problem. Therefore, there was a problem.

The thought that she might be party to this disinformation, that she might be hiding or redirecting that life-blood of the Silence—unthinkable. Not because—unlike everyone else he had trained—she had any undying loyalty to him, but because her true love and loyalty was to information. She truly believed that it *needed* to be free. The thought of impeding it would make her head implode.

Despite this, he trusted her to know who had protected her, who continued to ease the way for her to do her job without outside interference, or undue political influences. She would file away what was said here, would bring her mind to bear on what he pointed her at, and know everything there was to know—but she would not sell it to another player. Not while he continued to protect her.

He therefore merely held up a hand, indicating that she should drink her tea, and wait.

Jorgunmunder, his protégé/lieutenant would arrive soon, the third of the three he had called to this specific time and place. And then, they could begin.

One of the great dividing lines between Manhattan residents, even more than Mets versus Yankees, was "subway or bus?" Wren was firmly on the subway side. Subways had track problems, yes. And they ran late, and occasionally stank, especially in the summer. Buses were just as crowded, and got stuck in traffic, to boot. Add to that her tendency to be "overlooked" even when she was jumping up and down trying to flag a bus down…at least the subway trains stopped at every stop, no matter if they saw someone waiting on the platform or not.

Unfortunately it was also the middle of the morning rush hour, which meant that no matter what sort of mass transit you took, it was going to be packed shoulder-to-shoulder. Thankfully today was that in-between sort of day; cool enough that the levels of human sweat were down, and not cold enough yet that people were wearing bulky coats that took up twice the available room.

Some people claimed that New Yorkers were rude. Wren had asked Sergei about that once; he, being from Chicago, had merely shrugged, as confused as she was.

It wasn't until she had spent time riding the subways waiting for a target to appear before she understood what it was outsiders were reacting to; not rudeness, but extreme politeness. Everyone in Manhattan was living in their own space, the lack of eye contact or acknowledgment others bemoaned actually allowing their neighbors the illusion of privacy, keeping noses down in newspapers or books, or eyes closed and shoulders moving to noises from their iPods.

Wren's fingers twitched—the desire to Take overwhelming, for an instant, the fact that she had no desire to own an iPod, nor any market to sell one, even assuming she was interested in that. Which she wasn't. She was a Retriever, not a garden variety thief.

But sometimes, sometimes, that itch hit, a throwback to her adolescent stint as a thrill-shoplifter.

The moment passed, the way they always did. Self-control was key. Focus was everything, the only thing, and the foremost part of focus was self-determination. Wren found a spot in the corner, leaned against the wall, and rested her eyes on nothing, letting her mind run over the material she had read that morning online until an inner-timing sense warned her that the train was approaching her stop. She slipped through the crowded car, shoulder and elbow acting like the prow of a small boat, moving people aside without them even realizing that they had been moved.

Neezer had taken her to see *Chicago*, back years ago when it was on Broadway, when she was still a teenager and he was still sane. A birthday outing, it had been. That evening had convinced Wren that Manhattan wasn't so much a ballet as it was a Bob Fosse jazz routine, all hands and shoulders and feet constantly moving. If you did it right, you looked cool. Wrong, and you were a spaz.

When she had told Neezer that, expecting her mentor to laugh, he had merely blinked at her, long and slow, and nodded his head as though he'd never thought of it that way before but it made everything make perfect sense.

God, but she missed the old man. A lot. If he'd stayed, if he hadn't wizzed…

Is as it is, Jenny-Wren. His voice, sad and slow, across the years. He hadn't, he had, and she only had his memory to consult with, now. A memory that was starting to fade, no matter how tightly she clung to it. The things people think are forever? They're dust before you know it. Wren was surprised by how bitterly angry that thought left her.

Coming up the stairs to street level, Wren stepped over the homeless person sleeping in the entryway, resisting the sudden urge to shove him out of the way with her foot. If you didn't want to go to a shelter, that was your own choice. But there was no reason to sprawl in the path of people just trying to go about their day.

A tingle of guilt struck, and she shoved it down. Get rid of that anger, Valere. It just messes with you. She wasn't a bad person—a bad person *would* have kicked him. She was just cranky, was all. Maybe she should have gone to Starbucks, gotten a mocha mood-adjustment or something, before heading for home….

Let yourself start to procrastinate and you'll wallow in

it for weeks, she told herself sternly. *Go home. Get it done. Then it's mocha-time.* Maybe even a gingerbread latte. The only good things about November—molasses mashed potatoes at Thanksgiving, and gingerbread latte at Starbucks.

Her shoes crunched leaves that had fallen onto the sidewalk; random, not the thick, colorful carpet of leaves she remembered from her childhood. But it was enough to put her back into a more peaceful frame of mind, the crunch and crackle mixed with the odd, almost-unpleasant smell of autumn in the air.

By the time she walked the three blocks from subway to her apartment, Wren had decided on a preliminary course of action. Identify the piece of jewelry. Case the location. Blueprint entry and exit points. Execute. Cash checks. Nice, simple, unfussy. A photo of the item would be ideal, but unless Rosen got hold of a digital photo for insurance purposes, that was unlikely. So, a sketch, or, more likely, a verbal description. Aldo, on the first floor, was a decent enough pencil artist—she'd used him before to turn vague verbals into something she could identify.

The first floor apartment door was closed, which meant that Aldo was either working or sleeping. She left a note on the glossy white-painted splotch on his door with the grease pencil he left tied to his door for just that purpose. Just her apartment number and an exclamation point. He'd know what it meant.

In the meanwhile, she didn't have the luxury of sitting around and waiting for people to bring the answers to her. Time to hit the paperwork trail, earn that retainer, at least.

At least it was something to do, rather than waiting for another psi-bomb to land, or another fatae friend to be attacked, or another lonejack to go missing....

She took the last few steps to her apartment with caution, listening with her ears as well as her core. "May you live in interesting times" was great if you were a newscaster, or a photojournalist. But for a simple Retriever trying to make a living, it was a pain in the ass.

Nothing. For the first time in what seemed like months, there wasn't anyone lurking in the hallway. No spybugs planted in her ceiling. No demon waiting to pass news. Just her, and her new furniture, and the spotlessly clean apartment rebuking her for the amount of time she was spending away from it.

The door locked behind her, Wren dropped her keys in the dish on the counter and placed her obnoxiously yellow—and impossible to lose—bag next to it, shrugging out of her leather jacket and hanging it up, carefully. One lecture from Sergei about the care and feeding of good leather was all she ever wanted to sit through, thanks.

She opened the bag, pulling out the printouts she had shoved in there at Sergei's place. The lump of papers made the shoulder bag bulge strangely, and once again she thought that she might need to break down and buy a briefcase to replace the old one. It had died a grisly death, eaten by a disgusting bio-sludge that Walter, a Coast Guard ensign and moderate-level Talent, had accidentally let loose over the summer while he was trying to encourage a newborn kelpie harboring just off Ellis Island to eat all her proteins.

Humming under her breath, Wren set the coffeemaker to work, pulled a diet Sprite from the fridge to tide her over in the meanwhile, then grabbed the printouts and went down the hallway to her office. She could work anywhere in the apartment, but the vibes for concentration were best in that room.

"Damn. Also, damn."

Wren carefully placed the printout she was reading down on the floor in front of her, and stared at it as though the words were about to leap off the page and bite her. In a way, they just had.

She was sitting, as usual, on the floor, with her research materials in small piles around her. Also as usual, she had begun by sorting all the available material into "useless," "possible," and "bingo."

That printout absolutely went into the bingo pile. And then some. That changed everything. Or at least a few certain, possibly very important, things.

"I hate it when clients don't give you all the details." Although, to be fair, Rosen had told her everything Wren needed to know. The Retriever just hadn't realized it at the time.

"So that's how you knew the term Null," she said to her client. "Stepmomma used it on you one time too many?"

Because Melanie Worth-Rosen was a Talent. Like Wren, but unlike. Because one of the many social-page articles Wren had printed out that morning mentioned stepmomma as being a member of the Greater Hartford Crafting Society. The GHCS—a group that Wren knew from firsthand experience accepted only Talented members. Specifically, Talents who were also Council members, as opposed to lonejacks. Like the D.A.R., only magical.

"Are you a good witch, or a bad witch?" she wondered out loud. Being a Council member in and of itself wasn't a black mark, despite Wren's negative experiences with the leaders of the Council itself. She had tried explaining it to Sergei once, the difference between *Council* and being a Council member, but the best she could manage was that it was sort of like the difference between being a dues-paying member of a union, and being Jimmy Hoffa. That wasn't quite exact, but close enough for horseshoes, and he had pretended to understand.

Normally Wren didn't give a damn about the target of a Retrieval, so long as she knew ahead of time anything they might counterpunch with. Null or Talent, museum or private citizen, government or nonprofit. The situation outside of the Retrieval, though, was anything other than normal, and the last thing she needed was more reason for the Council (the Hoffa version) to start spreading rumors that she was targeting Council (union joe version) members.

"All right. Stop a minute, think this through. Client, Null. Target, Talent." She got up to pace as she talked, feeling her knees pop and crackle as she stretched. It was still easier for her to be in action than it was to sit still.

As much as she loved her apartment, as good as the vibes were, it had one major drawback: the rooms were too small to pace in. The T-shaped hallway leading from the bedrooms to the front door, however, was perfect.

"Client is a Null. Stepmomma is Council. What about dearly departed Daddy?" Nothing in her research had said, one way or another. It was easy enough to keep secret, if you didn't make a fuss about it, but Talent tended to marry Talent. Which would mean that Momma had also been a Talent?

The jury was still out on the influence of genetics in Talent, but it did seem to cluster in families more often than not. So odds were that one of the birth parents was Null, too. Based on Rosen's attitude…yeah, odds were it was Momma of blessed memory. So there might be some bias involved to go with the estate-squabbling. Did it matter? Maybe.

What bothered Wren more was stepmomma's affiliation.

"Council has made my life miserable for the past year, because they think I'm some sort of threat. Threat to what? Unknown. Council may or may not be—probably is—behind the recent disappearances of lonejacks of a specific age and ability. Mainly older ones, strong ones, who haven't wizzed or otherwise gotten anti-social. Rumor is: Council is up to something."

Seven, eight, nine steps, reach the door, pivot. Walk back to T. Go right, three steps. Pivot. Three, and another two, always forgetting that the top of the *T* hallway was off balance, and pivot again. Two steps, turn right again, walk down to the front door. There should have been grooves worn in the floor, after all the times either she or Sergei had done this, working through the details of a job.

"So. Assuming a suitable level of paranoia…is this also something they're up to? Or did I just get caught in a relentlessly normal family squabble?"

Worth-Rosen might be exactly what she looked like—a Talent who got greedy on the wrong Null. Or she might be a dupe of the Council, if not actually one of their catspaws. And if so… Sometimes, as her partner was fond of saying, paranoia was the only thing between you and the sharks.

So. A change in plans.

A phone call started things rolling, but it would take several hours before she would know the results. In the meanwhile, she still had to get the description from Rosen and talk to Aldo, then get her hands on the layout of the mark and…

And somewhere in there she needed to do some food shopping. She had tried ordering online, but after the sixth or seventh time she crashed the system because she got frustrated at not finding what she needed, Wren had decided that the old-fashioned way worked better for her.

Stopping in the bedroom-office, Wren grabbed the client info sheet off the floor. On her next pass down the hallway, Wren snagged the phone off the wall and dialed the number penciled at the top of the sheet.

"Anna Rosen? Yes, I'm calling about the discussion we had yesterday." Was it really only yesterday? Almost exactly yesterday, in fact. Twenty-four hours and all the chaos of the psi-bomb seemed to fade into happened-last-month. "I'm going to need a description of the item in question…you have a photo? No. All right, then." And she grabbed a pencil and a scrap of paper out of the junk drawer, leaning on the counter to write more easily. "Could you describe it for me, please? As completely as you can."

Rosen clearly had studied the necklace at length—she was able to describe it quite well. A silver mask of a woman's face, eyes closed and a slight smile—a smirk, Rosen said, but not an unkind one—surrounded by a silver-beaded headdress/cowl with tendrils off to one side, like a showgirl's headdress. A small silver skull was set on a chain hanging from the headdress, over her forehead.

All in all, Wren thought it sounded like a horribly gaudy bit of junk, the kind that Great-Aunt Hortense bequeathed to you and you sold at the rummage fair the week after, but the client clearly loved it enough to hire her to steal it back, so she wasn't about to judge. Everyone had different levels of emotional attachment, God knew. Maybe it was a Null thing.

Hanging up the phone, Wren looked at her notes, making sure everything was legible enough to read back to Aldo. She should have gotten all this from the client yesterday, during their meeting. Sergei would have. Sergei would have gotten the description, and the address of the target, and all the little things that yes, Wren could track down now but would have made life so much easier to have already.

"And you decided to do this one on your own, why

again?" The answer wasn't as clear as it had been when the first nibble came in. The nightmare still jangled on her nerves, and the normally comforting vibes of her apartment, the thing that had made her decide the first time she walked in behind the Realtor that this place was *hers,* was just making her feel jumpy and twitchy now.

She really, really wanted to feel the urge to brew tea that meant Sergei was walking up the stairs. Which, considering she had run from him—and the entire sense of being too-much-togetherness—this morning, meant that she was probably losing her mind.

Speaking of minds, and details, and the slacking off on them, she should check in with Danny, see if he'd found out anything about that psych-bomb. If it was Council work, that was another thing to consider. The timing was odd… Jesus wept, if it were tied into the Rosen case, and not the general intimidation shit they kept trying to pull…

"It would mean what, exactly?"

The voice was hers, but the logic was Sergei's.

"Would it change what you've already decided to do?"

"No," she answered herself. "In which case, stop worrying, and get back to working."

She picked up the phone again and dialed a number, this time from memory.

"Joey. It's Jenny. I know you're there, Joey, pick up. You really don't want me getting annoyed with you while I'm on the phone."

All Joey Tagliente knew about Jenny Valere was that his electronics had a way of going bad when she was around, which was why she was restricted to call-ins and e-mail. And why she always got fast service.

"Babe. So good to hear your voice. Tell me what you want and I'll tell you what it costs." He oozed, but it was a mostly harmless ooze.

"The address for a Melanie Worth-Rosen." She spelled the name out, just to be sure. "The real address, not a mailing drop or her bodyguards, or whatever well-to-do people are doing these days."

"You want the phone numbers, too?"

"Sure. Why not." The cost would all be added to Rosen's invoice at the end of the job, anyway. What wasn't covered by the retainer already sitting pretty in Wren's account. And, since she brokered the deal herself, did she have to give the usual cut to Sergei? God, she hadn't even thought about that.

"Anything else?"

"You got blueprints for that address, too?" Of course he did. Or he would, for the right money. He was an efficient little snoop, Joey was.

"Maybe yes, maybe no. Two for the first, another five if I can come through on the second."

She could have haggled him down to four hundred, probably, but Sergei had taught her that it was better to overpay a little to the valuable people. Make them think of you fondly, not with a curse. You saved the haggling for the really detailed, expensive jobs, where a percentage point or two made a difference, and they were padding the bill, anyway.

"How fast can you come through?" There was a sense

of urgency riding her shoulders that Wren didn't think had anything to do with the job itself; the storm clouds were building, and her core was pricking in response. But life went on, bills came in, jobs needed to be done...

"The lady in question has two addresses. One in Martha's Vineyard, the other in Manhattan. She is currently in residence in your fair city." He gave her the addresses, plus the lady's mobile phone number. Her main number, surprisingly, was publicly listed. Wren, used to folk who guarded their privacy, hadn't even thought to look first. Trusting lady, Ms. Worth-Rosen. Or one with reason to let people contact her without prior arrangement. Wren not only wasn't publicly listed, but she paid extra money every month to have her phone number "dropped" from the phone company's system.

The fact that this meant that the phone company had no record of her having a phone, and therefore never billing her, was a nice plus to the privacy, of course.

"As always a pleasure doing business. I'll drop payment later today." For a guy who lived for his tech, Joey wasn't much for banking, electronic or otherwise. Cash in a post office box, thanks much, and good manners got you twenty-four hours credit, like now. Her first year dealing with him, she had to pay in advance. That had given Sergei minor conniptions until Joey proved he was solid on delivery.

Leaving the notes on the kitchen counter, Wren went around the corner into the bathroom and turned the water on in the shower, shedding clothing as steam filled the tiled room. Her shoulder-length hair was unbearably tangled and she brushed it out, wincing as she hit knots, until the water had reached the perfect temperature. Shampoo, soap, loofa, and all the while she was mentally rearranging her brain. Identifying herself to Tagliente as "Jenny" had solidified the vague thoughts about approaching Worth-Rosen. Risky, on several fronts, but it had a strange sort of appeal, too. Being someone other than Wren Valere—a nice thought: shedding the responsibilities to friends and *Cosa,* if only for a little while.

Proving to Sergei that he wasn't the only one who could change personas was part of it, too; she was willing to admit that as she rinsed the last of the conditioner from her hair. He was so damn good at what he did, it was a challenge to try it, too. Being able to say, "Look, I can do this, too" would…well, she had no idea what it would do. Probably nothing. But what was done was done, now.

Not that you can tell him about it until you tell him that you took on a client without his knowledge…which you're going to have to fess up to, you know. He'll want to know where you are, what you're doing. Where the money you're going to deposit in his checking account came from.

"Nag nag nag," she muttered at the voice, turning off the water and reaching for a towel.

The clicking of her heels on the pavement was, in a word, unnerving. Wren kept thinking that someone was following her, until she recalled that she was wearing actual dress shoes, not her usual sneakers or soft-soled loafers. Charlie was sweeping the leaves and dust off the pavement in front of Jackson's E-Z Shopper; he waved, and she nodded in acknowledgment, but didn't stop to talk.

Hey!

At first, Wren thought it was just a random thought of her own, the nagging voice come back uncalled-for, until the nudge came back with a firmer swipe.

Hey!

She reached in and grabbed the mental touch, tagging it in return, a sort of delivery receipt to let the person pinging her know she was paying attention now.

Tagging was a game younger Talents played, fine-tuning their controls, typically as the setup for a practical joke. Or, with adults, as a way of challenging another Talent, letting them know that they were moving into territory that was already claimed.

This didn't feel like either.

She stroked a filament-thin strand of current, coaxing it up out of her core until it coiled down her arm, into her left index finger, ready for the next tag.

Valere. A sense of parlay, of truce, like a mental white handkerchief floating in the breeze. Nobody she knew, at least not well enough to recognize the taste of their mind, but the really good taggers could disguise that.

Lee had been one of the really good ones. The thought sent a spasm of loss through her, and she shoved it down ruthlessly. Not while she was working, damn it. A flick of her finger, and the current went out into the ether, following the swiftly fading trail the last tag had left.

Who?

She continued walking down the street; her only ex-

ternal acknowledgment of anything happening was a
change of direction the moment the first tag landed. The
subway was faster and cheaper, but a cab was more secure, if someone was trying to screw with her. Besides,
she rationalized, the persona she was playing would take
a cab, not the subway. Small, concrete details made the
illusion complete.

Sarah.

The name carried with it no sense of recognition.

Need to talk to you. Soon.

Wren wasn't naturally suspicious of other Talents, but
nothing in her life was normal these days, and just accepting any tagger's invitation to a sit-down was potential suicide.

Who? she asked again, even as she came to the corner of Hudson Street and raised her hand for a cab.

Sarah. This time the name came with a sense of self:
tall, ebony-skinned, teeth that should flash in an exuberant laugh now hidden behind a grim line of lips, eyes al-
mond-shaped and shadowed like an Egyptian queen's.
A scent of good, dark beer, and stale cigarette smoke, and
Wren placed her in the jumble of memories. Council-
raised, only she crossed the stream two, no three years
ago, now. That's when Wren met her, at the party a friend
of Lee's had thrown to welcome her to the lonejack fold.

Wren hadn't stayed long; coming down off a job that
had sucked all the sleep out of her, the last thing she
wanted to do was stand in a crowded bar and down over-
priced beer until she stank like last call. But one thing
about the evening had stood out, even three years later,

and made her interest in this unexpected tagging spike sharply.

Sarah was a Proggie. A Prognosticator.

A Seer.

Oh, shit.

A cab slowed, and Wren opened the door and got in before it had fully stopped, still immersed in the inner conversation.

"Where to?" The driver pulled into traffic without waiting for an answer, flicking the meter on as he did so. The heat was on, and the windows were rolled down all the way. Crazy.

"Central Park West and Sixty-eighth. Thanks." With luck, Eighth Avenue would be clear enough that they'd only pick up traffic going crosstown, so the meter wouldn't ratchet up too much.

Hello? A reminder that she had left Sarah hanging.

Another tug of current from her core, and Wren sent a final tag. *Tonight. Red Light?* A bar that had perfect acoustics for conversation—pick the right table, and while you could hear every word said, someone standing a foot away wouldn't be able to make out anything— and dark enough to make lip reading problematic.

Electronic eavesdropping wasn't really a problem, not with two Talents at one table. And, the way Wren was feeling, pity the bastard who tried to plant current-bugs on her again. She'd fry them, and him, and any unrelated electronics in the path between.

Will be there. A sense of the table Sarah was thinking of, the same one Wren had in mind.

You read my mind, Wren sent, and signed off just as the snort of psychic amusement reached her.

The sound of swearing in some foreign language made her look up just in time to see the cabbie slap the small black box set into the dashboard with the palm of his hand. The impact did nothing to reset the electric meter, which had gone from clicking off the quarter-miles to flashing "00.00."

Ooops.

And then the cab was turning the corner, gliding through clogged sidestreets to her destination. When he pulled to the curb, she handed the guy a twenty. Probably twice what the fare would have been, but she felt bad about wrecking his meter. Cabbies, like lonejacks, got shafted enough without her adding to it.

Taking a deep breath, Wren shut down the part of her that was awareness of her own life, letting the current rise and reach into every square inch of her body, tampering with her self-image.

Exiting the car, Wren gave herself over to the current entirely. She could feel her legs getting longer, the slim skirt and button-down blouse she had put on giving her the impression of height, while the professional-looking black leather pumps added a reassuring nudge of respectability. Her hair was coiled in a soft bun at the back of her neck, and the gentle smudges of eyeliner and lipstick gave the overall feeling of overworked competence. She based the look on the women she saw on their lunch breaks, not the ones rushing back and forth, but the ones who stopped, walked slowly, their faces up to the sunlight, taking time to remember to be thankful they were out of the office even for a few moments. That was who she needed to be: a woman who cared about the small moments, the shared intimacies. Who could coax the same out of another woman.

"I'm here to see Mrs. Worth-Rosen."

Even with her Talent-enhanced appearance, the doorman still would have turned her away without an appointment. He was that kind of employee, the sort who took the well-being of "his" building more seriously than the residents did themselves. But the woman had a listed phone number, which meant that she wasn't as peon-phobic as others in her position, and as a competent, well-tuned doorman, he had to be aware of that as well.

Scooping some of the current sizzling just under her skin, Wren gave the uniformed gatekeeper a shy, diffident smile, and Pushed a sense of her total innocence and usefulness toward him. Of all the skill sets Talents had at their use, the Push was the most useful—and the most open to abuse. The fact that she still worried about that, according to Sergei, was proof she wasn't about to run amok with it. Wren still worried.

"I'm Jenny Wreowski? The mediator from Darsen, Darsen and Kelvin?" Assume complicity, and most people will rise to the occasion. The doorman was no different; he knew that Mrs. Worth-Rosen was going through a tough time, and a legal mediator in the form of this soft-spoken, delicate-looking, Southern-sounding woman was surely harmless, if not proven helpful. He

went to get the appointment book, already expecting to
see her name listed there.

If you can get someone to that point, of anticipating,
it almost doesn't take much Talent to convince them to
see what you want them to see. In a matter of minutes
she was in the tastefully ornate elevator, being shuttled
up to the fifteenth floor where "Miss Melanie" resided.

"I'm sorry," the woman who opened the door said. "I
don't know why Jordan let you up here, but I don't see
anyone without an appointment and I'm sure…"

"No, you didn't make the appointment, Mrs. Worth-
Rosen. Another party hired me, to use my skills to prevent a small problem from becoming larger."

The target looked Wren up and down, puzzled, then
the light of comprehension cleared the confusion from
her eyes. "Anna. Anna hired you to talk to me."

"Yes, ma'am." Half-truth qualified as whole truth,
under the circumstances. This was the decision point. Either Melanie let her in, or she shut the door in Wren's
face. No safe ground between the two…

"All right. Come in."

Tea and biscuits were served out by a young Filipina
girl with large dark eyes and delicate hands, in a sitting
room filled with light and pastel watercolors hanging in
too-close profusion on the walls. Working with the
owner of an art gallery might not have changed Wren's
tastes much, but she had learned to recognize good pre-
sentation, and that wasn't it.

"I still don't understand quite how things went

wrong." The target shook her head, the soft waves falling just so around her face, so carefully made-up her features appeared completely natural in the muted sunlight filtering through sheer curtains. The room itself was larger than Wren's entire apartment. "It's as though Anna overnight became a different person. The sweet, loving girl I knew became shrill, coarse, accusing me of trying to cut her out, of stealing…. Anything of her mother's was hers, of course. That had been established long ago, before her father even fell ill."

Fell ill, Wren noted. Not died, or Anna's blunt "was murdered."

Melanie continued, holding her teacup in her hand and staring down into the oolong-scented liquid as though her script was printed there. "But the necklace was a gift, from her father to me. Anna refused to accept that."

Melanie's confusion over her stepdaughter's attitude seemed real. But Wren knew that the Push could be used on Talents, too, and if the older woman were better at it than she, Wren wouldn't be able to tell. That was always the risk; you could use your skills on a fellow Talent, and maybe they wouldn't realize it…and maybe they would. Wren preferred to fly under the radar, depending on defensive skills rather than offensive ones. The current keeping her appearance intact was subtle, so subtle almost as to not register, according to Neezer, back when he was first teaching her, and she'd only gotten better at it in the decade-plus since then. But Melanie was older, had been practicing longer, and so Wren couldn't take any emotional response at face value.

"She seemed so certain," Wren said, picking out a flaky-delicate butter cookie and biting into it with relish, wishing for a mug of coffee to dunk it into. That would probably give the maid a heart attack, if not Melanie. "May I ask…why not just give it to her, if it's so important? Forgive me if I intrude, but it seemed not a particularly valuable piece…"

Melanie's face twisted for just an instant, those lovely well-bred features showing an unpleasant cast before returning to their socially acceptable sweetness. Something Wren had just said struck home, hard. "Valuable? Not in the way most would think of it, no. But it has certain… properties that make it better to remain in my possession."

Mmm. Wren hadn't even blinked when the target's expression changed, but she had filed the moment down for later contemplation. Properties, huh? There was something going on there, something more than just sentimental—or even financial—value. Wren suspected suddenly that she was being played. She *hated* being played.

"I see," she replied, in a voice that said clearly that she was merely being polite. There were a handful of pointed questions Wren would have loved to have asked, but from the tone in Melanie's voice when she said the last, the Retriever didn't think she was going to get anything more out of her, no matter what the "legal mediator" might have to say.

"Well, still, this has been useful, indeed. Knowing where you're coming from? Helps me help my client understand, too. And maybe we can all get out of this without too much more upset?"

"That would be lovely," Melanie said with evident relief. "I miss my stepdaughter, Jenny. I truly do."

Wren believed her. But she also believed that the woman was not going to give up the necklace, not to Anna, not to anyone. There was something going on that was not sitting well with the sweetness and light and perfectly blended family pose she was giving off.

So. Back to plan the first. Retrieval, the old-fashioned way.

"Miss Melanie?" The maid was back, her serene expression broken by a frown. "Miss Anna. She's…here."

Damn it. Wren thought, struggling to not be thrown totally out of character by this new and extremely unwelcome news. Thankfully Miss Melanie seemed almost as disturbed, and for a moment Wren hoped the older woman would simply refuse to allow the girl access. But that, apparently, wasn't stepmomma's way.

"Mel, you bitch! I can't believe you changed the—" Anna stormed in, then stopped, taken aback to see Wren sitting there.

"Anna, honey." Wren stood, hoping that by taking the lead she could get them both out of there without further incident. "If you were going to hire me to talk to your stepmomma, you've got to let me *talk* to your stepmomma, no?"

Anna was upset, not stupid. "I hired you before I knew what she was doing. This is my home, too, you old witch, and you can't keep me out!"

She turned to Wren, her lovely eyes glittering with tears. Wren couldn't tell if they were of sadness, rage, or something in-between.

"She used her magic on the doors! The one thing Daddy would never ever let her do, and the moment he's gone…"

"Anna!" Melanie appeared flustered beyond measure, and for a moment Wren couldn't understand why. *Oh. Right. Me not knowing.* The last thing Wren wanted was to be outed as a Talent, so she headed that one off at the pass, as best she could.

"Anna, sweetheart, I think you're a little overemotional." She placed one hand on the girl's elbow, just below where her lacy little sleeve ended, expecting to be shaken off, but Anna let the hand remain there long enough for Wren to exert a very specific Push to make Anna trust her. God, she hated doing that. It made her feel dirty. "Why don't we just go sit down together, and Melanie and I can—"

Damn. Too much Push.

Because Anna turned on her then, irate as a betrayed lover. "You and Mel, huh? Since when has it been you and Mel? Take my money, say you'll help *me,* and suddenly she's got your ear and it's all 'cozy on the sofa'?" The anger pouring off her was so palpable, Wren and Melanie both took a step back. Anna might be a Null, but by God, she could project!

"Anna, you're being a foolish child."

Melanie's voice had gone sharp and hard, exactly like the parent of a five-year-old pushed to the final limit, and

Wren could hear the train alarms ringing, signaling blood about to hit the tracks.

Right. She was out of there. The maid could do cleanup. She was a Retriever, not a referee.

"Child? I'm a child? I'm more woman than you could ever be, relying on your tricks and toys."

"You ungrateful little…"

"Go on, say it." Anna taunted her stepmother, moving farther into the room. "You always wanted to call me that. I wasn't good enough, wasn't Talented enough. Too bad you didn't manage to pop out any *real* kids, make my daddy forget all about me."

Oh God, yeah. Wren was out of there. *Now*.

"Don't mind me, I'll let myself out," she said to the maid, who looked like she wanted to join her, and backed out of the apartment, deciding to take the stairs rather than risk waiting around for the elevator. She'd rather face a twisted ankle than be in the vicinity of those two another moment.

In the night's distance, a low-sounding horn called over water, a low-riding metal beast looking for its mate. Union rules had called it quits for the night, but lights still burned here and there, in small corrugated-side shacks and sturdier wood-and-brick buildings, as accountants and harbormasters went over accounts.

The rifle was a black, dulled-looking thing, more plastic than metal, but the ki-lyn facing the business end of it didn't doubt for a moment that it could hurt him. Probably kill him. If it didn't, he might wish he were. He knew the fate of his kind, taken by hunters. The black market was active in organ meats, giving false hope to the hopeless.

The human holding the weapon was a child, as the ki-lyn could judge such things; its head barely came to his withers. An older woman stood behind him, a weapon of her own—smaller, but no less ugly—held loosely in her left hand, ready to bring to bear the instant the child might falter.

Foolish old man, he thought to himself. *You were warned.*

They had found him down by the docks, where he had been waiting for transport home. This city had become unfriendly in recent months, and many of the fatae were fleeing, those who had an elsewhere to flee to, but he had wanted to finish his business out in a calm and dignified manner, not run like a startled doe.

At first, he had thought it a game, as the child darted out at him. Children were a gift, a treasure. He would never have thought to fear one, even as the small wooden bat it held came down first on one leg, then another, then a third before he could react.

"Why?" he asked now, as reasonably as he could while trying to hold himself upright despite what he was pretty sure were cracked kneecaps in three of his four legs. "What did we ever do to you? What crime did I commit, to so offend you?"

The child seemed unable to answer, his eyes wide and very very dark in his pale face. The woman had no such hesitation.

"You're a thing," she spat. "An animal. It's against God's will for animals to speak."

The ki-lyn considered that for a moment, as his kind considered all things: taking the four quarters of each question fairly, in turn, and with equal weight. "And yet, I speak, and think, and reason. Perhaps I am not an animal at all?"

He knew, the moment those words left his mouth, that they were the wrong thing to say. The woman's face twisted into such rage that anyone watching might have thought that she was the beast, and not he.

This was it. He would see his beloved homeland no more. Would never again see his own children, his mate of three-dozen decades.

"Monster! Abomination of magic!" Her eyes grew wide, the whites visible even in the dim lights overhead

He could have lowered his head and charged, even now, even with his legs giving way under him. But it was not right. Not the way a child should see its parent die, and he did not wish to kill a child. Not even a child such as this. Not even if it meant that he die instead.

If this was the Will of the Wheel, so be it. The child still stared at him, the rifle too large and too heavy for his hands.

"Kill it, baby," the woman crooned. "Show me what you've learned. Clean the earth of this filth."

The ki-lyn bowed his great horned head, and waited for the inevitable.

Forgive them, he thought to the Creator. *They act in fear, and fear is all that they know.*

"Momma..." he heard the child say, his voice wavering, and then there was a silvery ringing noise, a song too lovely to be deadly, and an impact, burning-hot and angry in his chest, and it was done.

The scaled and horned beast collapsed to the wooden docks. The boy, his rifle unfired, stared at it as though expecting the creature to rise and fight.

"Huh," the woman said. "Thought they'd be harder to kill, those scales and all."

They left the ki-lyn lying in a heap on the old docks, with only the seagulls sleeping on the light posts to bear witness.

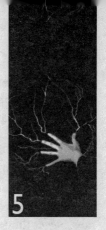

5

His cell phone was ringing. Or rather, it was vibrating, in the inside pocket of his suit jacket. Sergei was pretty sure it was Wren, just from the way the vibrations seemed to be off, somehow. Not that her current-magic could affect the phone that way, at a distance. At least, he didn't think it could. Wren kept finding new ways to surprise him, though. Being able to destroy his electronics just by calling was entirely within the realm of possible, if not probable.

He let it vibrate, and eventually it stopped. The lack of a beep said that whoever it was, they hadn't left a message.

"I don't want to get involved," he said to his companion. They were sitting in a small wine bar in midtown, surrounded by other men and women, also in suits, also drinking wine and picking at overpriced plates of dried meats, roasted peppers, and sliced cheeses before they went wherever they were going for dinner. After spending even the few days in Italy over the summer, Sergei couldn't work up the enthusiasm for what was called mortadella in Manhattan. Not even when the other person was paying.

Although the prosciutto was not bad.

"You *are* involved," his companion said, swirling the glass of wine thoughtfully, as though seeing answers in the straw-colored liquid. "As I go, boy, you go. Even now. Never think you don't. Never think, because we let you run your leash a bit, anything ever changed."

The bile that rose in Sergei's throat had nothing to do with what he was eating. That had always been Andre's mantra: where he led, they were expected to follow. You never felt the collar until you tried to balk.

"You didn't own me even then." Back when he had been a willing, in fact eager employee of the Silence, working tirelessly to use his brains, his wits, and his weapons to solve the world's more esoteric problems. "You don't own me now."

"Dear boy." Avuncular Andre replaced Tough Guy Andre. "Not a word was said about ownership. Merely…ties which cannot be unbound. Or cut."

"Everything can be cut." Sergei's words were as sharp as his meaning.

"Not without bleeding to death in the process." It wasn't a warning. Exactly. Andre sounded as though he were discussing a theoretical point of academic interest. Andre always sounded like that, even when the interest was life and death. Maybe especially then. He stepped back from emotional intensity, preferring to keep a shield between himself and those he helped. Sergei had never gotten the hang of that. Had never wanted to.

Life and death were too gritty, too messy, to be polite, or refined. Money, yes. He could be as refined as the next high-end salesman when it came to money. But blood was a different matter.

Especially his own blood.

Especially Wren's blood.

There were limits to his loyalty.

Andre had asked for this meeting. Not him. He didn't want to be involved. He couldn't afford to be involved. There were three priorities in his life: Wren, the gallery, and Wren's career. The second and third place priorities might move around, but the first was always first. It had been that way for over a decade now, since he'd fallen out of a wrecked car and seen those eyes in that pale face, and put a person to the name in a coded file. You could fall in love in minutes, even if you didn't know it for years.

"Boy…Sergei." Andre fiddled with the stem of his wineglass, and Sergei could feel his resolve wilt.

There were limits to his loyalty. But obligation lasted until death.

"You've got a problem," Sergei said, finally. That was an understatement. Andre had a disaster. "Withholding intel from you on the Nescanni case—it could just have been someone unhappy with Wren's retainer, someone trying to cause us to fail, make us look bad, so that the Silence would reconsider the entire arrangement. But more than that?" He looked at the notes he had, purely out of habit, jotted down as they talked. "A long-term pattern of disinformation, willful misinformation? No." He shook his head. "That's *your* problem, Andre, not mine." *Not ours,* he thought. *Not Wren's.*

And that's what this was all about: Andre trying to drag him back in, headfirst, to Andre's problems. Ironic, really. When he'd left them the first time, the Silence had let him live only because he had found Wren, and they wanted to use him to get to her. And so they had, through the Mage Council's arrogance driving her to them.

And now Andre, after playing the Silence's game for his entire adult life, suddenly smelled a skunk, and wanted Sergei's help in rooting it out of the woodpile.

For Andre—for the man who had taken a know-it-all, idealistic college graduate under his wing and taught him how to get by in the world with more than book-learning? For that man, Sergei would be willing to play the dog, do what needed to be done.

If there were no other considerations.

"Yes, that was what I had thought," his former boss was saying. "What I had originally hoped—that it was merely my workload, someone targeting your partner, as you suggested, or me directly. But it has become a pattern, this withholding of vital information, within the Silence itself. Not only in my cases, but others as well."

Andre tapped the table in front of him with slender, dark-skinned fingers as he spoke. They looked like the hands of a much younger man. Sergei compared them to his own, equally-well-manicured if less tapered, and then thought of Wren's hands: delicate and yet somehow battered, capable and somehow more honest than his or Andre's.

"You've been told this?" Sergei still didn't quite believe that. The Silence did not show weakness, especially not to your peers, and admitting that R&D wasn't giving you the full story meant not only weakness but vulnerability. Desk-pushers were worse than sharks; if they smelled blood, they would not rest until the injured member was not only taken down, but all traces of them were removed.

It was a depressing view of an organization that worked for the public good, however privately, but depressing made it no less true. Operatives—men and women like himself, who worked outside of the building's confines—were actually safer in many ways than those inside, in positions of power.

It was like Wren often said about being a Retriever: the trick wasn't in being invincible, the trick was being invisible.

"The fourth horseman rides by, I know," Andre said in response to his question. "Yes. I've been told. People are becoming nervous, finally. And nervous people do one of two things; they clam up and go very still, or they chatter."

"And you've been chattering?" Sergei was openly dubious now; too many years exposure to his former boss made him doubt the man *ever* chattered—without an ulterior motive, anyway.

"*They* have been chattering. I've been very still…and

listening." He swirled the wine remaining in his glass, a pale, golden-white liquid that caught the light in its depths, and placed the glass back down on the table-cloth, untasted. "And the one thing that seems to connect all of the cases where information has been withheld has been the supernatural element."

He had Sergei's attention again, as he must have known he would. "Talents?"

"I'd hesitate to narrow it quite that much. Call it supernatural."

Magic, then. Old, or new—unlike Wren, Andre didn't distinguish between the two variants. Sergei wasn't sure he could, even if he cared to. "Andre, that's barely, what, two percent of the Silence's caseload?"

"When you were full-time, perhaps. Things have changed since then." Andre's slick veneer slipped, and for an instant Sergei saw the face of an old, worried man. "Now the number of situations we handle, that involve the supernatural element in some way or another, has risen to almost forty percent."

Sergei almost choked on his Prosecco. *To borrow one of Wren's favorite phrases, Jesus wept.*

There wasn't much more to say, after that. Andre called for the check and headed back to the office, leaving Sergei sitting at the small table, pushing around the remains of his food and wishing, for the first time in almost twenty years, that he still smoked the cigarettes he carried around with him everywhere, like a talisman of will over cravings.

Forty percent. Forty percent.

Was it because they were the only ones left, the only ones interested in and able to deal with malign supernatural interferences? Or were the number of those interferences rising—and rising damn quickly?

The Silence had been founded in the early 1900s by wealthy men with guilty consciences, tired, finally, of earning money while others suffered. Their primary mission: to right wrongs. Their secondary mission: to prevent wrongs from being committed. Things had expanded, since then.

His code name there had been Softwing: the owl. Bringer of wisdom in some cultures—death, in others. He had found it amusing, once. Fitting. Had enjoyed being the blade that cut Gordian Knots.

He had specialized in knots with supernatural elements. Had been one of only three, then, who did so. They had not needed more.

How many, he wondered, were handling FoCAs, agents with Talent, now? How many of them—and their charges—were being put at risk because someone was withholding information?

More—how were they defining "supernatural"? Sergei hadn't bothered to ask Andre, and that might have been a mistake, of the sort he rarely made. The Silence was relentlessly humancentric; they barely recognized most of the fatae races that existed, much less granted them sentient status. By Silence standards, most of the arguments Sergei had observed over the years—including some rather spectacular bar brawls—involving fatae would have been seen as attacks against humans. A Situation to be cleared up, a wrong to be righted.

And never mind that a third of the time *humans* started it, and often all the participants ended up drinking at the same bar together the very next night.

Wren doesn't know what to make of what she calls my *fataephobia… Andre's would knock her backward into tomorrow.* And he didn't even want to think about the rest of the Silence, the ones who either had no exposure to the nonhuman races, or, worse yet, had been conditioned to see them only as troublemakers and wrongdoers.

"Svyataya deva."

When he had walked away from the Silence more than a decade ago, he had thought that was the end of it. Even hooking up with Wren, then a wise but inexperienced teenager with more Talent than she knew what to do with, had pointed him in a different direction. No more do-gooding through violence. No more trying to fix wrongs for someone else. Himself, and his partner, and the devil take the hindmost.

That had lasted for ten years, until the Council's threat to Wren seemed a greater threat than the Silence's possible or potential agenda.

Now, Sergei wasn't so sure.

Obligations were one thing, and all very well to honor. But first, he had a responsibility to Wren. To himself. To the people they both cared about. Andre, for all the older man had trained him, was not on that very short list.

* * *

The Red Light was just what the doctor ordered: crowded but not packed, noisy but not to the point of overwhelming your ears. The table was already occupied by the time Wren arrived, having stopped to change into something a little more suitable for bar-slumming—jeans and her battered leather jacket over a skimpy pink tank top.

Sarah looked older than Wren's memory of her. She supposed everyone did—memory stood still, time moved on, etc., etc., etc. But it was still disconcerting to expect to see someone in their energetic forties, and be confronted by an old woman.

On second look, Sarah wasn't old—but her hair, raven-black in memory, was now shot with silver, and the laugh lines around her mouth and eyes had been cut even deeper with worry.

Wren had never actually met the Seer who worked at Noodles her favorite Chinese restaurant, but she suspected that she or he was older than their physical years, too. Knowing too much weighed on you, aged you. Especially if you also—the way most Seers did—had the compulsion to tell others what you knew. Cassandra never did get to wash her hands and go dancing, instead.

"Valere."

Sarah's voice was the graveled rumble that came from vocal chord damage, not smoking. Like she had spent a lot of her early years screaming. Wren took a seat across the table from the woman, careful not to touch her or anything of hers. Psychometry was a skill that usually needed to be invoked—unless there was a lot of strong emotion invested in the object or person. Something told her that Sarah had a *lot* of emotion, and damned little of it got vented.

"I'm here. Talk to me." *Digame, digame.* She remembered none of the Spanish she heard as a child in the diner where her mother had worked, except that phrase, and the casual urgency it invoked. Sarah shouldn't wear all black. It just made her look more tired, if that were possible.

"You were at the Moot. I saw you."

"You and everyone else in the room," Wren grumbled. The Moot everyone kept referring to had pretty much ended when she called down lightning, literally, on thickheaded skulls. It had been, in her defense, the only way to get past the usual no-see-me vibes she generated like breathing, and make them actually *listen* to what she was saying. The end result had been, shock of shocks, to win her a few more enemies, both those who didn't like the fact that she advised moderation and caution, and the ones who felt that she had humiliated them, by making it impossible to ignore the fact that she was stronger than they were, could channel more current, more effectively.

But the Moot had failed; no combined action had been taken, no violence offered. No retribution taken.

At the time, it had seemed like the smart course. The only course. But it hadn't stopped Lee's death. Hadn't stopped other freelancers from continuing to poke the tiger that was the Mage Council, even if they used words rather than sticks.

"No. I wasn't there at that one." Sarah shook that past meeting off as unimportant. "The one that's to come. I saw you there."

"Oh…damn," Wren said, wanting very badly to say something stronger. She *knew* those idiots weren't going to be able to stop with that damned letter to the Mage's Council. She just knew it.

"I'm sorry." The Seer shrugged, helpless in the face of her own information.

Unable to take her frustrations out on anyone within reach, Wren settled for waving over a waiter—large, surly, and cute in a large and surly way—and ordered a beer.

"Make it two," Sarah said. "And a whiskey shot." Proggies, of all the Talents, drank copiously. The current in their wires that opened them to the future also overrode the usual dangers of drinking. The theory was that they Saw themselves getting stupid, and so automatically corrected to avoid that future. If true, Wren thought, it would be the first time anyone ever managed to completely avoid a Seer's foreseen fortune. Christ knew, she had never been able to manage that.

"So what am I doing at this Moot that hasn't happened but will? And do we have a time frame for it?" That was another neat trick of Seers: they didn't come with time stamps on their visions.

Sarah looked Wren over carefully, actually *seeing* her the way most people didn't. The weird magical hitch in her makeup—what made most Retrievers take up the career, and Wren called *no-see-me*—made peoples' eyes skip over her, leaving nothing but a blur in the memory. But Sarah was noticing details.

It made Wren surprisingly uneasy.

"Soon," she said, after their beers had been delivered. "You look the same. Everyone around you is angry. Shadows rising. Bring it…down? Bring *them* down." Sarah frowned. "No, that's not quite right, either."

Great. Not only a Seer, but a brain-fried one at that. Not wizzed—if Sarah had been wizzed every Talent within ten feet of her would have known, and acted appropriately; to wit, walking casually but quickly in the direction of Away. But the beer and chasers had clearly done their job, over time, on her brain.

So. Bring what or *who* down? And, specifically, *how*? Wren glared at her beer. Another useless Seer fortune, and not even a cookie to sweeten the deal.

To give her hands something to do, and to fill the awkward, postprediction moment, Wren raised her beer in a silent toast, then sipped at the dark, slightly bitter brew appreciatively. It had been too long since she'd kicked back and had a real lager. Sergei was a wine guy, not so much for the beers. Lee had been the one…

I'm sorry, she said to her friend, toasting him with the next sip. *And I know what you'd want me to do*. Lee had been a free market man, a lonejack's lonejack…but in the end, events had stuck too much in his throat to swallow comfortably.

Shadows rising. Rising and rising and rising, until you couldn't see the sun anymore. Wren didn't have a single thread of precog in her core, but the sense of foreboding that phrase sent through her couldn't be ignored. Bring it down. Bring what down? Shadows bringing something down? Was she supposed to bring something down?

"I don't suppose you can give me anything that's actually useful? What I'm supposed to say, who I'm supposed to say it to?" She already knew the answer.

Sarah shook her head regretfully, then lifted the shot glass of golden amber liquid and kicked it back without hesitation. "I wish I could. I'd sleep better at night."

"Yeah. Does that—" Wren gestured at the now empty shot glass "—help?"

"No," Sarah said. "But it makes the rest of me hurt to match."

"Waiter," Wren called, doing her best cool, lean-back-and-gesture-lazily-with-one-arm movement she could, considering the crowd. "Another round. Same again for both of us."

The walk home seemed longer than the walk over. The air had chilled off once the moon rose, and she was glad for the warmth of her jacket, not to mention the beer in her system, although she had pissed away a lot of it before leaving the Red Light. Sarah was still sitting in the bar, drunkenly morose. Wren made a mental note to never, ever, ever drink with a Seer again. They were just so damn *depressing*.

Still, as she walked, Wren felt her mood lifting slightly. Manhattan was a city made for nights. Daylight, it was rush-and-bustle, even the early mornings having an energy in them that made you feel the need to walk faster, be more aggressive, tougher than the next bastard scheming next to you. Nighttime, the lights came on, and a different sense of magic flowed up from the pavement. Made possibilities into probabilities. Renewed hope, faith. Sang like a siren in a good mood. Not even the mutterings of a sodden Seer could totally wipe that out, although to give Sarah credit, she had tried.

Traffic flowed, all the traffic lights synchronized perfectly the way drivers only dreamed of, and nobody felt the need to lay into their horn to protest being cut off by a manic cabbie swerving from East to West to drop off or pick up a passenger. Life in the big city was as it ought to be, for at least this instant. Prediction of shadows or no.

Shadows are mainly in the day, anyway. Night's all shadows…moon doesn't cast enough light for a shadow to be dangerous. All right, that wasn't exactly, technically, true. But night's shadows didn't feel dangerous to her. Not Manhattan shadows, cast out of neon and street lamps. To her, they were old friends, feral cats who lounged in your windowsill and stole your leftovers but never quite let you pet them.

She had just crossed Eighth Avenue and was turning downtown when her sense of pleasure in the evening was tempered by the awareness that one of those friendly shadows, wasn't.

Someone was walking too close, with too much intent. Intent, and current, damped down and controlled, but with the distinct tang of Council style, Council training blending with his individual current-scent.

"What now?" she asked. Resigned, because after all, how else could this day possibly have ended?

"What's the creed of the lonejacks?" Male voice, too close to her ear, so not a tall man, but depth to the voice, so broad, and probably strong, so stay calm, Valere, don't do anything stupid like take a swing because, after all, it's been that kind of a day. She had yet to win a physical confrontation with anyone, anyway. She fought with her words, as needed, not her fists. Not that she didn't have a decent left hook, if that was what it took.

"Don't get involved," she said to him. It was almost automatic, the way the words come from her mouth. First rule was "Don't get involved." Second was "Pick your jobs. Don't let them pick you." Third…didn't matter, when you'd blown the first two so spectacularly.

"Maybe you should pay more attention to what little your mentor managed to teach you and stay out of things that don't concern you."

The truth of the advice didn't stop anger from rising in her, hot, sweet and hungry, burning away the last of the beer; like current and unlike. Nobody but nobody talked about Neezer, poor, mad, lost John Ebeneezer, the only father she'd ever come close to having, with that dismissive tone in his voice. *Nobody*.

"You've made it my concern," she said, bitterness flowing with the anger. "The moment your people tried to play me." Almost six months ago, now, when the Council used her to try to cover up their own dirty history, and a bad deal by one of their own. A play that got so involved Sergei agreed to lease their souls to the Silence for protection, and things went from bad to worse, and no way to stay uninvolved.

Everything else—lonejacks, Moots, fatae meetings held in her own apartment, thanks ever so much, P.B.—it all came from that, somehow. Wren was certain of it. She had no proof, only a sense of patterns forming in chaos. An inevitable chain of events, movements within movements that set the entire set of works into motion, and it was all the Council's fault.

"I never had a beef with you. Never got in your way. Council lied to me when I asked them—" through Sergei, as proxy, and that's why he was in danger, too "—if they were involved in the Frants case. Tried to kill me, then tried to ruin my rep. I'm a lonejack, for Christ's sake. Did you expect me to be a meek little sheep and take it?"

Her current sparked, and felt an answering leap from the person next to her, responding to the challenge. *No,* she told her core, and locked it back down. *This was only a messenger.*

"So go take that back to Madame Howe and her band of merry mages. I didn't pick this fight. I didn't want it. I still don't, damn it. But you people wouldn't leave it *alone.*"

The deep-voiced shadow dropped away, and Wren walked on, a voice rising out of her memory, speaking inside her skull.

There's a line we dance on. On one side, control. On the other side, chaos. Both are terribly, terribly appealing. But neither is safe, and neither's very smart, either. Either one of them will suck you in, and never let you go.

Neezer had been talking about the risk of wizzing, when he said that, of going insane, as he eventually did. As too many Talents did, the really strong ones. The Pures, who didn't have junk in their systems, reducing the level of current they could channel. But it applied here, too.

The only way to win, to stay free, was not to play the game. But she'd already bought a ticket, suited up, signed on, whatever metaphor you wanted to use. She'd allowed P.B. to use her name to gather information, had acted on the information he had given her. Had spoken, even if it was only to say that she didn't want to get involved, in front of people who were already involved, already had her painted into the picture they were designing.

A Seer had Seen her. Had given her a fortune that did not allow for disappearing off the sidelines.

She was, in a word, fucked.

"Ti durak." It felt so good, she said it again. *"Ti durak."* She was pretty sure she was calling herself an idiot…that was the translation she'd gotten out of Sergei, anyway, who had a tendency to mutter it a lot when things weren't going well.

She was still muttering it to herself, savoring the sound, when she let herself into her apartment and knew that she wasn't alone.

This time, however, the sensation was a good one. Her partner had a…call it an aroma, for lack of a better term, that was unlike anything else she had ever sensed. It allowed her to find him in a darkened warehouse, to track him through a garden maze in the rain, and to know when he was sitting in her apartment, quietly thinking his own quiet thoughts. Some of it was his cologne, and the natural scent of his sweat, but there was an edge of something mental to it, as well. Not current—Sergei was mostly Null, if not entirely—but similar, as close to it as electricity itself was to current-proper. She thought sometimes it might be as simple as the living life force, what Eastern therapies called the chakra points, but had never had the time or energy to research it further. It was enough for her that that particular mix of taste and scent and mental touch was what she identified as "Sergei."

"Hi," she said quietly into the room where he was sitting, then went into the kitchen to deposit her keys into the bowl on the counter. Slinging her jacket and bag onto one of the stools, she wandered back to the main room to see if he had responded to her greeting yet or not.

He was still sitting deep in the brown tweed-upholstered chair, staring at the wall. The light from the kitchen played gently against the basic off-white paint, raising faint shadows that echoed in Wren's own unsettled mind.

"Hi," he said finally, just when she was going to leave him to it and go to bed. He shifted in the chair, and looked up at her. In the dim light, his face looked pale and desperate.

"Serg?"

"Come here." It was more of a command than she felt

comfortable with, but she let herself walk into the room, enfolded into his arms as he stood to embrace her. She rested her cheek against his chest and felt the steady thrum of his heart against her bones.

"Wh-ha!" she squeaked as he suddenly, without warning, turned and scooped her up into his arms. She almost went flying, her hands grabbing at the air in a failed attempt to regain some sort of control.

"Don't." His voice was harsh, still a whisper, and she subsided, letting him carry her down the hallway and into the bedroom. Her curtains were pulled back, letting just enough of the street lamp's light in for them to see the bed, the covers still rumpled, two pillows at the head, another tossed carelessly onto the floor.

He placed her down on the mattress, letting his elbows hold the weight of his own body off her, while still leaning in close enough to breathe on her neck, a warm, gentle breath that made a long shiver glide down her spine, right down to her groin. She hadn't walked in the door thinking about sex—but she certainly was now!

"Let me…" His hands slid under her tank, lifting it up. Her arms raised to help him, blinded for a moment while it went over her head and was tossed to the floor.

"Get you out of those jeans…" His voice was muffled by the fact that he had bent to her now bared breasts, not so much kissing as nuzzling her. The five o'clock shadow scratched pleasantly, the uncertainty and the adrenalin and the beer of the evening making her feel inclined to go along with his obvious plans. Her jeans and underwear joined her top on the floor, and she attacked the buttons of his shirt with growing enthusiasm. Your partner's need, sometimes, was the best turn-on.

She had read somewhere, once, that having sex with your socks on indicated a certain lack of commitment to the moment. That might have been true, but she wasn't worrying about it right now. Besides, Sergei wore cashmere blend socks, and there was absolutely no bad to cashmere on any part of the body, in Wren's opinion.

And then his body was naked—except for the socks—and he was touching every part of her body he could reach, skin-to-skin, and she was returning the favor, hands stroking and kneading and tugging closer, until he was positioned above her in a nicely classic mission-ary, his eyes still dark and shadowed but desperate in a very different way than before.

"Need to be inside you," he said, grabbing a condom from the nightstand, slamming the drawer shut in his haste.

"Need you there." No less than the truth, and when he slid inside, it was as though all of him were moving in her flesh, not just his cock. It still felt brand-new to her, sometimes, the sense of wonder, of fascination she felt for his body, something she knew so well, for so long, and now understood in a totally different way.

She could feel current wakening in response, her nat-ural core of the stuff thickening its strands, engorging it-self on the tension building in her body, the changes in her natural electrical charge. Sex-magik was old magic, and not something Talents were taught, as a rule…but some things you didn't need to be taught. Not when your body hummed along to it naturally. That was why so many people got into trouble with old magic.

She had never been tempted: sex was enough, as sex. But the power called to her now, seductive, appealing; the chance to feed her core off the power they were building, to use it to strengthen herself, to protect herself. Protect them both. Protect them all.

Shadows coming. Bring it down. Bring it on.

Not smart, she told the Seer, pulling back a little. *Not smart.* Not smart at all, no. Besides, no way even the most mind-blowing orgasm could generate that kind of current.

Shadows coming, the Seer insisted. *Be ready.*

"It's okay," Sergei told her, pausing midthrust as though he could hear her thoughts. Maybe he could. She knew what she took from him…maybe he was taking from her, too. Most of the population wasn't entirely Null…

He shifted, kissing her forehead, driving farther inside her, and that thought skipped town while current sizzled just under her skin in approval.

"Not…not smart…" He had no idea what she was talking about. No idea, even now, what he was telling her to do. She grounded in him, sometimes, when there was need. When she was working, and the overflow got to be too much, or something went wrong and she couldn't find bedrock. He was her bedrock. And that wasn't good, wasn't smart; he was human, and not Talent, and too much current could kill, if you weren't hardwired just right, and too much current could wiz, even if you were hardwired perfect.

"Let go. Zhenchenka, let go."

No matter what he was talking about, what he thought he was saying, she couldn't deny him, not when he asked with that tone in his voice. She opened the vein of power just a little bit, letting current spark though. Dark purples and greens danced along her skin, rising out of her shoulder to skip down her arm, running off her fingers where they spasmed, digging into the flesh of his backside. Where the current met his skin, the purple flared black-red for an instant, then disappeared into his body, sending a shockwave directly into his system, like a live wire touching water.

He came roughly, his fingers digging into the skin over her hips hard enough to bruise the bone, neck corded from the effort not to yell, his face contorted in pleasure that was easily mistaken for agony.

Wren closed her eyes, and let the waves of satisfaction coming off her partner send her down a similar chute, current safely contained within her own body coiled and sparking as she came.

Bring it down. Bring it on.

"Hoo." A long, drawn-out exhalation of air, and he collapsed on top of her, still comfortably inside her. His weight was a pleasant, solid reminder of the world around them, and she was reminded again that grounding could be done more than magically.

"Ow." He winced, and she found the energy to slide out from under him—carefully—and pushed him gently facedown onto the bed, stripping the sheets off to inspect his skin.

Sure enough, there were telltale marks where their skin had been in contact. Nothing too bad, but bad enough to see. The temptation to yell at him was intense, but she knew from experience that he'd shrug it off. Nothing was worse than Sergei when he didn't want to deal with something.

She reached into her nightstand for the tube of Bactrin she kept there and, sliding back down next to him, she squeezed a little out and soothed it into his skin where the marks seemed worst—his ass, thighs and stomach. Interesting, that the groin area seemed unmarked, although there might have been burn marks under his pubic hair. If he wasn't complaining, she wasn't going to force the issue. Yet.

He nuzzled at her neck, sleepy, satiated, and even in her annoyance she felt desire stroking her nerve endings again.

"S'okay, Wrenlet."

No, it wasn't. But it wasn't not okay, either. She didn't know if the ointment did any good, even, except make her feel less bad about hurting him…except it wasn't hurting him, he kept telling her that. It was a balance, a constant dance for her, between letting go and being swept away, and the awareness that Sergei would not tell her if she were actually, physically burning him. In fact, she suspected that he might prefer more of a burn; he clearly found it a turn-on. Within reason. She *hoped* within reason. She didn't know what to do, if it went beyond reason.

Capping the tube, she let it drop to the floor and lay down next to him again, letting the day's exhaustion take her down into sleep as well.

And then it hit her, just as her eyes were too heavy to keep open any longer, what had felt so strange about the deep-voiced shadow.

His accent wasn't from around here. Not even close. The *A* was all wrong, and the emphasis on certain syllables had been just ever so slightly…off. Unfamiliar.

Not local talent. Either the Mage Council was importing their bully-boys now, or…

Too much. Her brain hurt. So she turned it off.

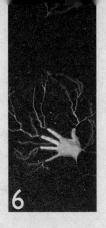

6

It was 3:00 a.m. and Wren was wide-awake, while Sergei snored lightly next to her, the coverlet drawn up to his chin. She slid out of bed and went to the single window in the bedroom, pulled open the heavy green curtain and looked outside.

Three in the morning in Manhattan looked like nothing so much as…3:00 a.m. in Manhattan. The sky was black, the streets oddly empty and silent, although she could still hear, faintly, the noise from the club down the street and around the corner. Ordinances against excessive standing-outside-club-doors had cut down on the really annoying street noise, in recent years; the clubs policed themselves pretty well, not wanting to risk the fines that could make the difference between breaking even or going under.

Wren had never been a club kid; no money for it when she was a teenager, no time or patience for it once she was earning decent money on her own. She also suspected that a Talent might not be welcome in most of those tech-heavy clubs; fire regs were usually overtaxed enough without some drunk current-user taking a hit off their power system to finish off the night.

Who needed drugs when you had a supercharged soundboard with umptygillion amps, and an entire room full of superheated lights to drain down? At least one major prank that she knew of had involved selective pinging of lights during the height of the disco craze, in one of the most popular clubs. She had been a toddler at the time, but the story was good enough to be retold—even Neezer, who generally disapproved of pranking overall, had loved that story, probably because everyone involved got exactly what they deserved.

But at 3:00 a.m. on a Tuesday night, in this decade, everything was quiet and low-key. Peaceful, even. Someone was walking under the streetlight, hands shoved into the pockets of a leather coat, intent on their own thoughts. The lamplight picked out glimmers in the thick black hair, but from the distance and the angle Wren couldn't even tell if the figure was male or female, human or fatae. Just a faceless, nameless New Yorker, on his or her way home.

Suddenly Wren wanted to talk to someone. Not just anyone, but someone who understood. Who grokked. Time was, she would have tracked down Lee, who was often working in his studio all hours of the night. That time was gone. Lee was gone.

Dropping the curtain, she padded in the darkness

down the hallway to her office. Lighting a thick pillar candle for light, she booted up the computer, then went to use the bathroom in the meanwhile. Just getting the computer up and running took forever, compared to most systems of comparable age, simply because of all the safeguards she had installed around it. Not virus protections, although she had those, too, but surge protections of the sort most super-secret government installations didn't worry about. Everything was routed and rerouted in ways she had absolutely no understanding of, courtesy of an MIT professor who was doing an ongoing and completely unofficial study of current, and still, every time she turned the damn thing on she held her breath. Current was the proverbial dual-edged sword—power on the one hand, irritation and annoyance on the other. There was so much you could do, if your body was set up to channel current, that was denied to Nulls. But Nulls could use cell phones and iPods and portable CD players, and all the things Wren could only look longingly at.

Life was fair, in its own way. It didn't play favorites, and kept the balance of perks pretty even-handed, in that regard. Besides, her computer start-time might take forever, but she wasn't entirely cut off from the online world. And some nights, that was the really important thing.

She came back to find the screen ready and waiting for her. Sitting down, she pulled the keyboard to her, scooted the chair out so that she could put her feet up on the desk, and logged in to check her e-mail.

For a person who couldn't use tech easily or comfortably, she was on an impressively high number of mailing lists. Most of them were low-traffic—one was old friends from high school, another a group of self-employed or small businesswomen, who traded tax information and medical insurance news in with the usual laments of working for yourself. Wren mostly lurked—of course—but she had picked up some valuable tips, which made it worth her time, and the risk.

She wasn't the only one who thought so, either. While a lot of the more conservative types shied away from getting online, or even close to tech—she didn't think Neezer had ever willingly gone near a copier, instead bribing the bio department's secretary to do whatever admin work was needed for his classes—there were just as many Talents who used their computer the way millions of Nulls did—as a social conduit to people you otherwise would never have met.

She sorted her e-mail quickly into "of interest," spam, and possible spam. The spam she wiped, and cleared out considerable space. The possible spam she skimmed over, and deleted anything that had off-kilter headers. Maybe yes, maybe no, but she had enough problems without hackers, viruses, or worms.

That left about a dozen e-mails from people she knew, or with headers that looked legit. Two, maybe three were maybe-possibly *Cosa*-related. And absolutely none of them were anything she wanted to deal with right now.

Taking a deep breath, she clicked on another software application. Intellectually she knew that how many screens she had running made no difference; it was *her* control that was the issue, not the RAM or hard drive, or anything actually inside the computer. But running too many things still made her anticipate disaster, and anticipating disaster seemed more often than not to create it, so she just avoided it over all.

No sooner was the new program running than she was pounced on.

<ohsobloodytalented> Awake! Someone's Awake over there! Long time no chat!

<downtowntalent> Actually I'm a figment of your imagination.

<ohsobloodytalented> Fabulous! 'allo then, Figgie. Wanna play?

Wren had never met the person on the other side of the connection. All she knew was that she was in her late fifties, had lived all over the world before settling in New Zealand, and was, like Wren, a Talent.

Wren didn't know if she was lonejack or Council. It had never seemed to come up in conversation before this, and she didn't know how to ask now without sounding rude. It was enough that she was there, at three in the morning—a decent hour of the afternoon tomorrow, Ohsos time—and ready and willing to talk.

<ohsobloodytalented> You still there?

<downtowntalent> Yeah, sorry. Half-dead and not much playful. Sorry.

<ohsobloodytalented> *sympathy* Need to chat it out?

Wren started to say *no thanks,* then paused. Why not?

<downtowntalent> Ready for a dumpload?
<ohsobloodytalented> Dump away, dearest. I'll never tell another soul.

Wren doubted that. But the distance made it all seem safer, somehow.

<downtowntalent> Right. A) We have a group of humans in town who seem to have made it their life's work to harass, harm, and otherwise be the best bigots possible to our local fatae.
<downtowntalent> B) Our local Council (and forgive me if you're Council as well, I, obviously, am not) has decided to goose step all over the lonejack crowd, with the intent of cowing us into signing up. Not only is it not working, it's making people…cranky.
<downtowntalent> C) I'm in the "your apartment or mine" stage of a relationship, and part of me resents like hell that I'm even considering giving up my place because, God, how parochial and patronizing, but he's got the way nicer space, and too much has gone on here and it doesn't feel like mine anymore, even when he's here but I still love my apartment— mine mine mine—and I resent the fact that I'm not 100% comfortable here anymore.

Wren stopped, amazed at what had just poured out of her fingers. She hadn't even known that she felt that way until she started typing.

<ohsobloodytalented>...You are having a shit week, aren't you?

<ohsobloodytalented> Can't tell you much about A—our local fatae aren't much for mingling, not that I can blame them, the laddies we have about here. Would think they'd be able to take care of themselves though, against Nulls.

Most people would think that. Either "their problem" or "who cares?" Wren still wasn't sure how she ended up being so concerned, either. It had to be P.B.'s fault. P.B. who looked so tough and sounded so tough, and actually *was* so tough, but there was only so much one tough midget-sized polar bear–shaped demon could do when faced with half a dozen humans with large sticks and ugly in their eyes. And Rorani? What would the dryad do if someone tried to hurt her tree, that beautiful centuries-old oak that shaded an entire picnic area in Central Park? It would be dire and dreadful, Wren didn't doubt that...but in the end, the tree would be damaged, and Rori would die, and the most the killers would get would be destruction of City property.

<ohsobloodytalented> C's easy, though. Where's the sex the best?

Wren laughed so suddenly at that, she choked on air. "Thank you for not saying that while I was drinking coffee," she told her long-distance companion. She could have pinged "Ohso" with the image/irritation, but that always felt like cheating, somehow. Besides, using current while at the computer, even in that relatively low-current way, was *really* tempting fate.

<downtowntalent> My bed's better, his shower's nicer. Sex isn't the question.

Although it was, of course, but not in a way she was going to discuss with anyone, even another Talent.

<ohsobloodytalented> Just remember to put that anti-slip mat down, in the shower! *snickergrin*
<downtowntalent> Oh God, that would be tough to explain to the EMTs, wouldn't it? On second thought, I bet they deal with stuff like that all the time. Thanks, needed the laugh.
<downtowntalent> Life's been grim, on other fronts.

She knew she should stop there, but her fingers wouldn't stop typing.

<downtowntalent> Any advice on *B*?

There was a long moment of silence, that *might* have been distraction on OSBT's part, or the time it took her to type, or anything totally nonworrying....

Just when Wren began to suspect she'd pushed too far, a response came.

<ohsobloodytalented> *B*—I'm Council, yeah, but our Council tried to toss weight around, can't see it would go over well here, neither. Doesn't sound right. Are you sure?

<downtowntalent> Yeah. We're sure. People are dead sure, emphasis on the dead.

Actually they didn't know that anyone was dead. They were just gone. Missing. Unreachable. In order to block a Talent from even the faintest ping, in order to make them untraceable, you had to either kill them—tough, if they're forewarned, but hardly impossible, even for the smart, strong ones—or block them off thoroughly enough that a concerted effort can't break through. The second possibility was even more damning to the Council, in a lot of ways. Anyone might have a grudge against Talents. It might be a coincidence that all the missing ones were lonejacks. It might even be coincidence that the missing lonejacks were outspoken in their opposition to the Council having any more weight in the *Cosa's* doings.

<ohsobloodytalented> I don't believe Council would do that. It's not in the charter.

The charter. Wren had heard it referenced, but never actually seen it. She didn't know anyone who had seen it, not even her few and far between Council friends.

Supposedly a list of Don'ts to guide the then newly formed Council in their benevolent dictatorship, written by several of the founding members who knew all too well what power could do to people, even well-intentioned. Maybe even especially the well-intentioned.

<downtowntalent> Is it prohibited in the charter? Forcing people to join, snuffing them if they won't?
    <ohsobloodytalented> Of course!
    <ohsobloodytalented> It has to be.

Another Council member who had never seen the charter. For the object that claimed to be the basis of everything the Council was, it seemed to *not* get around much. Honestly, people were too lazy to care. How many Americans, even well-educated ones, had ever actually read the Constitution, after all?

<ohsobloodytalented> The Council was formed to protect us from ourselves, not attack!

* * *

That much was true. Back in the electric age, when Edison was dreaming of lights in every home, and streets were being torn up to lay wires, every magic user in the country—and across the globe, as power lines went up and down—got flooded with more current than they'd ever had access to before. Ben Franklin had preached moderation when he captured current, but that old Talent had never been given such a feast. It took a saint— or someone with a totally nonconductive will—to resist.

Very few Talents were saints. In fact, Wren couldn't think of a single one. Tree-taller—Lee—had been as good a man as she knew, and he had been miles from saint-hood, by choice.

Then again, he had been a lonejack, hadn't he? For a reason.

The Council had been created to protect Talents from themselves. Balancing current's edge, especially in those early, heady days of easy-access power, was a dangerous thing. Open yourself up too much, and you wizzed, went mad from the overrush. The percentage of Talents lost to the flood in that first decade had reportedly *quadru-pled*.

<ohsobloodytalented> You're wrong. Mage Council is there to protect us. Turning on another Talent, even outside the Council…unthinkable. Like eating your young. Disgusting.

<downtowntalent> You're a good person. Not everyone is.

<ohsobloodytalented> You're accusing your Council…of murder!

<downtowntalent> I'm not accusing anyone of anything.

Wren felt her irritation level jump, and she tamped it down as gently as she could. Ohso was getting too upset, too angry, and the last thing Wren wanted to do was feed that.

<downtowntalent> It's just a localized phenomena. I'm sure your own Council is perfectly—

<ohsobloodytalented> No! No Council should be accused…the Council protects us from ourselves! It *is* us! Council would never—

Wren yelped and jumped backward as her modem—the modem that her tech guru swore could withstand a direct thunderstorm hit—sparked and gave off a whiff of something deeply unpleasant and all too familiar. <ohsobloodytalented> disappeared from her screen.

Wren pushed the chair forward gingerly, expecting at any moment for the entire computer system to blow up into a shower of burning sparks and flying electronic bits. But it remained intact, if offline.

The Councils had been established to keep Talents on an even keel, by grouping them into locale-based enclaves and giving decision-making abilities to chosen leaders. It was supposed to keep everyone honest—and safe. Lonejacks had rejected the need for it, gone their own way, made their own decisions, good or bad. The way the Council had been set up, they could have forced the issue, made every Talent join them or face penalties, ostracized until they fell into line. They hadn't, so long as the rebels didn't overreach themselves. Over time, it had evolved into a live-and-let-live philosophy. Mostly. Until now.

Possibly as a result, the first rule of the lonejack creedo was "Don't get involved." What it really meant was "Don't get overinvolved." Don't let emotions overrule common sense. Stay on the current's edge: balanced, not bleeding.

Wren looked at the remains of her modem, shorted to death by Ohso's emotional outburst and resulting loss of control, and wondered, for the first time, what damage the Council might have done to its own people, as well.

"Focus, Valere." Key words, especially now. "Gotta deal with your own backyard before you start looking into anyone else's."

With a sigh, she unhooked the modem and balanced it in her hand. If she'd gotten an internal modem, it would have fried her entire system, probably. Sometimes, old was better.

Dropping the modem into the trash, she shut down the computer, and went back to bed. Sliding in between now-cooled sheets, Wren stared at her partner's naked back, and thought very hard about just running away.

"Woman, your shower was built for dwarves and demon-folk." Sergei bent forward to rinse the last of the shampoo out of his hair, feeling his back muscles complain as he stretched. Once upon a time he'd been limber enough to adapt to undersized showerheads. He was pretty sure he remembered that.

It wasn't just that the shower was too short; it was also too narrow. He wasn't exactly oversized, but the enclosure was several inches too narrow for his comfort, leaving at least one bruise forming on his elbow where he'd knocked into the wall while trying to lather.

"I fit in there fine." Her voice came from the other side of the curtain, raised to be heard over the water.

"Because you're the size of a vest pocket."

"Fufffofff."

He translated the toothbrushingese, and grinned, letting the now-clear water run down his back. Thankfully the water pressure in this building wasn't amenable to that time-honored volley of apartment warfare—flushing the toilet while someone was taking a shower. His Wren was not above reaching over and jiggling the handle just for petty payback.

When Sergei finally got out of the shower, Wren had left the bathroom, the only sign of her passing the fact that the towel, which had originally been folded on the counter was now draped within easy reach.

He grabbed it, drying himself off, and went in search of his partner. She was already at work in her office, papers spread out on the floor in front of her.

"What're you working on?"

"Yahhuh."

He knew that sound. She hadn't actually heard anything he'd said. The lonejack ability to focus was fascinating—if he could bottle it and peddle it to grad students, he'd never have to sell another sculpture again.

He watched her for a few moments, then wrapped the towel more securely around his waist and went into the kitchenette to pick up the tea he knew that she would have left steeping on the counter for him. It was slightly bitter—he'd taken longer under the hot water than usual, trying to wash all the shampoo out of his hair—

but there was sugar in the canister behind the pasta, and a scoop of that made it drinkable.

Thus fortified, he went back down the hallway, clunky white mug with a local supermarket's logo on it cupped in his hands. He should check messages, see if any crisis had occurred at the gallery while he was out dealing with Andre, and then with Wren. He should be thinking about the installation they had coming in next month, worrying over the bills, the customer load, the daily to-do lists…

Lowell is a pain, and a snoop, but you trained him well. Let him prove it already. That had been the point of hiring the boy, after all: to train him to do the daily running of the gallery, so he, Sergei, could give more time to the Retrieval side of business. Sergei still wasn't sure he trusted Lowell entirely; there had been someone poking around his office over the summer, and Lowell had never warmed to Wren. If someone were to try to get to the Retriever through Sergei's assistant; well, that might be a weakness Sergei would have to take care of.

For now, though, the gallery was closed, and Wren was his only concern.

Wren half-heard the shower stop running, but the simple act of sitting down among the now familiar piles of paperwork had dropped her into a modified fugue state, where Sergei's normal morning routine became so much soothing white noise. It wasn't enough to make up for lost sleep, but it helped.

She did sense him standing in the doorway, even

through the fugue, and by the time he came back down the hallway she had shifted half of her attention from the research to conversation-mode. "Morning."

"Morning. You were up and at it early today." Again, he didn't say but she heard it anyway. She could work in the early morning hours, but it wasn't her favorite thing. Evening, when the shadows concealed, or afternoons, when there were crowds to lose herself in, those were when The Wren came alive. Mornings were for lazing about, sleeping late and doing the more mundane paperwork of daily life. Which reminded her, she needed to update her credit card balance. She tried not to carry her cards with her—the magnetic strips went kaflooey if she had them on her person too long—but they were damned convenient for automatic payments and phone orders.

No, normally mornings were for being lazy or, if Sergei were there, cuddling, talking things over, or not talking at all. She could have stayed in bed, faked sleeping when he woke up, let things progress from there.

Except after the recent downtime of no work coming in at all, not working when there was a job seemed... wrong. Only, as far as Sergei knew, there was no job.

He stood in the doorway, sipped his tea, and watched her until she started to squirm.

"What's that?" he asked, gesturing with the mug of tea at a pile of newspaper clippings and printouts

"Um. Project." She felt a moment of totally unfamiliar panic. Keeping secrets from Sergei—wrong, wrong, and wrong! *Damn it, how do I skate on this one?* "The psi-bomb."

"Ah. Good, good. Tell me if you manage to find out anything more." He was clearly preoccupied with his own thoughts, turning away without further curiosity and heading back down the hallway. If she weren't so relieved at not having to explain, she'd be annoyed. How dare he not be curious about what she was doing? What was going on, there? What was her partner up to?

You're an idiot, Valere, she thought, not without some amusement. Or she had a guilty conscience. When you're pulling a con, however gentle or harmless, then everyone else started to look like a con, too. If she was hiding something, then he must be, too?

She stared at the research she'd been trying to do, shoving a strand of hair out of her face in exasperation. It seemed pointless to even worry about this job—if the Seer was right, she had way more serious problems to worry about than Retrieving a gaudy little trinket from the middle of a family spit-war. But the mantra had always, but always been "Finish the job." Even if the world's going to hell. Maybe especially then. She had to focus on the job. Focus was the key. Focus was what made her a Talent, made her The Wren. Made her strong.

But for some reason, she wasn't able to concentrate.

Pushing the papers away from her in disgust, she sat upright, arms overhead, forcing her spine back into alignment. A slow relaxing of the arms, timed with a long, even exhalation of breath, and she reached for the fugue state. *Ground and center, ground and center…*

It wasn't coming. Instead of the calm quietness in her

limbs that was the ideal working stage, she felt twitchy, irritable. Jumpy, on the molecular level.

Ground and center, damn it! Neezer's voice, angry at her in a way he'd rarely ever been in life. His voice—the actual memory, rather than the idealized teacher-voice—was starting to fade in her head, finally, and the realization added to the unbearable weight growing between her shoulder blades.

Too many years. Too long since she had seen the man who taught her what she was, what she could become. Too many loved ones lost, along the road.

Neezer. Lee. I'm sorry. I'm sorry I couldn't save either one of you.

She could hear Sergei rummaging in the bedroom next door—he kept a couple of shirts and suits here even before they started sleeping together, just for convenience sake, but now that had expanded to fill half her wardrobe. Maybe at some point she should just give in and tell him to use the closet in the spare bedroom/ research library (the closet in the office being filled with filing cabinets). But that always seemed like the step to be taken further down the road, not right now. It was too soon. Too…permanent-feeling. This was her space, her refuge, the place where the nodes of current made her feel soothed. Except, recently, it wasn't so much soothed as spooked.

The jittery feeling in her bones persisted. Wren sighed, giving in to the unavoidable. What time was it? The computer was shut down, as it always was when she wasn't actively using it, but a small wind-up clock on the desk told her that it was almost seven-thirty. If she couldn't focus enough to work, then it was time for another cup of coffee.

She closed the door of the office behind her—to put the papers away might make them seem too important, raising additional curiosity in Sergei's mind, but closing the door wouldn't—and went into the kitchen to raise her caffeine blood level.

The coffee had been sitting too long, so she dumped it and started a new pot. How anyone could drink stale coffee baffled her. You might not drink it for the taste, but that didn't mean you had to suffer for it, either.

"I've got a client meeting at lunch." Sergei stood in the hallway, knotting an elegantly subdued silk tie around his neck. She took a moment to pause and just look at him. Even as a know-it-all eighteen-year-old, she had thought he was a seriously sharp-looking guy, with that squared-off chin, high forehead, and sharp cheekbones offset by surprisingly soft, pale brown eyes. The years had added creases around the mouth and eyes—all right, maybe less the years and more her, specifically, causing some of those lines—but she still thought he was, hands down, decidedly yummy.

It was the nose, she decided. Not quite hawklike, but not a gentle slope, either. The nose was what turned her on. And that mouth, and…

"Client for you, or client for me?" she asked.

"Maybe both." It happened that way, sometimes. He'd get a new artist in, or maybe an artist's agent, and they'd get to talking, and suddenly the client would start talking about this problem they had, a problem maybe with a work that a deadbeat collector won't pay for, or a museum was holding too long, or even just happened to be "stuck" in the house of an old lover, said lover refusing to give it up when it's needed for a showing...

It was a skill Sergei had: putting needs and people together to solve the need and enrich the people, in all cases Wren and himself. That skill that had made him first see, all those years ago, what a very good team they could be.

If he'd decided to go into politics, or used cars, the world would have been a much more dangerous place. And Wren would be flipping burgers in some joint somewhere, like her mother used to do.

"You okay?" He stopped fiddling with his tie and looked more closely at her, the way he hadn't at the paperwork.

Damn. That was the downside of Sergei actually seeing her. He *noticed* things.

"Yeah. Yeah, I'm okay." She wasn't flipping burgers. Between Neezer teaching her what she was, and Sergei helping her to fine-tune it, she would never have to flip burgers. So long as she finished the damn jobs. "Go. Sweet-talk the client. Make us some money."

"Right." He smiled briefly, reaching out with one hand to touch her chin in a way she hated from anyone but him. "I'll see you tonight?"

"Maybe. I'll check in later, okay?" Job first. Job last. And, truthfully, she was still feeling just a little too much togetherness right now. It was nice, but it was...too much. Together.

If her partner was hurt by her lack of enthusiasm, he didn't show it, merely finished polishing his look, smoothing down his hair until it sleeked back from his forehead in a fashionable but not too trendy 'do, and left, suit coat carefully folded over one arm, to keep it from wrinkling on the subway.

The moment the door closed behind him, Wren took her coffee and went back into the office, picking up where she had left off—with the blueprints for the apartment building she had visited the day before. Joey had delivered blues for the house Worth-Rosen owned out in the 'burbs as well; they had been left outside her kitchen window at some point during the night, wrapped in his usual baby-blue oilskin casing, but Wren was playing a hunch that dear, Talented Melanie wasn't going to let the contested piece out of her possession. She might even keep it on her at all times, which would make things… more complicated. Not impossible, just complicated.

Complications were what made the jobs interesting, but she didn't want an interesting job. She wanted a finished one. Wren wasn't completely out of touch with her psyche: she needed to get this done, so she could get ground back under her feet, feel confident again.

Figuring out the psychological underpinnings of your own stupidity was easy. Working them out was where the sweat and pain came in. And what she didn't have the energy—or concentration—for, not now. Not with the city-storm clouds piling up.

All right. Focus on what you can deal with. The physical aspects. The job. So, play the odds that it's still in the uptown apartment, and build a plan of attack from there.

She already knew that at least one doorman was susceptible to the Push. That would be helpful, if she had to resort to a traditional entrance. If she were prone to worry about such things, she would also count it a plus that her "legitimate" visit had left her DNA all over the place, to confuse the issue, but the sort of people she got involved in tended to not be the types to call in forensic investigators, not even PUPs. The only thing her DNA could be used for would be a Summoning, and she was pretty well protected against that, just like any Talent past first-year training. Tagging someone could be considered friendly, or a nuisance, or an assault, depending on the intent of the tagger and the mood of the tagee. Summoning—dragging someone by their current to where you were—was always perceived as an attack, and treated as such.

Still. She wasn't going to take any risks, not when the target was Talented, wealthy, and Council. Three really bad things for a lonejack to tangle with, even before the city got so tense.

"I need to know her schedule," Wren muttered. "Schedule, schedule…" She swirled her hand through the papers, as though conjuring just the right sheet of paper to leap into her palm like a trained parakeet. She had seen something, in the first run though Joey's offerings, on a sheet of paper, a printout…

There it was. A printout of a day planner, a monthly screen shot. She didn't want to know how much that little nugget of detail was going to cost her, since it wasn't in the original negotiations, but bless him for knowing what she'd need.

If he weren't so easily blackmailable in return, based on even the little she could prove he'd done over the years, she'd be worried that he knew her so well.

"Right. Where are you going to be, Melanie? When are you going to have to leave that lovely little apartment you no longer share with anyone…"

There was the maid, yes, but even the most loyal of help took nights off, or slacked off in the breakroom, or slipped out for a drink, a cigarette, or a bit of nookie.

And if they didn't…well, after facing down everything from sentient-spelled alarm systems to slavering hellhounds in the course of her career, Wren thought that maybe she had a handle on improvising around security surprises.

Don't get cocky, kid. Not a personal memory, this time, but a much-loved sound byte. Great. Even fictional characters were taking her to task, now. If the voice of Han Solo started in on her, she was going for a full psychic mindwipe of all her damn memories and starting fresh, she swore she would.

Memories, Valere. Tree-taller, sitting across from her in a coffee shop up in the fifties. His hair was wet from the rain, and his eyes and skin had an unbearably healthy glow to them. *Memories are what make us different from the animals.*

That we have them? she had asked. A much younger

she, new to the city and still freshly scarred from her first brush with bereavement.

That we cherish them, Lee had said.

Wren blinked, coming back to the present with an almost audible snap. The sense of ghosts at her shoulder was very, very strong.

Loss. Cherishing.

"Thank you, Tree-taller," she said under her breath. She didn't know quite what she had twigged to, here, but it *felt* important.

She reached forward to pull a fresh piece of graph paper out of the desk, and retrieved a soft-lead pencil from the floor. As always with her work, the Retrieval was going to rely significantly to how things fell out once the ball was rolling, but planning, planning, and planning were the secrets to good improvisation. She was better at planned stuff. She liked planned things that went according to plan. But she knew better than to count on them.

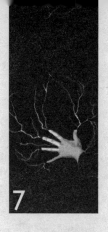

7

"Yeeeoow!" A body went flying across the grassy clearing—literally. Dragonfly wings beat the air madly, trying to right the body they were attached to before it landed, facedown, on the ground.

There was silence, then— "Medic!" a weak voice called from the motionless body. "Medic!"

"Get up." The voice of the man who had sent the body flying was cold, unsympathetic. "You'll be fine."

"I'm dead." The wings beat once, slowly, then came to rest folded against the bare, narrowly boned back. The voice was weak, pitiful, and in any disinterested observer would have invoked pity, or at least immediate sympathy

"No, you're not." The disinterested observer felt none of those things. Or if he did, he hid them well. "Come on. Get up."

"Morgan…"

"Get up. Or I'll walk over there and kick you into splinters."

The fatae rolled over onto its side, staring at the man named Morgan with oversized, bottle-green eyes. Its wood-dark skin and wings contrasted oddly with the gym shorts, knobby knees, and the Nikes on its delicate feet, making the creature look like a cross between a Rackham fairy and an unfortunate Phys Ed student.

"I mean it," Morgan warned, sounding as though he were about to commence the kicking. The fatae closed dark lids over those eyes, and let out a long, long-suffering sigh, but bent its knees at a painful-looking angle and managed to get up onto its equally odd-jointed elbows.

This human was cruel, its body language shouted. Cruel, and unkind and evil-minded.

"Well, that was…progress. Of a sort," Morgan went on in a slightly milder, quieter tone to the individual standing beside him. "Took the landing better this time, anyway." He shook his head in rueful dismay at the words. They had been working at this one move all morning, and the progress he mentioned was that the student had finally managed to land without splattering bits of blood from an orifice.

"We're not fighters." The fatae speaking, like the one on the ground, had a narrow build, with four elongated limbs—each with knobby double-joints—and a double set of gossamer-thin wings on each side of its body. The head was humanoid, if too narrow for any idea of human attractiveness, but the sound of the wings beating created a hum that was almost music.

Their teacher made a sound that might have been amusement. "You're not even arguers. And you're going to be corpses, if you don't get a clue, fast."

The vigilantes had been targeting the exotics mainly, he had been told. Morgan supposed it was because they were easier to spot than the nonhuman who blended into the general population, but he had quickly observed that the winged tribes had no sense of self-defense. Or much sense of any other sort, either, as far as he'd been able to determine. Attractive nuisances, he'd call them; except for the fact that they bled and died same as any, when those racist bastards caught up with them.

"A pity your race got large—those wings would have been useful in maneuvering, if they could support your weight."

The fatae fluttered its wings in agitation, watching the other figure pick itself up off the ground. "We are not dragons, to fly on hollow bones and hydrogen. Our wings are for display, to attract mates and keep—Morgan, this throwing and hitting and falling seems so…brutal."

Morgan nodded, unmoved. "It is."

The dragonfly fatae had a darker shade of green to its eyes, and the same expression of incomprehension. "And your people do this? For fun?"

Despite the seriousness of the situation, and the hours they had already put in, Morgan laughed at the incredulity in the creature's voice. "Some folk do. It's exercise, in addition to the defensive aspect of it. An art form, when you reach a certain level. Physical art…something you create with motion."

The fatae looked away. "I do not understand that."

Morgan shrugged, clearly tiring of the conversation. "You don't have to understand it. You're never going to be that good—you're just not built for it. You're probably not built to understand the enjoyment part of it, either. But you will know what to do when you're attacked. That's why you people hired me, isn't it? To teach you how to fight. To survive. Because I'm the best at what I do." The last was said without too much ego, merely a statement of fact.

"That. And…" The fatae hesitated. "And because you call us people."

The human stopped speaking, and looked up at the early dawn sky. He wasn't anyone. Just a martial artist wasting his gifts teaching overweight suburban kids how to break bricks with their heads, driving a truck for a moving company to make ends meet. There were masters out there who could dance around him and not raise a sweat, masters who could explain to him why, when these strange creatures had appeared one morning and asked for his help, he hadn't merely swatted them away and gone back to sleep.

He was just a guy, doing a job. That was all. No big deal.

"Get back into formation, featherweight," he barked to the figure who had finally gotten to his feet again. "You, too," he said to the fatae next to him. "And this time

I want to see some power behind that defense! Ain't nobody going to take pity on you 'cause you're so pretty!"

The two fatae shuffled into position, their bare toes *shussshing* through the dew-wet grass until they faced the human, enough room between them so that their wings had room to move. Morgan sighed. He would have to do something about that, eventually. Teach them how to fight even when they felt enclosed. But for now, he just needed to teach them how to fall without breaking anything, and how to get up after they fell. Survival tactics. That's why the fatae had hired him. If he could teach these two, and they could explain it to their people, and then he could teach another pair from another clan, adapt his knowledge to their body types...of all the damned fatae there allegedly were in the city, why were there so few who knew how to fight?

He watched them confer with each other, the smaller one looking over its shoulder at Morgan, those oversized eyes doing the slow-blink thing that meant it was nervous.

"Stop chatting, ladies. Here I come. Defense, damn it!"

He rushed them in an intentionally clumsy attack maneuver, the stick in his hand rising as an improvised club.

This time, rather than trying to duck out of his way, the larger of the two stood as though to block the blow. Morgan took him out easily, dropping him to the ground in a clumsy pile. Disgusted, Morgan raised the stick again. By now, the second fatae had presented his back to the human, wings fluttering in a confused clutter of sound and noise and wind. Startled—they had never done this before—Morgan hesitated. Only a second, a fraction of a second, but it was enough for the fatae on the ground to roll over and get to its knees, then back up onto its feet.

"Good!" They had surprised him. That was excellent.

The stick whirled, and knocked the first fatae behind the knees, sending him back down to the ground, face-forward.

It just wasn't going to be enough to keep them alive.

It wasn't a Fatal Friday, the traditional post-debriefing drink fest, but there were still a decent number of Handlers—the Silence employees who dealt with Operatives in the field—in town. You simply needed to know where to look for them. Sergei didn't—but he still knew who to call to ask.

Adam was oddly reticent, considering that the man had been one of the few still-friendly faces when Sergei came back to the Silence under Andre's arm-twisting, but he eventually coughed up the name of a few of the more popular hangouts.

Down three narrow, stone steps, turn left, through the metal door. "Into the last smoke-filled room in Manhattan," he said, shaking his head as he tried to see through the haze. Cigars were the inhalant of choice, everything from dainty cigarillos to the thick, pungent monsters he remembered his great-uncles smoking over their drinks, late into the night. Sergei hadn't thought of them in years, not since the last one of them died, reed-thin and cranky in a nursing home bed.

"Michael."

"Didier." Michael gave him a wary glance, then looked back down into his drink. The old man was sitting alone, in a bar where every single table was crowded. Sergei wasn't sure if that made Michael a good prospect, or a bad one, but it certainly made him a vulnerable one.

"You got time to talk to an old friend?"

They had been friends, once. Michael was already old when Sergei was a fresh-eyed recruit, but the two had hit it off over discussions of old blues and older wines.

"I got no friends. Least of all no old ones."

"So I see." Knowing Michael's penchant for speaking his mind, it was a wonder he still had a job, in this changed environment. Still, he always had a way of resolving Situations with a minimum of news or fuss, and that was the end goal, no matter how much everything else changed. Hall of Fame quality, was Michael, if the Silence were ever to indulge in anything that gauche. They didn't even have a Founder's Wall of portraits.

"We could make like we don't know each other, then. Just two outsiders, sharing a table."

"Look. I can't…." For the first time in the years he had known the old man, Michael actually looked *old*. "Please, don't ask me to do this."

For Wren, to get what he needed, Sergei could have driven Michael into the ground. He would have felt bad about it, even while he was doing it, but the training was deep in him, and the need would have driven him.

"Well. Look who the wind blew in."

"Jordana." He turned away from Michael with relief on both their parts, looking to the left where the voice had come from. Black hair. Black eyes. Sunless-pale skin contrasted by a bright red mouth. Deadly aim with a crossbow. He didn't know why that bit of information had lodged in his brain, when he couldn't even remember her last name anymore.

The woman waved a genial arm over, indicating that Sergei should join her table. There were two other women and a man sitting with her already, all with the same narrow-eyed expression and an erect, ready-to-move pose, even seated, that was the stamp of an active Handler.

Michael had been sitting slumped over, as though protecting his drink. Protecting his despair.

Sergei had worked hard to not remember his last Operative. Blond and ruddy-skinned, like some joke of a Swedish farmboy. More muscle-strength than current, for all that he tried to be the Perfect Soldier for Good. By the end, Sergei had wanted to lock him in a closet for his own good. You tried not to care about them, not too much. A good Handler didn't. A great Handler had to.

Jordana patted the seat next to her. "Saw you during the last Dump—" the reason for Fatal Friday, when all active Handlers reported on their current—no pun intended— and ongoing caseloads "—but you looked a little wiped out, so I figured you weren't in the mood to beer-trawl after."

Sergei took the offered seat, shaking his head and loosening the tie that was beginning to choke him, after fitting perfectly all day. He had gotten out of a wheelchair to report in, the day Jordana was talking about. A cab had taken him from the Dump, not to his apartment for much-needed sleep, but to Wren's, for a memorial service for Lee, the artist-Talent who had died during that job. That Situation, one the Silence had sent them on, with flawed and faulty information.

Not that Lee's death was the Silence's fault. Not directly. He knew that, even if Wren hadn't managed to accept it, yet. The blame for that death was square on the fatae, the small group of them who were blaming all humans, no matter what group they belonged to, for the attacks. Lee had just been in the wrong place at the wrong time.

"Wasn't much in the mood for socializing," was all he said now.

"So what brings you out here now?" She wasn't being particularly rude, but she wasn't as friendly as she'd first appeared, either. It was a subtle thing, and Sergei had a sudden fear that he'd gotten too paranoid, too personally involved, to judge the situation cleanly.

"Information," he said to her, leaning his elbows on the table, letting his body language suggest the hint of intimacy, of letting, all unknown, secrets slip. Odds were she wasn't going to buy it; she knew him too well. But one of the others might.

Jordana leaned back in her chair in direct response. "Getting, or disseminating?" A fair enough question, one Silence to another. And one he had no intention of answering. He wasn't Silence anymore.

"Depends on how much you already know. Or how much you know that you don't know."

Jordana looked blank at that, and the two other women looked away, but the man with her blinked. Sergei zeroed in on him.

"I'm looking for dirt. On R&D."

Silence met his statement, a combination of stunned disbelief and incipient laughter. R&D was the über of all departments. The domain of puppet masters. They didn't *have* dirt, they dished it.

"You're insane." That was the first woman, a sharp-featured strawberry-blonde with horn-rimmed glasses too trendy to be really needed and darkly mascaraed lashes underneath.

"Of course he is," Jordana said, bored. "He's Didier." His craziness was a given—the Handler who walked out on the Silence. The Handler who had been *allowed* to walk out on the Silence. And then brought back in. He had been the material of gossip, before. If he and Wren survived whatever was going around, he suspected a generation or two would make him into whispered legend, and, after that, if the Silence survived, into myth. It was a strange feeling, being able to look down the years of a probable path and see how his life would be twisted in the retelling.

"You think I'd know anything they didn't want me to know?" the man said, ignoring Jordana's comment.

"I think that you have a brain, and eyes, and the ability to do your job without a direct tube from Duncan's brain." Actually Sergei didn't think that about most of the people in the bar—even before he had burned out and walked, the quality of Handlers was sinking, mainly because the leashes were being held too tight. A good Handler needed room to run his or her Operative properly, room to evaluate and adapt, not blindly follow directives. Duncan, the head of Research & Dissemination, was a control freak, yes, but he also demanded competence from his people. Even the people who didn't report directly to him. R&D had that much power. It had never really worried Sergei before: he had never really bothered to think about it before.

Clearly Andre had.

"Sometimes, it's wiser to take the tube." The man stood up, picked up his glass, and walked a little too steadily to the bar, where he placed it on the counter with the precise action of a man who knows he's more drunk than he feels, and gestured to the bartender for a refill.

Sergei watched him out of the corner of his eye. "He can walk home from here, right?"

"What do you care?" The blonde, her powder-blue eyes wide-set and her pink mouth pursed in disapproval, practically radiated bitterness. "You hang with magicals, not humans."

"Clare!" Jordana seemed taken aback by that, but the strawberry-blonde nodded.

"He does. You know it. Only time he comes back to us is when he wants something. Something for *them*."

"'Them' meaning your FocAs? Or do they not qualify for human status anymore?" It was a shot in the dark, one he didn't want to hit, but he saw from the twitch in her eyes that it had.

"Right. Excuse me then. I won't waste any more of your time." Everything he had eaten all day suddenly wanted to revolt in his gut, and he controlled it ruthlessly, rising from his chair with smooth economy.

"Sergei—" Jordana said, as he stood and turned away. He looked back over one shoulder to see her still sitting there, her complexion pale green under the bar lights. "Be careful, Didier. For old times' sake."

"Careful." He almost laughed. "Right."

Careful was the only way to walk. Careful was the only way to survive.

Wren was sitting cross-legged on the floor in her office, studying the blueprints, a mug of coffee in her hand. The building was so straightforward it was almost tearfully boring, and she was reminding herself, over and over again, that boring was good, when she heard a sound coming from the front of the apartment.

Jesus. Had she locked the front door? She *always* locked the front door. Nobody had a key to the dead bolt, not even her mother. Only Sergei…Sergei and Jerry, who was, in his randomly used capacity, the super.

There was a moment of panic, then a familiar voice. "You chalked?"

Aldo didn't even bother knocking, just opened the door, came in, and yelled down the hallway. Either he was the prototype for every clueless, socially oblivious geek-artist ever joked about, or he had absolutely no fear of getting shot, stabbed, or otherwise dealt with as an intruder. Although, knowing him, both those possibilities were equally probable.

"Yeah," Wren said, as she came out of her office and closed the door behind her. Obviously, no, she *hadn't* locked the door when she came home. For the first time in how many years? Sergei would be appalled. Her mother would have conniptions. She was never going to mention this little slip to either one of them. "Got a request."

Aldo was anywhere between fifty and seventy, his snow-pale skin pulled tight and dry across features sharp enough to shred paper, with intense dark eyes and a hitch in his step that came, according to various stories, either from being shoved into the trunk of a car by mistake during a Mob hit, getting bodyslammed during a Ramones concert, or being too violently cuffed during the WTO dustups in Seattle. "Can I tap dance to it?"

"You can tap dance to anything, maestro." She had pulled the description of the piece from the folder she had set up earlier that morning: color coded, the way all of her case folders were. This one was bloodred; the only other active folders in her file were the ones she had set up on the anti-fatae vigilantes (electric-blue) and the forever-ongoing case of Old Sally, the stuffed horse of doom (green). She had never actually made up a folder for the Nescanni job, just thrown her notes and receipts and newspaper clippings into a plain folder and shoved it into the filing cabinet. Someday. Maybe. When things settled out and she had time to do things like back-case filing and cleaning behind old dressers…

"Here." She handed the sheet of paper to him. "I need as good a representation of that as you can manage."

"Now, or yesterday."

"Now would be good." She wanted this done with, but not urgently enough to owe favors.

"Right. Can do. Making stir-fry tonight, if'n you want to join us."

"Thanks, but no." Neither Aldo nor his partner were bad cooks, just always preoccupied with things outside the kitchen. It occasionally made for memorable meals, and never in the gastronomically pleasing way. Wren might not be any kind of gourmet cook herself, but she enjoyed food too much to see what they did to it.

"'K." He waved the sheet at her in an absentminded farewell, and went back downstairs, his size-tens a reassuringly solid *thump-thump-hitch-thump* on the wooden stairs.

Aldo was good people. Sometimes, Wren got so caught up in her job, and the recent chaos between Council and lonejack and fatae, that she forgot she was part of another world, too. Ordinary people, with lowercase *T* talents and skills. People who lived and loved and looked at her not as The Wren, the best Retriever of her generation, but as a neighbor, a friend, a comrade in the city….

A daughter.

Wren tapped on the door frame absently, then finished turning the dead bolts.

The Rosens had had a family, once, if photos didn't lie too badly. Now they were Talent and Null, torn apart over a thing, a simple, stupid thing.

Storm clouds rolling in. *Shadows rising.*

Wren chewed on her upper lip thoughtfully a moment, tugging at a strand of hair that had escaped her braid, and then came to a decision. Going into the kitchen, she lifted the old-fashioned, clunky phone off the hook and punched in a number.

"Mom. Hi. Oh, for— Who else is going to call you Mom?" Grinning, Wren perched herself on one of the stools, and settled in for a scolding. Her mother didn't understand her, didn't even pretend to understand what her only daughter did for a living, and didn't approve, at all, of her relationship with Sergei, if only because Wren's partner was a full decade older, but she had the fine and deeply appreciated gift of being able to see her daughter as an adult. That did not mean, however, that she was always able to let go. Entirely.

That was okay. Wren wasn't sure she was ever going to let go of her mother as "Mom," either.

"No, no reason for calling. I just wanted to check in, get my weekly dose of the 'burbs, remind me why I moved *here*…"

"Because all the boys here bored you, as I recall."

It was good, that her mother was so absolute a Null. That way, Margot could pretend her daughter was just like everyone else, letting her focus on the normal things, the everyday things mothers worried about, whatever they were.

There was a lot to be said for being Null, yeah. No

Council, no wizzing, no idiot lonejacks with death wishes. But Wren wouldn't ever choose it for herself.

Well. She looked up at the ceiling, where the stains from the spy-bug infestation could still be seen if you squinted hard, and thought again. *No. Not ever.*

But she was sometimes really, really glad her mom seemed incapable of remembering anything *Cosa*-related.

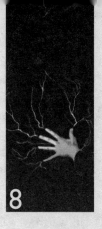

8

The clink of fine china and the shuffling of pens against paper barely disturbed the silence inside the room, until a voice raised in genteel inquiry.

"How many votes do we have?"

There wasn't a moment's pause before the answer came back—a man's voice, hesitant as though uncertain if his news would be taken as good or bad. "Seven. Eight, if Davey breaks the way he should."

KimAnn Howe stared out the window, her petite frame held like a ballet dancer's, almost casually elegant in her poise as though her shoulders had never once slumped, her back never been introduced to a curve. The view from the room was of a quiet tree-lined square, the very best neighborhood that money and influence could buy in Manhattan, but it could have been a blank wall for all the notice she took of it.

"Eight isn't enough. It would barely have carried us,

before." Her delicate hands rested on the window frame, only the papery texture of her skin and the carefully tended white of her hair betraying her age. "We need more than scraping past, Jacob. We need a solid, overwhelming majority. Otherwise the vultures will take us down, and everything I have done will have been in vain."

There were three of them, seated in a room dominated by a huge cream-colored marble fireplace. The interior was spotless, and instead of wood, in awareness of the still-warm weather, the grate had been replaced with a fan of golden straw and warm brown cattails that Martha Stewart might have envied. The furniture was mahogany, the perfect match for the massive boardroom table in the adjoining room, where the full Council would meet.

Even though the building around them was filled with assistants, clerks, and lawyers going about the Council's business, no noise reached into the room from outside, and none dared leave the room. No current was needed to ensure this; sturdy prewar construction assured it.

The only male in the room, an older gentleman given to portliness around the middle, but with an aquiline face that made him seem fierce even in repose, placed his teacup down on the small, round table next to his chair and looked up at the first speaker.

"What of Sebastian's side? How many votes will he be able to muster?"

She laughed, a delicate thing to match the bone china they were using. "He has less need to be diplomatic in his actions. They're all roughnecks out there, anyway, and seem to respect a leader who tells them what to think, rather than requiring that they be led about by a golden chain attached to their privates."

The third woman: a younger brunette wearing a subtle blue-checked skirt suit and tan heels, almost choked on her tea in amusement. "You would be bored with that obedient a Council," she said, using more familiarity in her words than most would, when speaking to the de facto, if untitled leader of the Northeastern Council.

"Hush, Colleen," the man said.

"No, the child is right. Never scold her for being right, Jacob. Sebastien has his own way of doing things, and I have mine, and we complement each other well. That is why I chose to approach him in the first place."

That, and the fact that the San Diego Council already had a reputation for maverick moves, unconventional behavior, and taking no guff from lonejacks, most of whom packed up and left for greener if more expensive pastures in Los Angeles or Las Vegas.

No, Sebastian Bailey suited her quite well. Suited her, and her purposes, and her plans.

KimAnn looked down at the slim packet of papers she still held in her hand, almost forgotten—but not quite. "And this—" she indicated the offending papers by the simple act of raising her hand, drawing attention back to them "—merely confirms that I was right to do so."

The single page letter had arrived that morning, not by fatae courier but Null express delivery service. Kim-Ann still was not sure if that was intended as some sort of commentary, or if they had simply not been able to hire a fatae willing to come here, to the heart of the Council.

Fools. She had nothing against the fatae, so long as they maintained their place, and did not try to interfere. And she would certainly never harm one merely for doing its job.

Unlike others within the Council she could but wouldn't name, KimAnn saw no point in killing the messengers for the failures of their employers. That was bad management. Kill an underling, you lose the use of it.

"I still say we should have made another attempt to neutralize the Retriever," the man said. "She's going to be a roadblock—she's already challenged us once, and gotten away with it. That sets a bad example."

Speaking of bad management—was she the only one here with any sense whatsoever? KimAnn pursed her lips, staring out into the lights of the distance, then shook her head. "Never, ever give your opposition a martyr-saint, Jacob. Especially one who is so much more useful alive and neutralized.

"Fact—her name is not signed onto this letter. She may agree with them, she may even meet with them but she has not cast her lot entirely in with these idiots. I've met the girl, taken her measure. Genevieve Valere is many things, but first and foremost she is a lonejack. And that means that she is selfish, self-involved, and, while not easily buyable, quite predictable. If we push *thus,* she will go in the direction we choose." KimAnn's voice was coolly neutral, a general evaluating a battle plan of her own devising. "I am more concerned with creating consensus within our own ranks."

"Meaning?" Jacob asked, his voice reaching for the same cool distance his superior had perfected.

"Meaning, what about Nola?" KimAnn asked, ticking names off in her steel-trap mind. "Where does she stand?"

"Squarely in the 'this is a bad idea' camp, I fear. She admires and respects you, and for that she has not spoken up against it, but she will not follow us."

The de facto Council leader dismissed that with a wave of her hand, the tapered fingers bare save for a simple white gold wedding band. "Will she oppose us?"

Almost forgotten in the moment, Colleen repressed a shiver at the even tone of those words. Not so much for what was being said, as what was being asked. Would Nola, a woman who had served the Mage Council for as long as Colleen could remember, who had family history of serving, back to the founders of the Northeastern Council—would she too be taken down without pity, without second thought, in order for Madame Howe to get her votes?

Jacob considered the question. "She is a practical woman. I suspect that she will soon evidence a desire to take on a new student, one whose skill level is such that it will demand much of her time and energy."

"Nola did always have the heart of a mentor," Kim-Ann said in agreement. "I would be sorry to lose her as a member of the Mage Council, but there could be no better use for her abilities, I agree."

The muscles between Colleen's shoulder blades unknotted slightly. *Her* loyalty was unquestioned; she would do as Madame Howe thought best. But there were better ways to show it, to her mind, than the stiletto, no matter how elegantly turned. The feel of the knife turning, the sound of the body as it hit the stones, the shocked and nervous silence quickly covered by nervous flutterings of social chatter, as they all, including her, pretended that nothing had happened…it wasn't something you forgot, anytime soon.

Please, Colleen thought to whatever power might be listening. Please, don't let anyone else oppose Madame Howe's plans for a Joint Council. Let them all understand, this is the only way to save us all…

"All right then."

KimAnn turned away from the window, finally, and Colleen uncapped her fountain pen and poised herself to begin taking notes.

"Inasmuch as certain changes have occurred within the community, involving all factions of the *Cosa Nostradamus,* I find myself torn between the traditions I have worked all my life to uphold, and the very real danger to the Mage's Council as it was envisioned, as a stand between the chaos of old magics and the rational use of the new.

"In order to maintain that stand, it is the opinion of this Council of the Metropolitan Northeastern Seaboard that further steps must be taken to demonstrate the seriousness of this threat to our unaffiliated counterparts, in the hopes that they will join with us, rather than with the forces of such chaos…"

Colleen kept writing.

* * *

After Aldo's visit, Wren had felt as if the walls of her apartment were closing in around her. She had grabbed the most intriguing of her materials, shoved them into her oversized, bright yellow shoulder bag/makeshift attaché case, and headed out the door.

She had meant just to go down to the coffee shop, have a couple dozen cups of spectacularly bad coffee and get some work done. Instead she had found her way to Sergei's, where the High Altar of Italian Caffeine waited.

The doorman on duty—by profession trained to see people without actually seeing them—merely looked up and nodded when she walked in. No excessive politeness, no solicitous greeting, just a faint nod and then back down to his newspaper.

Wren liked that. A lot. Maybe too much. She wasn't a doorman-type person, really.

Sergei had been home, much to her surprise. She had forgotten that it was Friday. The gallery was Lowell's domain on Fridays. Sergei claimed that he was training his assistant to someday take over, so he could retire somewhere warm and quiet. Nobody believed him, not even Lowell.

Wren didn't like Lowell, but she never thought he was stupid. Supercilious, stiff, arrogant and overproud of his limited abilities, yes, but not stupid. He wasn't expecting to inherit—just to learn enough from the best to go open his own place someday and compete. She could respect that.

Like the doorman, Sergei was reading the newspaper.

Unlike the doorman, he got up and greeted her properly. When she could breathe again, she waved the yellow bag in his face. He understood, and went back to his newspaper and tea, while she set up shop at the kitchen counter, spreading papers and starting the coffee to brew.

The invite had arrived a few hours later, via courier demon—not P.B., but a stranger—thin and hairless, but with the same dense musculature and dark red eyes that mark the breed. There was something about demon, something in their genetic stew, that made them gravitate naturally toward carrying messages, keeping secrets. Wren had never asked P.B. anything about his past—none of her business—but she did sometimes wonder about demon history. All anyone knew was that they were a mutation of an original, older fatae line; that they didn't breed true, assuming they bred at all, and none of them ever talked about it. Ever.

This courier had handed the invite to Wren and scuttled back out the door of Sergei's apartment without waiting for a response. A nice change from P.B.'s usual hand-over-and-open-fridge routine. But unnerving, too. There weren't that many demon in Manhattan: she hadn't had anyone other than P.B. courier for her in almost a year. And to have it delivered here, to Sergei's apartment rather than her own place, meant it was probably time-urgent.

And that the sender, whoever it was, knew where she was. That might just be innocent coincidence…or a warning.

She opened the letter carefully, using an ivory letter-opener Sergei kept on his desk. Blessed by some shaman or another, it was supposed to keep bad news at bay.

What it actually did—Wren had discovered while using it to clean under her nails, one afternoon—was prevent anything laced with current from "grabbing" at her while she opened the envelope. Useful—if she could ever track down the shaman, she would have ordered a dozen of them, plus another dozen door handles, to prevent nasty surprises inside.

Speaking of nasty surprises inside…

The invitation was drawn on the traditional vellum and with lovely, organic inks, which was nice, and used oddly stilted formal language, which wasn't. Wren knew that there were a lot of people who found the old ways to be charming, if not downright soothing. She wasn't one of them. Old wasn't better. Old magics were unpredictable; seven different methods got you eight different results. No, she wasn't nostalgic at all.

Invite was pretty to look at, though. Until the wording actually sunk in.

Another Moot, or meeting, this one specifically called to discuss and deliberate, in their words "the situation dire and dreadful brought upon us by our cousins of the Mage Council."

Unlike the last one, which she had been dragged to by Lee's request to stop it, here she was to be an honored guest and participant.

"Oh, lovely." She tossed the invitation down on the table so that Sergei could read it as well. He skimmed it, then raised one eyebrow in the way she really wished that she could imitate, the way that should have caused lots of Spock jokes but never did. Not to his face, anyway. Or hers.

"That's…interesting. You planning on going?"

He was sitting on the sofa, glasses perched on the edge of his nose, only a sliver of his attention given to Wren's news and reaction.

"No."

That got his attention. He put down the papers and looked at her over the top of his glasses until she relented.

"Of course I'm going to go. I got an invite. How can I not go?"

Sergei didn't look happy. He remembered all too well what happened last time. Well, so did she. Vividly. "When is it?"

"Tonight. I guess they didn't want to give me too much time to think about it."

She didn't tell him that she already knew about the Moot. Sort of. That she would be going, not because she felt any obligation, but because a Seer had already Seen her there.

You've got some serious shit going on here, Valere. Talk to the man.

Yeah, she would. When she figured out what she was going to say. "Hi, I took a client on without you, and by the way, Seers have been Seeing me taking a major stand in all the politicking going on, and I think that we all really really should leave town. Right now." That'd all go over well.

She'd much rather deal with a Moot. On her own. While juggling orangutans.

"You want—"

"No. Thanks." If the Seer hadn't seen Sergei there, or

at least hadn't seen fit to mention the fact of his being there—she didn't want him anywhere near it. It wasn't his job, it wasn't his fight, it shouldn't be his problem. She could take care of herself, damn it.

"You got plans for the rest of the day?" she asked, changing the subject.

"Had thought about going down to the gallery this afternoon, see if I can get a head start on the week's paperwork before the Kautsman delivery."

"Kautsman?"

"Avant-garde. You'd hate it." Sergei's dry tone indicated that he wasn't all that thrilled with it, either, but he thought that it would sell. He only took on new artists for one of two reasons: he thought they were brilliant, or he thought they would make him potloads of money so he could afford the brilliant ones. Fewer scruples would make the Sergei Didier Gallery a better-known name, but that wasn't what he was about.

Well, not entirely, she amended her thought. Her partner had expensive tastes, and no desire to give them up for a life of aesthetic poverty. She respected that—people who found dignity in poverty were generally people who didn't really understand what it meant not to have money. She understood, firsthand—it *sucked*.

"I'm going to go back to my place, do some cleanup work." Her grimace wasn't entirely feigned—she did have to do something with the Nescanni job paperwork, at some point. Having things unfiled messed with the essential planning part of her brain that needed everything in its place before it could function. Not to mention the twist it put into her year-end financials. She might not—thank God—have to deal with all the paperwork more legitimate freelancers were smacked with, but bank accounts and stock investments and IRAs all had to be documented and accounted for, one way or another.

"You going to come by after the Moot?" His voice was casual, almost deadpan, and she couldn't tell if he wanted her to come by, or wished she wouldn't. The parade of model-types he used to date flashed through her memory, impossible to banish.

"You want me to?"

His face gentled somehow, and he leaned back in the sofa to stare up at her face. It unnerved her a little, the way he always looked her directly in the face. Most people looked indirectly at her, if they noticed her at all. If she hadn't honed that skill so much as a teenager, to avoid notice, and then as an adult, to enhance her Retrieval skills, would her life have been very different? Or would she always still be the overlooked one, the easily forgotten one?

Sergei didn't overlook her. Sergei never forgot her. Sergei, she was starting to realize, scared the hell out of her.

She didn't want to love someone who saw her so thoroughly.

"I'll be here tonight, if you want company. If you don't, just let me know you got home okay, and I'll catch up on all the details later."

"Right." She shoved the paperwork back into her bag, then bent over to grab her shoes from under the counter and slid them back on her feet, thankful for the hair coming out of her braid and hiding her face from view. "Have fun with the paperwork."

He grunted, having already gone back to the newspaper. She let herself out, leaning against the elevator wall as it descended, letting herself feel the hum of the building at her back like a soothing waterfall. Even without drawing down any of the current residing in the manmade electricity, she was comforted by it. She might not rely on filtered current—her mentor would have had a fit, if she were to get that lazy—but it was nice to know that it was there, if she needed it.

Of course, the people she might need it against—her target, the Council goons, her fellow lonejack idiots at the Moot tonight—also had access to it. That thought was less comforting.

Which was why, rather than go back to her apartment and fling paperwork the way she'd told Sergei she was planning, she was going to do something about stacking the deck in her favor.

Half an hour and a downtown subway ride later, Wren came out in Alphabet City and drew a breath of relatively fresh air into her lungs. She wasn't smelling the slightly chilled breeze off the East River, or the exhaust rising off the street in front of her, however, but the intoxicating hum of power rising off the nearby East River Generation Station. Always there, always producing—always tempting, just to take a little bit, just a bit, first pulldown's free, little girl…

There was a café on the corner that made excellent

perogies, and didn't mind if you lingered over the newspaper and coffee, afterward. She went in and ordered a dish, grabbed a newspaper, and sat down in a prime corner table. Perogies—heavy Eastern European dumplings—weren't something she indulged in often: they sat too heavy in her stomach for comfort, but she was going to need something solid to focus on, with what she was about to do.

Every lonejack—hell, every Talent—knew how to draw down power from man-made and natural sources alike, but everyone had favorites which they used more often than not. Urban Talents, which was the majority of them, drew down from man-made sources by preference, and power stations were the most common target. In fact, in any given population sampling, there were proportionately more active Talents in cities than in the 'burbs, and almost none in the rural areas.

Wren, unlike many of her peers, preferred natural, or "wild" sources, when she could get it. It wasn't any kind of "back to nature" kick—a thunderstorm, or a natural underground ley line, gave her a buzz that was missing in artificially channeled current. Too much of that, though, and she ended up like a kitten on catnip: too buzzed to focus her eyes properly, much less her magic.

Something told her that she was going to need to be full-up and focused for whatever was coming at her tonight. Walking into a room filled with pissed-off Talents who probably also had recharged just for the event… yeah, not the kind of thing you went in half-empty and expected to win. Or even come out unscathed.

You're assuming there's going to be a battle.

She rolled mental eyes at the voice, which sounded suspiciously this time like her mother. *You think there won't?*

The voice fell silent.

Potato and cheese sitting warm and comforting in her stomach, Wren unfolded the newspaper in front of her, to give a reason to stay at the table, took a last sip of her overbrewed and undercaffeinated coffee, and let herself sink into a working fugue state.

Five...four...three...two...hello, baby...

If her inner core of current manifested as virtual snakes, sparking vibrant reds, blues, and greens, then the current gathered around the electricity generated by the power plant were sea serpents, ropy with steroid-enhanced muscles, glistening with sweat and dripping power from their fangs. Terrifying. Dangerous. Seductive.

Come to me. Feel my strength. Feel the appeal of my strength. Come to me.

You lifted current by being stronger than it. Control. Current responded to control. Without control, current ran insane, like lightning strikes sparking wildfires; like electricity burning flesh. The first lesson every Talent learned was focus. Failure was death.

Feel me. Come to me. Let me tame you, use you...

The current slowed in its restless stew, several jeweled heads turning in her direction. Their eyes flashed pit-black, lidless, and unblinking, and even knowing that they weren't really snakes, weren't really sliding toward her in such an unnervingly boneless manner, didn't stop the shudder from sliding down Wren's spine. She controlled it, controlled her revulsion and fear, and opened herself up, welcoming them. Enfolding them into her own core, and melting their outer skins down into a form that her snakes could consume.

I am in control. I control. I am control.

The heavy, impossible weight of lifted current settled into her core, weighting her down, making her feel as though she were nine months pregnant, impossibly queasy, bursting from her own skin…and then the sensations faded as her own current absorbed the power, reformatted it to her own body, sent it coursing into every cell. Her eyes felt brighter, her teeth sharper, her skin tighter and more sensitive. If failure was death, or burning out, then success was glorious. She enjoyed it for a moment, then tamped it down. This was business.

Five…four…three…two…

Wren came out of fugue state and stared at the wall opposite her, looking at the posted menu without actually seeing it as her eyes refocused and she reintegrated back into the world, the current changing from ugly outsiders to beloved enhancements.

Her coffee had gone cold while she worked, but she drank it anyway, watching the colorfully bizarre East Village crowd walk down the street outside and letting herself simply enjoy the moment, a New Yorker in New York.

The rest of the day, Wren virtuously spent in her apartment, doing as she had told Sergei she would: organizing her files and getting them back to her usual standard of compulsive organization. The Nescanni case had been hard for a lot of reasons, not only because the Silence did not give them anything close to the whole story about what they were supposed to Retrieve. It had required her to travel overseas for the first time—by plane, not a mode of transport she was entirely thrilled with. And the object Retrieved had turned out to be semisentient and vicious, the end result of old magic performed by a half-mad, entirely vindictive Mage.

She had almost lost Sergei to that old magic; only the bond they had, the knowing she had of him, had been enough to fend off the old magic's hunger.

They'd also become lovers during that job, finally. Just the thought made her smile. Even now, trying to figure out what fit how into each others' lives, rearranging the baggage of adult lives to coexist happily; even with the tensions they had to face daily, it still made her smile to think of him, warm in her arms.

But thinking of how they had finally hooked up led back to thoughts of the two teenage boys who had been their introduction to the Italian branch of the *Cosa Nostradamus*. That had been sobering: she had spent so much of her life working at being unobserved; discovering that her reputation as "the Talent who stood up to the Council" had spread beyond the city and overseas had given her considerable pause. Sergei could talk all he wanted about "the best PR" and "free advertising" but it wasn't *his* self-image that was being screwed with.

Wren stopped and stared at the papers she had been

stapling, paper clipping, and sorting. Receipts and no-
tecards, printouts and photocopies, newspaper clippings
and scribbled sticky-tags. It seemed like so little, in retrospect, to have covered so many changes in her life.

"What, because you expected a marching band and
media coverage? Grow up, Valere."

After the Nescanni files were in order, she did a once-
over of the rest of the year, just to reassure herself that
everything was as it should be. Like a wolf patrolling the
confines of her den, Wren was uneasy in ways she
couldn't quite put her paw on. Which was ridiculous.
Being told by a Seer that you were going to do something
was unnerving enough; add to that the fact that the entire *Cosa* was itching to do something stupid…

Giving it up as a bad job, Wren shoved the file drawer
shut and grabbed her exercise bag, heading out to the gym
to work some of the stress off on inanimate machines.

By the time she got back, sweaty and calmer, there was
only enough time to shower and change before she had
to head out again.

Getting out of the shower took an extreme act of will,
and the water going cold at a pivotal moment—she
wasn't normally a linger-in-the-shower type, but it was
so much nicer than what was waiting for her. Wrapping
a towel around her head to dry her hair, and knotting
another around her body, she padded down to her bedroom and stared into her closet.

"Dress for impact," she said, her gaze skimming over the
hangers filled with basic blacks and grays, an occasional
red or blue jumping out at her. She needed something that

would stand up to the chill air outside, but not stifle her in the doubtless-overheated meeting place. Finally she settled on a black T-shirt and black jeans, with a long black jacket over it. The look was classic Manhattan Yuppie gunslinger, wanting only a silver-tooled gun belt and boots.

She opted for black leather lace-up shin-kickers, instead, dragged out from the back of the closet and quickly spit-shined. Makeup was pointless, even assuming she *had* more than lipstick and a stick of eye shadow to her name; she wasn't there to look pretty, anyway. Hair half-dried, she braided it into a complicated knot at the back of her head, turning the edge under and clipping it with a jeweled pin she found under the dresser.

"You're no beauty, no," she told her reflection. "But you'll do."

Still staring in the mirror, she reached down into her overfed core with one virtual hand and coaxed one of the smaller snakes up into her "palm." The power surged through her, waiting for direction.

> "Because I need it—
> Strength and power to my voice
> So I may be heard."

Intent was everything, when directing current. Intent, and focus. She said the words thinking not about her actual physical voice, but rather how that voice was heard by others, how she was—or wasn't—seen by others. The spell therefore directed the power not to increase her voice in any specific way, but to affect others so that they would actually register that she was there, and hear what she said. Not quite charisma, it was the magical equivalent of boosting speaker power, only specific to her memorability, if that was a word.

When she spoke now, nobody would talk over her, or look through her, or not notice that she was there at all. It was cheating, yeah, and more than borderline rude to screw with people's perceptions so blatantly—but this wasn't just about ego. The need was real.

Need trumped manners. Even her mother would agree to that.

Armor on, internal and external, she grabbed her battered leather jacket and her pocketbook, and headed out the door before she crawled into bed and pulled the covers over her head until it was all over.

The last Moot she had attended—the *only* Moot she had ever attended, as the last one before that was decades ago, in 1973—had been held in a basement room out on Brooklyn. This time, they were set up in Manhattan proper, in an apartment up near the George Washington Bridge. It was a nice enough neighborhood, if not one that Wren spent much time in. A lot of bodegas, dry cleaners and liquor stores, but not as many nail salons as you found downtown. And a lot more people sitting on their front stoops, gossiping and yelling to their neighbors. Wren wasn't sure if they were just naturally friendly, if the TV on tonight was really that boring, or if some of them were lonejack lookouts, passing word if anyone who stank of the Council came by.

She found the building listed on the invite without too

much trouble, and stood outside, looking up at the third floor. She could feel the bodies gathering in there; at least a dozen, possibly more, all oozing current.

Her own core rose in response, sensing a threat, and she shoved it down. Not now, she told it. *There's no reason to react…yet.* She touched the spell for reassurance, and walked up the three steps to the double front doors, and was greeted by a guy who looked like every geek ever created, from the too intense look behind too thick glasses to the black socks worn with dirty white sneakers. Wren didn't actually know any geeks; even in high school the geeks—along with everyone else—had looked right through her. But Talent didn't discriminate, and it didn't automatically bestow any sort of coolness factor.

"You got a reason to be here?" He managed a reasonable toughness, for a geek.

"I got an invite."

"Name?" There was no clipboard or list in sight, but not everyone relied on writing information down the way she did.

"Valere."

That got the door opened for her. Fast. *Hoo whee.*

No elevator. Of course. She took the stairs at a slow and steady pace, not rushing. The apartment was empty of anything except people and folding chairs. There were more people than chairs. The chairs were all in the main room. The people were all milling about the three rooms, walking through the galley kitchen to get between two rooms and the third, where a narrow table was set up with bottles of soda and plastic cups. A large bowl was filled with ice that was slowly melting. A small plastic trash can under the table was filled halfway with used cups, indicating that people had been here for a while, but probably not more than an hour or so in any great number.

She touched the spell inside her again, feeling it hum as it waited for activation. After a moment, she noticed that people were actually looking at her, their gaze resting on her for a moment rather than sliding by without contact, so she knew her usual no-see'um wasn't kicking in under the presence of so many people and making her unnoticeable. That was a nice change. Maybe she wasn't going to need the spell, after all?

Dream on, Valere, she thought. They could see her now, in passive mode, sure. The moment she actually tried to *do* anything, she'd lay even higher odds than before that the no-see'um would kick into overdrive. It was an instinctive, responsive reaction she had learned to use actively as needed, not the other way around. Nature or whatever hadn't bothered to install an off switch, to make her life simpler. Of course not.

She got a cup of lukewarm soda, added a handful of ice to it and moved on. She didn't recognize anyone here. That didn't mean anything—her relationships within the community were more of a professional than a personal nature, for the most part. The fact that she had a partnership with a Null had pissed some lonejacks off; the fact that she was friends with fatae unnerved others, and the rest (including a lot of folk who used to at least acknowledge her) now seemed to think that her conflict with the Council made her walking bad karma and to be avoided entirely.

Of the three, she preferred the last attitude, which had the advantage of being refreshingly and reassuringly selfish.

It also made her invitation to this Moot even stranger, and made her more suspicious. What were they up to?

"All right. All right, people, can we get our shit together, maybe, and not be here all night?" The speaker was a tall, skinny black man in chinos and T-shirt, standing on one of the folding chairs and looking like he was about to start clapping his hands for order.

He clapped his hands to get their attention, and Wren mentally paid herself ten dollars.

"People! Let's not waste time!"

Wren found a seat in the back of the room with chairs. She might have to be there, according to her friendly neighborhood drunken Seer, but she didn't have to stand.

"We've already wasted too much time," a tiny woman with shocking orange dandelion hair called from the front of the room. "Sitting here yakking like a bunch of politicians."

"If you've got any brilliant ideas, Clara, now's the time to share them. That's what this is supposed to be all about." The black man got down off his chair, turned it around, and straddled it. Wren hated him immediately.

"Ideas? I've got one idea. We *do* something! Our people are being boxed in, cut down, curtailed—did you hear about that psi-bomb down in the Village? Tell me that wasn't an attack. Go on, tell me!"

Wren might have spoken up then, but something held her back, whispering, "Not yet, not yet" in her ear. It wasn't the usual echo of Sergei's voice, or even the memory of her long-ago-wizzed mentor, but she trusted it anyway.

"You're assuming that psi-bomb was meant for us. Who's to say one of us didn't sic it on a Councilite?" That was from a bored-looking man in a brown velour jogging suit, whose bald spot gave his otherwise ordinary face the look of a tonsured monk's, and causing Wren's heart to stutter a beat when she glanced over at him.

Not a monk. Not a Brother of the Binding. Those particular individuals were safe in Italy, minding—with more common sense now, she hoped—the deadly treasures entrusted to them. They were not her problem anymore.

"If I were going to strike at them, I'd make it count," Clara countered. "Psi-bomb's nothing but a media hound's Tinkertoy—lots of sound but not a lot of fury."

Obviously Clara's car hadn't been parked on the street when the bomb went off.

"So, what're you suggesting?" The velour monk leaned forward, interested.

"Take them down. Take them all down. We can do it, all of us. They're so hidebound, so lockstep, they can't think outside the box and that's all we do. All it would take is everyone working together—"

"Because we're so good at that?" The velour monk

had a good point. Lonejacks didn't get that name by being team players.

"You'd rather let them pick us off, one by one? Strike now, before we lose any more of our kind!"

"God, people! Is violence all you can think about?" That outburst from a woman in the back broke the dam of fascinated silence, and the room erupted into comment and countercomment, voices rising as everyone tried to be heard, everyone adding their own voice to the din.

"Now?" Wren asked her inner voice, slouching down and trying to stay out of the way if chairs started flying.

Not yet.

"Violence is all they've left us," Clara said, shouting everyone else down with a voice that was clearly Talent-enhanced. "You heard how they responded to our letter of protest!"

Wren sat up in her chair at that. She hadn't heard, no. They had sent the letter? As it was? *Idiots.* But at least her name wasn't on it. Unless the bastards had forged it…. If they had, there was going to be some significant beatings applied after the fact, as God was her witness, yes.

"So it proves that the Mage Council is a pile of diseased wankers. This isn't news. We can't assume—"

"The hell we can't! What about Shona? Francine? Janny? What about Mash?"

Talents, all. Lonejacks. Pillars of the lonejack community, all gone missing in the past three months; missing in the way only magic could silence.

"What happened with the letter?" she asked the man next to her, a redhead who had restricted himself to muttering agreement with some of the more bloody-minded comments, so far.

"They sent the damn thing back—imprinted on the courier's skin, like a damned tattoo."

Wren's vision swam with a disturbing shade of red, and she felt faint. *If they had hurt P.B...*

"Human, or demon?" she asked.

"You think we'd leave something that important to a nonhuman?" He seemed both startled and disgusted at the thought, but Wren didn't care about his fataephobia, in her relief. Only after did she wonder if the human messenger had been someone she knew. By then, her informant had gotten up and moved closer into the fray—or farther away from her, she wasn't sure which. By the time she got caught up on the various threads of argument, her mind had cooled down enough to think rationally again. The Council's reaction had been crude, for them, but not really anything more or less than what she had expected. So long as they weren't taking action against the specific names, or tracking down people who had contributed, she was—

Hearing her name?

"Everyone not for us is against us, haven't you figured that out yet? Ask The Wren, if you can find her. She's the one they've targeted the most."

Wren started. She was? Other than the psi-bomb... okay, and the Council trying to shut her livelihood down. And the bugging they did of her apartment, while she was away in Italy. The guy who shot at her during the Frants case had just been to sic her back onto Frants; just business, nothing personal.

All right, yeah. They were screwing with her because she challenged them, which was why she'd been willing to sign the damn letter in the first place, if they'd just made those changes. But the Council had been trying to take her out of the game, not punch her ticket entirely. Not like, oh, that idiot fatae, who got in the way on the last case; the one who had gotten Lee killed. Not like the ones who had gone missing. She was still here, wasn't she?

Sobering thought, that. Under all that, why *was* she still here?

"Hah. She doesn't care—she shut us down, last time. Told us to wait. Wait! And while we waited, more lonejacks were taken out of play. She's a traitor."

Now, the voice inside her said. *Now.*

Standing up, Wren made her way into the loose knot of people standing in each others' faces, yelling; she moved carefully around those still seated with caution, uncertain if any of them might try to stop her, for some reason or another. But none of them did, and she all too soon found herself in the center of that knot. The noise was like an overwhelming crackle of static, and it took her a moment to realize that the static was real, the result of so much riled current being loosed, not at a specific target, but allowed to shift around without directed.

Waste. Utter and total waste. So much the better for her, who was conserving, hoarding, waiting to use…

Now!

All right, all right, she told it. No need to shout.

She tapped the spell, hard, and commanded it to kick in. Her vision sharpened, her skin tightened, and tingles of energy raced form her core, up her spine, and into her throat, soothing and lubricating her vocal cords. It wasn't doing any of those things, actually. Nothing physical was actually happening, as far as she had ever been able to determine. But the sensations *felt* real. And, more to the point, the results were real.

"Traitor? Traitor?"

The words cut through the yelling, a shark speeding directly to flesh, and caused the same sort of sudden stillness.

"Watch what words you use, people. How can I be a traitor when the only truth to being a lonejack is 'Take care of yourself and your own'?"

A beat, waiting for someone to respond. Not surprisingly, nobody did.

She wished she was wearing a pair of kick-ass thigh-high, stiletto-heeled boots, instead of more practical ankle boots. Or something sleek and shiny, instead of jeans and jacket, however stylish she looked. No matter. She *felt* like she was decked for battle.

"You use as your 'proof' the fact that I've been targeted. True. And how many of you stepped forward when it *was* only me being targeted? How many of you crossed the street rather than give me aid, rather than come under the eye of the Council?"

Too many, she remembered. Sources had dried up, gazes been averted when she came by. Only Lee had damned the consequences and stood by her. And look where that had gotten him.

"How many of you?" she demanded again. "And you call me a traitor? Because I won't join in your little crusade? Because I *told* you all, months ago, that trying to use violence against the Council, that giving them a single large target to aim against, was suicide? For that, I'm a *traitor*?"

"That's The Wren?" she heard a voice ask, one sound picked out of the din. "She's not what I expected, at all."

Wren didn't—couldn't—let it faze her. The spell had kicked in, good and strong, and she was on a roll. Her voice felt like strong honey, and her core practically purred, and she *hated* it. The weight of so many eyes on her was like a brand on her skin, making her want to turn tail and flee the apartment, the street, the city. There was only so much even the best spell could do, and not even an act of God would turn her into a public speaker by choice.

"Wren Valere. Here to tell us what to do, again? You got some sort of insider information, gonna clear it all up for us lesser mortals?"

"Oh for…. No." She almost recognized the man who stepped forward, face twisted into an ugly sneer, and after a second her brain supplied his name: Geordie Whatsisname, who made a public tag-challenge the year before, and looked properly stupid when the other participant not only declined, but had no idea what Geordie was so irate over. A woman, if Wren remembered. Like being fought over was some sort of compliment.

"The only one of you who gave a damn, the only one

of you I personally gave a damn about, is dead. You could all join him, for what I care."

She paused, letting the truth of that sink in, for them, and for herself. She really didn't care. There was nothing in her, where concern for general humanity should have been. Interesting. So why *was* she here? Other than a Seer telling her she had no choice.

"You're still telling us, then, to just sit here and be picked off, one by one?"

"No." She knew that wasn't an option anymore. Not as angry as they were. Not with the Council pulling showy, message-sending stunts like they did with the courier. A horse's head in someone's bed would have been more subtle. She didn't care about them…but she had an obligation to them. For Lee. For Neezer. For the sake of this city, which really, really couldn't handle the additional stress of a Talent-war—but was going to get one now, anyway.

She turned slowly, trying to catch as many gazes as she could, pushing the limits of her spell as hard as she could to make sure that they by-God *heard* her. "I'm telling you to be smart. Be savvy. Be fighters, damn it, not sheep scattering under the scent of wolf."

She paused, then said the thing that none of them wanted to hear. "Be smart. Take the allies you've been offered."

"Allies?" someone asked, incredulous.

"She means the nonhumans." Geordie again, with the sneer you couldn't sandblast out of his voice.

"The fatae, yes." She ignored Geordie—all you could do, with that type—and focused instead on the faces that seemed responsive, the auras that weren't entirely shut down. Her senses were wide-open, all eight of them, and if anyone had tried to take a whack at her then, she'd have been hard-pressed to defend. But nobody did.

"Think about it! The Council has threatened them, too. The vigilante groups are targeting them. The fact that we Talents—their cousins, damn it, in magic—have done nothing about either of those things is turning them against us. And we *need* them. We need their strength, their numbers, their cunning. We need them to watch our backs. Be our ears where we're deaf, our eyes where we're blind.

"Offer them a trade. Make treaties with the different clans. Make plans, and use their strengths with ours. Offer them our protection, in exchange for theirs. That way, we both have a chance to survive."

In short, plan their response to the Council, their plan of attack, the way she and Sergei planned a Retrieval. Smart. Careful. Allowing for every possible option, making use of every potential bit of luck.

"It's the only way you—we—have any chance at all."

A bad slip, that, and one that made some of them waver, she could sense it. *Damn*.

"If you're so set against this, why help us? Why not throw your lot in with the fatae, then? Or just leave town entirely?" That from the thin black man, who had been silent since the shouting began.

She gave him the only answer she had. "Because this is my home, too. And I can't stand to see a job bungled for lack of thinking."

In retrospect, getting up in front of an angry and volatile crowd had been the easy part.

"You did what!"

"Calm down and shut up, okay?" She handed P.B. his beer, and sat down across the table from her partner, who was already nursing his drink, some unidentified amber liquid on ice. His expression would have been funny, if it wasn't directed at her. "It's not like I got stuck leading anything. If I had to shock everyone into remembering I was there every time I wanted to tell them something, I'd be a lousy leader. Hell, I'd be a lousy leader even if everyone could see me without opening their eyes."

"So instead you get to be the brain behind the bedpan."

"Shut up, P.B."

She had told them both to meet her at a bar halfway between her place and Sergei's, in the neighborhood she suspected was near P.B's crash space, dropped her bombshell, and escaped with their drink orders, hoping that by the time she fought through the crowd and back, they'd have calmed down a bit.

P.B., rather than being upset or horrified, looked like he was about to burst into giggles. After all the comments she had made over the years about idiots who volunteer, she supposed she deserved that. Her partner's reaction was less acceptable.

"I can't believe you actually… I knew I shouldn't have let you go alone."

"Excuse me?" She was not shrill. She was never shrill. But her voice did rise alarmingly on those two words. P.B. looked torn between wanting to dive under the table, and staying to watch the fight play out.

"You don't think I'll make a good second-in-command?"

Sergei put down his drink and reached over to touch her hand reassuringly. "I think you'll do an excellent job. Better than they deserve. But was it a smart thing for you to do?"

Wren snorted into her glass. "Of course it wasn't." Honestly, did he think she had totally lost all sense?

"All right…" He drawled the words out, totally at odds with his usual crisp enunciation. "Explain this to me once again. Slowly, and without commentary from the fatae gallery, if you please."

P.B. tried to pout, but his face simply wouldn't bend that way.

Wren took a deep breath, trying to remember the exact sequence of events. "They were determined to organize into some kind of pseudo-paramilitary defense organization."

Sergei nodded his head, remembering the Moot he had attended during the summer, when Wren had called down lightning in the middle of the meeting in order to put an end to that idea.

"Lonejacks don't organize well. We're all trained to be self-centered, self-interested, and selfishly survival-oriented."

"Freelancers," P.B. said sagely, nodding his furry head in agreement. Demon didn't play well together, either, for much the same reason as far as Wren had been able to tell.

"Yeah. But then I started to think, organizing might not be such a bad thing, in theory—if they actually organized the gossip lines, the way you and Lee were starting up before…" Her voice trailed off, then she spoke again. "But they had no clue what they were doing, or even what they *wanted* to do, except make some sort of stand. A physical stand. A *violent* stand."

"So you're going to tell them what to do?" P.B. didn't have eyebrows to raise, the way Sergei did, but he made a decent try. "You're not so good at that, Wren. Goes back to that whole 'people not seeing you' thing."

"Not people in general, you furry-footed doubter. Just four. A duly Mooted quad, one from each community, the way the fatae have things set up." She glared at P.B. before he could say anything. "And no, I didn't tell them anything about the fatae elders. It's just sort of a common sense thing, and yes, even lonejacks occasionally have common sense moments."

"Hey, I didn't say anything!" the demon protested. "No fair dissing me for anything I didn't say!"

"Back up. Lonejacks have communities? As in actual, formal groupings?" Sergei was practically quivering with the scent of new information. A momentary pause—did she really want to tell him anything that was just going to get funneled back to the Silence—was put down firmly. At this point, what the Silence knew or didn't know about Talents seemed seriously unimportant.

"Not so much, no. God, nothing formalized, are you kidding me? The first person to try to make us pay dues would end up flayed and roasting on the end of a stick. And it's not really—it's not the way the fatae have tribes, or the Council has territories. But there are vague identifications, yeah, based on where you settle.

"We managed to split it into four basics—the city and immediate commuter area, Connecticut, south Jersey and northern Pennsylvania, and the gypsies, the ones without any fixed address."

"The wizzed?"

Wren took a chug of her beer and shook her head. "They won't come to Moot, they won't speak— God knows they're not going to actually send someone or listen to anyone who got sent for them." Talents who had wizzed—gone insane from too much current in their bodies—were another thing she couldn't worry about now. So far, they weren't being targeted. Nobody had said anything about them being targeted. How would anyone *know* if they were being targeted, considering most of them could barely communicate with the external world anymore?

She and Sergei had tried to protect the wizzed, once. It hadn't worked very well.

All right, stop that now, Valere. Tail chasing, bad. And useless, more to the point.

"Look, it's a done deal, okay?" Listening to them voice their doubts was making her even less certain she had done the right thing, and she needed to be certain now.

No doubts. Doubts would be deadly. "I need you guys behind me."

"The power behind the power behind the thrones?" Off her dirty look, the demon subsided. "Sorry."

Sergei put down his drink and reached across the table to touch the back of her hand again, this time lingering. His fingers were cool, familiar, and impossibly soothing, just in that touch. "I'm here for you. Always."

The knot of tension that had been with her ever since the Seer told her of what she had seen—or even longer, since Lee's wake—loosened just a bit more. Always. No matter what she did.

Wren wasn't sure she believed in always. But Sergei did. Occasionally that scared the hell out of her. Tonight, it was exactly what she needed to hear.

Cherish the memories, Lee told her.

"So what are you going to do?" Sergei asked, pulling his touch away and putting on what she thought of as his Business Planning Face. Reassuring, and—even more than the supportive lover—exactly what she needed right now.

"Clean up a few details, first," she said. "Then…we're going to war."

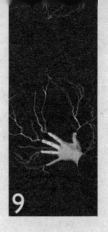

9

The next morning was a perfect late-autumn dawn: crisp, fresh air coming off the river, under a clear blue sky. Wren pulled the covers over her head, burrowing facedown into the pillow, even though very little sunlight actually came through the heavy green drapes.

"*Mmrrrmmmph.*" She could feel every strand of her hair, and each one hurt. They had gone from drinks to dinner, and then back to drinks to toast the birth of this new, as-yet-unnamed evolution in lonejack history, and her own intense stupidity in becoming part of it. Sergei had bailed after one-thirty, and P.B. had decided that they needed to try every single odd-sounding drink the bar had to offer. Including a few she was pretty sure they made up on the spot. Stupid, stupid, and even more stupid, for all it seemed like a good idea at the time. That seemed to be the theme of her life, right now.

"Note to self—demon digestion is not that of mortal systems."

When they had finally staggered out after last call, the memory of the Moot had faded under the liquid sloshing in her gut. Throwing up helped slightly, but not enough.

"Momma, why you raise such a fool of a daughter?"

That thought led to another, which made her sit bolt upright in bed.

"Oh, fuck."

"What?"

Wren shrieked, then subsided back under her covers as her brain processed the fact that the voice was familiar. And coming from the door, not the bed next to her. Or the floor, which would have been only a little less disturbing.

"Morning," the voice continued, and P.B. waved a paw, the other one busy with a white mug of something steaming hot.

"That better be for me," she grumbled, refusing to react further to the fact that the demon had spooked the hell out of her.

"I can get you one," he offered magnanimously

"You can give me that one and get yourself another."

Apparently Wren-in-morning-with-hangover was scary enough to give a demon pause. Useful to remember. After the second sip of coffee, she felt calm enough to deal with the thought that had jolted her to full awareness, earlier.

She was supposed to have lunch with her mother today.

By the time the mug was halfway through, she was able to get out of bed and slog over to her dresser, pulling out clean underwear, a bra, and a clean white T-shirt. A pair of khaki slacks that somehow still had proper creases in them and a dark brown linen blazer came out of the closet.

"Suburban sweetie," she dubbed the outfit. Perfect for soothing motherly concerns before they could even get aired.

Dropping the pile of clothing on the bed, she took the coffee with her into the hallway, down to the bathroom.

"You want a top-up?"

"You enjoy asking stupid questions?" She lowered the mug slightly so that P.B. could refill it from the pot he held, then went into the bathroom and, with her free hand, turned the shower on, hot.

She could deal with fatae running amok. Lonejacks working together for something other than a paycheck, for longer than a few hours. The Council taking out random lonejacks for some dire purpose. Even taking a case that left her working for a Null against a Talent, without her partner's knowledge or participation.

Her mother? Lunch, and the related Inquisition? Made her break out in a cold sweat. Resting her forehead against the tile and letting the hot water run down her scalp, soaking into her hair and making the abused tissue feel somewhat better, she realized that she was every adult daughter cliché. Knowing that didn't make it any easier.

The routine of getting from her apartment to the restaurant where she was meeting her mother was, contrary to most Manhattanites' theories about the terrors of suburbia, actually pretty soothing. The bus across the

George Washington Bridge left her off a couple of blocks away, and the day was nice enough that she enjoyed walking slowly along streets that were far quieter, wider, and greener than her own. The Patterdon Inn wasn't quite as quaint as the name sounded, had hundred-year-old plank floorboards and siding to match, and made a killer open-faced roast beef sandwich with real gravy.

"Jenny."

"Mother."

The woman who rose out of the green upholstered chair to kiss her cheek with real warmth was clearly, obviously, inevitably Wren Valere's mother, although on her frame—ten inches taller, before heels—what was forgettable on Wren became memorable, what was everyday became special. It was more than simply her slightly darker coloring, or even the far more noteworthy cleavage; it was more than the spicy orange scent she always wore. Margot Elizabeta Valere was just simply memorable in a way that Wren wasn't.

And it wasn't current-derived, either. Margot was more than a Null, she was an Absolute. Not only could she not handle current, she could barely even sense it, even when she carried Wren in her womb. She couldn't even remember it, not anything to do with magic, even when it stared her in the face.

"They have a special today that sounds wonderful," Margot was saying, waving one hand to bring the waiter over. "Veal."

"Sounds great, Mom."

She did like veal, but Wren went with the roast beef instead, to her mother's resigned sigh.

She couldn't help it. Patterdon-roast beef. She always returned to familiar foods when stressed. It was why the local delivery places all knew her address by heart.

At least, for the next few hours, the tension in her bones and muscle had absolutely nothing whatsoever to do with fatae or Council or her fellow lonejacks.

No, this was purely Mom-stress. The last time they had met face-to-face, it had been to argue over Wren's choice of bed-partners. Margot Valere liked Sergei Didier—as a partner and supposed mentor for her daughter, not as a lover. But, as Wren said once to Sergei, her mother not only had issues with men, she had an entire subscription, and nobody was ever going to be good enough for her little girl.

"So."

Wren braced herself, but instead of the expected inquisition, her mother launched into a recitation of the latest follies of the Lakeside Dental Associates. Growing up, Margot Valere had supported her daughter by taking any job she could find, including diner waitress and taxi dispatcher, but the past five years she had been office manager for the small practice within walking distance of the small A-level house Wren had helped her buy.

It was the only financial help Margot had ever accepted from her daughter, and Wren expected, any year now, to get a check back for every penny. Her stubbornness came down to her honestly, along the maternal line.

Her mother's mother was…well, "tyrant" came to mind. Also "bitch on wheels." But she cared, in her own way; had Margot been willing to name the man who got her pregnant and then abandoned her, Elizabeth Valere would have moved heaven and earth to find the guy, and force him, not to take emotional responsibility—nobody could force that—but financial, certainly.

"And so…"

Here it came.

"How is Sergei?"

Wren looked at her mother across the table. Her mother returned the look blandly, her eyebrow arched, her face as composed as it ever was. Nothing—not first learning about current, or her daughter's minor brushes with the law, not even running into P.B. at Wren's apartment over the summer—had ever shaken her mother's calm assurance.

Suddenly she wanted to shake that assurance, badly.

"Sergei's great. Working too hard, as usual. Mom…I need to know about my father."

Margot Valere blinked, then put her fork down and looked, long and hard at her only daughter.

"In all the years since you figured out that there needs to be a daddy somewhere in the equation, at least to start, that's the first time you've ever just come right out and asked."

Wren shrugged. "I figured, if you wanted to tell me, you would have."

"And you're right. So what's changed now?" An expression of alarm swept over her face, so fast Wren wasn't even sure she saw it. "Jenny. You're not—"

"God, no!" Wren's response was instinctive, and just a smidge too loud. "No, I'm not pregnant, Mom," she said in a lower voice, ducking to avoid the glances of the other diners. "I just…I've been thinking, a lot. Lately. About…what I do. And where it comes from."

Her mother knew about Talent—that had been Neezer's doing. He wouldn't take on any student without parental knowledge and approval. But magic didn't fit into Margot Valere's basic worldview, so she conveniently "forgot" about it, just as she "forgot" about the fact that she had met a demon on her daughter's doorstep, or the truth about what Wren did for a living.

There were things Wren wished she could forget so easily.

"Mom, please."

Margot picked up her fork and poked at the remnants of her veal. "If we're doing this, we're doing it over something with more calories." She put her fork down again determinedly and called the waiter over, demanding the dessert menu.

Small talk dominated the table until a plate of miniature éclairs were delivered, along with two massive mugs of coffee.

"Your…I can't even call him "your father." Father implies a lot more than donating sperm. And I can't believe I just said 'sperm.'"

"Mother." Wren was torn between amusement and

exasperation, resisting the urge to throw one of the éclairs at her.

"Well, we never even had that puberty discussion. Suddenly I'm supposed to be comfortable discussing this?"

"So call him my genetic donor?"

"That works as well as anything, I suppose. He was…" Margot stared off into the distance, less wistful than actively trying to remember details. "Tall, with broad shoulders. The first man who ever made me feel delicate." Wren was just a smidge over five foot tall, and her five-foot-ten-inch mother had always seemed an Amazon to her. If *he* had made *her* feel delicate…oh dear.

"So who the hell am I a throwback to?"

"Your grandfather," Margot answered. "You don't remember him, but he was built like Fred Astaire, all leg and lean, but not much taller than you are."

"And Grandma led him around by the hand, dancing backward and wearing heels?"

"That's your grandmother," Margot agreed, smiling for the first time since ordering dessert.

Grandmother Valere was legend among anyone she met—tougher than rawhide, classier than college, and more stubborn than anyone except her daughter.

So where did you meet? What was he like? What was his name? slid onto her tongue, but Wren bit it back. That was the one thing she knew from experience that her mother would never tell her. Not even now.

"I don't…it's embarrassing, but I can't remember now

what he looked like, exactly. Lovely eyes…dark blue, like velvet, and thick black hair…" She reached out to ruffle her daughter's hair, lighter brown, but just as thick.

"Well, at least we know where my overlookability comes from."

"Stop saying that," Margot said, returning her attention to her dessert. It was a long-running battle, and one neither of them fought with any vigor, anymore.

"We met in a subway car, if you can believe that. I was trapped in the middle of a crowd, trying to get out to join my friends, and he cleared a path—but got stuck outside the train with me when the doors closed again. So we invited him to join us. And the next morning…he was gone."

"Oh, God." Wren stared at her mother. "I was a one-night stand baby? Mother!"

Margot refused to blush.

"I need more coffee," Wren said, downing the last dredges in her cup and waving down the nearest waitress. She had originally just wanted to mess with her mother's mind. This, though—this was getting interesting!

But that was all her mother could—or was willing to—say. In the end, Wren had to be satisfied with finally understanding her mother and grandmother's running battles, from her mother's point of view. Did she play the disobedient pregnant single daughter, or admit that she had been foolish enough to have unprotected sex with a stranger? As much as Wren knew that her mother loved her—of all the things she had doubted in her life, that had never even made the list—there was no doubt that she would have had a vastly different—better—life if she'd not gotten pregnant at nineteen.

The last of the éclairs consumed over more general family gossip, and the argument over who was paying duly haggled over, Margot walked her daughter to the bus stop. Even in her demure white cardigan and business-length blue pencil skirt, she attracted far more admiring glances than Wren. Mother and daughter were both so used to that, it didn't even register.

It wasn't until the bus came into sight down the broad street that Wren said the thing she had actually intended to say, over lunch, before getting distracted by the family history.

"I need to ask you a favor. And I need you to do it for me, and not ask any questions, and not try to dance around actually doing it."

Margot waited. She did not make promises before hearing the details.

"I need you to leave town. Leave the area. Go visit Great-Aunt 'Tunia over in Chicago, if you have to, but don't be here. Not for the next couple of weeks, okay? Not until I tell you it's okay to come home."

Margot looked up to the sky as though asking the Lord for patience, then gave her only child a tight hug as the bus pulled to the curb.

"Whatever you're involved in…I'm not going to ask any questions. I don't want to know and you don't want to tell me. Yes, I'll do what you ask—although I'm *not* going to see that old hag. But be careful, Genevieve. Be careful. You're still my daughter and I will be very upset if anything happens to you." She paused. "Or Sergei. And if *he* ever hurts you…"

"You'll be second in line to kick his ass, I promise."

They parted with laughter, but as Wren settled into her seat on the bus, her expression sobered again. She wanted to follow up on the information her mother had given her—was his lack of memorableness due to being ordinary? That hadn't seemed likely, the way Margot had described him. You'd remember the guy who knocked you up, right? Or—more possibly—had he, too, been a Talent, with skill sets like her own? It was a question that dug at her, at stuff she'd been lugging around since she was a kid, but there was no time to do anything with it, not right now. She hadn't been overreacting, she didn't think, in asking her mother to be elsewhere. Clouds were forming around the city, coming in low and dangerous, all shaped like the Mage Council, and filled with violence.

And she still had a job to finish before the storm started to break. Time to clear the decks, tie everything down, any other storm-related metaphor she could think of, and time to retire it once and for all.

For now, she had done the important thing.

"I love you, too, Mom," she said, ignoring the odd look her seatmate gave her. "Be safe."

And then she put everything not related to the case in a small mental box, locked it, and shoved the key out of sight. The first rule was: Finish the job.

By the time the bus crossed the GW Bridge and disgorged its passengers into the narrow stairwells that led down from the bus lanes into the terminal proper, Wren had the basics of a plan in mind. Travel did that for her: something about enforced inaction, coupled with the hum of an engine, made her brain just work better, more effectively.

All right, it wasn't much of a plan, but then, it wasn't, all things considered, much of a job. Both client and target could have worked things out, but instead decided to draw lines in the cement and then spit insults across them, playing dare-me like they were still in grade school.

She used her transit pass to catch the subway home, on autopilot but still aware of the bodies moving around her as she jostled for a seat.

This entire job stunk like dead fish. Life was too short. Love was too precious and easily abused. Whining about how neither of those things was fair wasted time and energy and caused people like Wren to have to get involved for no reason other than pride. No matter. Her job wasn't to mediate petty little litter-box fights, just to Retrieve the object they were squalling over with minimal fuss and absolutely no muss.

So the target was Talent, and Council to boot. Whoop. Mages weren't any more powerful than lonejacks, just better-dressed. This was at heart a smash-and-grab; no real finesse or skill needed. The client had called Wren not because the job was difficult, but because she was used to hiring the best for everything. The Wren was the best. No argument there.

Some folk might get their noses put out of joint by

being asked to do something below their skills, something that wasn't a challenge. Wren wasn't one of those
folk. Sergei might have passed on this job, thought it
would be a waste of her time. Wren hadn't. She had, in
fact, been hoping for something simple, something that
wasn't going to require anything more than a chance to
stretch a few B and E skills. Well, she had it. So the timing sucked; maybe it wasn't such a bad thing after all.
Give her body something to do while her brain worked
on the larger problems the *Cosa* was handing her.

Yeah. That was workable. And if Miss Rosen was so
used to paying for the best? Wren could deal with that,
too, mentally adding a jumped-up fee to the nest egg she
was building for her eventual retirement.

Stretching her legs to their inconsiderable length,
touching the plastic seat in front of her, Wren closed her
eyes and drew on all the materials she'd gathered so far,
sketching in the details of the Retrieval in her mind.

This bit, here. That fact, there. And thus, to connect
the two…

The sink was too high for him to reach comfortably, but
there was a footstool in the small closet that made it workable. P.B.'s claws weren't ideal for dishwashing, as they
didn't retract all the way, but an opposable thumb made all
the difference in keeping the dish steady while he rinsed.

Housekeeping hadn't been the original purpose behind
his body design, but you made do with what you had.

Run water. Add liquid detergent. Dump every dish he
could find into the sink. Scrub and put in the drainer to

air-dry. There was a soothing rhythm to it, even if his fur was soaking wet up to the elbows. You could wash dishes and think—or not think, whatever your pleasure.

P.B. would rather not be thinking. It was enough, right now, that Wren was back on the hunt again, even if she was still denying that she wanted any of it. Maybe she didn't.

But she *needed* it. He'd been around humans for a lot longer than Wren—than anyone except another demon—suspected. He had seen a lot, some good, more bad, and he'd picked up a bit of knowing about the breed.

After that case last summer, when Lee died, Wren had drawn into herself in a way that was distinctly…unWren-like. Not that she was ever a social butterfly, or particularly fond of people in general, for that matter, but she had a real enthusiasm for what she did that had been lacking, even when the jobs finally started to come in again. She was trying, he'd give her that, but the spark was gone.

And sparks were what The Wren was all about. Sparks were what had drawn him to her, the first time he had seen her. On a job she'd been, hadn't she? Some stupid horse-thing she was tracking, focused and intent and totally self-involved, in the most wonderful way. He'd been captivated. He had followed her home, just to find out who she was.

She'd been a nobody then. New to the city, new to the game. But he'd picked the star to hitch himself to, that day, without even realizing it. After more than ten decades, he had finally found a new master.

That she became a friend was…a gift.

He dumped last of the pots into the drying rack and reached for a towel to try and soak some of the water out of his fur when a faint noise caught his triangular, tufted ears and made them twitch slightly. He lifted his head and sniffed the air, then slipped off the stepstool as quietly as he could, still wiping his hands. Not Wren's scent. Not Sergei's, either. The only other person who had a key to the apartment, as far as he knew, was Wren's mom. He had only met her once, but the scent had been close enough to Wren's that he should have recognized it again.

This was human, male, and unfamiliar.

Unfamiliar and human, in these days, meant danger. Hell, these days, *unfamiliar* meant danger. P.B. didn't know who was coming in the door, or why, but he wasn't going to take any chances. The kitchen window was open, as usual, to catch a breeze, and if he could just get there before—

Before the guy in the window came inside, holding a gun.

P.B.'s claws were thick black half-moons, and not there for decoration. His legs were short, stumpy, and corded with muscle under the thick white fur that made everyone at first glance think that he looked adorable and soft. He had no temper to speak of, no ability to hold a grudge, no need ever to have learned how to snarl.

But he knew how to kill.

A fast, hard leap and he had the newcomer backed up against the wall, claws at his throat, eyes the color of dried blood staring into the human's faded green ones.

"Live or die, your choice."

The human let the gun drop from his hands, even as the smell of urine filled the kitchen. P.B., straining at the hardwired instinct that kept him from ripping the human's throat out, let the terrified intruder drop to the ground. Giving him a kick with one callused foot in a place guaranteed to keep him down for a while longer, he then turned to deal with the other intruder.

Big mistake. Even as he turned, something slammed him hard against the back of his skull, and he went down, hard, onto the linoleum floor.

His last thought was that he did not want to die with his nose pushed up into a puddle of urine.

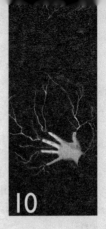

10

Wren was glad that she'd decided to stop at the gym after her lunch with her mother. Really. Not because it made her feel any better, or any of the rot exercise-junkies gave. Not even because it gave her an excuse to sweat the last bits of the job into place. Not even because she was proud of her six-pack abs, because she didn't have any. Fortunately, using current burned calories at an impressive rate, and it took significant gluttony to cause a Talent to become seriously overweight.

No, she went because getting winded, or not being able to get over a fence, or lift something, would be worse than embarrassing during a job. It could be fatal.

Workouts, therefore, were necessary, but not fun. She had been looking forward, the entire time she spent on the machines of torture, to going back to the apartment, taking a long hot shower, and curling up with a month's backlog of trade magazines to skim through. But the closer she got to her front door, the more she wanted to be Elsewhere.

She loved her apartment, no matter her words to OhSoBloody. It was her home, her refuge, her haven. And yet, in the past few months she had been shot at through her kitchen window, spy-bugged, and hosted the wake of a dear friend there.

Cigarette smoke would have been easier to clear out of the air than the memories that were starting to build up.

"Oh, screw this." She shifted the plastic bag holding a quart container of squash soup from Balducci's from one hand to the other, and marched determinedly toward her building.

"Miss Valere."

Wren stopped. "You've got to be kidding me."

Andre Felhim was sitting on her stoop, the elegant six-ty-something black man in an equally elegant suit and matte-shined shoes sitting on cold cement steps as though the seat of his pants didn't cost more than she paid in rent every month.

"I apologize for simply appearing like this, without warning, but I had reason to believe, based on our last exchanges, that you would not accept a phone call. Or, if you did, your emotional reaction might…create some static on the line."

"Oh, ya think?" Sarcasm dripped like butter on a baked potato. Static was the least she was going to give that smarmy, slimy, no-good, people-using bastard…

"Miss Valere, I had nothing to do with your difficulties during the Nescanni situation. I was not aware until after the fact that your contact had been intercepted—" taken out in a staged—and fatal—car accident, Wren interjected mentally "—and I most certainly was not aware that your dossier on the situation was not complete. I would never intentionally send my people out—"

"We're not *your people*." God, he understood *nothing*.

"I don't care about your little internal screwups and backbiting and political one-upmanship." She bit off each word as though if she got them sharp enough, he might just keel over and bleed to death. "I told you once and I'll tell you again—keep away from me, and keep your paws off my partner. We work for you—fine. Although I don't see how you're doing your bit, protecting me from the Council. But you have no call on us other than that. *None.* Don't contact us unless it's a paid job. Got me?"

"I got you," Andre said. "I had hoped that we could establish some sort of rapport, but if it is not meant to be…"

"It's not."

He stood and turned to go, then turned back to issue one parting shot.

"We *are* maintaining our side of the agreement," he said. "Why else do you think that both you and Sergei are still alive?"

And with that, he walked off down the street, lacking only a cane to be the stereotypical Mysterious Stranger.

If he meant to unnerve Wren with that last comment…he succeeded. But it made sense; they might not have many Talents in their organization, but they dealt

with them—and magic in general—all the time. It would
be logical that they'd developed some defenses against
it, somehow. Not all fairy tales were bunk, after all. You
could dispel glamours, ward your home against fairies,
that sort of thing.

She pulled her keys out of her bag and unlocked the
door, thudding wearily up the stairs. And stopped cold.

The apartment door was open. She didn't think it was
Andre's doing. He had too much style, too much class,
much as she despised him, to be that obvious.

Wren stepped backward, moving into the shadows of
the landing, and sent out a quick burst of current, a faint
yellow tracer that would let her know if there was anyone in her home who meant her ill. It was a nifty bit of
spellwork, something she'd read about in one of those
old books and been messing around with to see if she
could make it work.

The pulse came back negative. Nothing moving.
Nothing dangerous. Whoever or whatever had come to
visit, they were long gone. Assuming the spell was working properly, that was. Always a risk.

She entered the apartment, her knees bent, ready to
fight or flee as the situation needed, still wired from the
sugar and caffeine and trip home spent putting herself into
a working frame of mind, to say nothing of the gym
workout.

Nothing.

"I need to get new locks," she said, grousing to herself as she turned to do up the dead bolt and the chain
lock behind her. What used to be normal and acceptable-

for-Manhattan paranoia now clearly wasn't doing the job. And be damned if she was going to move. Housing in the city was insane, and the bubble didn't look to be bursting anytime soon. Besides, this place was going to go co-op sooner rather than later, and she was going to be on the inside to buy when it did.

This was *home*, damn it. No matter what sort of…

Sort of groaning noises she heard.

What *now*? Wren flexed her hand, trying to remember a single defensive cantrip that wouldn't also damage her home. The power she had pulled down from the power station was still in her, and the current practically sparked, but she had no desire to have to patch and repaint anything just because some joker thought it would be amusing to burgle her home.

"Get out get out wherever you are," she called in a soft, singsong voice.

Nothing answered. She moved forward into the apartment barely aware of the fact that silvery twitches of current were jumping from fingertip to fingertip. Neezer would have slapped her silly for wasting current like that.

The kitchen was the source of the noise: a pile of what looked like fur coat, tossed in one corner.

"P.B.!" She dropped to her knees beside him, grimacing when one knee came into contact with a sticky puddle of something disgusting. It wasn't his—demon blood was black, and their urine was blue-tinged. Unless he'd taken to throwing up yellow, the way one of her mother's cats had, when they were growing up…

"P.B.?" A hand came up to touch him; tentative, almost

terrified, and the current sparked, jumping into the coarse fibers of his fur and burrowing down into his skin

"Urrrgghh," he said again in response. *"Uuuurrrgh?"*

Wren exhaled, long and thankful. "Open your eyes, you ungrateful walking carpet," she said, using one of Sergei's favorite descriptive phrases for the demon. "Come on, damn you, open your eyes."

"I don't have a concussion," he said, opening his eyes slowly and staring directly into her own worried brown ones.

"How would you know?" She dropped the question as pointless. "What happened?"

P.B. struggled to sit up. Her hands, now bare of visible current, pushed him back down, carefully examining his head through the fur, checking for anything that might indicate real damage or bleeding or…she had no idea what she was looking for; anything that seemed wrong.

He put up with it for about twenty seconds, then slapped her concern away weakly. "Two guys. Humans. One through the door, one through the window. Have you ever thought about moving, Valere? This address is getting way too busy."

"And whose fault is that, that everyone knows where I live?" While she was in Italy, P.B. and Lee had used her apartment as a meeting-place for the fatae who would powwow with them. She had forgiven them—mostly. But not entirely.

Satisfied that he wasn't about to expire on the spot, she helped him sit up, propping him up against the wall.

There was a lump the size of a walnut that she was

pretty sure wasn't normal, but other than that he seemed to be recovering just fine.

"Valere, I'm fine…" he said, echoing her thoughts.

"Yeah. I seem to remember me saying that to you a few times, too. Didn't listen to me then, why should I listen to you now?"

He managed to stand up, then swayed a little, blinking nervously as though the room had moved with him.

"Room spinnies." He sounded surprised.

"Oh, for— Go lie down, demon, and be thankful you've got such a thick skull."

If a fatae had called him demon in that way, it would have been an insult, a way to remind him that he had no real place in the structure of breeds and clans, that he was part of a created race, a created being, fused together to serve, not evolve.

In Wren's mouth, the word sounded like…affection. Mulling that, P.B. let himself be shoved into her bed, careful to retract his dewclaws so that they didn't snag on the sheets, and suffered her to bring up the coverlet and turn out the light on him.

His head *did* hurt. A lot. He figured that he'd yell at her—and figure things out—later. After a nap.

Wren closed the door softly behind her and walked down the hallway before she realized that she was shaking. Not from cold, or fear, but anger. She had been attacked before; she'd even been shot at, before. People had tried to sabotage her career, spied on her, withheld information, shot at her, set off psi-bombs, made her open her mouth and get involved in a campaign she knew was doomed for failure, and generally made the past six months hellish.

But all the attacks, even the one that caused Lee's death, had been aimed at *her*. This time, even if the goons had come into her apartment, looking for her, they had attacked P.B., and there was no way anyone was going to tell her they thought she had suddenly grown a thick white coat of body hair.

It might have been a serious case of wrong place wrong time. It might even have been because he was a fatae. Hell, it might even have been because he was P.B.— the demon had a way about him that was the opposite of endearing, to most folk. Hell, he'd been attacked before, just for being a demon. It didn't matter. This time it happened here, in her home, to her friend, because he was here, in her home, *because he was her friend*.

She stopped halfway down the hallway, backtracked and went into her office. Sitting down at the desk, she picked up the phone, careful not to dislodge any of the jury-rigged wiring as she fit the headset over her ear. A number, recently memorized, and she was listening to the sound of a phone across town ringing.

"Speak." The voice was low, raspy, and almost hyper-naturally alert.

"Someone crashed my party today. I want a puppy over here pronto, to take readings."

The voice actually slowed down a little, as it recognized the caller, and processed the words. "You think it was Council? Already?"

"What, you thought they'd wait for one of your pretty lettered invites?" Sarcasm was too much of an effort for her even on a good day and she'd already used up her allotment on Andre; she let it drop. "I don't know who it was, damn it. At this point, nobody's getting ruled out, not even you folk. But you're the only ones I can call on."

"Bitterness noted and filed. I'll have a kid over there in fifteen."

"Make it ten."

She disconnected and removed the headset, then checked to make sure that her irritation hadn't futzed with the wiring any. Nope, still had dial tone, and the computer was still functional.

"I'm getting better at this," she said. Which was good, because she suspected that there would be a lot of tension, nerves, and irritation in her immediate future, and while blowing out tech could be a nice stress-reliever, it also tended to get expensive. And she already had a damn modem to replace.

She went into the kitchen and stared at the coffeemaker. It would probably be a really bad idea, to add more caffeine to her system. Not that something being a bad idea had ever stopped her before.

The faintest smell of ozone and a prickling of the skin that indicated a lightning bolt—or a wafting of directed current—was the only warning she got before someone knocked on the door.

She put the coffeepot down and went to the door, looking out through the spy hole.

Nothing there.

"Yes?"

"You called for a PUP?"

Wren unlocked the locks and opened the door. The P.U.P.I—private, unaffiliated paranormal investigator—was, literally, a kid; maybe legal to smoke, not to drink. Wren wasn't put off. Most of the PUPs were young—it was a pretty new and nervy field—and to find someone who could Transloc over so fast, they were probably not the highmost of techs.

That was okay. What she needed didn't take a magister.

"I'm Bonnie."

Bonnie was about twenty, short, thin, and pale, and white-blond the way that never comes out of a bottle. She was also dressed entirely in red—red silk shirt, red cargo pants, red sandals on her pale white feet. Her toes and fingernails were painted black, and she carried a metallic black toolbox on a strap over one shoulder.

"Come in."

Bonnie came in, gliding like a scarlet swan through the doorway. "So, where's the stink?"

"Kitchen." She had no idea where else the goons might have been, but the most residue was probably where P.B. had been slammed. "Think you'll be able to pick anything up?"

Bonnie patted her toolbox with territorial pride. "If it's there, we can sniff it out. Just give me a little time and space… Oh man. Totally retro kitchen. I love it. This entire place is just so totally—are there any other apartments available in this building?"

Wren blinked in surprise. "One, actually. Downstairs."

"Most excellent. The vibes in this place are…"

"Yeah, I know." Wren had rented this apartment because the moment she walked in the door, the space had called out to her, like some kind of ley line convergence, or natural pooling of current. For some reason, she had never thought to wonder why other Talent hadn't felt the same thing. You had to be in the right place at the right time, listening with the right sort of ears, probably. Maybe they'd just never come looking in this neighborhood. It wasn't like it was the very best address, after all. Just one of the more interesting ones.

"Right." Bonnie put her toolbox down on the floor and got down on her hands and knees to look around. Wren could practically *see* her gathering current, pulling it down and spreading it around the room.

That was what PUPs did—they were Tracers, only more narrowly focused. They didn't worry about things, or people, or anything larger than a thumbnail. They specialized in current forensics, and were trained to extremely specific protocols.

They were also totally independent—recruited from the Council and lonejack families evenly, based on skill-sets and inclinations, and trained to be impartial observers working not for glory, or even pay, but the sheer exhilaration of knowing whodunit, and how. The brainchild of a bunch of twenty-somethings too sharp and shiny for comfort, weaned on *CSI* and the *Discovery Channel*, set loose on an unsuspecting Talented populace.

Too early yet to see how the impartial part would play

out, but for now, Wren could use them to find out who had broken into her home, and know that they'd give her a straight and narrow answer supported by facts, not supposition or prejudice.

Out of the toolbox came a series of fine-haired brushes, three vials of black and silver powders, several rolls of tape, a series of three-by-five cards, and a roll of unused film, plus a pair of somewhat disturbing-looking latex gloves in flesh-pink.

The PUP snapped on the gloves, then looked up at Wren. "Do you mind…" Bonnie gestured, which Wren took to mean that she should wait outside the kitchen.

"Right. I'll be down the hall."

A pity—Wren would have liked to have seen what Bonnie did, specifically. For now, PUPs were too few to handle anything other than physical attacks. But eventually, some day, there would be enough of them trained to work other scenes. Like, oh, robberies. Fine so long as Wren stayed clear of Talented targets, but considering she was about to hit one…

Time to worry about that when it became a problem. For now, she had to focus on the job at hand, and let Bonnie do her job.

Going back to her office, she pulled the file she had started on Rosen and pulled the blueprints from it. Melanie hadn't left the city yet, so the site was still live. A popular apartment building, in the middle of a thriving, upper-class, and well-policed neighborhood, housing a Talent who was aware that she owned something under contention and liable to be stolen.

Wren could practically feel herself start to salivate over the extremely risky possibilities when she got a faint mental ping. Was it possible, she wondered irritably, to get an unlisted brainwave pattern?

What? she asked, not bothering to mask her emotions.

Then the message came through; from anyone else it would have been an order. Tailored to lonejack psyches, it was a strongly worded request. Wren sighed, and started packing up the files again. So much for getting this job squared away before the storm broke.

"Yo."

Bonnie stood in the doorway, managing to look directly at Wren and still give every indication that she wasn't seeing anything that Wren might or might not be doing.

"You've got something?"

"Yeah."

Oh. Good. That was fast. Wren waited, half-sorted files in her hand. When Bonnie seemed capable of standing in silence all night, she finally said, "Yes?"

"So. Your visitors left definite trace…nice and clear, like they weren't trying to hide anything at all." The PUP paused a moment. "In fact, I'd say, if I didn't know better, they knew you'd call us in and left their spoor behind like a calling card."

Day just kept getting better and better. "And the number on that calling card?"

"Council. Right down to the overlay of Her Ladyship on their hands."

Neither Bonnie nor Wren managed to look particularly surprised, although Wren did wonder fleetingly if

Her Ladyship—KimAnn Howe, the de facto leader of the local Council—had left actual trace of current on their actual physical hands, or if this was some weird PUPI lingo. And how they actually had samples to check against, if the former. She wasn't about to look like an idiot and ask, but made a mental note to do some research later, if the world as they knew it didn't crash to an end. A careful use of some slang, if not overdone, helped getting the best work out of specialists, she'd found.

"You shouldn't stay here," Bonnie said, breaking her pose of cool PUPI-indifference. "Cool as this place is. Not if they've decided to take you off the board." A nice way of not saying "kill you." There wasn't any incontrovertible proof the missing lonejacks were dead, of course. Merest hearsay and speculation on the part of panicked and fight-mongering radicals…

Wren hadn't even given the thought passing consideration, she was bemused to discover. It might not be the refuge it had once been, after so many others had tramped through it, but it was still her place. *Hers.*

"This is my home. They're not making me go anywhere." She grinned, then, and it wasn't a particularly friendly expression. "But I might just invite some friends to stay. For the duration." Sergei would give them pause—he was affiliated, yes, but not *Cosa.*

"Smart," the PUP agreed, her job-mandated I Don't Care expression back firmly on her face.

In a matter of moments, Bonnie had packed up her materials and Transloced back to the office, leaving behind a sheen of powdery gray dust over the entire kitchen. Wren went back into the office and shut the door on the mess. Time enough to deal with housekeeping, later.

Much later. She had other things—and people—to deal with, first.

"Hey."

Wren paused on the landing when she heard Aldo's voice. "Hey, yourself. You got something for me?"

"Not for you, no, but if your manager ever wants to stop by…"

"Manners, boy." A voice came from inside the apartment, but it didn't sound even slightly threatened. Aldo and Sean had been together forever and a year, and she didn't think either one of them had seriously looked at another guy since then.

"Sergei's not your type," she said anyway. "He's way too serious."

"Yeah, but imagine the…exposure he could give me!" Aldo did his best Groucho Marx eyebrow-waggling impersonation, which wasn't very good at all, and then handed Wren several sheets of three-by-five paper. "Best I could do. Hope it helps."

She glanced at the sketches, then tucked them into her bag, under the front cover of her notebook. No way to know how accurate they were, done third-hand, but it was more than she'd had before. And he'd given spatial references, too, which she would never have thought of, with notes on approximate weight and texture based on the materials used. A Retriever with support staff was a Retriever well-blessed. Especially when they worked for free.

"You're a doll face, doll," she said.

"I know, I know, it's my curse." He saw her glance down the hallway at the front door, and waved her on. "Go, flit, I won't keep you from your busy schedule, I'm just an old man, nobody has time to visit anymore…I'll just sit here. In the dark. Alone. With my love slave…"

She was still laughing as she walked out the front door. The air was crisp and cool, with the faintest smell of what might have been wood burning but was probably just exhaust fumes. Or mulch. The debris of the psi-bomb was gone, except for the occasional glitter of broken glass near the curb, and to look up and down the street a person would think that nothing more exciting than a broken hydrant ever happened here.

Wren liked that. She liked the combination of soothing and potency she got from the building, the "vibes" that Bonnie had mentioned.

So why was she spending so much time out of her apartment? She'd sworn, once, that nothing short of a gurney could get her out of there, but she was spending as many nights at Sergei's as she was here. All right, so his place was larger. And he always remembered to go food shopping, while she was lucky to have something non-green and non-peanut butter in her kitchen. And he had an elevator. Her sheets were of better quality—in her opinion—and the water pressure was just as good.

"Valere."

"Hey, Charlie." She had stepped into the E-Z as a reflex while her thoughts were on groceries, but now that she was here she realized that it was more to mend fences than to actually pick anything up. Charlie wasn't a reliable source, but he was a source, and they needed to be oiled and primed on a semiregular basis. Nothing much, just a touch. And she'd pretty much blown him off, earlier. Bad form.

"Hear you're being kept busy these days." He was a lonejack, but even more on the outskirts than most. In fact, Wren wasn't even sure his closest friends and family knew he was a Talent. Wren only knew because he'd used current to hold a would-be burglar in the store until the cops could respond to the silent alarm, back about three years ago. They'd never actually spoken about that day, but he knew that she knew, and that gave them something to talk about beyond the price of organic eggs and the quality of the apples available each fall.

"Busy enough." How much, exactly, had the *Cosa* drums spread? "You doin' okay?"

"Yeah, I'm good. Thinking about taking some vacation time, though. You got any ideas?"

"Not a bad idea, getting out of the city. See if there are any weekend specials down in the Carolinas, maybe? Hurricane season was pretty mild this year, not too many motels boarded up."

"Maybe. Was thinking about going up to Vermont, do some leaf-peeping, maybe. More interested in bringing on fall than hanging on to summer, you know what I mean."

Wren paid for the bag of apples, and took one out of

the bag, biting down into the white flesh underneath red skin.

She chewed, swallowed around the sudden lump in her throat. "Yeah. I know exactly what you mean."

"Oh." Charlie wouldn't have known Lee. But he would have heard through the grapevine, even on the outskirts. If nothing else, the wake being held in Wren's apartment would have made the rounds, with Talent and fatae mixing openly and semiamicably. His eyes went wide and he blinked at her like a nervous owl. "I didn't—"

"It's okay, Charlie. It's okay."

It wasn't, no. But it would be. Someday.

Despite distractions and delays, only three of the four-wheeled troika had arrived by the time Wren made it up-town to the meeting, held in a small, distressingly quiet restaurant on the West Side, near the Javits Center. The buildings to either side were gray brick tenements, the kind that development had promised to get rid of, and the restaurant itself didn't look all that much better de-spite a newish green awning; without even going in, Wren knew she didn't want to eat anything that came out of its kitchens—or, for that matter, drink any water that came from their pipes. Fortunately, after the apple, she didn't have much of an appetite.

Inside, it was—surprisingly—much nicer, with pale salmon-colored walls devoid of the usual kitschy post-ers of foreign lands, and an appealing aroma of garlic in the air. She still wasn't hungry, but thought that maybe a side of garlic bread, or maybe an appetizer plate of mussels, wouldn't hurt.

It all depended on what happened once she sat down. This wasn't a Moot, which at least had some vague historical precedent. This…Sergei had, snarkily, referred to it as a staff meeting. She'd had to cancel dinner with him for this, so he was entitled, she supposed, to some snark.

Bart, Michaela, and Rich made noises of greeting when Wren walked over to the table.

"Metro North's screwed up again," Michaela said on the heels of her "hello," in the tone of voice that suggested she had said it several times before, already. "Steph will get here when she can."

"There should be bulletins put out when it's *not* screwed up," was Wren's opinion as she looked up and down the table for a free chair to sit in. The representative from Connecticut could walk in anywhere from now to several hours from now, depending on the cause of the delay. They used to give specifics, up to and including "body on the tracks," but now most delays were either "signal malfunctions" or the ever-popular "police activity." In the subways you still occasionally got "sick passenger," which could mean anything from a little kid tossing his cookies to a stiff in the seat next to you.

Still beat the hell out of driving in Manhattan, though.

The three leaders of the lonejack consortium who had made it in represented New York and Central New Jersey— Bart—South Jersey and northern Pennsylvania—Rich— and the gypsies, the lonejacks who didn't really settle anywhere but roamed the tristate area—Michaela. There were apparently more of those than Wren had ever really thought about; the idea of not having a home-spot to go to wasn't something she'd enjoy, but they seemed to thrive on it. Different strokes, she supposed. More power to 'em.

Several other humans sat at the table as well, some of them leaning forward, anticipating some great words of wisdom and leadership, others just as plainly not wanting to be there at all. The troika had brought their own cheering squads, it looked like. Joy. The more people involved, the less likely they were going to accomplish anything.

There were a number of water glasses on the table, and a pitcher of what looked to be either cola or iced tea, but no wine. That was good. Talents, overall, didn't react well with alcohol, and the last thing this meeting needed was for someone to get plastered and unruly.

She found an unoccupied chair, kicking someone's feet off the rungs so she could pull it out, and sat down.

"So, do we wait for Stephanie, or get started?" someone down the table asked

"We start," Michaela decided.

At that, the three leaders and their cohorts stared at Wren, who stared back at them. Several of them blinked, looked uncomfortable, but nobody said anything, or looked away.

"Oh, Jesus wept," she said, finally, uncomfortable with being in direct and steady view for that long. "Look. I'm not here to tell you what to do, or when to do it. That's not what we agreed on." At least, she didn't think it was. "I can listen and tell you when you're being idiots. Judge plans. Give you my experience. But you're the ones who speak for the lonejacks in your area." She paused, a horrible thought striking her. "You did all manage to get some sort of feedback from your area before calling this meeting, didn't you?"

Bart and Michaela nodded their heads. Rich, leaning back in his chair, suddenly wasn't so interested in looking at her anymore.

"Oh, for…" Wren was tempted to just get up and walk out. But the reasons she had agreed to be here in the first place still stood. Maybe even more so. Talents were, well, Talented. Very few of them combined what they were with what they did the way she did. And while Sergei was the business guy, she was the one, technically, who ran the business. They needed her…oh, call it her practical knowledge.

"We all know what needs to be done." Bart was almost a cliché, as the representative for the NYC and central New Jersey area lonejacks. Where the other three reps had gotten their jobs because they had somehow managed to not piss *anyone* off, Bart got his position because he had pissed *everyone* off, at one time or another. If you asked someone from Omaha to pick the New Yorker out of the bunch, they'd pick Bart, every single time. It was just the vibe he gave off, somehow. "We need to find a way to present a united force against the Council, without—according to you—actually giving them anything that looks like a united force. Piece of cake."

Wren hadn't forgotten how annoying Bart was. She had just forgotten how badly she wanted to slap him into the day after tomorrow. His heart-shaped face was topped by a mop of silvering blond curls that looked disgustingly natural, but an otherwise Ivory-soap appealing look was ruined by the sly smirk he habitually wore.

Rick was about as opposite as could be arranged: short, dark and arm-wavingly Italian. His hair was pulled back into a braid that put hers to shame, reaching halfway down his spine and tied with a metal band. He rode the dark purple Harley that she had seen in the parking lot outside the restaurant: he had given her a ride home once, after a party. She didn't remember much of the ride, other than the fact that it had reminded her of being drunk without actually being out of control. She supposed that was why he drove it, although she didn't feel that she knew him well enough to ask something like that.

Michaela, a tiny dandelion-puff with dark blue hair, was unknown to Wren, and vice versa. But the look of irritation on her face when Bart spoke boded well for their ability to work together, her and Wren.

"The feeling among my people," Rick said, learning forward earnestly, while the man beside him pulled a water glass out of harm's way, "is that we need to find a weakness within the Council itself. A back door, something that, even if we never have to use it, can still make them nervous."

"They're already nervous," Michaela said, dismissing that idea. "If they weren't, we'd either be left alone, or already all dead."

The gypsy was a bit harsh, Wren thought, but not altogether wrong. Something had made the Council uneasy enough to start picking on lonejacks in the first place. What was it?'

She asked that question out loud, then again, for those who had managed—surprise—not to hear her the first time.

"So why, after so many decades, are they nervous? Nervous enough to break the tradition of all those years of leaving us alone?"

It wasn't a new question to anyone at the table; it was the first thing anyone had asked, the first question in that failed letter they'd sent: why?

"Something's going on inside the Council," Bart said. "It's the only thing that makes sense. Something that made them feel like they had to show strength to the membership, to keep them in line."

"What?" he said, off everyone's look of surprise. "I'm an ass, not an idiot."

Wren settled into her seat, planting her elbows firmly on the tablecloth, and claimed an untouched glass of water. "Maybe so," she said in response to Bart's comment—which one, she didn't specify. "If the Council—pay attention, people!" as attention started to wander off her. "If the Council is having their own traumas, then we need to know what it is. That's their weakness, maybe our back door, if we need it. So how do we uncover it?"

Not everyone heard her, but the three or four who did started talking, and they all heard those voices. Wren took a sip of her water and sat back, sorting through what was being said, and who was saying it. This, she could do. Trigger a commotion. Let them fight it out amongst themselves, and she'd be able to give feedback to the troika, after.

The waiter came over with a menu, and she took it. She was going to need protein for this, she suspected.

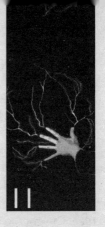

11

"I hate everyone," Wren announced to the world at large. The world seemed unimpressed.

Ten-thirty was an off hour for NYC subways: after the last trickle of rush hour, but before the club-goers started heading home. In the city that never slept, this was the hour for mass transit to catnap.

Wren was seated in a row all to herself; the only other person in the car was an old man halfway down, reading his newspaper and occasionally muttering to himself about something he read there. She had a notebook filled with notes from dinner, and the discussion after, but had put them aside in favor of the sketches Aldo had made for her. Time enough to hate her fellow Talents and their idiotic arguments later. She needed to get some serious cash-paying work accomplished. The city might go down in current-fueled flames, but the bills still needed to be paid.

By now, she had committed almost all the details of

the sketch to memory, and thought that, if needed, she would be able to track the necklace by her own sense of it. She wasn't a very good Tracer, though, so hopefully that wouldn't be necessary.

The blueprints had likewise been memorized, and she entertained herself for a bit by mentally walking through the apartment, the two rooms she had actually been in filled with detail, the ones she hadn't been in shadowy blanks. Trying to imagine what might be there was a bad idea: you got too hung up on filling in the details that inevitably were wrong, and that could throw you off when the job went down.

Tomorrow, she thought. A few hours sleep, and she'd get it done tomorrow. There was no point in procrastinating; she was only going to get more wound up and caught up in the *Cosa* crap.

Family, indeed. It was all about family, this job, and how much shit they could drop into your life. Mainly because, as far as Wren could tell, they *could.*

She folded the sketches and put them back in her bag, then leaned her head back and stared at the ads that ran along the top of ever car. Half of them were in Spanish, and Wren read along with the familiarity of someone who spoke not a word of the language but recognized words from content and repeated overexposure.

She didn't need life insurance to take care of her children, or a fast, discreet AIDS test, so the ads only held her interest another two or three minutes. So when the train pulled into the Twenty-third Street station and someone got on, she looked up, hoping for a distraction.

"Man, just piss off, all right?"

"Aw, wassamatter? Can't take a joke?"

There were five words in the English language that when put together, were reason enough for justifiable homicide, to Wren's way of thinking. And those were, "Can't you take a joke?"

From the look on the boy's face, he agreed. But the two kids who had followed him into the car out-muscled him by at least three-to-one odds. Wren frowned, watching the boy move. Something…

He hunched his shoulders under the bright red Rutgers University sweatshirt he wore, and that something clicked in her brain. Hunching like that, and that look of intense concentration, like something you needed to itch but couldn't? Winged. Wings bound, so you can't spread them: specifically, a feathered wing, bound down.

Angel. The boy was an angel.

Wren had nothing against the angeli. She had nothing for them, either. Arrogant little snots, most of them. But this was just a kid—okay, so he might have been four centuries old. But he looked like a kid. And not every angel was a shit—although it would be tough to prove that based on her own experience. If demon were mellow and mostly mild-tempered, angels were cranky, full of themselves, and…

Outnumbered, two to one.

The taller of the two humans leaned into the angel's personal space, features that might have been handsome ruined by a cruel sneer. "Not so tough now, are you? Not so tough, all alone."

"I'm never alone." The angel might have sounded more convincing if his voice hadn't wavered. Normally he was right—angeli traveled in packs, more or less. What you did to one you did to all his brothers, and they tended to get pissy about that. But Wren had seen an angel taken down by humans who knew what they were doing, and it hadn't been a pretty sight.

The shorter bully put a foot up on the plastic seat next to the angel, effectively boxing him in between leg and wall.

Idiots, Wren thought. *This is going to end very, very badly.*

For the angel, almost definitely. For the humans, too, once the subway came topside and his brothers could reach them.

For Wren, if she was caught anywhere in the vicinity. Angeli didn't like *anyone* who wasn't angeli, and in a bad temper they didn't always discriminate. The Old Testament got that much right, at least.

The train swerved around the track, throwing everyone off-center, and the lights flickered. Wren braced herself, and gave up any pretense of not watching the three boys. She had no idea what she could do—on her best day she wasn't a fighter, and this was very much not her best day. The smart thing would be to lay low and hope the train didn't get stuck anywhere underground. Let the angeli take care of angeli.

The lights flickered and went out again as the train went around another bend. It slowed down slightly, and

Wren let herself hope—but then the train kept going, by-passing a nonlocal station.

Damn. And thrice-damned.

The light, when it came back on, flickered on metal. Blood, on the tip.

The angel was grinning, showing unnervingly white, perfect teeth, while a thin cut dripped down one side of his face.

"Crazy-ass freak," the shorter bully muttered, his hands clenching into fists, as though he were anxiously await-ing the moment his leash would be slipped and he could get physical. The taller one, the one with the knife, was leaning back. Not as though he were about to back away; this was more the movement of a cobra about to strike.

"Grinning, are you? Think your winged pansy broth-ers are going to rush in and save you? Not down here they're not. You're in human territory now, *freak*."

Damn it, Wren thought again. *Frickin' vigilantes.* Of course. Because there wasn't enough shit going down al-ready, to complicate her life.

The knife-holder flicked his wrist again, and an-other cut slowly opened on the other side of the an-gel's face. The grin never slipped, but there was a tremble in those shoulders, as though he were trying not to cry. Or those feathered wings were struggling to break free.

Wren touched current, careful not to pull any out of the subway car around her. It was tempting, but she'd already pulled in too much recently. Current hangover would totally screw with her plans for tomorrow.

And ending up in a hospital with knife wounds, won't?
Just do it, Valere. Whatever it is you're going to do…

The knife-wielder spun, startled, and was on the metal floor before Wren was even able to finish her thought, the knife spinning across the floor to rest under the molded seats opposite the action. The newspaper-reading old man was standing over the vigilante, holding a heavy wooden cane like an offensive weapon—which was exactly what it had become. The angel looked as startled as Wren felt, which was nothing compared to the expressions on the faces of the two human bullies. She scuttled around in her seat, not wanting to miss a moment of the action.

"You want to play rough?" the old man asked. His face, seamed with age, was suddenly like granite, and the eyes that had barely skimmed print were now laser-focused. But he was still an old man, totally without any Talent at all, that Wren could sense, and there were two of them…

The shorter human was clearly thinking just that, and lunged without warning—only to be brought up short by the heel of the cane square in his throat. The boy gurgled once, his eyes going wide, then dropped.

The one on the floor tried to get up, and the angel stomped one boot-clad foot on his wrist, clearly putting all his weight into it. The human's eyes measured the distance between himself and the knife, then wisely lay still.

"Tired of these damned bigots," the old man muttered

to nobody in particular, stomping back to his seat. "Idiots, can't leave others just *be*."

Wren wanted to kiss him. She settled for getting off at the next station the train pulled into. It was still a ten block walk to her apartment, rather than the three blocks of her usual stop, but it was a nice night, a good night to stretch her legs, and she'd rather burn the calories than stick around any longer. Let the angel deal with the vigilantes. They wanted to mess with fatae, they get to deal with the consequences.

You're leaving them to die.

Oh, shut up.

They don't deserve to die.

They made their choice when they decided to go after an angel. One of the other fatae breeds? Might have walked away. But the angeli still had blood to avenge, blood that group had spilled. And if it came down to choosing sides…

Wren found she was very much a member of the *Cosa Nostradamus*, at heart.

The steps up to her apartment felt like miles of hard road, but she finally reached her landing. Bag and keys were dumped in their usual spot on the counter, then she went into the main room and turned on the stereo, flipping stations until soothing jazz filled the space. She realized, only after the fact, that this was the first time she'd listened to music since… Well. In a long time.

She felt dirty. Every dealing with those…bigots made her feel grimy, ill. She dealt with greed, desire, anger, etc., on a daily basis—without them, she had no job. But the bile these Human-only types carried with them…it was ugly, simply put. Ugly of a sort to make God cry.

Going back to the kitchen she prepped the coffee machine, setting it to start at 4:00 a.m. At that hour, she might be awake enough to drink coffee without spilling it on herself, but making it would have been more of a challenge.

You left those boys there to die.

Shut up.

The newly bought chairs and table seemed an affront, somehow. They didn't fit, were odd intrusions into her normal pacing space. The walls of the hallway were too close, the faded brown carpeting too dingy, the light fixtures too bright. Everything familiar was dreary, anything new was offensive, and Wren suddenly, really, didn't want to be there anymore.

"You're exhausted," she told herself. But she wasn't. Not in the needing-sleep way. She needed a detox, maybe. Shake everything out of her system, fill it up fresh. No man-made current, no fast food, nothing but lightning and green tea and whole grains…

"Ugh."

What she wanted, suddenly, was not to be alone. Not that she wanted company, but the sound of someone else breathing in the apartment would have been…comforting. Someone to sit and listen to, just quietly sitting in the same room with them, until her own system unwound and calmed down.

"You need a fish tank," she said, not for the first time.

Fish were soothing. They could be left alone for days at a time, and didn't stare at you reproachfully when you finally came home.

Of course, with her luck, she'd have a current flash, and end up with a tank of expensive fried tropicals.

A turtle. A turtle would be good. Slow-moving, lettuce-munching, blood-pressure-soothing.

You left those boys—

Shut *up!*

She could call Sergei. She could wake him up and listen to him breathe. Better than a turtle, any day.

But he'd want her to come uptown, then, and she'd had enough of traveling across the city for one day. Or he'd come down here, and she didn't want that, either. She wanted to be alone. But not lonely.

Shedding her clothing in a trail down the hallway, Wren crawled into bed without bothering to turn on the light. She should have brushed her teeth, washed her face. Gotten all of her shit together for tomorrow.

Time enough for that…later.

The street lamp cast light through the window; knowing she had to get up early, she hadn't bothered to draw the heavy velvet shade the way she normally did. Shadows lay heavy on everything, rising and falling with the pattern of her breath.

You left those boys there to die.

I know, she told the voice, finally. I know.

She fell asleep, finally, watching the illuminated clock hands tick over to 1:00 a.m.

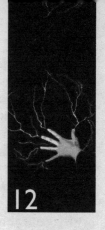

12

Six twenty-nine in the morning. Wren paused on the
street to get a feel for the rhythm of the traffic: taxis and
early-morning car-bound commuters cruising down the
avenue, a lean, middle-aged jogger in white T-shirt and
black running pants moving up and down in place as he
waited for the light to change, a blond Rasta dog-walker
with two dachshunds on the leash coming down the
southbound side.

More traffic than she had expected, but nothing she
couldn't handle.

Her brain had woken up sharp-edged and focused.
Her body, however, wasn't quite with the program. Coffee hadn't been enough to get her going. Coffee, and a
hot shower turned cold in the last instant had barely
been enough. Stopping along the way to jolt herself on
freshly made Krispy Kremes had, finally, done the job.
They were disgusting, but the sugar coursing through

her system made it impossible for her to even think about going back to sleep. And now that her body was finally awake, she could get to work.

Dawn might not have seemed like the wisest choice for a break-in, but it actually made a great deal of sense. People were in that groggy half-awake state where yes, they might wake too easily…but they were also much more likely to slap their snooze alarm and go back to sleep, not get up to investigate a strange noise the way they might in the middle of the night. And she was counting on Melanie to be a snooze-bar hitter, assuming she set her alarm at all. When you don't have to work for a living, slow wake-ups are the rule, not the exception.

Wren put down the case she was carrying and bent down onto one knee to relace her flexible-soled black boots, using the action as a cover to scan the sidewalk all the way down to the building's entrance again from that angle. She'd run into more than one home defense system that was set up not at the usual shoulder-height, but the more difficult to avoid ankle-height.

Not that she expected anyone here to be sneaky enough to do anything that, well, sneaky, but you survived in this business by being mean, nasty, and suspicious, and then assuming your target was meaner, nastier, and more suspicious than you were.

That was why she wasn't using the front entrance. The fact that she had already been in that way actually made it easier—she could have made herself look familiar, again, and eased passage, even this early in the morning. But easier wasn't always, long-term, smarter.

Smoothing the way sometimes left traces in people's minds that a well-asked question could trigger, to her misfortune.

That meant doing it the harder, smarter way.

While on one knee, she let her arms relax, forced her shoulders to drop slightly, and pushed down on her tension from ears on down to her toes, like forcing toothpaste all the way down the tube. It was harder than it looked, requiring an odd combination of work and a Zen-inspired sense of not-working to get it right.

When she felt almost boneless from the lack of even normal stress, Wren touched the subway running underground, under her feet, and let herself fill up, not with tension, but siphoned current. It flowed into her core, refreshing the natural energy that was always there, and spread out along the current-channels in her body, the channels that made her a Talent rather than a Null. The temptation was to overfill, to again hold reserves against trouble, but that temptation was false security; there was a real danger in carrying too much, too. You could burn out, filling up that much. Being a Talent didn't mean you were indestructible—far from it!

Banishing those thoughts, Wren took another deep breath, then let it out even as she gathered current and shaped it with the focus of her will and her words:

"Like the dawn
On little cat feet;
No-one sees."

The outfit she was wearing might, on quick glance, look like a particularly trendy cyclist's outfit, if she had a bicycle anywhere in sight, except that where a cyclist would want to be seen, her slicks were nonreflective, absorbing the light and encouraging the eye to move on past her. The cuffs came down to the top of her boots, and strapped under the heel to keep from riding up, no matter what she did, and the cuffs draped over her wrists, a loop waiting to be adjusted over her middle finger, to cover her entire hand. There was a wrist enhancement that went over it, for climbing, but carrying it in the city was more of a risk than Wren felt comfortable taking. Right now, she was dressed oddly. With the claws, if she was stopped, any half-awake cop would suspect they were for more than scaling the gym's rock-climbing wall. Worst-case scenario, she was carrying a concealed weapon and looking at some serious explaining.

Besides. The day she couldn't get into any apartment building without toys to help her, she'd hang up her slicks entirely.

With a faint tingle, she felt the cantrip finally kick in, an almost physical blurring of her edges to match the no-see'um impulse she carried within her on a daily basis. If there had been a mirror nearby, she would not have been surprised if she were smudged where skin met air.

It was an enhancement of what happened to her normally, turning what some might consider a negative into a career-enhancing plus. Lemons into Limoncello, as it were.

Wren stood up and stretched, fingers reaching over her head, rising up on her toes so that she was an unbroken line of muscle from the heels of her feet to the heels of her hands. Her body sizzled, the sugar and caffeine and current fusing into pure sparkling energy. *As ready as you're going to be*.

Picking up her small soft-sided case—not so coincidentally made of the same light-absorbent fabric as her slicks—Wren adjusted the strap over her shoulder, and walked past the doorman who had handed her out of the cab on her previous visit to the building, pausing at the narrow alley where the trash cans were tucked discretely out of view.

In a newer, or more trendy building like Sergei's, she might have had trouble. But the apartment buildings in this part of town clung to their original looks with a determination matched only by Hollywood starlets, and the rough-edged brick building still had old-fashioned fire escape ladders. In far better shape than the one P.B. used on her own building, true, but the mechanisms were still the same. Reach up, swing the bar down, and climb up.

Only a tyro, a total clueless newbie, would use the fire escape. Wren bypassed the obvious—and inevitably alarmed—entry and instead braced herself against the building on the other side of the alley. A hard shove of her feet against the ground, and the current she had siphoned off reverted to the original purpose of the electricity it had traveled with, treating her body like a subway car to be moved along the tracks.

So long as she was able to concentrate on "laying" tracks up the wall, the current should continue to move her. If she lost concentration, or ran out of "tracks…."

Don't, she told herself. *Make like John Henry and lay dem tracks...*

Pushing an inch at a time, feeling when the external wall changed from brick to cement, scratching through the too-thin fabric of her slicks, Wren made her way up the wall. She could have had the current reform into a softer gel-like texture, smooth the flow, but she didn't want to risk her focus.

Don't look down. Whatever you do, Valere, don't look down. She wasn't afraid of heights, as such. It just didn't seem like a good idea, as she passed the eleventh floor window and neared her goal.

Dark blue curtains were drawn against the view; the rooms on the other side, she remembered, had cream-colored drapes that were open to let sunlight come in.

"End of the line. This station stop, target achieved," she told herself. "Time to disembark."

Easier said than done. Not that she couldn't do it; she just didn't *want* to do it.

You're not *going to fall.* Her brain believed her. Her body wasn't so sure.

Flexing her fingers against the wall, she twisted current into the whorls of her fingerprints, dark purple sparks twisting and turning into a sort of paraphysical Velcro, or suction cups.

If you think about it, you're going to be here until the city goes down in flames around you, and hey, no payment, then.

That was the ultimate incentive. *Cosa* and Council could go *mano a mano* and take everyone down with them, but her landlord would still want rent, her credit cards would still want payments, her student loans would still demand their pound-plus of flesh. Just because you were Talented didn't mean you got a "Get out of real life free" card.

Taking a deep breath, she crouched, as best she could while still pushing against the wall, and forced her body to jump from one wall to the next.

There was just enough time for her to think *ohmygod-sweetjesus* before she was clinging to the other wall like a sticky-toed tropical frog.

"Well," she whispered in amazement. "That actually worked."

The window she chose was, according to the blue-prints, the guest bathroom. She preferred coming in through bathroom windows, when she could: even if she did happen to startle someone, they were bound to be somewhat incapacitated, giving her the essential extra seconds advantage. And a guest bathroom, especially with the target at odds with the client, was likely to be unused.

Wren hoped. In the end, too much of the job always relied on best guesses and hope.

The window gave under her touch, the faintest bit of current sliding under the wiring of the security system and making it believe that it was still connected. It wasn't a difficult maneuver, any more than picking a lock was all that difficult, but it took a certain level of delicacy and concentration. Adding the difficulty of doing it while stuck to the side of the building…well, that was one of the reasons why she charged more for her services than the average burglar. Or even the above-average Retriever.

Sliding the frame up as slowly as possible, she let her senses extend gently into the room. Normally she would be more aggressive, but knowing that target was a Talent changed everything. Current took the flavor of its user, and the longer you held it in your core, the more it "smelled" like you. That was why she had siphoned off current just before the job began rather than drawing it from inside: if the target did sense her, it would be as an unidentified Talent, rather than "someone who seems familiar." Or, worse yet, identifiable by name.

Bathroom. Check. Damn, that was a nice bathroom. Silvery-gray marble, subtle pattern in the cream-on-cream tile, dark-colored towels that—she gave into impulse and stroked one of them—yes, that felt as thick and soft as they looked. Nicer than her L.L. Bean sale specials. And this is what they had in the guest bath? Wren hated being impressed by massive amounts of money, but sometimes it was just there to be impressed by.

Focus, damn it!

Once inside, some of the tension she'd been carrying around slid off her shoulders and dissipated, as she'd known it would. When she was working, everything fell into place. Whatever happened outside these walls? Whatever she had done, hadn't done, was going to do? None of it mattered. Only the plan, the execution of the plan, the finishing of the job: that was all that mattered, here. That tight focus gave Wren a serenity she'd been lacking in herself for too long, now.

There were ten rooms in the apartment. The difference between her neighborhood and this one was more than doubling the number of rooms, though; it was also about square footage. That was more than doubled, here. The house Wren had grown up in had been smaller than this apartment.

Guest bathroom. Guest bedroom, off to the left. Down the hall, the maid's room, plus a much smaller bathroom. Wren would guess it probably had marble, too, if not quite so much. Maid was off today, one of the reasons Wren had picked today for her attempt.

To the right, the living room/dining room combo where she'd been received, before, which led through French doors to the entry foyer. That was all she'd seen of the place, previously. Luxe, in that understated way old money had. A library. The deceased husband's office. The kitchen was in the center as well, toward the back of the apartment—the side she was on now. Avoid the kitchen—if there was any activity this early in the morning, it would be the target, fixing an early breakfast for herself.

On the other side of the entry foyer, the master bedroom suite. Bedroom, sitting room, dressing room—what sort of person needed a room to sit in and a room to dress in?—and another bathroom. Wren was guessing that one would be entirely marble. The target didn't seem to be the sort to stint herself in the slightest.

The urge to nick a few pretties for herself, as long as she was here, was almost overwhelming. Normally Wren did the in-and-out without hesitation. But normally she was in places with less personally appealing temptation—museums, offices, that sort of thing.

Bad idea. Bad urge. She was a Retriever, not a thief.

You really think there's any difference? You really think the rest of the world gives a damn?

Sergei does.

For the moment, that put the question to rest. But it was a sign of the stress she was under that the thought had even come up. She needed to do something nice for herself, and soon. Or she was going to do something stupid.

While she was thinking, she was moving. Slowly, sliding rather than stepping, her feet making no sound at all on the cool tiled floor, staying off the narrow Oriental runners so that there would be no imprint left behind, however faint. Slicks didn't shed bits of itself, even when torn: that's why they were so damn expensive.

All right. If you were a small bit of jewelry, not very expensive but potentially very important, where would you be? It wasn't really a question; or rather, it was one that she had already answered.

Not in the library—darling stepdaughter would know all the hiding places already. Ditto the office, if father and daughter were really all that close. Bedroom, though…bedroom was probably off-limits to a grown daughter of a different marriage.

Besides, people liked to keep things like that close, to reassure themselves it was safe.

Ironically it was that very instinct that made such things so easy to steal.

A touch of current, stretched farther out, confirmed what she had suspected: other than the external wiring of the alarm, the house was mercifully free of traditional modern security measures. Fine for an office, perhaps, or public space, but no adult Talent wanted to have to be so careful of current overflow in their own home, for fear of shorting something out and having the cops arrive minutes later.

So that left current-traps. Tricky, in that most ways of protecting oneself from them—using current at more powerful level than the creator used in building them—were also what set them off. Fortunately Wren had an answer to that, one that was as obvious as it was effective.

When the traps are set "up," go down.

Wrapping the current more tightly around her sense of self, Wren "brushed" at it, softening and blurring the edges of her perceived outline even more. The spell, set earlier, was a passive one, the sort that a resident might set to enhance sleep, or make sure paint dried evenly, or any of a hundred boring uses. Small. Passive. Noninvasive. Unlikely to set off anything sniffing for disruption, even before the don't-see-me aspect of the spell was taken into consideration.

If anyone ever figured out what to actually do, in order to discern or repel a Retriever, Wren would have to rethink her career. But for now, people continued to be trickier than they needed to be. And that was fine by her.

Taking a deep, silent breath, she slid through a partially opened door and crossed from the empty side of the apartment into the occupied part.

This was where her "other" training kicked in. The

noncurrent work she'd done with retired sneak thieves and pickpockets, hanging out with old locksmiths and retired cat burglars.

Resolutely not looking at the antique silver tea set, or the small, impressively expensive knickknacks scattered on tables and sideboards, Wren ghosted across, not touching anything. Her body was a shadow, soft-moving, like a dancer on ice. Her slicks picked up the shadows, rather than the light, and her hair, braided and darkened with specially tinted talc, did likewise. To human eyes and minds, and most fatae, she was invisible.

The double doorway off the foyer led into the public rooms. Wren bypassed that, and went directly on to the smaller, less eye-catching but still gorgeous cherrywood door. It opened onto a short hallway with another door at the far end, which should lead to the sitting room.

None of the doors were locked, which wasn't a surprise—who locked internal doorways? If they had been, she had a kit in her bag which would have made short work of them.

She moved carefully through the doors, alert to anything that stirred the currents or smelled of elementals. If she used them as telltales, there was nothing to say other people couldn't, as well.

But the target clearly wasn't as paranoid as she was; not surprising, few lonejacks were, and even fewer Council members, protected as they were by Mage Council proscriptions against poaching on fellow members, etc. etc., ad nauseum. Being a Council member was all about being proscribed, one way or another. And that was what they wanted to enforce on lonejacks. No, thanks.

Mind on the job, Valere.

The sitting room was dark and shadowed, with darker spaces indicating furniture. Three doors led off of it: one, ajar, led to the bathroom. The other two should be to the dressing room, and the bedroom.

The rise and fall of snoring through one door told her that the target—assuming the target hadn't invited a friend to an impromptu sleepover—was still in bed. Short of having the target locked in the bathroom with some dire digestive disorder and a Saks Fifth Avenue catalog, that was best-case scenario.

Reaching into the small case she carried with her, Wren pulled out a small globe about the size of a tennis ball. Hand-blown glass, it looked almost unbearably fragile, but was actually remarkably sturdy. Inside, sparks of current flickered and danced wherever her fingers made contact with the sphere's surface. Cheap electronic rip-offs of the idea could be found in every cheap mall gimmick store, but the real thing was considerably more expensive. There was an entire string of scientific babble to explain it, involving the breakdown of current and related electricity and bands of somethingorother that kept the prepared spell-work inside from escaping, but all Wren cared about was that it worked.

She could have just done one up herself, she supposed, but the workmanship of glass was what you paid for, and it was worth it just to make sure nothing broke too soon.

Placing the globe on the floor in the center of the sitting room, Wren pushed the two closed doors open just enough to allow a sliver of light to pass through. Returning to the center of the room, she raised her foot and, whispering a hushed prayer, brought the heel of her boot down gently on the globe.

It shattered silently, with a gratifyingly gentle spray of glass that dissolved almost immediately on losing its shape. That was another thing you paid through the nose for: minimum debris left behind for someone like Bonnie to trace.

The current that was contained within the globe now released, it unrolled into tendrils, flickering pale silver.

Anyone could premake a spell, but very few people did. Beyond the tedium and expense of finding something that could contain them without contamination, the fact was that current was lazy—it wanted to follow the path of easiest transport. That was why it traveled with electricity—and why, unless you were totally in control, and directed your current specifically, it would revert to its original form, and become inert, useless in an emergency.

A lot like most lonejacks, actually.

"Now released—
Remember your goal.
Retrieve it."

The tendrils wavered, then, reinforced by her own determination and the picture of the object she held in her memory, formed into three distinct arms, one for each open door. Slipping through the open space, they went in search of the object to be Retrieved.

It would be better if, someday, she could direct this kind of search from off-site, but if there was anyone who had that much control, she hadn't met them yet. And she thought that maybe she was thankful for that small blessing.

Control plus current meant power. Wren had yet to meet anyone with that much power who didn't also have an agenda. There were enough agendas floating around the city already, without adding more to the mix. Thank God it wasn't an election year, too. If she had to listen to any ads—

Focus!

Her mentor's voice, cutting through the fog that threatened to clog her brain.

Damn it, Jenny-Wren, pay attention!

She shook her head, a small movement, but violent enough to clear out her brain somewhat. Her eyes refocused, and she had a momentary flash of coherence, enough to make her aware of how far she had managed to drift.

Closing her case and draping it over her shoulder again, Wren let herself float with the fog a moment, trying to get the flavor of it. Threat? Or just something otherwise harmless piped into the ether, some kind of Talent-specific sleeping aid?

No. There was a definite focus at the base of it. *Something's screwing with me…* Without letting go of the current-tendrils, Wren sent a gentle probe out to see what was up.

sssssszzzztttttt

Wren yelped, the sound echoing loudly in the room. The hours of training Neezer had put her through during her mentorship, enhanced and maintained in the years since then, was all that kept her connected to the searching current-tendrils.

Fuck, that hurt!

The elementals around her settled back down, having warned her off their territory, and determining that she was no threat to them. Meanwhile, the shock of touching them, ungrounded and unprepared, was fading slightly from her system. Wren took a few seconds to resteady herself, finding her center and focus again.

This time, alerted, she was aware of the elementals, able to discern the comforting drone they were emitting that had fogged her brain to begin with. Another sharp shake of her head was able to shake some of it off, and being aware of the influence helped…but not enough. Damned current-happy elementals. They were useful on occasion, but like the current they lived on and in, they tended to lapse into lionlike indolence unless specifically directed.

Unless they had been directed to send out those mind-fogging vibes, as part of a passive defense program. Unless someone was meaner and sneakier and lazier than she was… Oh, shit. Wren didn't like that thought, not at all.

Find it! She sent a quick, barely psi-audible order to her tendrils, reinforcing the urgency over caution. One of them responded in the affirmative, the silver flashing through their connection to a vibrant ruby-red.

Not the bedroom, which surprised her. The dressing room. Private, maybe even more private in some ways than the bedroom. A safe, maybe?

Not waiting to see if anything defense-wise had been woken by the elementals' sting-back, she slipped into the dressing room and looked for the telltale red glow.

In the closet. A small wooden box, up on a shelf. Not where you put something of great personal value, generally—but a good place to stash something until you figure out what to do with it.

The target had been lying through her collagen-enhanced lips when she said she wasn't keeping this little memento of Mommy from her stepdaughter. Not that Wren cared particularly—she wasn't being hired to care. Just to get it back.

The shelf was too high for her to reach, and it was too far back on the shelf to stretch-and-grab. A quick glance around showed no handy stool or other climbable furniture. There was no help for it but to go on the offensive.

Taking a deep breath, Wren directed a sliver of current to shove the box off the shelf, sending it directly into her waiting hands.

The box screamed.

Every nerve in her body flayed by the noise, Wren dropped the box through sweat-slicked hands, sensing more than hearing it hit the floor with an almost-alive, fleshy thud.

Fuck.

Shutting down every bit of current in use and shoving it back down to her core, Wren didn't wait to see if any-

thing more active than an elemental was coming after her,
but beat feet out the way she had come in, retracing her
steps and already planning for her exit out of the building.
It wasn't going to be graceful, but if she could manage to
stay quiet, if nothing bigger or meaner than she was showed
up to stop her, she just might make it. Might. Maybe.

The current-alarm was still screaming in her head. A
thin veneer of current tried to rise through her skin and
shut the damned thing up, but she shoved it down again.
At this point, everything would have her signature all
over it. The damage was done—better to keep them focused on the box, on making sure that it was still safe,
still in their possession.

"Joey? Is that you?"

A sleepy voice, followed by a much more awake cursing and the sound of someone fumbling with something
heavy and metallic, followed Wren down the hallway and
across the foyer. Bracing herself for a blast of current,
Wren was unprepared to hear sirens in the distance, and
the crackle of a security system telling its owner that the
alarm had been sounded.

*Cops? She called the cops? What kind of Talent calls the
cops? There's the door—brazen it out? No, stick to your
original plan. Don't deviate! Don't get caught somewhere
unprepared.* More *unprepared.* All that went through her
head in a fast-forward voice, too quick for any real words
to be formed.

The bathroom window was still open. But there was
a red light flashing over it, where the wires she had mo-

jo'd had clearly gotten their act together—or the alarm had been triggered elsewhere.

An electrical alarm system? I'm going to be the first Retriever to ever get nailed by an ADT system. Without completing the Retrieval. The Council can stop worrying, the humiliation alone will kill me.

The sirens got louder, and she could hear someone in the apartment behind her.

You can't afford to get caught. You know too much. If the rumors were true, if the rivalry was getting this serious— if the Council was as determined as the lonejacks to have their way, then the Council would have no hesitation in using her, whatever they could get out of her, the same way her fellow lonejacks had, only more so. They'd use this Retrieval as whatever proof they needed to hold her. And the voice was right; she did know too much. Who and where and what and when. For the first time in her life, something other than her own concerns were tied up in her actions. Getting caught meant more than her reputation would be hurt.

Wren turned even as she was running, pushing the bathroom door with one elbow, shoving forward off her toes and grabbing the window frame with her free hand, twisting so that her body glided out the window into a sort of free-form dive.

Headfirst umpteen stories down to the sidewalk below.

Well. The voice almost sounded impressed. *That was particularly stupid.*

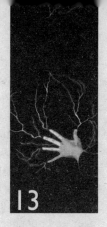

13

"Another one, honey?"

"Please. Yes."

The ground coming up too fast, too hard. Clutching the box, unable to close her eyes. And then, suddenly, Neezer's voice, hours after she went out of the window or was it half a second? Neezer's voice, shouting in the back of her head, and Sergei's touch on her hand, and a gust of wind slapped her in the face, putting her rightside up and slowing, slowing her, skin feeling like it was ripping off from her bones, the box slipping from her hands and hitting the pavement, the pendant falling out.

In her memory, she caught the pendant, scooped it up, ran with it. The truth was, it hit the floor of the dressing room, the face of the pendant right under her nose. The object had been right there, within reach. And she had left it there, and run. Fled the scene like a scalded chicken. Failed.

She had *failed*.

Caught up in self-disgust, Wren hadn't noticed until she was three blocks away from the apartment building that her hands were burning. Literally. Dark green flames, licking around her fingertips, under the fingernails. The flame ached rather than injured, but it was disturbing. And, from the odd looks she was getting from pedestrians, visible even to Nulls. It had taken almost half an hour of deep breathing and centering, hunched over in a doorway, for her to make the flames go away.

Her fresh drink came, and the old glass was whisked away. She supposed that she was running a tab, at this point.

Wren looked at her hands, wrapped around the glass of some drink she didn't want when she ordered the first one, and wanted even less now that she was on her third, and carefully didn't suspect that the medallion—no innocent tacky keepsake—had anything to do with those flames. At all. Because the only thing, that could scream like that, the only thing, that would leave such a residue of current around her, without ever making direct contact, was an Artifact.

Artifacts—objects of power, things that held current naturally—were to be reported to the Mage Council, to be recorded and studied and kept safely out of circulation. Even the most renegade lonejack knew that. Even the most wizzed wizzart knew that. It was the one thing, to the best of her knowledge, they had never faulted or faltered on.

Why hadn't Melanie Worth-Rosen reported it? Hell,

why hadn't dear departed Momma—no, and Wren checked herself—Momma hadn't been a Talent, had she? Papa, then. He had to have known what his wife was wearing. Why hadn't he reported it? Not a good Council boy, was he? Not a lonejack; that would have come up in her background search, even if she wasn't up to Sergei's standards. No affiliations at all, Mr. Rosen. Rare, but not unheard of. Second wife was the one who got on the radar; and she was the one who realized what it was Anna was supposed to inherit, and snatched it for her own.

That was Wren's theory, anyway.

So why did Rosen the Younger want it? Momma's legacy? Or was something else going on behind those pretty eyes?

Too many questions. Too many possibilities. Her headaches were getting worse, not better.

Rather than going home, Wren had peeled off her slicks and folded them down into a flat package and shoved them into her case, into the space where the pendant was supposed to go, and went in search of a night-shift bar that wasn't going to look askance at a small-framed woman getting soused all alone.

She ended up, unsurprisingly, here in Kalli's, down off Christopher Street. It was a corner dive, an unlikely gay bar that catered to blue collar workers. She had found it originally when she first moved to Manhattan, mainly because they had a small but free hot buffet until midnight. The buffet had gone the way of skyrocketing real estate prices, but the bartenders were still cute, and the drinks were generous, and nobody looked twice at a woman alone, except to wonder if she didn't mean to go to Henrietta's, down the street.

Plus, a twenty-dollar tip on the first drink got her left alone, except for the occasional refill, and the music on the jukebox was eighties kitsch; perfect for not letting her brain do anything other than play "Name That One-Hit Wonder." But despite the nauseating distraction of The Waitresses claiming that they knew what boys liked, Wren couldn't stop wondering about that box, the pendant, her rather impressive if brainless learning-to-fly act, and what she might have gotten herself into, yet again.

The Artifact was troubling, yeah. And the fact that she'd screwed the job, had left it unfinished, and, worse yet, alerted the mark that someone was after it…. That was all really, really bad.

The flying thing trumped all that.

Wren still didn't know how she had done what she'd done, that she wasn't dead, or otherwise splattered on the uptown pavement. She suspected that it was some latent skill-set coming to the fore under pressure, the way most new current-related skills were discovered. But she didn't *know*, and that not knowing was making her nervous.

It was, Wren thought, a really bad day when a major on-the-job screw-up took second place on the *odd-*ometer. A really, really bad day.

"You could just tell the client the job's off, and be done with it." That would be the smart thing to do. That's what Neezer would have told her to do. "Or go to the Council and turn the target in…or just drop it off, all anony-mouslike." Lee would have counseled that; get free of anything to do with it, dodge the karma that probably came attached to it like psychic sludge. Because didn't she have enough stuff focusing the magical universe's at-tention on her, already, even hiding behind—what had Sergei called them? The four-wheeled troika?

Sergei. Sergei would tell her…finish the job. So she screwed it up, first go-round. So she wasn't as damned perfect as her press claimed. It was a relief, actually.

Wren took another sip of her drink.

Yes, a relief. After the hero-worship she got from the boys in Italy, after having to fight off the Council's at-tempts to shut her down, after all the pressure of being the best at what she did, without actually being able to stand up and take credit for any of it…

She wasn't perfect. She was just damned good. And damned good still allowed her to be human. To screw up a job.

To get a second chance.

And how the hell had she managed to call up enough wind-current to counteract gravity? Without conscious thought or willful direction? Assuming that was what she had done, and not…

"Christ, I don't even know what I did, much less how, much less if I ever can do it again." Or if she would ever want to, for that matter. If it took being about to die…

"I'll worry about that after I've finished worrying about everything else," she decided, finally. Only thing she could do.

"Ah-hah. There you are."

Wren instinctively moved her foot so that she was in contact with the case, making sure that it was still securely hidden under the table. There was nothing really incriminating in there, precisely, but it would be expensive to replace her slicks if this were an attempted bump-and-grab. Only then did she half-turn in her seat to look at the newcomer.

"Oh. Hi. How'd you find me?" she asked, wishing she could feel more surprise.

"Followed my nose," P.B. said, the black nub-shaped object twitching as he spoke. Wren had never actually gotten a straight answer on him about his sense of smell, so maybe that was the truth. Polar bears were supposed to have really good sense of smell, right? Maybe demon did, too.

She turned right-side back in her seat and picked up her glass again. "Uh-huh." A wealth of skepticism came out in that vocalization, more than she'd thought she was feeling.

"Okay, actually, I got a call from Dopey," P.B. said, pulling a stool over and hauling his short, stout body onto it, garnering only a few bemused stares from the other patrons nursing their midday beers. Apparently four-foot-tall white-furred demon weren't any more of note here than females.

"Dopey?"

"Dopanisimano. Bartender." And the demon jerked his head in the direction of the bar, where a tall, square-shouldered bald man was wiping down glassware with far too much attention to the task, aware of her sudden scrutiny.

"Right. You put out an APB on me, or something?" Wren really did wonder, sometimes, about P.B.'s extensive network of contacts in the City. It seemed to run from the top of the social strata to the bottom without prejudice on their part—or his.

"Didn't know where you'd disappeared to. Made me nervous."

"You're not my mother."

"Yeah—she shaves her legs. Look, normally I wouldn't bother someone so clearly in the middle of important work—"

"You're starting to annoy me, P.B."

"Too bad. Your day's about to get worse."

She raised the glass, holding the cold surface to the side of her face. "Oh, goody. Can I pay you not to tell me?"

He ignored her. "I just came from a powwow."

P.B. was right. Her day was already worse. "What now?"

Powwows were what P.B. called it when the fatae, the nonhumans, got together for a bitch-and-solve session—although they were more prone to the bitching than the solving. She supposed it was a blessing—the idea of all the fatae tribes and clans actually coming to agreement was the only thing that made her more nervous than lonejacks organizing, which was her current active nightmare.

His silence gave her a clue. "Oh, Jesus wept. They're reconsidering standing with us, aren't they?" That had been the great accomplishment of the summer: making the fatae understand that the lonejack community was horrified by the racially motivated attacks on nonhumans by humans, that Talents had nothing whatsoever to do with it.

P.B.'s face wasn't the best for conveying expressions—his foreshortened muzzle could bare teeth in a grin that looked menacing as hell, but that was it. But somehow he managed to convey exasperation extremely well. "They think you're going to lose. Against the Council. And they don't want to go down with you."

"But they're willing to reap the benefits if we win?"

P.B. made a helpless gesture, black-skinned paws raised to the ceiling. "Like your people are all that different? We're not joiners. We're not fighters. We're survivors."

"Bloody damned hell." The temptation to put her head down on the table and just not ever lift it again was, well, tempting.

"On the brighter side—there's someone new in town I want you to meet."

She rested her face on her hands. "Jesus wept, Polar Bear. I'm really not in the mood right now. It's already been a long day, and now you just dro— Hey!" Wren had thought that her body had overdone itself on surprises today, but the sudden appearance of a tall, skinny gecko at her table was outside of enough to warrant a jump and a yelp.

"Genevieve Valere, this is Seiichi Shigenoi. He's fatae."

"Yeah, 'cause I hadn't figured that one out," Wren said. P.B. looked as abashed as his face could manage.

"He's also a Talent."

All right, that was unusual enough to warrant real interest. Most fatae were magical in their own right, but it didn't often translate in the ability to *handle* magic the way a Talent did. Mostly they were old-style users: limited, specialized, and unpredictable.

"You're Japanese?"

"You could not tell?" Unlike most of the reptilian fatae, Shigenoi spoke without even the trace of a sibilant in his consonants.

But not entirely reptilian, Wren noted with interest. Between his eye-bumps, a thick but narrow ruff of blond fur stood on end, like a pony's mane shorn into a mohawk. When he turned his head slightly, she could see that it ran all the way down his back, probably down to his tail, assuming he had one.

"I've never met a Japanese fatae before, at least, not a native." There were a lot of immigrant tribes in the New York area, and she wasn't entirely sure about the origins of all of them. "You want a beer? I don't think they serve sake here."

"Just as well. Sake makes me, what is the term?" He made a gesture with one webbed paw that indicated regurgitation.

"Toss your cookies?"

"Yes. Alcohol does not metabolize well in my species. Soda, please. Ah, seltzer water."

P.B. nodded, then looked at Wren. "I'm good," she said in response. "So, Shigenoi. How was your trip over?"

"Not…enjoyable, I fear. Travel is difficult," he said. "I hate traveling cargo. My scales dry out, and my fur gets staticky. But the seats are…difficult to stay in for extended periods of time."

Having just recently taken her first transatlantic flight, Wren could sympathize. Even without a tail.

"So what brings you to Manhattan?" Please, God. Not fatae-Council stuff. Please don't let their problems have spread out of the area...

"Ah." Wren wasn't sure geckos could blush, but his pale green skin did seem somewhat...rosier, even in the bar's mediocre lighting. "Business. I have a rather thriving, um, small company. Import-Export."

"Oh. Smuggling?"

"Valere!" But P.B. was laughing. "Why do you assume everyone I know is on the nonlegal side of things?"

"I don't assume that at all," Wren said. "It's just that usually the ones you introduce to me tend to be."

"No, no, nothing at all... Well, I suppose it would depend on your point of view."

"My point of view's pretty wide-angle lens," Wren said, encouragingly.

When the visiting fatae hesitated, P.B. tapped the table with one claw. "Shigenoi. This is *Wren Valere*." When Shigenoi didn't seem to understand the emphasis, P.B. sighed, a deep, dramatic sigh that involved all of his considerable chest. "The Retriever? Like you?"

"You're a Retriever?" Wren was fascinated. There weren't all that many Talents who were Retrievers, worldwide, and she had never heard of a fatae who was one.

"It is not something I generally advertise—" and he shot P.B. a glare that Wren could so appreciate "—but, yes, I am. Forgive me for not recognizing your name. I can only humbly blame jet lag. You are, of course, quite well-known to me, by reputation, at least."

"Yeah. Rep's a fabulous thing," she said, in a tone that indicated anything but.

Geckos should never try to grin. Or even smile. "Yes. And yet, to be known to your peers, and respected by them, is not a thing to be dismissed."

"So long as it doesn't lead to any testosterone-bumping. So. How do you know my courier-running amigo over here?"

"Our acquaintance goes back some number of years. When I knew I was coming to town, he kindly offered to show me the sights."

"And keep him out of the places he shouldn't go," P.B. said. On the surface it might have been friendly needling, native to tourist. But recent events had shown Manhattan to becoming less friendly to unwary fatae. Everyone should have such an alert guide. She approved.

"Anyway. I thought you guys might have stuff to talk about, and he's an art collector, too, so maybe Sergei…" P.B. stopped to reconsider. "Or maybe not."

Sergei's fataephobia wasn't something he was proud of, but P.B., being the fatae her partner saw the most of, was bound to have picked it up.

"He's always glad to meet a friend of mine," Wren said. She hoped.

"Great! I was thinking getting Shig's opinion on Noodles."

"That's Chinese, not Japanese. Honestly, P.B.…."

"Hey, it's Asian. He'd know more than we would how decent it is. I know you love the place, Valere, but I swear, it gives me indigestion every single damn time."

"So don't eat my leftovers," she said tartly. "Anyway, I wasn't planning on eating out tonight. No offense," she said to the visitor.

"Oh, no offense taken at all. And certainly I was not expecting you to change your plans for us," Shigenoi said, protesting. "We would be intruding, at such short notice. You might have other plans…"

Her only plans had involved stressing over what to do about the pendant. Wren blinked, then looked at both the fatae in a way that immediately made the demon nervous.

"What?" P.B. said.

"What, what?" she asked him.

"There's always a what when you get that look, human."

After the day she'd had, Wren felt it was probably inevitable that she'd break out into giggles at the aggrieved tone in P.B.'s voice. It was either that, or hit someone, hard. "Go get the drinks," she commanded him. "I want to talk shop with my fellow Retriever."

Leaning across the table, she rested her chin on the palm of her hands, and asked, "So. Have you ever run into an Artifact?"

Shigenoi sat sideways on the chair, and leaned forward in a mirror of her actions. His pop-set eyes seemed to glisten, and an inner eyelid dropped over them. "Myself? No. Have I heard others speak of them? Yes…."

When P.B. came back, Wren had picked Shig's brain as best their mutual exhaustion could allow for, and she had decided on a course of action. It wasn't one she was happy about, but it was probably the best of bad choices.

"You got your cell on you?" she asked P.B.

"It's turned off. I know better than to bring anything loaded near you. Either of you, for that matter."

"Turn it on. Call Sergei. Tell him to meet us at Noodles this afternoon."

"No takeout?" he asked, getting his mobile phone out of the courier bag he carried everywhere.

"My apartment's getting too many visitors these days, don't you think? I'd rather not assume it's leak-proof, as it were."

"Good point." The demon rubbed his head as though it was still tender. "Real good point." He dialed a number, his claws delicately picking out the keys, and held the phone to his mouth, having to tilt his head oddly to adjust for the nonhuman distance between his mouth and his ears.

"Yo. Didier. I'm just carrying a message so don't hang up on me. Dinner, tonight, Noodles. She doesn't want to go home, I guess. Oh, man, she's a woman, what the hell do I know from how her mind works?" He made an apologetic moue at her, and Wren rolled her eyes. "Yeah, and I'm bringing a friend, so mind your p's and q's. You'll see."

It wasn't unusual for someone to be burning the post-midnight oil in the midrise building that housed the Silence. To the rest of the neighborhood, the unmarked brownstone was merely one of the many not-for-profit organizations that dotted the Manhattan landscape, utilizing property bought cheaply, or left to them by prosperous donors. The people who went in and out were well-dressed, unflashy, and although not rude, not overly friendly, either. They patronized the local take-out deli, and the coffee shop down the street, and occasionally stopped in for lunch at the pizza place on the corner. They were good neighbors, was the most anyone would ever say of them. Never any trouble. Kept their sidewalk clean in winter, never left trash out front, never had any unruly incidents, and even the few employees who gathered outside for their daily cigarettes did so in a quiet and considerate fashion.

Darcy Cross didn't drink. She didn't smoke. She hated pizza with a passion. But she knew everyone who indulged in all those things, and if she didn't know them, she had eavesdropped on them, one way or another. Her job was information; the getting, the collating, the sorting and resolution of that information into useful reports.

She should have been assigned to R&D. Only Andre Felhim's intervention years ago had kept her out of Duncan's clutches. Because once Duncan took something, he kept it. Or them.

She'd have been paid more, working in R&D. But there were things more important than money. In R&D, the information would have been pulled from her before she was ready to share it. Andre, on the other hand, understood that she needed time to let it simmer through her brain; that she needed to *understand* it, before she could share it.

And she didn't understand what she was seeing.

The Silence existed to correct things which had been

put wrong by malign intent. That was the charter; that was the mission statement: that was the Cause, the reason for everything they did. Not so much to help the individual—that was a plus—or even to keep those with power from enforcing their desires on those without, but to keep the balance of the world even. To ensure that people were able to live their lives without interference.

Someone was interfering. Someone was restricting the flow of information, the lifeblood of the Silence. Someone was manipulating events for a specific purpose.

That didn't bother Darcy; she had no illusions about the corruptibility of anything or anyone, least of all her co-workers, or the organization for which they worked. What bothered her was that she could not determine the purpose of the manipulation. The end event was hidden from her, no matter how she shifted the data, no matter how many times she ran scenarios or evaluated logic flows.

It made her want to kick something. Throw something. Scream at the top of her lungs, until the empty hallways rang with her frustration.

Instead she tapped her keyboard in irritation, closely trimmed nails making a dull clicking noise against the plastic, then went back to inputting raw data.

"You really need to relax a little."

She had heard him coming down the hallway; while everyone asked for her on jobs, damned few of them came to visit her. She preferred it that way.

"Are you relaxed?" She didn't really care if he was or

not, it was just habit with her, to mine out any available nugget, no matter how seemingly useless.

"I never relax."

She shrugged then, as though to say, "Well, there you are." He sat down behind her, on the stool she used in order to reach things her delicate four-foot, five-inch frame could not manage, and she gritted her teeth in irritation. Of all the rudeness…

To return that rudeness, she kept working. But the space between her shoulder blades itched.

"Why are you working so hard on this?"

"Because Andre asked." That was a no-brainer. Andre needed something, she provided it. End of story. Besides, it was a challenge. So little in life was a challenge, anymore.

"Good answer. Loyal answer. But loyalty's not the only driving force in life. Sometimes, you have to take care of yourself, too. Andre understands that."

Andre exemplified that. Andre took good care of himself. Taking good care of himself meant taking good care of Darcy. Her fingers didn't pause, her eyes still scanning the screen-in-screen for new info, even as she was inputting what she already knew into the existing database, building and refining the available information.

Into that database she added the following fact: Andre cannot rely on his second in command any longer.

And then: knowing I would enter this, he came to me anyway. Which means…what?

Another bit of the puzzle, to wriggle out.

Darcy heard Jorgunmunder leave, but didn't bother to

acknowledge him. He had sounded her out. She had given her answer. They would both do what they needed to do.

That was how the world worked.

Noodles used to be a tiny little hole in the wall: one cook-owner, Jimmy, two interchangeable delivery people, and an ancient figure of unknown gender sitting in the back, writing the fortunes that were far too accurate for anyone's comfort. If it weren't for the fact that Noodles also had the undisputed best Chinese food in all of Manhattan—no small feat, that—Wren would refuse to have anything to do with the place. Or so she told herself.

Over the summer, Noodles had moved into a larger space down the street, effectively doubling the kitchen space, and adding a dining area. It was strange to actually sit at a table, with chairs, to eat Jimmy's food. The balance of the universe was set askew, somehow. But the space was clean, and the tables had paper tablecloths you could doodle on, and the waiter was actually reasonably unsurly, for all that he spoke not a word of English.

And, more to the point, they were fatae-friendly. In fact, the waiter, without them having to ask, found and brought over a backless stool for Shigenoi to use comfortably.

Sergei, for once in his entire life, was late.

"You want to bet he went to the old spot?" P.B. said.

"Sergei would never do something like that. Only major disasters make him late to anything." Which was a terrible thing to hope for, but if he had forgotten about the move… Wren wasn't sure her system could take another shock, today.

They had just settled among themselves what they were going to order, and were starting on the bowl of fried noodles, when Sergei finally did walk in. His eyes bulged out almost as much as Shig's when he saw the fatae sitting with them, but had remastered his cool by the time he crossed the dining room and sat down. Wren had to give him props; her partner might have been a bigot, but he was one who was trying really hard to change. So did that make him a bigot, actually? Or just misguided at an impressionable age?

"Glad you could join us," she said.

"Sorry—Lowell had a question about the new database he absolutely needed answered before we went any further with the new installation, and…" He shrugged, indicating his helplessness in the face of his assistant's determination.

All right, it wasn't a major disaster. But the idea of Lowell being a pain and a jerk kept her universe in balance anyway.

"Hello. I am Seiichi Shigenoi."

Sergei, who had just sat down, stood up again when Shig did, then pressed his hands together, palms facing each other, and made a shallow bow. "Konbanwa, Seiichi-san."

I really do love this man, Wren thought, handing him a menu. He barely even looked at it, ordering kung pao chicken and a bottle of Tsing Tao.

"So, how do you know these two?" he asked Shig, handing the menu to the hovering waiter and pouring himself a cup of tea.

As P.B. had predicted, Sergei immediately glommed

onto the fact that Shig was in the import/export field, and started pumping him for information on Japanese customs and import laws.

"You thinking about expanding the gallery?" Wren asked, when the two of them finally paused for breath.

"If I had an agent in Asia whose judgment I could trust?" Sergei shrugged, not indicating yes or no. "A smart businessman always keeps his ears and eyes and options open."

The waiter came then with their appetizers, which they fell on like nobody had been fed in a week. Since Wren knew what P.B. had stolen from her fridge the day before, she was less than sympathetic.

"My metabolism is different," he protested, when ribbed about how much food he had ordered. "I have to eat a lot. Look, not an inch of me is fat!" He offered his arm to be pinched, for proof. Sergei and Shig both declined, but Wren reached out and gave his arm a thick pinch-and-twist, until he yelped.

"What was that for?"

"I don't know, but odds are you did something today that deserved it."

"They are related?" Shig asked Sergei, who almost choked on a bite of Wren's shrimp-roll appetizer, which he had snitched off her plate. "Not that you could prove it," he finally said, after washing down the offending bit with a sip of tea, "but I've often wondered."

"Bite me entirely," P.B. said.

"Hey. Where do *you* get off being offended at being related to *me*?" Wren asked, mock-offended.

"Children. Eat."

Sergei's voice was indulgent, amused, but when Wren looked closely at him, she noted lines over his hawk's nose that hadn't been there a few days ago, and a drawn cast to his face that was worrisome. Plus, beer. On a weeknight. She rethought her decision to bring him into the matter of the Artifact. It would only worry him more.

And if—when—he finds out, after? If you've kept things from him not once, but twice?

Shut up and stop being so practical, she told the voice that sounded suspiciously like her mother this time, watching the waiter hand around platters of deliciously steaming food. *I'll wait until he's finished dinner. He's always calmer while he's digesting.*

"Gods above and below, this smells good. It never smells this good the day after in the fridge."

"Maybe if you ever bought any of it for yourself, instead of cadging off me like the endless stomach of a mooch you are, it would smell better?"

P.B. actually considered that for a whole sixty seconds before shaking his head. "Nah...."

Shig looked both fascinated and frightened, as though discovering some particular dangerous snake performing street theater. She supposed, in a way, he had.

He's such a little brat, she sent along a pulse of current, unsure if that means of Talent-to-Talent communication would work with a nonhuman. From the way he carefully busied himself with his chopsticks to hide one of those weird amphibian smiles, she figured it did.

Most unique, your relationship, he sent back, his silent

words flavored with a feeling of understatement, and the scent of damp moss. Interesting. Most humans smelled, psychically, of dryer things, like sand and red wine and fresh-mown grass.

Oh yeah, he's one of a kind, that demon.

As are you.

She bowed her head slightly in acknowledgment of the compliment, unsure of how far to take it without turning the brief exchange into an uncomfortable love-fest. To delay the decision, she scooped her chopsticks into the orange chicken for second helpings when P.B. changed the topic entirely, for the entire table.

"So, Wren, what are you gonna tell your client about the Artifact, anyway?"

"P.B., you little pissant piece of dead meat…"

Sergei's eyebrow went directly into his immaculately groomed and gelled hairline.

"Client?"

His voice was calm, only vaguely inquisitive, and if Wren hadn't sworn it was impossible, P.B.'s fur turned an even paler shade of white at the sound of it.

"Your timing sucks, old, soon-to-be-dead *pal.*"

"Um. It's a gift." He swallowed, then got indignant, his tufted ears practically quivering with it. "Hey, how was I supposed to know— How the hell, no, *why* the hell are you taking on clients without Sergei's knowing about it? That's not how the universe works, damn it! You're messing with my reality!"

Despite the not-as-she-planned-it nature of his revelation, Wren hoped that she would be able to salvage something. So she was totally unprepared for the expression on Sergei's face.

The bastard was *amused!* Pissed, yeah, but she knew those cocoa-dust eyes. He was trying really, really hard not to laugh. Her, or at P.B., she didn't know, but rather than being relieved, she felt herself getting angry. Why wasn't *he* angry at being left out of the loop?

"We'll talk later," was all he said, and went back to his kung pao, turning to discuss trans-Pacific shipping routes and import rates with a clearly relieved Shig.

Wren kicked the demon under the table, her legs barely reaching underneath to his own shorter ones, and went back to her own meal.

"Why am I always the one who gets kicked?" P.B. asked the universe at large, then waved down the waiter for more tea before anyone could explain it to him.

After the day he'd had—fending off Lowell with one hand, and Andre with the other—Sergei had not wanted to go anywhere but home. Much to his surprise, the dinner had been an enjoyable interlude, and even P.B.'s revelation of what his partner had been up to hadn't been enough to spoil the relaxed mood he was in.

Besides, he had known that she was up to something. Wren was only ever that casual when she was trying to keep a secret.

He was even feeling mellow enough to pick up the check. Not that there was much choice to it; P.B. was a mooch, Shig probably was on limited funds, and it was just habit for him to pick up Wren's share, especially now.

She let him only because it was easier than arguing about it. He appreciated that about her, that she could pick and choose the battles. He'd just put it against his commission from this unknown client.

"You two be careful," he said to the fatae as they parted outside Noodles. He didn't think they'd have any trouble—the last time the vigilantes tried to go after P.B., it had ended badly for them, not the demon—but that had been months ago. Stupid people didn't learn from examples.

"Yessir," P.B. said, only a little mockingly, and the humans watched while their companions made their way up the neon-lit street, weaving in and out of clumps of humans, clearly involved in some sort of lively discussion, from the way Shig's hands were moving.

He turned to his partner, gesturing for her to start walking alongside him. She did, silently, not leaning in towards him the way she usually did.

Oh, hell, he thought. *What now?* He looked down, and saw that her face was back in the pensive, not-talking-to-you mode. He bit back a sigh.

"What?" she asked, not looking at him.

"What, what?" All right, that wasn't quite fair. He knew exactly what she was whating about—she could hear a sigh, even internal, ten paces away.

Wren walked a few more steps down the sidewalk. They had, without discussion, headed for the subway up to Sergei's apartment. "You're supposed to be pissed at me."

"Why?" he asked as reasonably as he could, mainly just to see the steam rise from her ears. It was bad form, to pick a fight with your partner, but sometimes it was also needful. She'd been chewing on this all through dinner; better to let her get it out of her system now, rather than let it build any more. He'd never seen her so upset over such a little thing—she'd even forgotten to open her fortune cookie, and she usually just *had* to know what was coming, claiming that putting off one of Jimmy's fortunes just made whatever was coming down the road at you hit that much harder.

Impossible, even if you did believe in predetermined fates, but she was usually stubborn enough about it that he didn't disagree.

Reminding her of that fortune now, though, would be very, very bad poker.

She kicked at something invisible on the street. "Because I'm not supposed to take on jobs without you!"

"No, you're not." He was, vocally, calmly agreeable. Guaranteed to piss her off. "But you did anyway. Were you looking to cut me out of the commission?" He hoped not. That would be tacky.

"No! I was going to tell you." She reached up to pull at her braid, then let her hand fall. "Eventually. When…"

"When what? When you had proven something to yourself? To me?"

"It wasn't like that." But he could hear in her voice that it was, at least a little bit.

"Oh, for…" Sometimes, she drove him insane. "Do you remember why we both agreed on how we do business? Jobs matched to strengths, not weaknesses? We each have our specializations, Wrenlet, and negotiating contracts? Not yours, to say the least."

As he spoke, he felt a coal-hot heat rising up from somewhere in his chest. He *was* angry, after all, although clearly nowhere near what she expected from him. And that thought made him even angrier, that she had thought he'd be—

"What, did you think I was going to take you over my knee?"

Wren turned a sullen expression up to him. "I thought you were going to yell at me, yeah. Which is exactly what you're doing!"

"I am not—!" He stopped, realizing that he, in fact, was yelling. He took a deep breath, then another. They didn't help.

"Jesus, Valere, you'd drive a saint to psychedelics. Yes, I'm angry, damn it! We're in the middle of some sort of gang warfare, Council against lonejacks, and you've put yourself not only in the middle of it, but leading the damn charge! And don't give me that bullshit about not being a leader, because everyone except you knows you're the one they're looking to for answers. Not to mention the fact that you hang around with nonhumans who have damned targets painted on every inch of their bodies for this damned vigilante group, and then you go and take a damned job without clearing it with me and then go *do* this damned job without telling me, and what makes you think I want a partner with a damned death wish?"

"I do not have a death wish!"

"Then you're an idiot."

Wren was, literally, spitting mad. Sparks rose from her skin, looking iron-red and painful. Current wasn't a tamed thing; as far as he'd been able to understand, the best you could work for was to stay in control and convince it that you were the one leading the dance. Most days, it worked. That was what mentorship was all about, apparently, convincing you that it worked.

"If you didn't hover so damn much—"

"Me? Hover? I do my damned job."

"Is that what I am now? A job?" Wren stopped dead in the street, staring incredulously at her partner.

"Ah, for the love of... Genevieve. You *know* that's not true." He stopped as well, but refused to look at her, staring instead out into the street, at the evening traffic passing by.

"You didn't even notice I had a job, did you? I wasn't even registering on whatever's important in your life right now..."

She hit a nerve with that one, and he knew she knew it, had seen the way his body jerked upright, just the littlest bit, but she was ready for it; she was looking for it. A damned good poker player, her partner, but even he had his tells.

"All right, now you're just being insane," he said, stung equally by the fact that she thought it, and that it was, at least a little bit, true.

The moment the words came out of his mouth, Sergei knew he'd made a terrible mistake, even before the current-sparks hit him.

"Na huy...?" He'd been hit by a taser once, part of his

training with the Silence, and he'd always thought that was what it might be like to be on the receiving end of a pissed-off Talent.

He'd underestimated.

Talent didn't go insane. They wizzed. Wren's mentor had wizzed, leaving her the lonejack equivalent of an orphan at sixteen. He couldn't have hit a more open wound if he'd studied for years. Which, he supposed, he had.

"Ohmygod." Wren, on her knees next to him. Funny, he didn't remember going down to the pavement. Pedestrians looked at them curiously, one or two of them looking as though they meant to come forward to help, but giving it second thought at the sight of Wren, still sparking. Now, the sparks were—he squinted, not sure if it was her, or his sight being wonky, but it was as though she was surrounded by an entire kaleidoscope of colors, popping and hissing at him.

"You're all sparkly," he said, half in awe, half in warning.

"Are you burned? Did I burn you anywhere?"

She fumbled with his shirt, unbuttoning the cuffs to check his arms, then moving on to his chest.

"Dizzy. Wanna go home."

"Right." She helped him up, and with his arm slung over her shoulders, taking a portion of his weight, he could feel her shaking. A cab stopped—did she call it? How long had they been waiting?—and he felt himself fall forward into the seat. She climbed in after, and gave the cabbie his address.

By the time they got to his building, Sergei was feeling a little more himself, but the ziiizing of the current-slap still resonated under his skin in strange ways. Not like it did when they had sex, although there were similarities. And he was absolutely, positively hard as a rock.

Probably not the time to mention that to Wren, though.

The high-speed elevator made him woozy all over again, but he leaned against the wall and concentrated on the nausea going away, and it did.

Now, if he could only will away the soreness on his skin and in his muscles, everything would be just peachy. As far as ending fights went, this was effective, but probably not practical on a regular application.

"I think…we need to save this for extra-special arguments," he said, his voice sounding huskier than usual, even to his own ears.

"We're not doing that ever again."

"What, arguing?"

That got a snort out of her, at least. "We never used to argue."

"I like it when we argue," Sergei said, skidding off his shoes and leaving them by the foot of the stairs before beginning the slow climb up the spiral staircase to his loft bedroom. Wren was right behind him, in case he couldn't make it. "It means you're standing up to me, not just taking every damn thing I say as gospel. Nothin' worse than that. Nothin' more boring than that." He was starting to slur his words, something he normally did only after multiple shots of something much harder, and wetter, than current.

His partner laughed, a shaky, not-quite-certain laugh,

but a laugh nonetheless, and he could feel the tension in her begin to ebb. What he had intended to do, before he lost his temper, but not quite in such an…extreme way. For all that getting slammed by current was a rush—all right, he admitted it, probably a kink—it was also damned dangerous, and more than a little stupid. Fortunately it seemed to be very specific to current with Wren's touch in it, not just any Joe or Jane Talent.

She sat him down on the bed and carefully stripped off his shirt, checking more thoroughly for current-burns. There was a tube of ointment in the table by the bed, and she uncapped it and started spreading the cool gel on his skin without comment.

She had a soothingly light touch, none of her anger at herself translating to him. If he hadn't known her so well, he'd have thought that she was perfectly calm. There seemed to be an awful lot of skin she was covering—he didn't think she had hit him that hard.

Then again, he was having a difficult time thinking at all.

"Need somethin' t' drink."

"Yeah. Hang on."

She went back down the stairs, and he heard her rummaging in the kitchen, below. When she returned, she had a glass of ginger ale in one hand, and a pitcher of something in the other.

"Soda first, then water. Drink as much as you can handle. I should have thought of this right away."

"Ne' time, we'll know."

"There's not going to be a next time." Her voice was tight, brittle as old leaves.

Control, he remembered. Control was the almighty thing with lonejacks. She had lost control, and that was what she was angry at. Not him.

"Shhh…" He put the glass down on the table and reached for her. She resisted a moment, then gave way, sliding onto the bed with him, so he could enclose her in his arms. "It's okay, Wrenlet. It's okay to be angry."

"No, it's not. It's…"

He silenced her with a hand across her mouth, gently enough that she could have broken his hold without effort. She nipped at his palm, but without real vigor, then reached up and moved the offending palm, just enough to speak clearly.

"Go to sleep, Sergei."

Wise advice. He could barely keep his eyes open, no matter how important it was that they get this dealt with.

His eyes closed, and his hand slid from her mouth down to her shoulder, adjusting his hold on her.

A thought roused him, sleepily, long enough to ask, "Did you get a percentage up-front?"

She sighed. "Yes. Already deposited and cleared. Rest should be coming as soon as I inform the client that the job's completed."

"Goo'girl"

She whapped him halfheartedly with a pillow, and he went back to sleep, content.

As his breathing evened out, Wren settled next to him, one hand stroking his hair.

She hadn't gotten a fortune cookie. That was unheard of, from Jimmy's. It worried her.

Sergei had gotten one, but tucked it into his pocket without sharing it with her. That was also unusual. And worrying.

Across the city, two beings were settled in for the night as well, although it involved two ceramic cups of chilled sake and a pair of comfortable leather hassocks.

"So. What did your fortune say?"

"What?" Shig had been inspecting the bottom or his cup, as though expecting more sake to suddenly appear.

"Your fortune. The thing that came in the cookie, after dinner. What did it say?"

"It's important?"

"Absolutely.

The amphibian fatae closed his internal eyelids and recalled a memory. "'You will dance on edge of disaster, but learn many new steps.'"

"Huh. Interesting, but nothing too horribly dramatic. Be thankful. Mine was actually boring. That always worries me. A lot."

"And The Wren's? I saw you sneak her cookie, after they left."

"You think it works that way? If I take it, it's mine, even though it was put on her plate?

"If this Seer is as good as you think he is, then he might have known you would do so. Or he cannot focus on such small, short-term moments, and did not know, in which case it is hers. In either situation, she is not here to read it, and you are."

Tough logic to argue with, even from a gecko sitting on a hassock, chewing thoughtfully on a bamboo stalk.

"Right." He reached into his pocket and broke open the cookie.

"What does it say?"

"'This fortune not for you.'"

"You are making fun of me."

P.B. wordlessly handed his friend the slip of paper.

"I would take this Seer quite seriously," Shig said, thoughtfully.

"Yeah. Yeah, we do," P.B. said, collapsing back onto his bed and staring up at the ceiling. "We do."

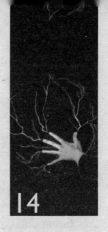

14

The next morning was a quiet one. Sergei woke up first, but came out of the shower to find Wren already sitting at the kitchen table, poking absently at a bowl of cold cereal with her spoon.

He finished toweling off, then draped the towel over his shoulder and leaned against the wall, watching her. His apartment was on an open plan, so there was no real wall dividing the spaces. It made for good paranoid planning, or ballroom dancing, but lousy for leaning indolently in a doorway, since there weren't actually any to lean in.

"You want me to make you some eggs?"

"Nah. Thanks. Not really very hungry, anyway." Her voice was even, noncommittal.

"Suit yourself." He went to the refrigerator and started pulling out supplies. Time to face the music, as it were. He was many things, of variable social acceptability, but his mother had raised neither a coward nor a hypocrite.

If he was going to be angry at her for trying to go out on her own, locking him out—and it amused him again, briefly, that he was angry about that, and not the keeping secrets thing—well, it meant that he had to own up to a few side ventures of his own, too.

In his pants pocket, a tiny scrap of paper had a short, succinct message: "Bring it on." Jimmy's Seer, the mysterious figure who wrote all his fortune cookie messages, never made sense; but always gave good advice. Assuming you could figure it out.

Bring it on. Right. Face it, he supposed the Seer meant. Stop ducking and dancing around what needed to be done.

It was damned easy to write a fortune. Tougher, always tougher, to deal with it.

By the time he had finished scrambling the eggs and dicing the leftover grilled salmon, she was salivating like a starveling kitten, as expected.

As good a time as any, he supposed.

Time to rinse the skillet, and leave it to dry before turning to face her again. "You're not the only one keeping secrets, beloved."

Wren didn't even stop shoveling the food into her mouth, the cereal pushed, half-eaten and forgotten, to the side of the table in favor of the savory plate in front of her.

"You have another woman on the side?" She wasn't taking him seriously. Not yet.

"It's the Silence."

That got her attention, fast. She didn't quite put down the fork, but her rate of consumption slowed noticeably.

"What now? I'm not taking on another job for them. Not now. Maybe not ever."

Not even if she had to give up the damn retainer. She still hadn't forgiven Andre for showing up at Lee's wake. He could hear the litany as easily as if she'd spoken it out loud again. The bastard. Oily, overfriendly, condescending cold-blooded bastard. Not that she was bitter, or anything.

"Genevieve." That got her full attention; he knew it would. "Andre's asked me to come back to the Silence." Before she could splutter anything, he went on. "He thinks that he's being undermined from within. That someone's trying to subvert the Silence to a personal agenda. And cutting him out. That's why we didn't get enough information on the last situation. None of the Ops with Talent are getting full disclosure."

He leaned back against the counter, and waited.

She stabbed her fork into the salmon and eggs with renewed vigor, carefully not replying until she'd run through a choice few retorts in her head, and discarded them.

"And I'm supposed to care about this—why?" He was still a bastard. And he was maybe even more of a bastard, for trying to get to Sergei without her. She'd warned him about that, when he tried to get her away from Sergei. They were a pair. A partnership.

You haven't been acting that way, recently, a little voice told her. *Which he knows, now. Why are you expecting Andre to do any different, when it's not in his best interest?*

Oh, shut up, she told the voice. *I'm not in the mood to be logical. Or forgiving.*

"You aren't," Sergei said to what she had actually said

out loud. But his voice said differently. His voice said he wanted everything in his world to go smoothly, all the bits and pieces of it to play nicely together.

She would do almost anything for her partner. Especially after the current incident last night. Almost. "Forget about it, Sergei. The bastard wants absolution for screwing us over. I'm not giving it to him."

"Wren, think about it." He took his own plate to the counter, sat down. "If there are factions moving within the Silence…"

"If? You told me once that everything within the Silence was layers and layers, secrets on secrets."

"All right. Point taken. Doesn't lessen the fact that anything that can make Andre uneasy is something that makes me uneasy, even at a remove. Especially since thanks to that damned contract I drew up, they can still call on you—and we have no guarantee that we'll get the full dossier then, either. Not if Andre hasn't tracked down the source and neutralized it."

"You say that like it's an odor. 'Neutralized' it." Her distaste was plain.

"All right. Taken steps to normalize the situation. Does that sound better?"

Wren relented. "No. But at least it's a little more honest." She didn't know for certain, but what exposure she'd had to Andre and his henchboy Poul, not to mention the way Sergei reacted to anything Silence-related, suggested that their ways of "normalizing" the situation often had more to do with the handgun her partner still owned than any kind of verbal negotiations. "So why tell me now? Secret for secret? Or did you agree to anything I need to know about?"

Sergei shrugged helplessly, shoving food around on his own plate. He was sitting across the counter from her, elbows on the marble in a rare show of relaxed manners that was contradicted by the obvious strain in his spine and the set of his shoulders. "I didn't want you distracted, that's why I didn't tell you." Then, with the air of a can being pried open, "I don't like working apart from you, not telling you things. Makes me break out in hives."

"Those aren't secrets, Didier, those are your burns, healing." *And I can give you more if you don't watch it* was implicit in her words; she heard the threat, and flinched from it. He, predictably, didn't. Not really a threat, if he liked it. Although that wasn't fair. It wasn't pain he liked, as far as she could bring herself to figure it out. It was the risk, the tinge of danger to go with the passion. Which she supposed she could understand. A little. Maybe. Although not the pain part of it.

The silence went on too long, after her comment, and she was starting to get uncomfortable.

"He came to see me. Andre."

"What?"

"Uh-huh." She wasn't hungry anymore, as good as the food still smelled. "He showed up on my doorstep, literally, couple days ago." She counted back, mentally. Before the busted job, the afternoon P.B. got himself busted. "Two days ago."

"And you're just now telling…" He visibly caught

himself. "Right. I think we're destined to be living examples of why really good sex doesn't always indicate perfect communications."

Another direct hit for the guy-side of the team.

"And what did Andre have to say for himself, to you?"

She shrugged. "I didn't really let him say much of anything. I think he was on a make-nice mission. Which, based on the timing of what you're telling me, I think means he was trying to butter me up so I'd green-light you going back to work for him, with my blessings."

"I told him—" Sergei's frustration was clear. The bastard *had* been playing both of them independently.

"And I told him again. I don't think he's listening." Her voice softened with a curious blend of regret and pride. "He really needs you. I don't think he ever let go of you, not really."

"He invested a lot in training me." Sergei's tone was calm, neutral, and Wren felt herself getting angry all over again.

"You're going to do it, aren't you? You're going to help him. No matter what I say or do."

"I don't know yet."

"You don't know? Jesus wept, Didier, he—"

"He's not the Silence. He's a man. And, more to the point, he's a man who has in the past and can in the future do us some good. That's the bottom line." She had not only touched a nerve, she'd zinged it, hard, to get that kind of flat-line reaction.

"So." *Self-control. Focus.* Stop the cycle now, damn it. "What happens now?"

Her partner sat back and regarded her with a steady gaze. "I don't know." They'd had fights before. They'd even had serious arguments before. But this was a strange roadblock of the sort they weren't used to, another person coming between them, paths seemingly diverging, and neither of them seemed to know how to move it. "I think this is where we're supposed to run out to the bookstore and buy a relationship self-help book."

"'When Your Secret Lives Conflict With Romance'?"

She shrugged, and picked up her fork again, even though the eggs had gone cold and she had no appetite.

"We used to be a good team, Wren. Well-oiled. Fast to respond. What happened? And don't say sex, because that's a cop-out. Besides, the sex is where it's still damn good."

Wren laughed, as he meant her to, but there was sadness in it as well. "Don't need a book to tell you that, smart guy. It used to be just the two of us. For a well-trained Silence lackey dedicated to the Good of the Many, you adapted really well, really fast to the lonejack code."

"First, worry about yourself. And all the related jazz that goes with enlightened self-interest."

"Yeah."

"It's a good code." He had thought so from the very moment he head heard it, burned-out from the Silence's insistence on the Larger Picture above and before all other considerations.

"It's a *smart* code, anyway. Not so sure how good it is." She shrugged. "Useless point of debate, now. More players. More things to consider. More obligations."

"Obligations that bind both of us," Sergei said. "Even when only one of us makes them."

Ouch. All right, so they were back on the clock, original-argument-wise, then. Claiming that he wasn't involved in all this would be pointless, and also stupid. Even if they sometimes forgot that they came as a matched set, nobody else did.

"Look. I just…"

Sergei reached out and snagged Wren around the waist, pulling her off her chair and onto his lap.

"Hey!"

Then whatever she was going to say got muffled by his mouth on hers. He tasted salty-sweet, like eggs and ketchup, and those narrow lips were way too familiar with the kind of kiss she liked.

By the time he eased his hold on her, they'd settled that discussion. So much for self-help books.

"So. How much did you soak the client for?"

Wren rested her head against his shoulder, feeling the slow thud of his heart all the way down into her bones, and felt absurdly, impossibly at peace.

"You'd have gotten more. But I need to Retrieve it, first. She's going to move, now, if she hasn't already. I fucked up."

"You had an unexpected interference in the execution of the job. Not the first time. Probably won't be the last, although we're getting better on our percentages. Can I help?"

Sometimes he couldn't. Sometimes, having another brain—a sneaky, left-brained, cold-blooded reptile brain—was exactly what was needed. She reached out and pulled her bag to within easy reach and pulled the papers out. "Here. Look at this."

He looked. "The Artifact P.B. mentioned?"

"Yeah."

"All right. So this is the focus. Where would target make a run for, knowing someone's after it?"

They were back in the groove, she could feel it. Too easy, far too easy, and there would be things to deal with later, under the surface, but they were grooving again, and that was the important thing.

"Second home, out of the city. Full suburban territory, better than standard guards, although nothing expansive. Probably the husband's doing—she seemed the trusting sort." Although not so trusting that she'd stick around, now.

"She's not the sort to be able to throw everything into a bag and flit. Apartment will need to be closed up, unless she keeps the maid there."

"She's a live-in?"

"Five days a week, on a flex schedule. So maybe, yeah. But even so, it takes time to pack up a wardrobe like hers. But she won't be more than forty-eight hours, even if she has to call ahead to get the house in the 'burbs all aired out and provisioned. There's a staff of three, there. Maid, cook, and guy-of-all-else. They all live off-site. I guess housing's not such an incentive out there."

"You want to wait, make a try for it there?"

"Tempting," Wren said thoughtfully. "It's in the same area that damned horse was last seen in, I could double up my workload…"

"You and that damned horse." A stuffed horse from way back in the whateverish medieval period, in full prancing regalia, that appeared wherever something bad was about to happen. Wren had been chasing it for years now, to the point where even the original clients had given up. But she was determined, someday, to track the damned thing down and Retrieve it. It was a matter of pride with her, now. "I hear a 'but' in your voice."

"But I get the feeling that it needs to be done fast."

Sergei looked down at her. "The necklace?"

"Is bad stuff, maybe, yeah. But…I don't want to be out of the city, if I don't have to be."

Sergei clearly wanted to comment on her feelings, but took one look at her expression and moved on.

"So, a second pass at the town house. But she's going to be on her guard."

"Yeah." Wren got up off his lap and started to pace around the kitchen. She picked her fork up again and slapped the back of it thoughtfully against her palm as she spoke, like a conductor using a baton. "Yeah. She's going to be extremely guarded. Especially if she knows it's another Talent who's going after it. But…is she going to know that? The Client's a Null. Total Null, didn't feel the psi-bomb coming at all, had no clue after. Doesn't know anything about the necklace being an Artifact."

"Are you sure?" That was her Sergei, always willing to be the cynical one.

Wren recalled Rosen's face, the look in her eyes when she saw Wren sitting in her stepmother's parlor. "Pretty sure. Almost definite. She doesn't have the feel of a manipulator, except as how she's young, attractive, and wealthy. Anything twitchy, she's being twitched from the outside."

Sergei raised one of those well-groomed eyebrows, asking a question.

"No. It's not that kind of Artifact." Not actively malevolent, like the parchment they'd been sent after, that had taken all the ill-will in the city and fed on it. "I was only near it for a second, I know, but it felt like pure power. Untapped, untainted."

"Wait a minute." Sergei raised a hand as though asking teacher a question. "I thought you said power took on the personality of the user."

Wren nodded, realizing that she was now using the fork like a pointer, and put it back down on the table before she did damage with it, accidentally. "It does. The moment you touch current, it conforms to your specific tone, your individual signature. After a while it can fade."

"Or not," Sergei said, remembering the madness of the Talent who had wielded the last thing of power they'd dealt with.

"Or not. But this one's pretty clean. Which means whoever's been holding this—presumably the target, since the client's mother died years ago and the father isn't likely to be wearing anything as…distinctly female as this necklace—hasn't been using it."

Sergei looked all sorts of thoughtful again. "I like this woman already."

"Yeah." Wren shoved her hands in her pockets and stared at her toes. "Me, too."

Someone who could hold an object of power, and not touch it, not even just to run her fingers through the pretty fire? Maybe, just maybe, she should be leaving the Artifact with Melanie. Except that wasn't the job. And the job had to get done, or her reputation—the only thing she had, the thing her life was built on—was gone. Who would hire a Retriever who got sudden moral qualms about what she was sent to Retrieve?

Morality. Responsibility. Familial ties. There was something she was missing in all this.

Melanie cared about her stepdaughter. She was a Talent, a Council Talent. But not a powerful one. Not in the high-and-mighty ranks. Not in the loop. Keep things out of the loop, or they become corrupted.

Power corrupts, but we need electricity. Even funnier to a Talent, that joke.

"It's not about the magic."

Sergei looked up from the pencil rendition. "It's not?" His expressive eyebrows got all expressive again.

"Anna. Why she's doing this. It's a mom thing," Wren said. "Your dad marries someone else, there's always this feeling of disloyalty. Or…something." She shrugged. "You're the one who told me to take that psychology elective in college."

"But you said that she liked her stepmother. Originally."

"Yeah. Especially then."

Sergei was no slouch at following logic trails. "She

feels guilty about liking the woman who replaced her mother, especially since the new woman is a Talent, unlike her mother—and unlike her. Someone the client thinks might be seen as a better match to her father. And her father's dead now, so he can't ease those fears. So she's overreacting to this one thing, that she may or may not actively care about, in order to strike back."

"You're starting to scare me, Didier." That had been *exactly* what she had been thinking. Oh, Anna had her own reasons to want the necklace—even a Null had to know it was of some value, somehow. But this made her behavior make sense.

Not that any of it mattered, in the long run.

"Does it worry you that in less than a year we've run into two different Artifacts?" This, and the Nescanni Parchment, which had been an Artifact of a much nastier sort.

"No. Should it?"

"Yes." Wren was certain about that. Artifacts weren't exactly thick on the ground, even in Talent-crowded Manhattan, home of eclectic collections both public and private.

"All right, I'm worried. What am I worrying about?"

"Just worry in general. That's what you're good at—worrying while I rush in."

"Like an angel?"

"Very funny." Angeli only rushed in when they scented blood.

Sergei was worried, actually. But he could see that something was turning over in her brain, and relaxed a little. She'd been stuck, but he had faith she'd get loose again, out of the rut and back on track. He set up the deals, but she was the one who executed them. Although he'd be there when she needed *his* skills—or a grounding influence, whether she wanted to admit it or not. "So. Got any plans for later tonight?"

Wren nodded slightly, her lips beginning to turn up in a smile that her partner knew very well—knew, and had missed seeing, recently. Oh, yeah. Goodbye, rut.

"Yeah. Yeah, I think I do. And so do you. Cancel whatever you thought you were doing today. And did you get Shig's contact info?"

If they expect you at night, go during the day. If they're double-locking the windows, go in through the front door.

The Wren always worked alone. Except when she didn't.

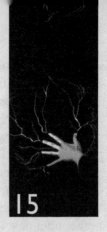

15

The moving van was smaller than Wren had expected, but it was still perfectly placed by the curb, a smidge too close to the fire hydrant, and the movers were perfectly out of central casting: two young guys and one older but still bulky with muscles, all of them clearly related on the Mediterranean side. They shouted to each other in a language Wren didn't know but suspected that Sergei would. He kept pulling languages out of his hip pocket, just to, she suspected, annoy her.

The sun was warm overhead, but the air was November-crisp, and if she hadn't been so tightly wound up inside, she might have stretched like a cat for sheer hedonistic pleasure of the day. A good solid meal inside her, the sitch with Sergei all warm if not fuzzy, and a job on the plate and a Retrieval in play. Life really didn't get any better than this. Assuming you could forget all the

Cosa shit piled high and deep, just waiting to be stepped in. But for now, in this instant, everything was perfect.

And there was the target, looking only slightly harried and not the least sleep deprived in pressed chinos and a dark blue, gauzy-looking shirt. She came down the steps of the building, clearly giving the older man directions on the handling of the boxes he was carting out. He looked unimpressed by her words.

The moment the target had cleared the building, Wren shifted her position slightly, still to all intents and purposes lounging against the bumper of a candy-red sedan that was screaming "ticket me," but minutely more alert, as though she were a Prohibition-era lookout who had just seen a cop coming around the corner

That was how P.B. would have described it, anyway. He was the only one on the street who had any knowledge of Prohibition firsthand—had, in fact, been a lookout for several local speakeasies in his day—and it wasn't relevant, so he was quietly amused by the fact and kept it to himself.

The shift, minute even if you were able to focus on Wren, was their signal to start the action.

"*Oi!* Help! Someone help!"

The first rule in a mugging was yell "fire!" at the top of your lungs. People would come out and look at a fire. They're not always certain to look at a mugging. But in this case, they didn't want too many people looking. Just the right ones.

Shig staggered out from the alley, holding a hand up to his head and looking dazed. At least, P.B. thought he was trying to look dazed. Or drunk. Tough to tell. Sergei was right behind him, moving hard, one hand raised up as though to catch the fatae by the shoulder, and clearly not with friendly intent.

Watching, knowing that it was all staged, P.B. still felt a surge of alarm. Sergei could be a mean-looking bastard, when he wanted to.

"Ugly abomination," Sergei said, just loud enough to carry. It was a risk, this plan. But all the best plans were risky, it seemed. Risk went hand in hand with payoff. Shig was a newcomer to the city. Sergei, at first glance and unless you knew Wren well, was just another human. But if the target had done any of her own homework…

"Leave me alone!" Shig cried again, adding a whine of pain to his voice, and two of the three movers turned to look, a young one, and the older guy. The other man was in the truck itself, and probably couldn't hear.

The target stopped, midscold, and turned to look as well, just as Shig did a half-turn and threw himself up against the wall. It looked, from a distance, as though Sergei had done the tossing. Not bad for only a few hours' of practice.

"Morgan," the younger man said, half in warning, half "look at that" mode. But neither of them showed any surprise at all. P.B. wondered if they were used to seeing fatae: he thought he knew most of the *Cosa*-owned business in town, and Menachem Moving wasn't one of them, but you could never tell with individual employees.

The older man—Morgan—stepped forward, his stride the movement of a man trained to use his body to do more than haul furniture, and clearly not going to help out Sergei.

P.B. tensed. He was far too well-known to be involved in the stagework. His role in all this was to keep anyone from getting significantly damaged, no matter what side they were playing for. If that meant tackling a human whose only crime was to try to prevent an apparent beating, well, he'd apologize to the guy later.

Although it would make for some very weird human-fatae relationship twists in an already pretzel-shaped world.

It looked as though he wasn't going to be needed, though; the target had put a hand on the older guy's arm, pulling him back. Typical Council bitch, not wanting even her hirelings to get their hands dirty on a fatae getting what she probably thought he deserved—

And then Sergei staggered back like he'd been slapped with a giant hand, arms flailing as he tried to keep his balance. The expression on his face was surprise, followed hard-on by a calculating sort of relief.

Current. Someone had used current to stop him. And since it wasn't Shig, who would have had no reason to, and it didn't seem to be either of the movers, it had to have been one of the only two other known Talents on the street.

Wren, which was unlikely as to be impossible, or— the target. Who stood there, eyes locked on Sergei, her face drawn into a patrician look of disapproval.

All right. So she didn't want to make a scene—but she

wasn't willing to let a newt get slapped around, either. He took back half of what he'd been thinking about her.

Speaking of Talent…out of the corner of his eye, P.B. saw that Wren was gone from her position across the street, and was now, in fact, halfway down the street, walking away from the target and related chaos. He hadn't even seen her move, despite it being part of his job to watch over her, too.

Damn, but she was good.

And ready, and go.

The moment Shig made his move, Wren was already halfway across the street. The fugue state came down easy, encasing her in a sense of strange but familiar calm. The pulse of the world was the pulse of her own heartbeat, and she moved in easy rhythm with it. Her core, rather than roiling the way it usually did during a job, slithered in an equally calm way, sliding up her spine and into her veins. But the sense of ready anticipation was the same, the inevitability of something happening, and not being sure what it would be, or how it would all work out.

The buildings seemed sharper, somehow, their edges more distinct, as though they could cut flesh if she walked too close. The flesh of other people was deeper, thicker, and at the same time fluid, like she could fall into them, and the closer she got to Sergei, the more his scent pulled at her.

She hadn't been deep in fugue near him since the battle at the Friesman-Stuzner building, when she'd had to tie a virtual rope of herself to him, to keep him from being sucked into some sort of nonexistent dimension or something. It felt as though that rope was still attached, somehow, even though she clearly remembered pulling her current back inside, trying to resuscitate Lee…

Don't go there.

And then she was walking toward the target, walking past her, toward the moving-van guy carrying the boxes, and the middle one was flickering with flames, so hot and vivid she almost cried for the beauty of it. And a flick of current down one particular channel, holding her breath and praying that this part, the most important part worked, and why didn't she just swallow her pride and ask Shig to do it even if it did mean she'd have to cut him in for the payoff…

"Lady of fire
I command thee, make the jump;
Her possession—mine."

The shiver that ran through her as the Translocation spell worked was a double relief; first, that it had worked at all, second that she wasn't facedown puking her guts out. She was getting better at this. Although there was no rush to try and Transloc anything larger, over a further distance, anytime soon.

The amulet was a heavy weight around her neck as she walked past the movers, even as the older one started toward the "mugging victim" and his "assailant." She hoped, with the part of her mind that wasn't totally immersed in fugue-workings, that the boys would be able to get out of that without her help, but mostly she was concentrating on keeping herself smooth and silent and out of sight, even as she walked off, Retrieval accomplished and no one, not even the target, any the wiser.

Damn, but she was good.

16

"She defended me." Hours later, Shig was still having trouble with that. Wren was listening to them nattering in the background while she did all the serious work. As usual.

"Yeah. I'm going to have to rethink all my thinking," P.B. said, sounding annoyed by the notion.

"You've been thinking?" That was Sergei, polishing his best sardonic inflections.

"Shut up, Didier," Wren said, not even looking up from the box she was constructing out of gold and copper–shimmering current.

Her comment made P.B. grin, a drop-jawed expression that made the nondemon in the room who were looking at him suddenly aware of the veracity of his nickname—and wonder once again what might happen if he were to someday become bored with pizza and Chinese food.

The four of them were sitting in Sergei's living room,

three draped in various positions of we're-proud-of-ourselves on the sofas, while she was seated, cross-legged on the floor, weaving strands of current like a macramé project, building a box of demurely sparking red and gold thread.

She used to work primarily in blues and greens. She hadn't noticed when so much red crept into her work. She wondered if she should be worried about it.

"This is to protect us from the Artifact?" P.B. said, leaving the boys' discussion in order to lean over her shoulder and watch her work.

She batted at his muzzle, warning him to point his nose elsewhere. Bad enough so many Talents had their fingers on it, and Nulls, and who knew what else. She didn't want to find out what fatae cooties might do to it as well. "No. It's to protect it from us. Melanie managed never to use it, for whatever reason." She knew the reason now, having picked that up, along with the Artifact. Honor. Honoring a promise. Honoring a dead woman's trust in the man she had married, and the woman who followed her. Honoring, Wren suspected, her stepdaughter's innocence of the real darkness that waited outside her money-protected world. "I'm not so sure of myself, to be that strong, and I don't know that any of you can be trusted, either. Apologies, Shig."

"None required," the fatae responded, rising off the ottoman to bow to her in response. "You are wise to think of such things. But what will you do, once you contain it?"

Wren stared at the necklace, the woman's face smil-

ing serenely back up at her through the cage's bars. The
Artifact wasn't fighting the enclosure, which made her
feel almost guilty. *It's not sentient,* Valere, she told herself.
Just a power-source, not anything alive. Not like the parchment, that malignant bit of bloodwork they had encountered over the summer. She had learned, out of necessity,
to construct a current-cage for that thing. This container
was a variant: less powerful, less draining on her, but still
effective to keep the firepower out of reach. Anyone's
reach. And only she, or a Talent who understood what
she had done, could break the bars.

"I don't know," she said, finally. "I don't know."

Shig had told her, on the way home, to drop it into
the ocean and let Benten, Queen of the Sea, take care of
it. Wren, not being quite so confident on the willingness
of the elder fatae to take care of anything—they had gotten a reputation for capriciousness and willfulness honestly, after all—had declined that option, although a
lead- and current-sealed lockbox might end up being the
best idea, in the end.

An Artifact should be given to the Mage Council.
That was tradition, decades of tradition. For all that they
were arrogant, they were also organized, and had the fa-
cilities and wherewithal to keep these things safe.

But…did she trust them? Could she trust any of
them? Or would it be like giving a loaded pistol to someone who had threatened you?

She hadn't voiced her concerns, but Sergei was picking up on them, as usual.

"So, the target is a Council member, if not actually sitting on the Council, as far as we know." Serge paused to contemplate what he had just said, then shook off the contradictions implicit in the words as one of those things about the *Cosa* that just naturally made him crazy. "And doesn't have anything against fatae in general, at least not enough to warrant allowing one to be beaten into a bloody pulp simply because they're not human."

"That doesn't mean anything." P.B. had decided that it was less about giving a damn about the fatae than it was her not wanting a fuss made anywhere near her belongings. After all, the woman hadn't actually stopped the attack, just given Shig enough time to run, and then let Sergei go.

"It means that, whatever the Council may or may not be thinking, with regards to the fatae, it hasn't gotten all the way into the ranks," Wren said.

"That matters?"

"It matters a lot," Wren said, biting back a heavy sigh of exasperation. "Stop thinking of Council members as being lonejacks with money, P.B. That's not it, at all. There have been a lot of lonejacks who were filthy rich."

"But no Council members who were dirt poor."

"No," she had to admit. "But that's the thing. Adhering to the Council means you adhere to their dictates. That's what earns you the Council's protection—and, to a certain extent, ensures your financial security, if it comes to that, yeah. You choose security over independence, to put it as boiled down as possible. And you stick to that, or pay."

P.B. was stubborn, and willful, and in his own way as bigoted as Sergei. But he wasn't stupid.

"So if the Council had laid down the law about how to treat fatae, then she would have had to toe the line, or risk losing all the pretty toys. Which means either they haven't, or she flouted them."

"'Zactly," Wren said. "And either way, it's good news for your people."

"Except it doesn't mean that the Council isn't still behind the vigilantes. Only that they haven't made it policy, yet. What an individual does is not always indicative of the greater governing body, even on the Council. In the Council. Of the Council?" Sergei had to come in and lay down the spoiler, before anyone started making assumptions.

"In the Council," Wren said. "I think. A Mage Council member sits on the Council, but a member is in… My head hurts, now."

Sergei shook his head, his own brain past hurting, trying to follow the conversation. And he'd thought that the Silence was bad?

"You people couldn't have come up with an easier way to figure this?"

"Mage Council was, before there were Council members who weren't also Council." Shig leaned forward on the coffee table, warming to the topic. "They did not Foresee such growth in population."

"He said Foresee with a capital *F*, didn't he?"

"He did," Wren agreed.

"Nah." P.B. rejected all their grammatical musings for a

matter of more pressing practicality. "What it really means is, if I'd decided to hang with a Council member instead of a lonejack, there'd be better quality beer in the fridge."

"There's no beer at all in my fridge, P.B.," Wren said.

"Exactly my point!"

Before Wren could throw anything at him, Shig had chucked the last of the pizza at the back of the demon's head, leaving a rather impressive shmear of pepperoni grease between his ears.

"I think I begin to, how is it said? Get the hang of this," the fatae said happily, wiping his delicately scaled hands on a napkin.

"Next person to throw food in my home gets thrown out the window," Sergei said. P.B., who had been trying to decide if he would rather eat or retaliate, decided to shove the last piece of pizza into his mouth, instead.

"Seriously, though. The Council, et al, doesn't seem to be as anti-fatae, overall, as they are, for example anti-lonejack. And even that's pretty localized. I've spoken to Talents in Italy and Down Under, and Shig here knows folk in Japan. Not a whiff of trouble. It's only here, and by here I mean East Coast, although I've been seeing some weird references and asides from *Cosa* in other spots that make me think everything's not peaches and cream there, either. Detroit and San Jose, specifically, although Katie out in Houston had made a comment about maybe it not being a good time for anyone to visit…..

"We've been operating under the assumption, not entirely unfounded, that the anti-fatae bias was Council-wide, because it fit with them wanting to shut us, lonejacks, down. What if the rest of the community hasn't been forced to make a choice yet?" Wren was tugging at the thread of an idea, but she wasn't quite sure where it was leading to, yet.

"All right." Sergei was willing to play what-if. "So…"

"So, what's policy, and what's just prejudice?"

Sergei considered the question a moment. "Does any of this really matter? I mean, so not every Council member may be on the kick-the-fatae page. Does it matter, if the Council itself, is? Is it going to change the fact that the individual members aren't, according to everything you've told me, not independent at all, but members of—for lack of a better term—a hive mentality? What the queen bee decides, eventually everyone picks up, right?"

Wren deflated. "Right. Either that or they swarm to pick another queen bee. Even if we got one or three or a hundred members to back down, the majority would still adhere to policy once it was made. But I think it might be important, anyway."

If Sergei was right about KimAnn, that this entire thing with the Council was some sort of personal power play, then Wren didn't dare give over another potential weapon into her hands. And there wasn't time to leave town and find another Council leader who could be trusted…especially if KimAnn's ambitions went beyond Manhattan, threatening other area Councils…

"Let it be important later. Like I said, if Madame Howe is up to what I think she is, there's nothing you can do about it anyway. Don't get distracted from the problem at hand, which is this Artifact. Can you hold the necklace, for now? Or is the client going to insist on it back right away?"

"She can ask all she wants. She's not getting it back. Or at least, not the original."

"Lawrence?"

"Lawrence." An artist Sergei featured on a regular basis in his gallery, Lawrence was also a refabricator, someone who made copies of antiques, for daily wear when the original was too valuable to be risked.

"I'll put a call in." He got up to get his cell phone, which he had carefully left, along with his PDA, at home when he went out that morning. Standard operating procedure, when on a job with not one but two Talents, involving a third Talent. As much as there was an SOP for something like that.

Considering the slap of current he had gotten, it was a wise decision. Regular backups didn't make having to buy a new PDA any less annoying.

Meanwhile, P.B. had his own idea about what the next step should be.

"What's important is that we get your people and mine back on the same damn page. Because it may not be policy yet, but the Mage Council hasn't done squat-all about the vigilantes, and if the lonejacks don't, either, soon, we're going to be looking at some serious fracturing of the *Cosa*. And not just here, either. Wren, if more fatae die…"

"Yeah, I know. Haven't forgotten." There was no way she could forget that. The *Cosa* couldn't survive, if they didn't learn how to stand together. That had always been the idea, as well as the ideal. She'd seen that in Italy;

when the fatae warned the local Talents away from the House on the hill, Talents had avoided it, no questions asked, and probably saved the sanity if not the lives of at least a dozen of their children over the generations. The trick was getting each side over here to admit to it— and stick to it.

"So what are you going to do?" Sergei asked. He was tapped flat out of ideas, himself.

Wren looked up at the ceiling, feeling the weight of two pair of eyes on her. Shig, being more polite—and a newcomer—turned his gaze away while she thought.

Family ties. Responsibility. Somewhere along the line, people started thinking only about the *Nostradamus* and forgetting about the *Cosa* part of their nickname.

Family.

This was what the seer had Seen, she suddenly realized. This was what had been inevitable, all along.

"I'm calling an All-Moot."

Sergei watched as his partner's words put the demon into motion. Shig, being new to town, wasn't able to help much, but P.B. had the name and contact info for every single clan in the city who had indicated their willingness to deal with humans in this matter—and a few who hadn't been willing at all.

"We're only going to get one shot at this, you know," he warned the humans. "Bringing them all together like this—it's not like what we were doing, me and Lee, all those meetings in your apartment. It's not one-on-one, talking sense."

Wren remembered, all too well. The last time she had tried to bring the fatae to the table, at P.B.'s request, none of the many clan representatives had been happy with the situation. Few of them were willing to believe that the human side of the *Cosa* meant them no harm. And then KimAnn, Madame Council Chairwoman, had shown up with her own damn agenda, and Wren had barely held things together by her fingernails.

"I hate all this," she muttered to Sergei, as P.B. went off into a corner of the office to make his calls. "Like herding six-legged, two-headed cats." Three-headed cats, if you included the Council in on it. An All-Moot was exactly that—all members of the *Cosa* were included. Wren suspected that the Council would put the kibosh on any of their people actually attending, though.

"Speaking of which." He raised a hand, hesitated, then went for broke and stroked a stray hair back into her braid, letting his hand linger until she turned her face into the caress. "I have to go. Meet with Andre. Find out exactly what's going on—and see if he knows anything that we can use."

She really didn't want to hear that. "I need you here."

"I'll be back. I promise. But I need to see him. I owe him that much, if nothing else." To warn him what might be going down, if a storm broke among the *Cosa*, the way Wren seemed to think it would. What Andre did with that information…

"Hurry back."

"Before you even know I'm gone." He kissed the top of her head, picked up his jacket, checked for his keys and wallet, and was gone out the door before she could come up with any compelling reason why he should stay, and damn Andre to his own personal hell.

The old man had asked to see both of them, actually, in his last phone message. Sergei was not going to tell his partner that. She would probably have agreed, and then one way or another Sergei would have blood on his hands. Better to keep the two of them on opposite ends of the city, for as long as he can. Hopefully a very nice, long time, like forever. Wren was many things, but forgiving had never been on the list.

It was indicative of the way things were going that Andre had not asked him to meet in the downtown office, or even in any of the usual, known meeting areas scattered around. Not that you could keep anything secret from the Silence—Duncan was a bastard, but he was the most efficient bastard in the Western hemisphere—but meeting in an off-site, off-route location was a good way of letting people know that you didn't want to be obviously eavesdropped on, and would in fact take measures to prevent it, so nobody's nose should get put out of joint if they couldn't join the party.

Still, the choice of Bryant Park was a surprise. From a run-down and dingy embarrassment to the city, the space behind the Public Library's main building had been turned into a lovely spot for office workers to brown-bag their lunches in the summer, listening to music and soaking up sunlight reflected off high-rise office buildings. There was even a small carousel, and a Starbucks' booth.

Sergei bought himself a chai tea, and walked slowly down a side path until he saw Andre, sitting on one of the wrought-iron benches.

Darcy was with the old man. That was also a surprise. Even more of a surprise was that Jorgunmunder was nowhere to be seen.

Off in the distance somewhere with a high-powered rifle? Sergei wondered. *All right, now you're just crazy-paranoid. Stop it. Just because Andre's desperate enough to go for yet another end-run at us....*

"I won't waste your time," his former mentor said, the moment Sergei sat down beside them. Darcy looked completely out of place out here; he couldn't remember ever actually seeing her outdoors, and her pale, soft, screamingly white skin attested to that fact. "Will you work with us, to root out whomever, whatever is keeping us—" and by "us" Andre meant "me," and the people I use to achieve my goals "—from the information we need?"

Will you come back to heel, Sergei mentally translated. *Will you be my dog, once again, my faithful, well-rewarded hunting dog?*

He braced himself. "No."

"No?" Andre was having trouble accepting the word, and Darcy reacted as though she had been slapped across the face.

"No." Sergei held firm...for about thirty seconds. "Damn it, I can't, Andre. Not now. Hell's breaking loose elsewhere in the city, closer to home, and I have to deal with that, first. Your agenda's going to have to wait."

"My ag— Do you really think that any of these so-called agendas stand separately, boy? Do you really think that your problems with the Council—yes, I know about the disappearances, my lines of information may be blocked, but they're not dead yet—do you really think that they're not all connected?"

The Silence employed Talented operatives, but only on a small, weak level. No matter how many they might have on payroll now, they didn't have their hooks into the powerhouses—except Wren. And that was his fault. His, for negotiating that devil's bargain, and Andre's, for not being able to let go, ever, of anything he thought was his.

"If they are, Andre, if the Silence has anything what-soever to do with what's going on, if your problems are even remotely connected, then it's because you and yours helped to create the situations in the first place, spewing your bigotry and your hate into the ears of everyone around you, playing Holier Than Thou while playing with people's lives like rubber-soled gods, immune to current because you willed it so.

"Think about that, *boss,* while you're up to your ass in alligators and you've alienated the only folk who could have drained the swamp."

Rising from the bench in a smooth, elegant move, Sergei crumpled his now empty cup in one hand and shot it into a nearby trash can. Like his past, like everything except what mattered now. A flutter in the trees overhead caught his attention: a piskie, an adult, watching them. Small, uncute, and mostly harmless, piskies had been the first-hit by the vigilantes, the worst-hit. Sergei gave a quiet nod to the fatae, who watched him a moment with its ugly, large-eyed face, like a human-lemur cross, and then nodded back, equal to equal.

A small moment. It probably meant nothing. But, under the current—*bad pun, Didier*—political conditions, Sergei felt, somehow, that he had won a far more important victory than the one he'd just scored in saying no to Andre.

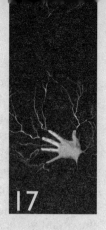

17

The main room had become a control center, of sorts. Wren had dragged the corkboard out of her office and leaned it against the far wall, stripping all her old materials from it and leaving it bare so that Shig could stick the names of clans up as they responded, either affirmative or negative. So far, the largest column was still "no response."

P.B. was still making his calls in her office—he tried coming out once, and the cell had immediately dropped the call with a hiss of static. Trying to use the landline was even worse—Wren was too agitated to even have the stereo on, at this point, and that was usually pretty stable. He had threatened to go up onto the roof and take his chances there, if she didn't lock it down.

Shig had offered her one of his Valium, hoarded for the trip home, but she wasn't a big fan of drugs, over the counter or otherwise. Control was better than loss of control, no matter the situation.

No matter what Sergei might think, sometimes.

Thoughts of her partner brought mixed emotions. She needed him here, damn it. Not that he could do anything, but the lack of his physical presence was a space in the apartment that nothing else could fill, and she resented that. Resented needing that. Resented that he was elsewhere when she needed him, and why wasn't he back yet, already? She kept waiting for the urge to brew tea to kick in, indicating that he was on the way home.

Although she hadn't felt that urge lately, had she? After a decade of knowing when he was coming up the stairs, the lack of that warning was disturbing, and if she had any brain at all left to fret over it, she would.

"All right, we need a place to hold this dance party," she said. "Make like a wedding and assume everyone will come, especially the ones you wish wouldn't, and how many is that?"

"Couple—three hundred," P.B. said, coming out to hand Shig another slip of paper to thumbtack to the board, this one in the *yes* column. "So far you were right—not a single Council drudge has bothered to RSVP, much less accept. Gossip says they're being sat on, hard."

"Fine. It will be easier to keep things calm and productive without them, anyway. Three hundred bodies means four hundred opinions, to begin with."

"At least," P.B. agreed. "But you know an All-Moot without all involved isn't going to be binding…"

"It will be binding," Wren said, grimly. "And it will bind the way it needs to." She had no idea how she was going to manage that, considering she couldn't even get her four-wheeled troika in line on a plan, but it was, by God, going to happen.

"So many people, Noodles as a gathering place is not possible, then?" Shig asked.

"Hah," P.B. crowed. "Another convert!"

"The food was very good," the other fatae agreed calmly, his webbed paws handling the small tacks with a small amount of difficulty. He had refused her two earlier offers of help; they all felt the need to do *something*, however small, to keep involved.

Hers was pacing. And thinking out loud.

"There's a place around the corner, doubles as a recording studio, might be large enough, but would cost the earth, and…"

"And bring a bunch of Talents into a *recording studio?*" P.B. looked at her as though she had just spouted multicolored feathers and a tutu, and done the Dance of the Dying Phoenix to a reggae tune.

"Right. Not one of my brighter ideas, huh?"

P.B. just shook his head and went back into the office.

A sudden sharp noise made them all jump, and look at each other in confusion. It was repeated again, somehow more urgent, and Wren blinked in realization.

"Oh. It's the intercom."

"You have an intercom?" P.B. shook his head. "And someone uses it?"

"Sergei had it fixed. And not everyone comes in via the kitchen window."

P.B. stuck his tongue out at her, and crossed dark red

eyes, making his normally amusing face look like an actual demon's face. "Grow up, Polar Bear."

He stalked off down the hallway, grumbling, while she went to the control panel and hit Speak. "Yes?"

"Miss Valere?"

For an instant Wren had flashbacks to Andre—the only person she had ever told to always but always refer to her as "Ms. Valere," even in his thoughts—but then common sense sunk in. This voice was female.

"Who is this?"

"It's Anna Rosen?"

She sounded like she wasn't quite sure if she was or not. A far cry from the self-composed little rich girl who had come here that first day.

"Now is not a good time, Miss Rosen."

"I need to have an update, Miss Valere. I need to know what you're up to!"

Wren was tempted to tell her to go away and leave things to the adults. But the last thing she needed right now was some hysterical girl making a scene outside on the street. So she hit the door button, and buzzed her in.

Rosen looked like hell. Her long blond hair was only pulled back into a sleek ponytail today, and her pale green eyes were red-rimmed and smudged with charcoal-colored half-circles underneath.

"You didn't get it. She still has it. What went wrong?"

Those were the girl's first words in the door, and Wren had to fight down the urge to backhand her right back out onto the landing.

"You hired me to do a job. Let me do it."

Interesting, that the girl knew about the failed attempt, but not the successful one. Did Melanie dearest know that she'd been robbed? She must, by now. But how did Anna know? Wren couldn't imagine Melanie telling her…which meant that the client had her own sources.

Shig had made himself scarce as well; she suspected that both fatae were down the hallway in the office, safely out of sight. Just because Rosen knew about Talent didn't mean she knew piss-all about fatae. Or needed to know that two of them were hanging around in The Wren's apartment.

"I hired you. That means you report to me. So, report."

She must have learned that stance from Daddy, before he died. Or watching too many episodes of *The Apprentice*. On her, it wasn't very scary.

"You hired me to do it my way. My way doesn't involve reports, memos, or any kind of daily metrics. Get over it, or fire me."

Firing would be good. Firing would be a way out of this bind, once and for all. Firing would also be very very bad. She'd never walked away from a job, and she'd never, ever been fired.

"I *need* that necklace!"

"Why?" Wren didn't care why, actually. It was enough that she had been hired; justifications, like legality, was a thing she worried about on her own time, not the clients'.

"Because, I…"

The change in Rosen's voice alerted Wren to snap out of her own internal musing and pay attention. Damn it, Sergei was the schmoozer. Sergei knew from getting people to talk about themselves, spill more than they meant to, and give away the entire candy store.

"Anna? Why do you need the necklace? Want, I can understand, it was your mother's. But you told me yourself that it was a trinket, and your stepmother confirmed it. So why is everyone so intent on keeping it for themselves?"

She knew why Melanie wanted it, obviously. And she knew why she had it trapped in a lockbox. But why did Anna, lovely Anna the self-proclaimed Null, want it? This was more than personal. This was borderline terrified.

"I…someone approached me. They want to buy it. Mel won't sell. She won't let me sell, either. And that's not fair! It's mine, it was my mother's and now it's mine, and I should be able to sell if it I want!"

Never enough money in the damn world, to satisfy some people, Wren thought, not without some compassion. She wasn't sure there would ever be enough money in the world for her, either. But nobody was lining up to let her find out, worse luck.

But this was a woman who was willing to sell a treasured trinket of her mother's, a seemingly worthless item, for cold hard cash. And to people who scared her enough to do anything in order to make that sale.

A drop of foreboding tickled along Wren's scalp. Who was that scary? Who wanted this necklace so much, to intimidate a young woman into stealing from her own family? And how had they heard about it in the first place? All that suggested Talent…more, Council. Which, to Wren, specifically spelled out K-I-M-A-N-N.

Not that it mattered much, since Wren had already determined KimAnn wasn't getting her manicured talons on it, but…

"Come into the kitchen, sit down, let me make you some tea," she said, taking Rosen's arm. The client let herself be walked into the small kitchen and seated on one of the stools, waiting like a rag doll while Wren was setting the kettle to boil, picking out the tea bags, and pouring the water, all the while keeping up a line of gentle cocktail party chatter that would have impressed her grandmother, snob that she had been.

"I need to know—" Anna broke in, and Wren nodded soothingly.

"Of course."

Wren almost felt guilty as she gathered up the current from her core, stroking it until it stretched, sleek and dark purple, like a vein up out of her core, up her arm, into the hand that offered Anna her mug of steaming hot tea. As she did so, Wren touched the skin of Anna's hand, the fleshy part between thumb and forefinger, and with scalpel precision, Pushed the thin line of current slid from her into the Null space that was Anna Rosen.

The Push was a skill Wren hated using—and seemed to be using more and more often. It made her feel like she needed to take a shower.

Reaching into Anna's brain, into the space in her hypothalamus where the memory and awareness was stored, Wren's current flowed in over Anna's questions, quieting them with a gentle murmur of its own, replacing questions with contentment, queries with complacency, and a sense of all things being well and well-explained.

It was delicate work, and the temptation was great to go in a little deeper, and burn away every memory of the necklace, as well—or, if she had the time, to craft a new memory, one of having sold it, and spent the money on a new pair of shoes.

It wouldn't be a bad thing. It might even, in the greater scheme of events, be a Good Thing. Certainly, it would ease Anna's life considerably, to remove her from the path of self-destruction she seemed determined to pursue, because while a Talent might mold an Artifact, the stories said, Artifacts almost always molded Nulls, and almost always in really bad and fatal ways.

Even if whoever wanted to buy it took it from her, and paid her, and let her live, she would still be effected by the magic stored within.

Stepmomma was trying to protect Anna, as well as the Artifact. Pity nobody thought to explain it to the girl. And now it was too late: thanks to whoever had tampered with her, she would never believe it wasn't just another ploy to keep the poor, pitiful Null from what was rightfully hers.

Yes, using the Push to make her "forget" about the necklace would make life easier for everyone—but it was in the end, all each Talent had was an internal meter of how far they were willing to step into the gray areas, and Wren's was already pinging the red line.

Taking the mug out of Rosen's now unresisting hand,

Wren stood and led the client like a rag doll back out to the front door.

"We're all set then, Miss Rosen?"

"Yes. All set. Thank you for being so patient with me. I simply want what belongs to me, you understand?"

"Totally," Wren assured her. Offering the client a handshake on it, Wren made one last Retrieval, taking back the awareness of Wren's home address and contact info, excising it neatly, without any space left behind.

No guilt, there; self-preservation trumped all other concerns. When the replacement was made, Wren would send it to the client in the usual manner—through a blind drop that Sergei would arrange. She was over the incredibly stupid urge to do everything on her own. She thought. Probably.

Down on the street, there was no sign of the driver or his big bad car. Anna must have braved the subway, poor little rich girl. Wren watched out the window while Anna walked down the block, a normal-looking vigor in her stride, increasing as she got farther and farther away; the walk of a woman who had gotten exactly what she wanted.

"Life would be easier if I were a nicely amoral, cold-hearted bitch, intent on only my own agenda, like a proper lonejack."

She was about to call Shig and P.B. back for another round of find-a-Moot-location when she realized that she had gone back into the kitchen and set the kettle to boil again, for a fresh pot of water. The front door opened just as she started to laugh, and Sergei came in, looking like he really needed that tea.

The look on his face triggered a memory in her own brain, of an old Math teacher of hers stressed beyond belief by the willful ignorance of her charges, and she blurted out, "The old high school!"

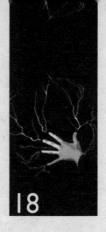

18

Technically speaking, Wren thought, watching the bodies mill about in the space below her, P.B. was right, and
this wasn't an All-Moot. But with lonejacks and fatae both
represented, it was the closest anyone could remember
ever occurring. Redcaps and an odd-looking feathered
creature sat quietly against one wall, watching intently
while three or four piskies flitted in the air, piskies being
one of the few winged species who could still actually fly.
A Nassunii, or water serpent, was by the door, talking to
one of the feathered serpent-types, and two troll were arguing with a basilisk—thankfully an immature male, or
the argument could have gotten ugly, fast.

None of them were talking to humans, no. But they
were there, almost sixty-five percent of the fatae who
were invited. That was better than she had hoped for: a
majority were still willing to listen.

But no dryads. Rorani had not shown up. Wren was

disappointed by that, but hopeful the dryad—mother of the fatae, she was called—would show up before the evening was over. They needed her, to give whatever happened validity.

A heavy hand on her shoulder: she managed, barely, not to flinch.

"Are you sure about this?"

"I'm not sure about a damn thing. But we all agreed, something had to be done."

"Yeah." For all his annoying personality, Bart was about as pro-fatae as they came—he employed a bunch of them in his landscaping company, and not just because they worked cheaply. "Separately, the damned Council's just gonna pick us off. You notice? Since we started organizing? No more grabs."

No more lonejacks gone missing, no. But more fatae were dying. It was escalating, in fact.

And the psi-bomb set off outside her house wasn't the only one reported: three other lonejacks reported similar blasts, each of the three doing considerably more damage than her own. That report had come in last night; late, because the lonejacks involved had been injured, and were only now getting in touch with their area representatives.

On one hand, it was good to see that the plan, such as it was, was working: lonejacks were sharing information in a coherent and timely manner, not just exchanging gossip over coffee, the way they used to. It was a tribute to Lee's memory, for a lot of them. The formal gossip-mining he and P.B. had started, over the summer, was being carried on.

On the other hand, it showed that the Council wasn't backing down from their plan to intimidate lonejacks into coming in under their oh-so-protective umbrella. They had just taken a different approach.

She didn't bother pointing any of this out to him. He knew. They all knew. As much as the fatae needed them, they needed the fatae, too. They had to learn how to work together, all of them: not in a block, the way the Mage Council insisted Talents work, but as cohesive individuals.

Wren hadn't been a stellar student, even when she was paying attention, but she did remember her history classes well enough to remember one particular phrase: "We must all hang together. Or assuredly we will all hang separately."

She didn't bother mentioning that to Bart, either. Instead she scanned the crowd below them, leaning on the railing with her fingers curled around the iron rail. Sergei threaded his way through the crowd, his normally noticeable height and shoulder-width not as obvious among the larger fatae.

"You know what to do?" It felt odd, speaking to someone like this. It wasn't like working with Sergei and the others, arranging the Retrieval—that had just been a question of reassuring herself that everyone knew their parts. Once set in motion, she hadn't had to pay attention to them, only herself. Here, she was the one directing the action; she had to keep them all on the page.

Bart nodded. "Yeah. I got it. You really think this is going to work?"

"It has to," she said. Which wasn't really an answer.

Stephanie entered the room, and everyone turned to watch her walk, even the straight women and gay males. She just had that kind of a walk.

Wren was aware of an extreme—and extremely annoying—flash of jealousy when Sergei's head turned as well. She used to handle it much better, his being red-blooded and breathing. Weird, that being in a relationship made you more aware of your own insecurities, rather than less. Or maybe it was just that you actually had something of value to lose…

"People! All of you, winged, weirdboned, and otherwise!" Her voice carried throughout the room, actually a former gym. Wren and Bart were standing in what used to be the track circle, above. Weirdboned was a term Wren hadn't heard in years—it was an old, old, old-fashioned way of referring to Talents. Old as in Revolutionary-war, old. She knew it only because Neezer had referenced it once, in one of his endless lectures on Why She Shouldn't Use Current to Shoplift, and she, curious, had looked it up.

A piskie threatened to dive-bomb Stephanie's head, and she grabbed it by the legs and pulled it down to face level, staring directly into its eyes before letting it go. Its roost-mates snickered and settled down, more amused at her being caught than the treatment she received. Piskies were like that. They took as good as they gave.

"Thank you for coming tonight."

Wren had vaguely been aware of Bart leaving her side,

but it was still a bit of a shock to see him step onto the raised dais, along with Michaela and Rick, to join Stephanie. Together they looked pretty damn impressive, she had to admit. Almost official-like. It helped that they'd dressed up for the occasion: Rick and Bart were both wearing dress slacks and shirtsleeves, and Stephanie was every inch the Connecticut Professional in a skirt and jacket. Even Michaela had made an effort, trading in the worn, ripped jeans and cammo tank top of the earlier meeting for a neater pair of black jeans and a white cardigan-style sweater.

"Thank all of you for coming tonight. We're aware that this is, in a word, unprecedented. But times change around us, and we either change, or we suffer for it."

There was a vague noise from the audience, one that Wren thought indicated agreement, but she wasn't entirely sure. She held her breath, hoping that they'd be able to stick to the script that had been hammered out...

"We have no secret, no hidden agenda." That was Michaela stepping forward, the lights glinting in her blue-dyed hair, that and her so-fragile bones making her look almost fatae. "No pre-decided plans. No decisions already made—we're not going to insult you like that."

The noise this time was a little louder, more obviously positive, if not entirely believing. They liked that, the crowd did. Good.

"Is there anyone here who doesn't know why we've called this Moot, this rather exceptional, inclusional Moot?"

A few of the fatae made as though to say they didn't, but seemed hesitant to speak up around so many humans. She had thought about using P.B. or Shig to jump-start discussion, if needed, but they each had their own, different problems. P.B. was too well-known, too closely linked with herself, and through her the lonejacks, while Shig was too unknown, too obviously a stranger, and therefore suspect.

"Because you need us," one of the fatae finally said. A Leshi; shaggy-shouldered, with a two-pronged rack set into his skull. Young, then, but adult enough to have a voice within his tribe. His body language practically screamed testosterone-aggression. Wren had only encountered one of them before, in a run-down, fatae-friendly hotel in midtown when she and Sergei had helped fend off one of the earlier vigilante attacks. She wondered if they were related; she hadn't thought that there were many in the area.

"Because we can offer each other what we need." Rick might be out of his usual leathers, but he still moved like he was wearing them, and the belligerent fatae-buck backed down a step.

"You've never given a damn about us before."

"If you believe that, why are you here?" came a shout from across the room. "Go back to your caves!"

"Hey!" Rick still had a leather-wearing voice, too.

"Not all humans treat us like animals." A quieter voice, near the front. Wren craned her neck to see who it was. Winged, and elongated, and no species she recognized, not that there was any great shock in that. "For the killers who hunt us, there are those who help us. We—my people—have a champion who teaches us to defend ourselves, because he does not wish to see fatae blood spilled."

"You hired him to teach you," someone else said, dismissing that claim.

"And he takes our money, and teaches us well. What more do you ask?"

The winged fatae made his—her?—point. It wasn't discrimination if you were being treated the same as everyone else, in terms of services offered.

"We're not asking you to join us," Bart said. "We're none of us big on the joining thing."

Some laughter there. Good.

"But you know we've been having problems. And we know you've been having problems. So maybe we can help each other out, neighbor to neighbor. *Cosa* helping *Cosa*, the way it was supposed to be."

"Don't see Council here. Council's *Cosa*, too."

"Are they? Not by my book they're not!" An angry voice, from the back of the room. Wren couldn't tell if it was fatae or human. Not that it mattered, she supposed. It was—

Her thought stopped cold, running into some kind of mental wall. Something wasn't right. Wren couldn't put her finger on it, but the tone, the underlying feel of the room, had changed. There was still the orderly arguments below; the foursome and she had agreed that they wouldn't expect anything other than arguments for the first hour, until everyone had it out of their systems, more or less. Danger or no, extraordinary Moot or no, these were still *Cosa* they were dealing with; still lone-jacks. They *needed* to argue. Otherwise they wondered why everyone was humoring them, and got defensive. This was different.

Wren let the sounds of the debate going on below her fade to the back of her awareness, like watching television in the background. Resting her hands lightly on the banister, feeling the cool steel under her fingertips, she summoned fugue state; not a heavy working trance, just enough to let her focus cleanly.

Slipping down a gentle slide, feeling the tendrils of her core embrace her, wrap around her, she opened them up, transforming them into psychic ears of a sort.

Nothing.

A wall of dead air outside, like a stormfront stalled and quiet.

Too quiet.

She felt ill, the tendrils turning inside her restlessly, searching something familiar. They didn't like the dead silence, either; it made them uneasy, waiting for a storm to break, a blow to land.

Nothing was that silent. Nothing living. Not unless…

She had a sudden flashback, a memory of the summer past, when she encountered a dark space for the first time; a location entirely Null, impenetrable to current, unfriendly to magic.

This felt like that. But that was impossible. There was no Null space here, not in the middle of Manhattan, one of the most current-charged, electrically alive places on earth. Was there anything that could mimic the feel of a dark space? If so, Wren wasn't sure she wanted to know about it.

A memory, resurfacing unwanted. *Fourth of July, when she was, what, ten? Maybe nine. Her mother was dating a guy who lived in Manhattan, and he had invited them to have dinner and watch the fireworks. Huge crowds, people in tight masses of excitement and anticipation, and Wren, all four-foot-something of her at the time, pushed and shoved by adults and teenagers who didn't see her there, despite her bright red T-shirt and green Statue of Liberty headpiece. Her mother held her hand tightly, looking up to the sky at the exploding sparks, and couldn't understand why her daughter, who usually adored the crackling energy of fireworks, started to cry…*

People. Outside. Nulls.

A lot of them.

Sergei. She had to get to Sergei. She had to get his attention, somehow…

But he was down there, in the crowd, and she didn't want to do anything that might cause a panic, not with the mass down there already on edge, not until she knew for certain…

Sergei. The *sense* of him, always close under her skin, too many years of working together, feeding off each other, emotionally and current-wise. The endless dozens of times she had grounded herself in him, taken from him and fed back into him. Even before they were sexual partners, there had been a bond Wren had counted on. Had depended on. Had used, most recently, to save his life, his soul, from the all-consuming hunger of the Nescanni parchment.

She reached for that now, and, trying hard not to panic, not to startle him, reined in the impulse to tug the bond, instead treating it like a whisper-thin thread, stroking it like the sinew of a harp. Listening to it resonate, she followed instinct and impulse, moderating the sound from random music to words.

Part of her wondered how she knew to do whatever it was she was doing; the other part focused back on the sense of the dark space, moving ever-closer.

Sergei. Partner. Don't react. Just listen.

She had no idea if she was getting through, just continued shaping the words out of the thread-music.

Trouble coming. Human. Null. Outside. Not sure what kind.

It might be nothing. It might be a busload of theatergoers, coming in from the Greater Suburbia, synthetically-Null from job-stress and exhaustion. Might be anything.

There was a knocking noise, a dull, almost rhythmic sound, from outside, and Wren felt rather than saw the attention of the crowd shift. The four-wheeled troika felt it, too, and scrambled to get their audience's attention back, just before the front door of the gym slammed open, and the first *Cosa* member went down under a baseball bat.

Alarm! It wasn't needed, now, but Wren was already in fugue state, and she could feel how quickly confusion and surprise was turning to panic and chaos. A little di-

rection never hurt any brawl. Especially direction from
someone with an overhead view of the action.

*Coming in from the front door, side gate; stage-left win-
dow.* The others were barred, probably to prevent basket-
balls from crashing through glass, or other activity-related
damage. Small blessings; it kept all but the smallest fatae
from escaping, but also limited the ways the vigilantes
could come at them.

No guns. At least as much as she could sense; pneu-
matic pistols or the like might be flying under her awareness. She wasn't very good at this sort of thing, damn it!

*Those who can fight, focus on the ones with bats. Those
who can't, or won't, drop down and get out of the way!*

Some of them heard her; too many didn't. Bodies went
down under the attacks, and screams and shouts rose up
into the air.

Current could be a decent weapon—if you were prepared. But very few Talents could jump into action without warning, and the fatae were…fatae. Useless. She
could use current—but how to make sure she only
harmed the attackers? No way. She was a Retriever, damn
it, not a fighter.

The scent of blood mixed with sweat, and rose into
the air. Wren almost gagged, the trauma sending her rising up out of fugue state. Only extreme force of will kept
her there, kept her focused.

Sergei! A yank, now, on that bond, and he responded.
Anger, a hint of fear—for her, for those around her—and
a growing desire to find the attackers, do them violence.
Normally she avoided thinking about the levels of anger

and violence that lived inside her partner. Right now, it might be their only hope.

Sergei prided himself, rightfully so, on never losing his cool. Ever. It was what made him effective. Efficient. He could step outside the moment and do what needed to be done in order to close the deal.

So it bothered him not at all to shoot a man in the back.

Partner!

Wren's cry sounded in his head, and for an instant he was confused—was it an echo of her earlier cry, or—

The sharp burn of a knife cut answered that. *Damn, damn damn, she couldn't have yelled, "Duck!" or, "To your left"?* Shutting down his awareness of the pain, Sergei backhanded the guy with the knife, gratified to see his attacker go flying across the floor on his backside, knocking into another knot of fighting and scattering those players like bowling pins.

Too many, he thought, using the moment to size up the room. Too many, too organized, even for vigilantes. He was making an assumption there, but it seemed warranted, since most of the attacks seemed to be aimed not at the lonejacks, but the fatae. Someone had set this up. Someone had told the vigilantes that the fatae would be here, in number.

Someone had sold them out. Someone who didn't care if a few restless, unaffiliated magic-users got killed, too.

"Valere!" A bellow, a war-cry. "Valere, out!" The hell

with the rest of them; he had to get his partner out of here.

He risked a look up to the balcony where she had been playing Field Marshall, and swore. She was still there, leaning too far over the railing and calling out warnings to those below in the fight. It would only be a matter of moments before the fighting moved up there, if not sooner. And while Wren could hold her own in a fight, all the tricky moves in the world didn't help against a brute with a large enough stick and the willingness to use it.

Ducking an overmuscled goon with the aforementioned stick, Sergei headed for the stairs.

Three steps into the melee, and his handgun was useless. Even if he'd been willing to fire into such a closely packed crowd, the number of agitated Talents made the risk too great. Not that they could use current to affect the weapon directly, not without coming into contact with it, but the noise might startle them into an unplanned, unfortunate release of current.

He didn't mind taking damage when needed. But getting whacked with a bolt of current wasn't high up on his to-do list, despite what Wren thought.

"Knees! Knees!"

A tiny form whizzed past Sergei, almost tripping him up.

"Knees!"

The voice was P.B.'s, chanting under his breath as he ran alongside Sergei. The human was puzzled for a moment, then as another small form swarmed past them, he realized that the demon was giving instructions to the half-dozen piskies moving with him. As per instructions, they would peel off periodically and attach themselves to the kneecaps of Null humans—how they could tell the difference, Sergei didn't know—and bit down, hard, in the fleshy area behind.

Pisky teeth were sharp. Without fail, their victims staggered and went down.

"Knees!" P.B. said again, and started up the stairs half a step ahead of Sergei, even with his much shorter legs.

Someone grabbed Sergei from behind, around the neck, and he felt himself being pulled backward.

"Get her out of here!" he managed to shout. Hopefully it wasn't too garbled. There wasn't any need to specify who he meant. P.B. would understand—and understand why, too. Wren might think she was merely an advisor, but this alliance wasn't going to work without her. If this attack was designed not only to take out as many fatae as possible, but to prevent them from gaining possible allies, then Wren was as much at risk as any of the fur-skinned, bark-haired, bewinged creatures around them.

Reaching backward with the flow of the attack, Sergei grabbed his assailant's elbows and pulled forward even as he dropped down, sensing the pressure on his throat dropping. Swinging in place even as the chokehold eased, Sergei ended up facing a very surprised goon who became even more surprised when Sergei head butted him in the face, hard.

Freed, Sergei got to his feet and raced for the stairs again, grabbing at elbows that got too close, twisting and shoving without any consideration of friend or foe. If they were between him and Wren, they were to be moved.

Get to Wren. Get to Wren. The voice in his head chanted the mantra until voice and action melded into a sick symphony, drowning out the yells, crashes and swearing around him. But one fact was clear: the vigilantes were trained, armed, and winning.

Useless. All these Talent, totally useless in a fight.

The memory of Lee came to him—a tall, too slender man, an artist, a maker of beauty, heart and soul. A man who used his Talent only to create—spending his last moments turning those skills to hold off a fatae set on killing Wren.

Not all useless. Just undirected.

"Forearms!" he yelled, hoping that someone would hear and understand. "Hit 'em hard on the forearms!" He held up his arms in example. A hard enough blow, even untrained, and odds were good that the victim would drop whatever he was holding. Like, say, a baseball bat.

That hope thrown out into the sea of battle, Sergei took the stairs two at a time, reaching the balcony in time to see Wren turning, a look of dismay and anger on her face, to deal with two humans who were clearly not there to ask her for her autograph.

"Valere!"

She heard him, thank God, and then…

Disappeared.

He knew she could do it. Her entire career, in many

ways, was based on her ability to slide under the mental radar, to become so obvious, so overlooked, that your mind literally didn't see her standing right in front of you, taking your valuables.

He had heard her talk about how she did it, the technical details, the preparations, the effect…but he'd never actually seen her do it. Or not seen her, as the case might be. For some reason, even when she put the mojo on, he had always been able to see her.

Not this time.

Someone came up the stairs behind him, and Sergei turned, determined to throw the son of a bitch over the railing.

"Come! Come!" The Leshi had lost one of his prongs, and his patrician nose was bleeding, probably broken, but his flat, even teeth were bared in a fierce grin, and not all the blood on his face was his. "More come. We go."

"Finally," Sergei muttered. "A fatae with a lick of common sense. Wren?"

"Here," a voice murmured, and a cool hand touched his, and then was gone.

Bart gave up even pretending to eat his scrambled eggs, and looked around the table. "All right. I hereby call this meeting to order, yada yada yada. What was the final roll call?"

"Full house—almost thirty fatae of various clans, probably a hundred lonejacks, maybe more. Tough to tell—not everyone had checked in, and more were still arriving when all hell broke loose." Stephanie tallied it up, her Connecticut Suburban Matron Cool still holding, but only barely.

"Losses?" Wren didn't want to think about it, but they had to.

The dark red flaking off P.B.'s matte-black claws was noticeable only when he flicked some of it off, a nervous twitch Wren would prefer never to see again. The last time she had seen blood on his claws, it had been her own, after he dug a bullet out of her shoulder.

They were sitting in an all-night diner just outside the Lincoln Tunnel, surrounded by off-duty staff from the local hospital, a guy who was probably an undercover cop, from the way he was sitting, and a scattering of workers wearing the uniforms of a major office cleaning company. The paramedics gave them an occasional professional once-over because of the number of bandages and bruises they were sporting, but otherwise the only person paying any attention to their table was their waitress, and even she was doing a half-assed job of it. P.B. finally had to get up and grab the coffeepot off the warmer himself, to give everyone a refill.

"Too many. At least half the fatae are down, maybe out." The Leshi had borrowed a file from Bart's truck and evened out the ragged edge of his antler as they fled the city, giving him a disarmingly rakish look. He picked at the edge of his salad, shoving the hard-boiled egg to the side of the bowl with a grimace of distaste.

Wren had only ever met one Leshi before, back when the vigilantes were becoming a real problem, and he'd been a hell of a fighter, too. She wondered if it was the antlers that did it, or if they had developed the antlers because they liked to fight…

Michaela got a vague look in her eye for a moment, listening to a report from someone still on the site, doing cleanup work. "Seven lonejack dead. Another dozen in various stages of walking wounded. Two more had to be sent to the hospital with head injuries, no word on their condition."

Current could seal up minor skin damage and do wonders for bone fractures, but anything more delicate than that and it got tricky. Healing yourself was generally considered a major no-no—you couldn't separate out your internal organs from the current, and sometimes really bad things happened.

There were seven of them at the table. Michaela, Stephanie, and Bart, Wren, P.B., the Leshi whose name, amusingly enough, was Clyde, and another lonejack Wren had never met. Nobody had seen Rick since the attacks began. You didn't want to count Rick out, but…

Sergei had dropped them off at the front door, then commandeered Bart's truck, saying something about the Null going to get gas while they compared notes. That had been an hour ago. She figured he was either lost in the swamplands of Jersey, or checking in again with Andre. Either way, he was on his own. She had to deal with the crisis of the moment.

Although his calm mind would have been useful, right about now.

"How many Nulls?"

Wren shrugged, wincing as she felt a muscle twinge. She'd managed to avoid getting hit, being out of the main fighting, but being no-see'um had its own disadvantages—someone had slammed her with a chair, aiming for someone else when she was in the way. "Didn't stop to count bodies. Anyone else?"

A round of heads being shaken, all around the table.

Wren ate the last strip of bacon on her plate, then wiped her fingers on a napkin. "There looked to be at least two dozen of them. Maybe more. I doubt we did much damage. Even if we all knew how to land a punch, we were taken by surprise."

"How?" That was Michaela, finally asking what everyone had been avoiding for the past several hours. "How the hell did they know where we were? Who told them?"

"Someone told them. Someone who knew. Not that this was exactly a secret, considering how far the word went out—"

"You think it was Council?"

The question fell on the table with an almost literal thud.

"It had to be someone who knew ahead of time," Wren said, not answering the question directly. "You don't get that many people together in half an hour, not unless you have an entire army sitting around waiting."

"How do we know they don't, the Council? Ready and waiting to make their final move against us?"

The tension level, already high, ratcheted up at Bart's question. Wren could feel it, all the current coiling tight in her own gut, echoing the actions of her fellow Talents. Even the fatae at the table got tense.

"All right. Enough." Stephanie, taking control of the conversation before anyone let exhaustion and fear mix badly. "We got hit, and we got hit bad. Proof, if anyone doubted it, that an alliance is not only a good idea, but a necessary thing. The first prong of the attack was not aimed at lonejacks, but fatae. Alone, our cousins would have been slaughtered."

"Then if the freaks hadn't been there, we wouldn't have been attacked in the first place." The unknown lonejack, Shawn-something, his name was.

Bart slammed his meaty fist down on the table, making his unused silverware jump, and the coffee, left cold in his cup, shimmy unpleasantly.

"How did you get out of there?"

There was silence.

"I'm talkin' to you, Shawn. How did you get out of there?"

"I followed you," he said sullenly.

"And how did I get out?"

The lonejack glared at Bart, then looked down at his plate. "You followed the fatae."

"The fatae has a name," P.B. muttered, then subsided when Wren kicked him under the table.

"And why was I following the fatae?" Bart pushed.

"Because…" Shawn gave a long-suffering, put-upon sigh, then said, "Because he was clearing a path."

"With claws and muscles that only a fatae would have.

With claws and muscle he knew how to use—and was willing to use, to get us out."

Point made, Bart leaned back in his chair, still pinning Shawn with a glare.

"It didn't matter who they were there to attack. The point is, we made it out as a team, where alone we would have died. The vote was taken in blood, *our* blood. We're *Cosa*. We stand together. Got me?"

"Yeah. I got you."

Wren wasn't so sure the message had actually gotten through, but she had never given a damn about winning hearts or changing ideals—she just wanted people to stop screwing with each other so she could get back to work.

She was a simple girl, really, with simple desires.

"Wren."

Okay, and she was a simple girl who was slipping, if her partner could sneak up on her like that. A simple, very tired girl, who had at this point been awake for almost—God, almost forty-eight hours. No wonder she was starting to get groggy; there was only so much adrenaline and caffeine could do.

"We need to talk." Sergei's face was even more poker-still than usual, and there was no sparkle in his eyes, at all. Wren was on her feet before her body thought about moving.

"Wait." Stephanie, frowning. "What can't be said here, in front of everyone?"

"Retriever business," Sergei said, not even bothering to look away from Wren's face.

"Bullshit," Bart said. "You've discovered something, and don't want to tell us. What is it?"

Something flickered then, deep in Sergei's expression. Wren felt her breath catch.

"You were sold out."

"We figured that already," Shawn said in disgust. His body language shouted that he didn't see what this Null could do for them, or why he was even being allowed at the table.

"You know who," Michaela said.

Sergei gave a tight nod, his eyes still holding Wren's. Her insides twisted in a way that had nothing to do with current.

Someone at this table. Someone we trusted.

She wasn't sure what happened next; he might have let something slip, some body language or change of expression. Or maybe the traitor just panicked. But the table went flying onto its side, pushed with a blast of current that knocked them all off their chairs and onto the linoleum floor. Diners around them scattered, clearly expecting some sort of brawl to break out, and in the corner of her eye Wren saw the cop start to reach for a holster.

"No guns!" she shouted, a dual message: for Sergei not to pull his own weapon, and for the cop to understand that this was going to be settled without bullets.

Talents had different ways of doing things.

Bart grabbed for Wren's hand, and after a moment of panic, she grabbed it back, her much smaller fingers engulfed in his meaty and callused paw.

Paw. A memory rose, something she'd never had time

or energy to follow up on: P.B. offering himself as a source during the battle with the energy-creature, back in the Library over the summer. *"It's what I was created for,"* he had said. She hadn't understood it then. She didn't understand it now. But she didn't understand half of what she did; she just did it, and it worked, and that was all the moment needed.

The thought had no sooner come to her than she felt claws scratch her shoulders, felt the warm, musk-scented fur of her friend at her back, and once again sensed that deep, heavy strength coming up under her own core, supporting and feeding the current without actually having any of its own to compete or interfere. Total surrender, total trust.

Some day we're going to talk about this, she told him before falling down onto the offered strength, reaching out with tendrils to coil around Bart's offered current, feeling Michaela taking her other hand, sending Shawn's weaker offering coming through Michaela.

Any of them could have been point. But only she had P.B. at her back, and Sergei's influence guiding her mind, coolly, calmly, dispassionately. Doing what needed to be done.

And current lashed out, cracking in the air, destroying cell phones and PDAs and laptops throughout the entire diner, shorting lights and bringing the entire kitchen to a standstill.

Wren fell out of the gestalt, and looked across at the shattered, bloody remains of what used to be the Connecticut representative, then over at the cop, who was blinking in shock, sitting back down slowly as though aware that there was nothing at all he could do.

I hope we didn't short out the entire town, she thought, then leaned forward and threw up.

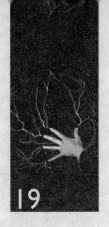

19

The sound of polished stones being placed on the table sounded muffled, despite the excellent acoustics of the room. They appeared into the air above the table, untouched by obvious hands, and dropped slowly onto the cherrywood, not even smudging the surface. Seven, eight…nine stones, each the size of a well-groomed thumbnail, all glossy quartz. Six were milky-white, two a dark glossy green so dark they looked black, and one was clear, shot with webs of smoky-gray.

A sigh seemed to rise into the air, breathed collectively by the eleven bodies in the room.

The Arbiter, the somber tones of his dark gray suit off-set by a pale pink bow tie, gave the stones a careful once-over, then nodded. "It is done. It is witnessed. The Mage Council has voted."

The words were ritual. The satisfaction in his voice was not. Clearly, he—like everyone else in the room—had an opinion about the vote.

KimAnn Howe, the architect of the vote, smiled pleasantly at nothing specific and everything in general, every
inch the genteel little old lady in a slim-styled business
suit and demure heels. Only one Mage Council representative had abstained; old Washington, and KimAnn
was not about to waste energy resenting someone who
had cost her nothing; everyone knew that Washington
would not take sides. The two who had voted against her;
well, that was a different story. But for now, in her victory, it made no sense to be vindictive. A split decision
was often more useful than a unified front. The Council
needed a loyal opposition. Just so long as they stayed
loyal. And the de facto, acknowledged leader of this
Council was pretty sure that she had ensured that.

The individuals seated around the table raised their
hands, palm upward, to show that they held no more
stones. "As the will of the Mage Council moves it, so
shall the Council be moved."

Those words, too, were ritual, binding the vote into
inevitable, unstoppable action. With the soft clunk of the
voting stones, and the binding words over them, the
greater New York Area Mage Council voted to become
a larger entity, merging Sebastian Bailey's San Jose Mage
Council into their own, creating a larger, more powerful entity. Against all tradition, defiant in the face of the
original charters, and with the full awareness that the
five other Mage Councils of North America might take
it amiss, they had done this thing.

KimAnn met the glance of Jacob, sitting in the offcorner
quietly making notes, and exchanged satisfied nods. A

merger of equals, yes, but one with clear leadership—her own. It would take a while for the kinks to be worked out, and everyone to find their comfortable placement, but in the end, the Council would be strong, healthy, able to face the decades to come and not falter.

A fitting legacy to her name, to pass down to the generations. Even the lonejacks would see that, soon enough.

"Michael, if you would ring for service, please?" They had come directly to the Council Room that morning to vote; although she had enjoyed a leisurely breakfast upon waking, it was unlikely that the others had been able to down more than coffee before—

"Madame Howe."

The voting over, the stones recalled, the barriers on the Council Room doors had been released, and Colleen stood in the doorway, carefully looking directly at Kim-Ann, avoiding the table and those still seated around it.

"Yes?"

"Madame, there is news." At KimAnn's raised eyebrow, the girl continued. "The lonejack Moot. It was…attacked."

That got the attention of everyone in the room, Council members looking at each other with concern and not a little suspicion—they had all heard of the disappearances, of course. Those messages had been as much to keep her own people in line as to encourage the lonejacks to come to their senses. Angela looked a little pale—KimAnn remembered that she had a relative who had gone lonejack, almost a decade ago. It happened, now and again. No fault was attached to the family.

"Attacked by whom?" She had not ordered any discipline—would not have done so on such a wide scale, regardless.

"Madame. We—we don't know."

KimAnn sat back slowly in her chair, the only sign that she was disturbed by this intelligence. Not that she cared if a few lonejack were brutalized—if it made them feel insecure, or threatened, then so much the better. Her own plans had been predicated on the fact that it was far easier to bring home frightened children than defiant ones, after all.

But an organized attack on an entire Moot of Talent indicated someone who was not afraid of current. And that—that bothered her a great deal, indeed.

"Gentlemen, ladies." She nodded to the others seated at the table. "We shall adjourn for breakfast, and follow up on this disturbing news after we have had time to contemplate it. For now, let us celebrate our new, stronger identity. Members of the San Diego Mage Council have traveled in expressly to meet with you; please, feel free to make new friends!"

Gentle laughter met her words, and if any of them wondered at the confidence that allowed her to bring the San Diegoans in before the vote was taken, none voiced it out loud.

As they rose and filtered out of the room, KimAnn waited, her expression pleasant. Underneath, she could feel her current roiling, and soothed it back into quietude.

"Michael." Her secretary came like a well-trained dog to heel. "I do not like being without information. Find out who called the Moot. If they survived, set up a meeting with them. If they did not, find out who their second was." She paused. "And I expect, by then, to know who instigated the attack." She had been using a stick to herd these particular cats. Perhaps it was time to use tuna, as well.

And if neither of those means worked, then it was time to rid the city of cats, entirely, once and for all.

But she kept that thought, very silent, to herself.

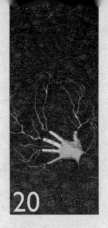

20

"I so very, very, very much do not like this."

"So you've said." She didn't like it, either. "Madame Howe was pretty clear about it, though. Lonejacks and Council only. No fatae…and no Nulls."

"They let me speak for you before." The previous summer, he had acted as her proxy when approaching the Mage Council, to determine if they were involved with a Retrieval she had taken on. They had lied to his face—all right, Sergei admitted, they hadn't actually lied. But there had been a good deal of dancing around the truth. "So why am I suddenly not good enough now?"

Wren didn't even bother to answer that. He was griping because he was unhappy at being left behind. P.B. had done the same thing last night, when the invitation had come. Parchment, handwritten: all very traditional. The remaining troika—Rick having been recovered from the hospital bed where nurses had tried—unsuccessfully—

to make him stay put—had received theirs already; she had wondered if the Mage Council was going to ignore her. She had, honestly, hoped that they would.

No such luck.

7:00 a.m. The Cloisters. There are things we must discuss. No outsiders.

None of the fatae had gotten invites. Big surprise. Not.

"They've already tried to kill you. Twice."

"That sniper was totally unrelated to all this."

"That sniper was what started all this." The Mage Council, trying to muddy the waters over their involvements in the death of Jamie Koogler, an architect whose murder was the base of a spell cast decades ago, a murder Wren helped to uncover, had hired someone to shoot at her, hoping to distract her.

It had just resulted in pissing her off.

"And the psi-bomb—"

"We don't know for certain the Council was behind that. Anyway, it was hardly a fatal blow."

"It was supposed to be."

That stopped her. "What?"

He hadn't wanted to tell her. But the news had been chewing at his mind ever since the Moot three weeks earlier; every day that passed, he expected them to try again.

The message from KimAnn hadn't soothed his concern any. If anything, he was convinced this was a trap; taking out the three remaining lonejack leaders and their most visible supporter—he paused a moment to appreciate the irony of that—in one swoop.

"Talk to me, Sergei." He had her full attention now, rolling over on her side, the sheet barely covering her body. It was damned distracting, the way the fabric kept sliding down, and he reached up to tuck it more securely under her arm.

"There were two other attacks, the same day," he said.

"Yeah, I heard. Nobody was injured though, right?"

"Not seriously, no. But they got lucky—one of them was in working mode, and was able to deflect most of it, the other was asleep. Something about REM acting the same as a fugue state?"

"Yeah, that's the theory. Tough to test…we don't exactly make good subjects to hook up to electrodes."

"I imagine not," he said dryly. "But the point is, the intel I got—" she, mercifully, did not ask where or who he had gotten it from "—they were able to deflect the blast, and protect themselves. You weren't working, weren't prepared…and yet sustained less damage. And, according to sources—"

She had long ago stopped trying to figure out Sergei's sources, although finding out about the Silence went a long way to explaining some of them.

"—the area around your building took more damage. Which is unusual, for a psi-bomb, right?"

"I guess. Not something I know a hell of a lot about. You think…" She frowned, sitting up in bed and staring at him. "What are you thinking?"

"I'm thinking that that bomb was meant to be a lot more deadly than not. And no, I don't think that Andre's people were able to do anything to mitigate the effects, no matter how they may be patting themselves on the back for it."

"Okay, fine. They were trying to take me out. So why didn't it work?"

"I have no idea. And, frankly, other than being damn glad it didn't, I don't care right now. I just don't see why you're so willing to walk into another chance for them."

"Because it doesn't fit the pattern. And the Council is all about the pattern. If they've been behind the attacks—and I think we're all pretty much in agreement they are—then they're doing it *sub rosa*, without a mandate. If they don't have a mandate, if the entire Council hasn't voted on it, they can't turn around and do anything with their fingerprints all over it."

"Jamie all over again."

"Yeah."

Jamie had been an architect, a good man unfortunate enough to be working for a very bad man, years before either Wren or Sergei had been born. He had been murdered as part of a spell cast without Council sanction, but the Council had known and allowed it, and three generations later they had been willing to kill to hide that fact.

"All right."

As easy as that, Sergei backed down. Sometimes, even now, he amazed her. She leaned forward and kissed him lightly, first on the tip of his nose, then his chin, then down further, on the side of his neck, then, sliding under the sheet, on his sternum.

"Valere…."

"Shut up, Didier. I'm working, here."

"You've got twenty minutes before you've got to be in the shower, getting ready. I'll take a rain check, thanks."

"Spoilsport," she muttered, sliding back up out from under the sheet in a manner designed to leave him with a reminder of what he was passing up.

"Just for that, I'm not going to leave you any hot water."

"Hey, I wasn't the one invited to the party. I don't have to get out of bed at all."

Half an hour later, Wren was pouring her second cup of coffee while the water heated for Sergei's tea. The threat of using all the hot water had been an idle one; Sergei's building didn't do anything as déclassé as run out of hot water. Her building, on the other hand—great pressure, but the boiler had a mind of its own, and a distinctly malicious sense of timing. She'd swear sometimes the entire building was alive.

Alive…a theory started to form in her mind, about the psi-bomb, and she shoved it into a box and slammed the lid down. She needed to be focused. Focus. Get the focus working. KimAnn Howe was the toughest of tough old ladies, no matter how sugared her coating. Especially if Sergei was right about what was motivating the old woman. Even if this wasn't a trap—and she hoped to God it wasn't, because otherwise Sergei would never let her live it down—Madame Howe wasn't going to sweeten the bait with anything useful, not intentionally. Anything they got out of her, they were going to have to steal.

Fortunately their side had the best damn Retriever working today on the case.

Wren grinned, a tight, evil-minded grin, and took another sip of her coffee.

"I don't like this place."

Wren got out of the cab and looked at Rick curiously. "What's wrong?"

"I don't know. I just…" The biker had always had a fair streak of precog to him, enough to evade speed traps and DUI busts, and not much more. If something ticked at him, it might actually be a bomb. Or it just might be nerves scraped and strained from coming *thisclose* to dying.

"Is it emotional, practical, or currential?" she asked.

"That's not a word."

"You understood what I meant, didn't you? So it's a usable word. Like piratical." She put her hands on her hips and mock-glared at him, the wind blowing hair into her face and ruining the glare entirely.

"That's a totally pointless argument. Just because I could figure out from content does not make it a word. Neither does stealing from Gilbert & Sullivan." He was huddled into his jacket, peering out of the cab's door and looking miserable. He hated cold weather; was always threatening to move to Florida, or somewhere even warmer.

"So what does?"

"Continued usage." He was adamant about that.

"Fine. Currential, currential, currential. You want I should continue?"

"You're insane," he said, grinning despite himself, allowing her to manhandle him out of the cab.

The squabble thus having served its purpose, Michaela paid the cabbie off. He sped down the roadway out of the park, clearly thankful to have the four very cranky early morning passengers out of his car, not bothering to ask why they were going to the Cloisters hours before it opened.

Wren stood in the open air outside the endearingly ramshackle pile of stones that housed the Metropolitan Museum of Art's collection of medieval art, and wondered if the sense of unease she felt was the same as Rick's, or just echoes from the House of Holding, back in Italy. That building had been a dark space, a location that nullified current, and she did not have fond memories of it at all.

"Come on. Let's get this over with."

They'd actually put together a plan, of sorts. As much as you could, going into an unknown situation with unknown parameters and an unknown desired end result, other than "information." It came down to what the plan had always been: the remaining three wheels of the troika would do the talking, and Wren would do the listening.

Every Talent had different ways of going into work mode. For Wren, it was a relatively simple slip down into fugue state. Out here, her feet solid against the bedrock of upper Manhattan, home ground in the truest sense possible, it was even easier.

Her eyes fluttered closed, as though she was falling asleep, lulled by the early morning birdsong and relative quiet of the park. The voices of the troika became background noise, then faded, as did the birds and the distant sound of traffic on the parkway, until all that was left was the sound of a gentle breeze through the trees, sliding her down into her own velvet-lined core, where tendrils of current reached up to embrace her with their lethal coils.

Hers, hers, hers. It was a litany you could never forget, or the power would turn on you, destroy you. But you couldn't embrace it too tightly, either, or it would send you wizzing into madness, unable to differentiate between current and flesh, open to every flash of power that wafted nearby.

Focus.

She gathered the current, slid into her core, and set up residence. Externally her eyes opened and her body moved with the others, but everything that mattered, everything that was *Wren,* was protected, hidden in her core. If this was a trap, if the Mage Council did strike, even if they managed to get to her down there, she would still have time to tag every single lonejack within the island and let them know. And she'd go down fighting, too.

Around her, the others were setting up their own protections; nothing that would offend the woman waiting to meet them, but rather reassure her that they were taking her seriously, giving her the respect due to an honored opponent.

Sergei's idea. Sergei was the one with the training in shit like this. It was all beyond the normal lonejack experience; they'd rather conclusively proved that political maneuvering was not their thing, although Sergei seemed to think they'd actually done pretty well in the past few days. But Wren had always held that anything that didn't evolve, died.

Lonejacks were even worse at giving up and dying than they were at working together, or politicking.

Together, the four of them moved up the walkway to the large wooden doors. They were locked, the museum's alarm system running, but Wren and the alarm system of the Met were old friends, and it only took her a few minutes to wrap herself around the wires and coax them into letting the door open without notice. The physical locks took a few minutes more, but Wren was a firm believer in old-fashioned handwork, too, and the toolkit she carried with her on every job worked its usual metaphorical magic as well.

"Up there," Bart said, pointing up a narrow stone staircase. Their footsteps echoed in the quiet, moving one at a time up the steps until they came out into the open foyer. Michaela picked up a map from a holder on the information desk, and led them to the garden the note had indicated. Filled with the scents of herbs and some sort of spicy flowers, it had a lovely view over treetops of the Hudson River below that, on another day, Wren would have found extremely peaceful.

Deep in her core, however, she now picked up on what Rick had felt on arrival. Layered on top of the more ancient emotions, and darkening the more common feelings of awe and satisfaction felt by daily visitors, was the taint of blood. Darkness. Betrayal.

Someone had been murdered here. Recently. Within the month, give or take a few days.

No matter. Focus. Focus on the moment. Focus on what is important.

"Good morning. I thank you for meeting with us on such short notice, and in such a remote area. We felt, in light of recent events, that waiting until a more proper location could be arranged would not be wise."

"Madame Howe," Michaela said, taking the lead in greeting their opponent. The other two fell behind her in a neat triangle, with Wren a step behind them and to the left. Distract the eye, spread the area of potential attack. Sergei's advice, again.

KimAnn Howe was as trim and elegant as ever; Wren suspected that she could be tossed into the tapir's pit at the Bronx Zoo, and still look classy and composed.

"The place and the time were not a problem," Michaela went on.

In fact, they were almost suspiciously ideal. The Cloisters had a state-of-the-art alarm system, and respectable wiring, but the very nature of the building and its distance from midtown meant that it wasn't filled with distractions—or pooled areas for Mage-current to hide behind. What you felt was probably what was there. If Wren wanted to set someone at ease, she might have chosen the same place and time. Why did KimAnn want to set them at ease?

"We heard what happened to your people." KimAnn's voice remained as smooth as ever, but Wren could See, deep inside her core-fueled eyes, the waves of concern that rippled inside her. But concern about what? Wren wasn't ready to dig any deeper: right now, her job was just to stay low, and listen.

"If there is anything we can do to aid—if any of your people still need medical attention, or—"

"We," Wren noted. Plural use, indicating the Mages of the Council were in agreement on this, or was Kim-Ann being Royal?

"What's the price tag? Your sort never do anything without a price." Bart, the bitterness always lurking in his voice coming to the fore.

KimAnn raised her elegant white eyebrows. "A lone-jack, griping about supply and demand?"

"That's not the price your sort take."

"We take only what is offered," the Mage said. "No one has ever been forced to join the Council."

That was true. Coerced and pushed, yes. But never forced. Distinction without too much of a difference.

"We've taken care of our own, thank you." The cost had been high, but less so than anything the Council might ask for aid. That was a historical truth.

"As you wish. We heard, as I said, and were distressed that our sisters and brothers had been set upon in such a fashion. No matter the differences in…philosophy we might have, we are all *Cosa*, after all. What affects one, affects us all."

"Even the fatae?" A dig, not so subtle, reminding them all that no Council member had attended the All-Moot. No Council member had been injured.

"The fatae have always gone their own way, even

among their own kind. But we have a history with their kind which does not go unrecognized."

Wren felt nothing from KimAnn off those words. Not a ripple, not a flutter, not the faintest fluctuation. Whatever her personal feelings about fatae, they were locked down deep.

Not that this made her much different from most of the human side of the *Cosa;* that was the problem. But it wasn't a problem to be dealt with right now. Now, they had to determine where KimAnn stood. And if the entire Mage Council stood with her.

"You note there are only three of us here." Michaela, going on the offensive.

Four, actually. Wren kept her mouth shut. She was working. Being overlooked was part of the game plan.

"Should there have been more?" KimAnn took another look at their faces, and sighed. "Yes. I had noted that Stephanie was absent. Might I hope that she is well?"

"She's gone."

In another language, gone would have layers upon layers, ranging from "left for the bathroom" to "taking a long trip," to "obliterated out of existence by a blast of massed current." In English, it was a flat, uninspired word. But KimAnn seemed to understand it.

"Ah."

And that was all the epitaph Stephanie got.

"You've had spies among us," Bart said.

"The Council has friends in many places. Some high, some low. The river between us is not as great as you like to believe."

"No," Michaela agreed. "But it is as treacherous to cross."

"You have been gathering in secret, massing, and making alliances. Without contacting us. It would be remiss of the Mage Council if we did not make an inquiry."

"Queries involve querying. Not spying."

Sez you, was the answer implicit in KimAnn's simple shrug. The very movement set off the differences between them: Madame Howe in her elegant suit and heels, pearl earrings and expensive shoes, against Rick's jeans, biker boots and leather jacket, Michaela's flowing gauze skirts and denim top, or even Wren's and Bart's casual khakis and pullover tops. They were dressed for agility, speed, and comfort. She was dressed for business.

"Yes, Stephanie was passing along information to me. But not as much as you might choose to believe, else why would I be standing here before you?"

"To me," not "to the Council." Wren, thinking that she sensed an opening, nudged a feeler of current in Howe's way, only to have it slapped down by...something outside of Madame. Shellfish—Talents who bodyguarded not the body but the core; their own bodies safely hidden away, their entire existence subsumed into being the shell-protection around their client's core. It didn't keep her from being attacked, but would turn any but the most persistent touch away like an unwanted Seventh Day Adventist at the door.

Shellfish were legend. No self-respecting lonejack would give up their existence to protect another. The

Council… Wren wondered, suddenly, if becoming a Shellfish was a choice…or a decision made for you.

Focus on the moment, Valere!

"It might have been a trap, to take out three more lonejacks who stand against you," Michaela countered.

"Lonejacks have always rejected the Council. It is what makes you lonejacks. Why should you four be any different?"

Four. She saw all of them. Including Wren, who had been promoting her no-see'um since they walked through the door. That fact was noted and ignored as being irrelevant right now.

"An excellent question," Michaela responded. "What has changed, in the past few years, that we have become a noticeable thorn in your side? What has changed, that you feel the need to clean house of the riff-raff cluttering your nice clean, well-organized house?"

Careful….Wren warned her companions on a soft Push of current. They didn't want to get sidetracked; the answers might be interesting, but it would also distract the Mage's attention, and Wren needed it as focused as possible, for her to read the reactions.

"The Council was not responsible for the attack on you." Blunt words, laid down with the sizzle of current. How much of it was true, how much an act?

"You admit to picking us off one by one, and yet expect us to believe this was not your act?"

"We have admitted to nothing, except differences of opinion." KimAnn seemed to soften, just a shade, and Wren was immediately suspicious.

"My sisters, brothers. The Council had nothing to do with the attack on you, or the fatae in your company. We wish you to join us, yes. And we have taken steps, on occasion, to keep those who would harm us at bay." What steps, and what they considered "harm" were left open to interpretation, and Wren couldn't read anything off her. Madame Howe was good, damn good.

"And the fatae?"

Wren held her breath, and KimAnn looked puzzled. It wasn't an expression that came naturally to her.

"What of the fatae? We have no place for them in our organization, nor would they wish to join us, any more than they have ever joined with you."

A fishing expedition. *Hold*, Wren warned the troika. *Keep yourselves stilled. Give nothing away.*

"Madame Howe." When Bart got polite, it was time to worry. "You placed an informant within our inner councils. A traitor, who chose to die rather than be unmasked."

Not exactly true—they hadn't stopped to give her a choice. But the strength of her reaction to discovery had exonerated them of too much guilt in that matter. For Wren, at least. Or maybe she has just pulled an overskin of "Sergei" over the sore until it healed.

"Forgive us if we do not believe any protestations of innocence—or even not-guilt—which comes from the Council now, or any time in the future."

"I can assure you—"

"No. You can't." Michaela, as hard-voiced as granite. Although Wren could judge the flips and flares of current, there was no such thing as a truth seer outside of fairy tales; mind-to-mind doesn't mean you can't lie, especially someone as strong-minded as Madame Howe. The lonejack representative was laying down the cold hard facts. "You've given us nothing to make us trust you…not even an explanation for why a member of an outside Council was in town—and seen meeting with a known anti-fatae vigilante."

That was a revelation, and only Michaela's gentle pressure back on Wren's current kept her from zipping her head around to stare—or glare—at the gypsy representative.

"If a competing Council member can be in your city, working to means you claim not to support, without your knowledge, then how can we possibly trust your ability to control your side of the *Cosa?* And if this was done with your knowledge and approval…" The implication of that was left to an ominous trailing-off of Michaela's voice.

Wren could see KimAnn forcibly relaxing herself, inch by inch; Michaela's news had come as a surprise to her as well, then, although not all of it.

"You knew another Council was in the city." Wren spoke without thinking, in her shock. That as almost unheard of: the Councils were encouraged to be territorial, to keep them as isolated as possible. An alliance was not—

"You invited them here." Wren didn't know why she was so certain, but she was. It was the act of an insane person…or a supremely smart, savvy, and confident one.

"You alone, not the Council entire." Sergei had been right, had been dead-on about what was happening.

Rick made a move as though he wanted to put the Council leader into a headlock, then checked himself.

"What game are you playing, Madame Howe?" he asked, instead.

Wren could hear the wind overhead, outside the stone courtyard, but inside the stones it was still, as though even the plantings were waiting to hear her response.

"One you have chosen to sit out," the older woman said finally. "You were invited—" that got a snort of unamused laughter out of Bart "—yes, invited to join us. Perhaps our methods were extreme at times, but we tried only to show you how very much safer it was within the protection of the Council rather than floating, alone and aimless, at the fringes."

"Safe, the way Mash was safe? Is he safe now, Madame Howe?" Mash had been an older Talent, a lonejack of considerable reputation, much loved within the *Cosa*, who went missing from his home one day, without warning. Without any clues even the best PUP could find.

"The end justifies the means," KimAnn said, an indirect but damning reply, and Wren felt her core begin to seethe with the need to do something—anything—to wipe that arrogant expression off the older woman's face.

"This meeting is over," Rick said. He turned without waiting to see if the others were with him, and walked out of the courtyard, back into the dimly lit recesses of the Cloisters.

After a moment, the other three followed him, leaving KimAnn alone with her shadows in the morning sunlight.

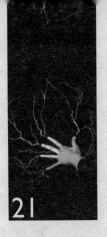

21

"Hi, honey, I'm home." Sergei walked in the door, then did a double-take at the stranger sitting with Wren. "Oh. Hi."

Wren waved her hand, quietly amused at the blush staining Sergei's cheekbones. "My partner, Sergei. Sergei, this is Bonnie."

"Pleasetameetya," Bonnie said, half-rising from her chair.

"Likewise, I am sure." He gave Wren a casual once-over, and she nodded. The visitor was okay, no worries.

Reassured, Sergei hoisted the large-ish canvas bag he was carrying and, humming gently under his breath, went down the hallway with it.

Bonnie sat back down, and Wren shook her head in mock sadness. "Do you have any idea what you're getting into?"

The sunlight filtered through the kitchen window, and

the crisp air that came through it carried the smell of someone somewhere charring meat over a grill. Probably the couple in apartment #4, up on the roof again. Familiar sights, sounds and smells… Lee's ghost was still in the woodwork, everywhere she turned, but that was okay.

The world was tipping enough on its axis, Wren wasn't ready to give up the things that were right, just because they were difficult to live with, sometimes, day by day.

"The landlord's not always good about repairs. And apartment #3—that's Clyde—likes to wander around nude—which no, isn't a good thing. At all."

Bonnie leaned against the back of the chair she was straddling, and merely smiled at Wren. "If you're trying to scare me away, it's too late. I already signed the rental agreement."

"Once P.B. learns there's another lonejack in the building, he's going to be raiding your fridge, too."

"I have two brothers. I know how to lockbox my food."

Wren blinked, then grinned. "Without spoiling the food? You're going to have to teach me that little trick. Consider it payback for letting you know there was an apartment available."

"I already had my Realtor looking into it," Bonnie countered. "But since I would never have known about this place without you calling us in, I think I can do that one small thing."

They shook hands on it, then Bonnie looked at the old-fashioned wind-up clock on the wall and made an exclamation of dismay. "And I was supposed to be at work twenty minutes ago. I'll catch you later, 'kay? Neighbor." She waggled her fingers, nails painted a sparkly pink this time, and disappeared.

"Show-off," Wren muttered. Translocation was one of the few things she was very very bad at, and it was still a sore subject. Still. Bonnie seemed nice enough, and having someone with those skills handy wouldn't be a bad thing…but they were going to have to set some guidelines about Translocing in and out of the apartment like that, without warning. Wren had things she kept private. Especially from a professional snoop.

Reaching down below the table, Wren pulled the small, current-shimmering box out from under the chair where she'd hurriedly stashed it when the PUP came calling, placing it back on the table proper.

Technically she was in breach of her agreement with the client, having Retrieved the item and then substituting a forgery in the exchange. But if you were going to play technical, had Wren known what she was being asked to Retrieve from the beginning…

Stepmomma hadn't been wrong to try to keep the Artifact from Rosen: her mistake came in not sitting the girl down and explaining it, instead of trying to protect her.

But love made you do stupid things, sometimes. Wren only hoped that the two of them would be able to repair the relationship, someday. Melanie might be Anna's only hope of escaping whoever had set her up in the first place, when they discovered the necklace she gave them wasn't real. Although if Wren's theory was correct and KimAnn was behind it, she was also the source of Anna's knowledge of the failed attempt, and would know exactly what had been done, and why.

As Sergei had said, none of them could do anything to stop KimAnn. Not until she revealed more of her hand, anyway. At least they weren't alone in the waiting, anymore. The troika's decision to offer an alliance to the fatae had been considered, accepted and ratified by seventy percent of the attending species, and more were falling into place as gossip spread.

And if KimAnn did blame Anna for the fake necklace? If…

If anything happened to Anna, Wren would tell Melanie who had been responsible.

It wasn't just a question of finishing the job. You had to finish it *right*.

The sounds of hammering came from the hallway, followed by a sharp burst of cursing in Russian, and Wren winced. A package had arrived yesterday afternoon in the mall, addressed to her—a small brown parcel containing the most exquisite piece of silk Wren had ever seen; pale green, with delicate brushstrokes evoking a stand of bamboo and a tiny bird, almost invisible until you spotted it, and then impossible to miss. The enclosed note that said, simply, "A thank you for letting me play in your city."

Shig, back home and doubtless dining out on his adventures—and adding to the overblown legend that Wren's reputation was becoming. At this point, Wren could only grimace and accept it. She never *meant* for things to get that complicated…

Sergei had taken one look at the chop, or signature, on it, and guestimated its worth at least several thousand dollars, then promptly gone down to the Gallery to get the proper hanging tools.

For a guy who spent most of his adult life selling art, he wasn't too handy at actually hanging things, though. For a moment, she almost missed his overbred, overpolished assistant, who despite his other flaws was actually pretty handy with a hammer. Not that she'd ever let him into her home, not unless it was life or death and he was the last paramedic on earth.

The cage in front of her glimmered, a pale shade of green racing through the red, and she touched the current lightly with one finger, bringing it back to a steady red shade.

Too many distractions here. It needed somewhere calmer to rest. Somewhere less likely for current use to stimulate it.

Somewhere less likely for someone to lay hands on it, even accidentally. Even with the best of intentions in the world.

There was a piece of fabric on the table, folded into a neat square. She unfolded it, shaking out the heavy, lead-lined cloth, and draped it over the current-cage.

Then, almost despite herself, like watching someone else move her body, she stood and walked over to the phone, lifting the receiver and dialing her mother's cell phone number.

"Mom. Hi. Your youngest." She didn't think that her voice sounded *that* odd, did it?

"I just wanted to say thanks for lunch. How's Toronto?"

Her mother started telling her about the lovely restaurants, and the lovely hotel, and the lovely weather. Wren murmured the right responses, but mainly just let the familiar voice wash over her like a verbal security blanket It was enough that her mother was out of the line of fire, for now.

She watched the Artifact, carefully, while she listened. Left alone, red current-sparks flickered and flared under the lead-lined fabric, almost like the pulsing of a squared-off heart. It was going overseas, to the monastery. The monk in charge there owed her a favor, by God. Whatever this thing was, the need to own it broke apart what had been at least a friendly relationship. It wasn't anything she wanted anywhere near her. And she won't trust the actual Mage Council with mud, at this point. Not after they had—as far as the *Cosa's* best sniffers could tell—funded the vigilantes into taking out the fatae as part of their plan to break the lonejacks' independence. A move that was not, apparently, supported by all Council members.

That was the most worrisome thing, to Wren's mind, the distrust growing within the Council of its own leadership. Bart had started digging, after their meeting with KimAnn, and what that annoying but effective badger had dug up had made a lot of things suddenly start to make sense. In addition to the lonejacks who had gone missing, several members of the Council were unaccounted for, as well. Unexpected vacations, or running off with their secretaries, or merely taking a rest cure…

nobody was talking. Unlike lonejacks, when Council got scared, they stopped gossiping. And that explained why Worth-Rosen hadn't gone to the greater Council with the Artifact on her own, once she inherited it. Her husband might have died from an illness, rather than being murdered as his daughter claimed…but Wren highly doubted that the illness had happened without a push, magical or medicinal.

Worse, members of another Council were in town. Specifically, highly placed members of the San Jose Mage Council, including KimAnn's counterpart, Sebastian somethingorother.

That was forbidden, by rule and tradition. And Kim-Ann Howe had always come down hard on the side of rule and tradition.

No, the Mage Council was no longer to be trusted, not with anything. They were no longer *Cosa*. It didn't take a Moot for that to be decided; word was already spreading throughout the city. A month from now, by the time the weather changed toward winter, new lines would be drawn.

Wren thought, fleetingly, of running. She had a reputation, she could work anywhere.

But where would she go? This was her home.

She would fight for it.

"Valere!"

"Hang on a sec, Mom," she said into the phone, cutting her mother off midrecital.

"Come take a look at this," Sergei said, appearing around the corner. "I don't want you bitching later that I hung it crooked."

Wren smiled, saying her goodbye to her mother with a promise to call soon, and followed her partner down the hallway.

They'd fight—tomorrow. Today, there was art to display.

* * * * *

Chapter One

In the middle of a copse of trees, bordered on the side behind her by a dry creek bed and in front by a low stone wall covered with moss and bird shit, Wren Valere crouched, her backside an inch off the leaf-strewn ground, her palms resting on her knees, and her knees complaining about the whole situation. She was tired, sweaty and pissed off at the universe in general and one person in particular.

"Annoying, ignorant woman," she scolded that person, hidden inside the house on the other side of that wall. "You couldn't have taken the kid to Boston, or Philadelphia, or somewhere semicivilized? No, you had to go all bucolic and pastoral and…leafy." Wren reached up to pull another damned twig out of her braid, and wiped sweat off her forehead with the back of her hand. It was a lovely, autumn-crisp day, pale blue skies overhead, and she was sure that there were hundreds of people driving up and down the winding county road a few miles back for the sole purpose of enjoying the scarlet and orange display of the maples and oaks and whatever else those trees were. More power to them.

Wren Valere was not a nature girl. The leaves were pretty, and she was glad it was a nice day, but she wanted to be home, on concrete and steel, surrounded by the familiar and comforting hum of current running through the city. Home was Manhattan, where magic fed on and was fed by the torrents of electricity running in the city's veins. A Talent like her—a current-mage, a practitioner of modern magics—had no business being out here in the woods, miles from anything more powerful than a solar-powered bug-zapper.

Genevieve, you're exaggerating, she heard her mother's voice say, exasperated. All right, she admitted that she might be overstating things slightly. It still felt like middle-of-nowheresville to her: too quiet, too green and too still, electrically speaking.

The thought made her reach instinctively, a mental touch stroking the core of current nestled inside her, deep in a nonexistent-to-X-rays cavity somewhere in her gut, just to make sure it was still there. Like a bank, you could overdraw and forget to refill, and even though she *knew* she had enough in there, it was a nervous twitch, obsessive-compulsive, to make sure, and then make sure again.

Current was similar to but not quite identical to the electrical energy the modern world had harnessed to do its bidding. They were, so far as anyone could determine, generated off the same sources, and appeared in the same natural and man-made situations, but with a vastly different result when channeled by their natural conductors. Metal, in the case of electricity; Talent, in the case of current.

The more abstract and technical distinctions between current and electricity were lost on most of the *Cosa Nostradamus,* the worldwide magical community, except those very few who made an actual study of it.

Wren wasn't one of those few. She wasn't an academic; she was a Retriever. She came, she stole, she went home, with no interest in the whys, so long as it worked. Although she freely admitted that the feeling of it simmering inside was nice, too. Some Talent described their internal core of magic, the power they carried with them at all times, as a pool of potent liquid, or birds flocking together, their feathers rustling with power. For her, it was a pit of serpents, each thick-muscled neon beast sliding and slithering against each other. The touch filled her with a quiet satisfaction, a sense of power resting under her skin, ready if she needed it.

Reassured, she moved forward through the trees, only to be pulled up short by something tugging on her braid, before realizing that it wasn't an attack—or at least, not one she needed to worry about.

Reaching back, Wren removed her braid from the grasp of a branch and scowled at it, as though it alone were responsible for her bad mood. "I hate camping. I hate bugs. I hate trees."

She didn't really hate trees—Rorani, one of her oldest friends, was a dryad, in fact, which made her an actual, honest-to-god tree hugger. She had never needed to go camping to know how she felt about it. She preferred luxury hotels to sleeping on the ground.

She did hate bugs, though. Wren grimaced and reached a hand down the back of her outfit, scratching at something irritating her skin. She pulled her hand away and made a face, shaking the remains of the unidentifiable insect off her fingers. She especially hated bugs that kept trying to crawl under the fabric of her slicks to reach the bare skin underneath.

"Ugh." She wiped her fingers on the grass. "Next job? High-rise. Climate controlled. Coffee shop on the corner." She kept her voice low, more from habit than belief that there was anyone around to hear her. "God, I'd kill for a cup of halfway decent coffee…."

She really shouldn't be in a bad mood at all, even with bugs and twigs. Coffee and the rest of civilization would be waiting for her when she got home, same as always. This was just a job, and it would be over soon. And money in the bank made every job better in retrospect.

Tugging the hood of her formfitting black bodysuit back up over her ears, making sure that the braid was now tucked comfortably inside the fabric, Wren kept crawling forward until she reached a low hedge of some prickly-leaved bushes. Rising up to her knees, she scowled over the shrubbery at the perfectly lovely little cottage on the other side of nowhere.

All right, she told herself, enough with the griping and the moaning. Showtime.

She let herself reassess the scenario, just to get the brain in the right place. The area was on the grid. She could feel the quiet hum of electrical wires—man-made power—overhead, not far away. There wasn't a lot, but if she suddenly had a need it was there to draw down on. Comforting. And the house wasn't totally isolated— despite the screen of trees, a half-hour hike would bring her back to the highway, and it was probably only a few minutes' drive from the front door to the nearest coffee joint. If, of course, you had a car.

The job had specified no traces, though, which meant that renting a car, even using one of her many fake IDs, was out. Frustrating, but manageable. The client was paying large sums for this to be a spotless, trouble-free Retrieval, and that was what The Wren would deliver. No muss, no fuss, no anything the courts could use at a later date against the client. Everything had to be perfect.

It was more than just ego at stake, that perfection, although she was always about that. This particular job had come to Sergei, her partner/business manager, not through the usual route of the *Cosa Nostradamus* or his art-world contacts, but through a retired NYC cop now living upstate, a guy named McKierney who moon-lighted as a bounty hunter. The client had gone to him originally, but this kind of grab wasn't McKierney's scene. He had heard about The Wren through his own contacts, and had given the client her name and Sergei's contact number as the go-to girl for this particular job. A totally nonmagical job.

She didn't get many jobs out of the urban areas, where most of the *Cosa* congregated. A satisfied client here, among human Nulls, could open up a whole new market for her, and there was no way she was going to give less than everything to it, even if it involved trees and bugs and crawling around in the dirt. Sergei had drummed that career advice into her head years ago: you never knew when the next client was going to be the million-dollar meal ticket.

Yeah, the job stank, on a bunch of levels. Money—and clients with money—got her into a lot of situations she didn't enjoy. But this job had something even better than money to offer: there was absolutely no stink of magic to the Retrieval. After spending a year of their lives immersed in a literal life-and-death struggle, when what seemed like half the city suddenly set out to wipe the streets clear of anything that looked like it might be magical, and then having to give over another nine months to the job of cleaning up the aftermath—and getting her own life back into some kind of order—Wren was more than ready for something distinctly unmagical. Even a be-damned custodial he-said she-said, with a four-year-old kid as the prize.

That was the job she was on, right now. Mommy had grabbed the kid and ran. Wren was here to Retrieve him for Daddy, who was the client.

Wren shifted on her haunches, still feeling the creepy-crawling sensation of bug legs on her skin. That was the real reason she was griping, not the green-leafy-buggy-nature thing. Live Retrievals were a bitch. She'd only done two before, and both of them had involved adults. One she'd been able to reason with, the other she'd had Sergei along to help conk the target over the head when the reasoning didn't work.

She steadfastly didn't think of the third live Retrieval she had done. That had been different. That…hadn't been her, entirely.

Hadn't it?

Nobody had judged. Nobody had said anything, after, except thank you. She had restored a dozen teenagers to their family, broken the spine of the anti-*Cosa* organization, the Silence. But Wren didn't list that Retrieval in her (nonexistent) CV. She didn't talk about it. She tried not to remember anything about it, the hours of cold rage and hot current spinning her out of control, making her—for the second time in her life—into a killer, however justified those deaths were, to save the lives of others. She hadn't been entirely sane at the time.

Inanimate things were easier to Retrieve, every way up and down. Adult live Retrievals were bad enough; it was seriously tough to stash a four-year-old in your knapsack. They tended to squirm.

And yet…the challenge was irresistible. The benefits for a job well done were deeply rewarding. So here she was.

Wren didn't let herself think about the morality of the Retrieval, either way. If possession was nine tenths of the law, The Wren was the other tenth. Not that she didn't have standards about what was just or fair, she just didn't let them get in the way of an accepted job. If something set off Sergei's well-honed antenna for fishy, she trusted him to say no before she ever knew the offer had been made. That was his job.

"And you need to be getting on with yours already," she muttered, annoyed at herself. Taking a deep breath, she felt her annoyance, acknowledged it, and then let it go, slipping away like water down a drain.

Dropping behind a hedge, Wren settled herself into a more comfortable crouch on the damp soil, and let herself sink into fugue state.

She pulled current from her core, shaping it with her will and intent until greedy tendrils of neon-colored power stretched outward, touching and tasting the air, searching for any hint of either current or electricity.

Nothing. A void stretched in front of her: no defenses, and no house, either. Nothing but trees. Impossible, if she believed what her eyes told her. Even if they had built a house without any electrical wiring whatsoever, she should have been able to sense the natural current within the wood, stone and metals, much less the flesh and blood entities moving within those walls.

Some Talent trusted their magical senses more than their physical ones. Wren wasn't that arrogant or that dumb. When the two senses disagreed, something was hinky. Either the house itself was an illusion, or something she couldn't sense was blocking it from being found by magic. Both options were…disturbing.

Giving her Talent one last try, she stretched a tendril of current out, not toward the building, but down, sinking it deep into the soil and stone, reaching for anything that might have been laid in the foundations, deep enough to be hidden to even a directed search. Wren felt a cramp starting, low in her belly, and ignored it, extending herself even as she remained firmly grounded in her body. Sink and stretch, just a little more, just to make sure…

What the...? She touched a warmth, a hard, sharp warmth, tucked underneath the crust, deep in the bedrock where there should only have been cold earth. It spread beyond the house, covering a wider range, suggesting that the house was only secondary, protected as an afterthought. Was that what was blocking her? She pushed a little more, trying to determine the cause. Wh—

At her second touch, something shoved back at her, hard. Unprepared, the magical blow almost knocked her over, physically.

The hell? she thought, pissed off as much at being caught by surprise as at the assault itself. She touched it again with a handful of current-tendrils, not quite a shove in response, but not gentle, either.

That something in the bedrock expanded, filled with thick, hot anger and a wild swirling sense of frustration that escaped containment, swamped her own current and shriveled the tendrils where they connected, like twigs in a wildfire. Angry, yes, and sullen, and a feeling of bile-ridden resentment that threatened to consume her, and something worse underneath, something darker and meaner and rising fast.

Yeeeah, outta here, she thought in near-panic. *Outta here* now.

And you think *magic* is complicated?

Acclaimed author

laura anne gilman

returns with the gripping Retrievers tale

curse the dark

Wren and her partner Sergei are off to Italy in search
of a missing artifact, knowing only that it's very old,
very dangerous and everyone who gets too close
to it disappears. But compared to talking about their
"relationship," with a supersecret magic-watching
agency trying to wedge them apart, this Retrieval
mission is looking like a piece of cake. As if!

LUNA™

Available now!

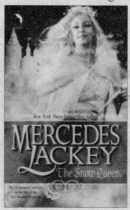

nocturne™

New York Times Bestselling Author

REBECCA BRANDEWYNE

FROM THE MISTS OF WOLF CREEK

Hallie Muldoon suspects that her grandmother
has special abilities, but her sudden death
forces Hallie to return to Wolf Creek, where
details emerge of a spell cast. Local farmer
Trace Coltrane and the wolf that prowls around
the farmhouse both appear out of nowhere, and
a killer has Hallie in his sights. With no other
choice, Hallie relies on Trace for help,
not knowing if the mysterious Trace is a
mesmerizing friend or a deadly foe....

Available June wherever books are sold.

www.paranormalromanceblog.com   SN61812